CW01508591

VALKIA

'SEE THIS AND mark it well. Such is the fate of the betrayer.'

She let the dying man squirm for a while, watching as his struggles grew weaker and then took up his sword. She turned the blade of the weapon downwards towards him. The first stroke crunched awkwardly into the bones of the traitor's neck. The second severed his head in a welter of gore and silenced his voice forever.

'Bring them both,' said Valkia, stepping back. 'My father for the rites due his position and the traitor as an example.' She turned her attention to Eraich. 'I made you a promise,' she said. 'And I keep it. But your people are no longer yours to be concerned about.' As her blade flashed from left to right across Eraich's neck and darkness rushed in to claim him, the faintest suggestion of a smile crossed his features. The last words he heard were Valkia's declaration.

'They are mine.'

By the same author

THE GILDAR RIFT
A Space Marine Battles novel

· **WARHAMMER HEROES** ·

WULFRIK
C.L. Werner

SIGVALD
Darius Hinks

THE RED DUKE
C.L. Werner

LUTHOR HUSS
Chris Wraight

VALKIA THE BLOODY
Sarah Cawkwell

SWORDS OF THE EMPEROR (October 2012)
Chris Wraight

A WARHAMMER NOVEL

VALKIA THE BLOODY

Sarah Cawkwell

BLACK LIBRARY

For my boys: Ben, the man who can... Jamie, the boy who will... And my big brother Stephen, who always chased away the shadows.

A BLACK LIBRARY PUBLICATION

First published in Great Britain in 2012 by
Black Library,
Games Workshop Ltd.,
Willow Road, Nottingham,
NG7 2WS, UK.

10 9 8 7 6 5 4 3 2 1

Cover illustration by Cheoljoo Lee.
Internal illustration by John Blanche.

© Games Workshop Limited 2012. All rights reserved.

Black Library, the Black Library logo, Games Workshop, the Games Workshop logo and all associated marks, names, characters, illustrations and images from the Warhammer universe are either ®, TM and/or © Games Workshop Ltd 2000-2012, variably registered in the UK and other countries around the world. All rights reserved.

A CIP record for this book is available from the British Library.

UK ISBN: 978 1 84970 185 3
US ISBN: 978 1 84970 186 0

No part of this publication may be reproduced, stored in a retrieval system, or transmitted in any form or by any means, electronic, mechanical, photocopying, recording or otherwise, without the prior permission of the publishers.

This is a work of fiction. All the characters and events portrayed in this book are fictional, and any resemblance to real people or incidents is purely coincidental.

See Black Library on the internet at
www.blacklibrary.com

Find out more about Games Workshop
and the world of Warhammer at
www.games-workshop.com

Printed and bound by CPI Group (UK) Ltd, Croydon, CR0 4YY

This is a dark age, a bloody age, an age of daemons
and of sorcery. It is an age of battle and death, and of the
world's ending. Amidst all of the fire, flame and fury
it is a time, too, of mighty heroes, of bold deeds
and great courage.

At the heart of the Old World sprawls the Empire, the
largest and most powerful of the human realms. Known for
its engineers, sorcerers, traders and soldiers, it is
a land of great mountains, mighty rivers, dark forests
and vast cities. And from his throne in Altdorf reigns
the Emperor Karl Franz, sacred descendant of the
founder of these lands, Sigmar, and wielder
of his magical warhammer.

But these are far from civilised times. Across the
length and breadth of the Old World, from the knightly
palaces of Bretonnia to ice-bound Kislev in the far north,
come rumblings of war. In the towering Worlds Edge
Mountains, the orc tribes are gathering for another assault.
Bandits and renegades harry the wild southern lands of
the Border Princes. There are rumours of rat-things, the
skaven, emerging from the sewers and swamps across the
land. And from the northern wildernesses there is the
ever-present threat of Chaos, of daemons and beastmen
corrupted by the foul powers of the Dark Gods.
As the time of battle draws ever nearer,
the Empire needs heroes
like never before.

ONE
The Schwarzvolf

SWOOPING WHORLS OF colour lit the night sky with their vibrant shades. Vivid reds, deep blues and virulent greens twisted and blended into one another, producing an entirely unnatural display unlike anything anywhere else. Only the Northern Wastes could boast such stark, murderous beauty as presented by the snowy tundra. They culminated in this spectacle, the magnificent aurora that crowned the top of the world. Nowhere else was there such magical fallout.

Her eyes wide, the child stared up at the fury of the skies, stricken mute by their very majesty. By her side, the warrior clad in blood-stained furs reached down to scoop her up in his arms. With ease he lifted her onto his shoulders that she might better see. She was getting rather large for such treatment now that she was older, but she was still slender and lightly built. The warrior had no difficulty in bearing her weight. She shifted slightly to make herself comfortable.

'They say that when the Axefather is pleased with our efforts, the tides of the sky will flow and ebb with darkest red, leached from the blood of our enemies. On the day that happens, Lille Venn, our people will rise far above all others.'

Her father smiled. He did not have to see her to imagine the look of wide-eyed wonder on his ten-year-old daughter's face. She was a beautiful child and although he loved her dearly, her ever-growing resemblance to her dead mother brought a fresh wave of bitter loathing towards the enemies that the Schwarzvolf faced. The war between the two tribes had raged for nigh on twelve cycles of the moon and the elders of the Schwarzvolf had foreseen that the morrow would see victory or death for Merroc and his people.

The child wound a lock of dark hair around her finger and continued to stare into the skies. Words were few and far between from his daughter. She had always been an introspective and thoughtful child, intelligent and sharp beyond her years. The death of her mother at the hands of their enemy a year ago had hurt her, but with the easy pragmatism of all her people, she had borne it with stoicism. Occasionally she would speak, invariably to make an observation or to ask a question. She was inquisitive and curious and this pleased Merroc. He may have produced no sons of the union with Valkia's mother but this girl, his first child, was his pride.

'How does it happen?' Her question, when it came, was demanding, as though she accused her father of arranging this spectacular show of magic purely for her benefit.

'None of us truly know, Lille Venn.' Lille Venn, he called her. *Little Friend.* 'There can be little doubt that such a miracle is the work of the gods themselves.'

'Where are the gods?' She absently tugged on his scraggly beard, winding it around her little fingers.

'Far to the north. Further than any of us have ever travelled. None who have ventured there have ever returned to tell of what lies beyond the mountains.'

'When I grow up,' she said with the fierce determination of children everywhere, 'I will go there.' When Merroc laughed, she narrowed her eyes at him. 'Why is that funny?'

'I believe you, Lille Venn,' said Merroc, his laugh becoming nothing more than a smile. 'If anybody could make that journey, it would be you.' His words mollified the little girl and the flash of anger left her eyes. She was like her mother to look at, that much was true. But her bearing, manner and attitude were Merroc's through and through.

He loved her for that alone.

Together, the two of them watched the winds of magic and the virulent display of colour in a companionable silence for several long minutes. Eventually, the girl spoke and this time it was not the petulant voice of a child, but the self-assured tone of a young woman who knew what she wanted.

'I want to fight with my people tomorrow,' she said, tapping Merroc on the shoulder as an indication that she wanted to be lifted down. Within the tribe, it was not unusual for a child of her age to fight. But Valkia, despite her ferocity, was female. It was customary to refrain from allowing any female child of the tribe to enter battle without having produced at least one live offspring.

'Lille Venn, you know that I cannot allow this thing you ask.'

'I am not asking you, Papa. I am *telling* you what I want.' He indulged her outrageously, but then he always had. He could not help himself. She was utterly charming when she wanted to be and a hard-hearted little bitch the rest of the time. But in this matter, he could not forsake hundreds of years of tradition.

'I forbid it.'

'I defy you.' It was an old game of theirs, one which she could maintain far longer than he could. He would deny her something and she would taunt him until a smile would cross his face and he would give in to her piping demands. But this... was unthinkable.

'You will not.' There was a hard tone in her father's voice that Valkia had never heard before and it shocked her to silence. She had rarely seen her father the chieftain. She was used to Merroc as being just her father. The thought that he would deny her what she wanted brought a pout to her lips. Merroc hunkered down until his eyes were level with hers.

'You are my only child,' he said. 'If I were to take you into battle tomorrow, it would be inviting your death. You have to grow and bear a grandchild before you can take the field of battle.' He felt briefly awkward discussing this with her; her eyes were like little emeralds, hard and green, and bored into him. 'Your mother bore you when she had known fourteen summers. You have yet to reach eleven. Do not be so quick to wish for your death, Valkia, for it will come. It comes to us all in time.'

He stood and tucked his long, dark hair which was shot through with threads of silvery-grey, behind one ear. He looked up at the aurora. 'I can't give you what you want, my daughter, not this time. You cannot fight. I will not lose you to those animals. You are too precious to me and to the future of our people.'

She looked up at Merroc and considered him. He was tall and broad of shoulder, his well-muscled body made larger by the addition of the furs that he wore as proof against the northern cold. He seemed very old to her, although he was perhaps only twenty-five years of age. If you lived to see thirty summers, the people of the Schwarzvolf considered you ancient.

His face, whilst too battle-scarred to ever be called handsome, was nonetheless proud and arrogant. There was an undeniable purity in his appearance that told of his good stock. The reigning family had held the chieftain's cape for seven generations, the mantle passed from father to son. Merroc's marriage to her mother had produced only two living children: Valkia and her sister Anya, who had died before the first year of her life was out. Three sons had been born to Merroc and his wife and none had been born with breath in their lungs. Merroc tried to deny the whispers, but he had come to believe them over time.

He was cursed.

'I see.' Valkia's two words were spoken through pursed lips and he looked down at her fierce, determined little face. He forced the smile from his lips and reached down to take her chin in his hand.

'I cannot allow you to take up arms and fight in the battle tomorrow, my daughter,' he said. 'But

I will speak to the Circle this night. They may per-
mit you to take up a shield and join the ranks of the
shield maidens.' She jerked her face free and looked
as though she would argue, but Merroc caught her
again. 'Listen to me, Valkia. I don't care how much
fuss you make. You *will* understand that this is the
way it must be or I will beat it into you. I cannot buck
the traditions of our people for your childish whims.'

'I am not a child.'

'Then stop acting like one.' She looked crushed and
he softened slightly in his attack. 'I will do what I
can, but I make no promises. Come now. The Circle
meets soon and I have tarried too long here.'

'You promise you will speak to them?' Reluctantly,
the little girl relented and slid her hand into her
father's bigger one.

'When have I ever disappointed you, Lille Venn?'

She had no reply she could give to that, only a cold,
penetrating stare which was far too old for her and
which left him feeling very uncomfortable.

THE CIRCLE WAS a group of seven tribal elders and
leaders. As the tribe's chieftain, Merroc sat at its head
but frequently felt that his words went unheeded.
He had come to the mantle at a young age, barely
sixteen, and they had never stopped treating him
like a youth.

They met in Merroc's semi-permanent dwelling;
a yurt made from animal hides that had spent long
hours tanning in the sun. They were stretched across
rigid poles and treated with animal fat that acted
as proof against the cold and the moisture. A small

opening at the top funnelled the smoke from the fire in its centre. The remains of a deer trapped a day or two before turned on a spit over it and the Circle frequently reached up to hack a slice from the animal and gorge noisily upon it.

The conversation had largely been strangely optimistic, given the fact they knew the dawn would bring either success or eradication. None of the Schwarzvolf were given over to pessimism before battle. If they did not believe they would win through, then they would not. It was quite simple.

'They will strike at first light.'

The words came from Ammon and all eyes swivelled towards him. The tribe's Warspeaker, he was only a year or so younger than Merroc and the closest that the chieftain had to a true friend. He had guided them through seemingly endless battles against their most rapacious enemies. The tribe who had so hampered them for months had never been granted the honour of being recognised by a name. The warriors of the Schwarzvolf called their enemies 'they' or 'them'. To give them a name was to ascribe something humane to them. And they were anything but.

The Schwarzvolf were widely considered one of the most ferocious tribes in the north lands and with good reason. Tenacious and fearless, their young warriors had been known to fight with limbs severed or their intestines held in by their shield hand. But they... *they* were of a different ilk. They liked to take prisoners, something which the Schwarzvolf found strange. They harboured a belief that if something was too weak to be free then it was too weak to live.

Torture, sometimes followed by slavery, would follow and to Merroc and his people, the concession of freedom was not something they subscribed to.

Ammon got to his feet and moved to the flap of the animal skin tent. He gave a piercing whistle into the darkness and a lithe, slender figure slid from the shadows and entered Merroc's tent.

'My chieftain.' The young man inclined his head with respect in Merroc's direction. Radek, his name was. He was one of the most shrewd, canny warriors in the tribe and his ability to hunt and scout was so astute that there were occasionally whispers that he must have made particularly dark pacts with the gods to acquire such skill. Fleet of foot and deadly with his bow, he had risen to the position of Pathfinder with alacrity. He was, Merroc recalled, Ammon's nephew.

'Radek. What news from beyond the camp? What do we have on our side for tomorrow's battle?'

'We have the land with us, but little else. Their numbers equal ours, if not exceed them.' The scout accepted a cup of wine, mulled and heated in a cauldron that hung over the fire. Not really strong enough to intoxicate, the wine was nonetheless welcome and he took a long sip from it, savouring the flavour. It was sweetened and given its pungent aroma by a mixture of spices, and the berries which made its base were in plentiful supply at this time of the year.

Radek set down the wooden cup and looked at Merroc. A slight smile played on his lips. There was a faint shadow of downy fluff on his chin. He was remarkably young to have come so far. The thought flickered through Merroc's mind but he almost immediately chided himself. Just because Radek was young was no reason to judge his competencies. 'There are two things we have that they do not, however. I got as close as I could to their camp earlier tonight.'

'And those are...?' Merroc left it hanging and reached forward to flense another slice of venison from the deer. He chewed on the meat, its juices dribbling down his chin and slicking his beard.

'We have more shields than they do. We can hold our lines far longer.'

Merroc nodded. 'The line will hold. This is a good start. The other?'

Radek's faint smile became an impish grin. 'Sobriety, my chieftain. They are drinking heavily, perhaps as a way to numb the cold in their bones. They are not used to being this far north. Come the dawn, they will be suffering for it.' This generated a ripple of laughter through the yurt and Merroc nodded, wiping grease from his face.

'This is excellent,' he rumbled. 'None of our warriors will be drinking this night. Tomorrow, when we have watered the earth with their blood... then *we* will drink.' The ripple of laughter became a combined grunt of approval. Merroc turned his head to the right. 'Godspeaker?'

The man sitting at the chieftain's right hand had been called Fydor at birth, but in this council, he wore the name Godspeaker. The tribe's shaman and doctor, his knowledge and gift of foresight were deeply revered and respected. Just as Ammon the Warspeaker sat at the chieftain's left hand, so the Godspeaker took the trusted position on the right.

'I am yet to read the omens,' he replied. The God-speaker was the oldest man currently living within the tribe. He had seen no fewer than forty summers and some whispered he had seen sixty. The hand that reached out to accept a cup of mulled wine was darkly tanned and liver spotted. 'I will do so shortly.' His eyes, dark and depthless in his ancient face, bored through Merroc in much the same way that Valkia's had a few short hours before.

'You have a question for the Circle,' observed the Godspeaker. Merroc wound a lock of his beard around one finger and let out an exasperated sigh. There was never any doubt that Fydor was exception-ally gifted. Whether with premonition or the simple art of understanding body language and distraction didn't matter.

'Aye,' replied the chieftain. 'It is a small thing. I was waiting for a suitable time.'

'Now is as good a time as any.' The Godspeaker opened out his hands, palms spread. 'Speak, chieftain.'

Merroc shifted slightly uncomfortably, uncrossing his legs and re-crossing them. The Circle sat comfort-ably amidst a number of cushions scattered on the floor. He took up his cup and sipped the wine. As he did so he gathered his thoughts carefully, know-ing that how he phrased the next sentence could be instrumental in its success or otherwise.

'It is not a question,' he said in due course. 'My daughter wishes to take her place in the battle tomor-row,' he said and there was such challenge in his voice that, for a moment, he wondered if he had been too aggressive with it. 'And I have agreed that she can take her mother's place as a shield maiden.'

'You are asking us for our approval?'

'No, Warspeaker.' Merroc shifted his gaze to Ammon. 'I am *telling* you.'

'It is unseemly. She is too young. Far too young. She has yet to produce an heir. If she were to fall...'

'If she falls, then I will take another woman of the Schwarzvolf to wife.' When Valkia's mother had died, Merroc had been grief-stricken enough to say that he would not re-marry. The promise he made here was spontaneous and he almost immediately knew regret because it sparked the conversation he had avoided for nearly a year.

'You know the Circle's views on this matter, chieftain. We have told you that we feel the time is right for you to take another woman to wife anyway. You need to produce an heir. If you do not and you should die, then there will be great upheaval amid our people.' It was no exaggeration on his part. Should the line of the chieftain fail, there would be a fight for the mantle that would potentially halve their number. 'You do not surely wish to impart such a legacy to your people?' The Godspeaker was calm and his voice measured. Merroc recognised the spark in the older man's eyes and felt the defiance that had so marked his leadership of the Schwarzvolf bubble to the surface.

'I already have an heir.' Merroc's voice was as fierce and proud as Valkia's had been when she had made the suggestion in the first place. 'She will take her place as the leader of our people when the time is right.'

'Pretenders to your position will kill her before the day she takes up the mantle.'

'She will likely kill them first.' Merroc was surprised at how much he believed the words he was saying. His dark-haired daughter was barely ten years old and yet she had already demonstrated great tenacity and courage.

But she was a child still and more – she was female. There had been female leaders of the tribe over the years but every one of them had been assassinated within days, sometimes within hours, of taking their place. Equality was one thing and the Schwarzvolf would gladly fight with their women at their side. But to defer to their command was to call into question centuries of belief and structure.

The odds were not in Valkia's favour. Not for the first time since she had torn her way into the world, Merroc felt a pang of sorrow for the hardships she must inevitably endure.

An uncomfortable silence had descended on the tent, broken eventually by the chieftain. None of those present had protested and he took that as his cue. 'Then it is agreed. Valkia may take the field of battle tomorrow.'

A ripple of assent passed across the assemblage. The only man present whose eyes met those of the chieftain's directly were those of Radek the young scout. Merroc was not sure whether the expression he saw there was a good thing or not, but he did not dwell upon it. He didn't need the approval of the young. He was the tribe's chieftain.

* * *

THE WARSPEAKER'S PREDICTION had been reasonably accurate bar a single detail. The enemy struck just before dawn rather than at first light. They launched their attack whilst the erratic and forbidding bale-moon was still low in the sky, taking its presence and the absence of its pale cousin as a good battle omen. Fiery gold stained the horizon, tarnishing the sickly green light and cutting shafts of grey which threaded through the velvet night. There was a biting sharpness in the air that carried the threat of more snowfall.

Their early attack earned them no advantage however. The warriors of the Schwarzvolf had been prepared for what felt to one young girl hours already.

Valkia had slept poorly the previous night. She had dozed fitfully whilst waiting for her father's return from the Circle and when he had ducked his head to enter their yurt, she had sat bolt upright and fixed him with her disturbingly intense stare.

To learn that she was able to take the field of battle had sent a thrill through her. She had never experienced such a feeling before; a surge of adrenaline that set her stomach to churning. She would never have acknowledged that such a sensation was akin to fear because the people of the Schwarzvolf did not know fear; only recognising it as a weakness that needed to be overcome.

Across her right arm was strapped a huge, bronze-shod round shield that was almost as tall when resting against the ground as Valkia herself was. Her left hand remained free, giving her the ability to bear the shield with both hands should it be required. Although she was only a child, she was not so small that she was completely lost in the shield line. To either side of her were women of the tribe she knew by face but not name. They had merely glanced down at the small girl and shown her how to hold the shield correctly.

She wore a thick leather jerkin that was several sizes too large for her but which had been cinched in at the waist with a belt. It was long enough that it came below her knees and there was no flesh visible between the edge of the tunic and the tops of her leather boots. Her tangle of dark curls was slicked back from her face by rendered animal fat and pale woad, in the same style as all the warriors of the tribe. A warrior's queue, or ponytail, would give an enemy a potential handhold and whilst the fat stank, even in the chill of the morning, it was better by far than having your head removed from your shoulders whilst your enemy held on tightly.

Valkia wrinkled her nose at the smell of the grease on her hair, but none of the others were showing any sort of discomfort so she tried not to let them see. She shifted position slightly, the movement earning reproachful looks from the women either side to her.

'Keep still,' the one on her right snapped, not unkindly. 'Do not fidget. Remain as still and straight as you can manage. If the enemy see a weakness in the shield line, they will exploit it.'

Valkia would normally have snapped back, but instead she nodded, appreciating that the words were given as advice and not admonishment. The woman smiled briefly and reached down with her free left hand to squeeze Valkia's shoulder. The girl looked up, made slightly bolder by the display of camaraderie.

'What's your name?' The taller woman, seemingly not much older than Valkia herself, seemed surprised by the question.

'Kata,' she replied, returning her gaze to the fore. Although they had been prepared for a while, there was still no sign of the enemy. 'And you are Valkia, chieftain's daughter. It would seem that you are finally ready for your first taste of battle.' She looked back down again and the smile was back. 'It is my first battle, too. When we return victorious, perhaps we can regale one another with stories of our bravery.'

'I would like that.'

'So would I,' Kata replied. She did not need to expand on the fact that she would also like the opportunity to present herself before the chieftain. The entire tribe had gossiped about his need for another woman since the death of his wife and Kata was unwed and of child-bearing age.

There was the sound of approaching running feet and Radek, along with several of the other scouts, emerged from the edge of the thin forest that was the natural border between the Schwarzvolf and their encroaching enemy. The young scout was in a state of dishevelment but still held himself with pride.

'They are coming,' was all he said.

'Then we take the fight to them,' cried the Warspeaker. 'We do not stand and let our enemies break upon us!'

A roar of agreement came from the skirmish warriors and the women of the shield line and Valkia raised her own piping voice along with theirs, caught in the thrill of it all. Soon, she would taste war.

Soon, the course of history would change.

FIRST CONTACT CAME far sooner than Valkia could ever have imagined and for a few heart-racing seconds she wondered if she would live to see her father again. The fore shield line, the more experienced women and younger warriors who bore weapons as well as shields, absorbed the initial impact. Numbering at least a hundred, the enemy tribe were largely armed with the axes so favoured by the people of the north and they hacked repeatedly into wooden shields sending splinters flying in all directions.

The air was filled with the screams and shouts of more people than the little girl had ever seen gathered in one place. It was a riotous clash of sound, sight and smell and she could barely take any of it in. Her world seemed almost to shrink until there was only her and those who stood either side of her.

She tasted a moment of abject terror as she stared around what was rapidly becoming a battlefield. She took in the sights of people she knew wading into the attackers, their own weapons flailing and hacking. Her eyes sought out her father, the bloody red sigil of the Schwarzvolf on his jerkin. The other warriors wore symbols too; but none wore the red of the chieftain's house.

Merroc was already in the thick of battle, having burst from the shield line with the others and utilised the jarring shock of impact to their advantage. His furs were splattered with blood and what little of his face could be seen behind the leather helm that covered most of his head was similarly stained. The two-handed battle-axe that he wielded with such aplomb swung slowly, decapitating and dismembering wherever it went.

There was so much blood. It ran like a bloody river, saturating the ground underfoot and she slid several times. So much blood. So much death. Everywhere there was the smell of copper as it stained the snow, dirty and slushy from the trudging of hundreds of feet. The scent of it tickled the child's nostrils and she found herself inhaling deeply rather than trying to avoid it.

Something was fired deep inside her soul as she breathed in. This was what she had been born into, this ceaseless violence and horror. This was her birthright. If only she could take up arms and step into the breaches that were appearing in the battle line as warriors fell, dead or injured...

'Step!'

The order came from somewhere to the left and Valkia was jarred into alertness once again. Her hold on the shield slipped a little and she groped to catch it again, her small hands tightening around the grip. She found herself moving forward with the rest of the line, her shorter legs meaning she had to half jog to keep up.

'Step!'

Another shouted order and Valkia moved forward. She looked up at Kata and saw the grim determination on her new friend's face. Without realising it, she automatically mimicked the expression. The shield line moved forward, closer to the fray, and Valkia felt once again that strange mix of thrill and fear. A few more feet and the line would be close enough to engage and protect the warriors.

Her attention was caught yet again by the flash of her father's sigil and she turned her head. If she strained hard enough, she could make out broken words. Using her own intelligence and understanding, she filled in the gaps as best she could. He was bellowing at the Warspeaker. They were both shouting at the top of their voices in order to be heard over the cacophony that surrounded them. Ammon was, like her father, covered from head to foot in the blood of the enemy and his face was grim.

'...barely making an impact on their numbers, my chieftain.'

'We need to keep... They will fall eventually. They're undisciplined.' Merroc indicated around himself, pointing and shouting instructions that Valkia could not fathom. The noise was overpowering, the press of bodies claustrophobic. Daylight was in evidence; a dull, heavy light that was choked with leaden, snow-filled clouds and which would later be filled with the greasy smoke of funeral pyres. There would be no bright sunlight this day.

A sudden dip in the noise level allowed Valkia to catch the tail end of her father's words.

'Their leader is in the middle of the attacking warriors. He is surrounded on all sides by his strongest and best. If we chew their force from the sides, then we can get to him. And I want him brought alive.'

'As my chieftain commands.' Ammon inclined his head.

Valkia didn't understand strategy, but her father's suggestion struck her as remarkably shrewd. The enemy were definitely all facing forwards; even those at the very back – at least as far back as her reduced height would allow her to see – were intent on ploughing through the solid line of the Schwarzvolf.

'Radek!' The Warspeaker turned from his chieftain and sought the head scout. He bade the youth carry the message to the outlying warriors and with a sharp nod of his head, the scout set off at a run.

Valkia watched him go and turned her head to meet the gaze of her father. Merroc gave her a tight smile and she felt immediately certain that they would win this battle. There was no way her father, such a great man, could lose to a rabble like this.

She was proved, over the course of the next hour or so, to be quite right. As soon as the skirmish began to break up, as the enemy were forced to meet the new challenges from either side, the rival tribe's already decidedly scrappy line began to completely lose cohesion. Once that happened, it became easy for the Schwarzvolf fighters to pick them off in droves. The shield line, of which Valkia was a part, was ordered to break and do what they could to aid the slaughter.

Some began to flee, many being cut down before they even made it as far as the woods through which they had marched, but most were killed and left where they fell. Nobody told Valkia that she must not take part in this massacre and as such she took up a dagger dropped by one of the fallen and threw

herself into what remained of the fray. Her blade
hamstrung several of the enemy and their last sight
before they toppled to the ground was that of a dark-
haired devil child darting away from them. In her
wake came death. Always death, brought swiftly and
without mercy by a warrior of the Schwarzvolf. Valkia's passage did not go unnoticed. On the far right
flank, her father watched his daughter and felt great
pride in her actions. He moved with alacrity to follow her and joined her. He darted from enemy to
enemy, the broad smile of his axe lopping the heads
and limbs from enemies with lethal precision.

Gradually, almost imperceptibly, the noise began
to die down as the numbers thinned to a handful.
Some had surrendered and they would be judged
for suitability for auxiliary warriors. The tribe may
not have taken slaves, but they had no compunction when it came to offering a place within their
number for those of worth. The females amongst the
enemy who had been spared death would be used
for breeding. Valkia knew this and although was still
somewhat ignorant of the true hardships of the tribal
existence, often wondered if death was not a preferable option. The Schwarzvolf would head to the
camps of their fallen enemy and claim any breeding
women and children for their own. In this way, the
tribe expanded.

'It is over, Valkia.' Her father stood before her and
reached out his hand to take the dagger from her.
'There is but one thing left to do. Come with me.'

With obvious reluctance, the child handed over the
dagger and slid her hand into that of the big warrior.

He led her through the fallen, past the dead and the dying.

Valkia was slowly regaining her awareness of the here and now. As well as the corpses of the enemy, there were bodies of her own people. She looked around anxiously for Kata but did not see her. She found herself hoping that her new friend was not dead.

Merroc led Valkia to a group of people who were gathered in an approximate circle around a single man. As big as Merroc and knotted with rangy muscle, this other man was the leader of the enemy. Valkia knew this even before Merroc could tell her. He looked up at their approach. He was lying on his side, his armour in tatters and his body drenched in gore. Something resembling a stylised skull had been crudely branded onto his chest. It was a strange symbol and it appeared to writhe and change even as she stared at it. She looked away, realising that her eyes ached if she attempted to look at it for too long. A great gash in the man's thigh pumped arterial blood into the ground beneath him. It was more than evident that he was not going to survive.

A string of harsh syllables grated from his lips at Merroc but Valkia could not understand him. The words he spoke were in a language she had never heard and she looked between the dying man and her father. Merroc held himself with even more pride than he usually did and didn't even flinch when the man on the ground drew back his head, hawking a gobbet of bloody phlegm at the chieftain.

'A barbarian of the worst kind, my daughter,'

said Merroc and he turned to Ammon, holding out his hand. Ammon put a finely carved spear into it, which Merroc angled thoughtfully at the warrior on the ground. 'No,' he said eventually. 'No. This kill belongs to you, Valkia. It was your strike to his leg that felled him and the honour of his slaughter is yours.'

Without another word, he handed her the spear. It was bigger than she was and it felt awkward to hold. She felt the weight of expectation on her shoulders and knew, without understanding how, that her actions in the next few moments would somehow define her very future.

The enemy lying at her feet swivelled his gaze from Merroc to the child and the pain and hatred on his face slowly became a sneer. It was all the incentive Valkia needed. How *dare* this creature treat her with anything less than the respect due to the daughter of the chieftain of the Schwarzvolf? How *dare* he look at her as though she was beneath his interest?

How *dare* he?

When the spear slid into his chest, Valkia savoured the sensation of it slipping into his heart. A gout of blood spewed forth from the barbarian's mouth with projectile force, covering the little girl. But she did not even flinch. Instead, she put her entire weight behind the spear, driving it ever deeper into her enemy's chest. She twisted the spearhead viciously, opening up the wound, and only released the pressure when she felt it drive through his back and into the soft earth beneath.

The warrior gave several violent spasms and choked

up a last mouthful of blood before he died, his eyes staring glassily into space. Valkia returned his earlier gesture and spat on his corpse.

From his vantage point, Merroc watched with pride that could barely be contained. It didn't matter that she was not a son. His daughter had more than proved her mettle here on the field of battle. She was a warrior at heart and she would rise to greatness. Of that he was sure.

TWO
Ambition

THE SEASONS TURNED as they always had since time began. Winter melted into spring, became the temperate summer of the north and finally, following the autumn rains, settled back into the near-constant snow and ice of the long winter.

They turned in this way for years and the child Valkia grew into foal-limbed, awkward adolescence and then through to young womanhood. She saw eight summers from the day she had driven that spear into the chest of the enemy chieftain, and in that time she had grown in ways far more than the physical.

It was the physical changes that gave her the most difficulty, however. From the age of fourteen, she had been pressed to find a suitable mate amongst her people and she had resisted with a stubborn pride that infuriated Merroc. In time, none of the men of the tribe even made the effort to court her favours.

The girl was far from unattractive; indeed she was beyond simply pretty and had stepped across the threshold into the realms of stunningly beautiful. There was a coldness to her beauty though; her skin remained alabaster pale despite the life outside and it gave her a marble chill that many men yearned to warm.

When she had turned thirteen and her budding womanhood had become apparent, her father announced that his daughter was ripe for marriage. The initial rush of interest in this was swiftly curtailed by Valkia herself. The little wildcat had soured the best intentions of her would-be suitors with her foul mouth and even more improper attitude. More than one of the young tribesmen who had fancied their chances with her had left the tent of the chieftain in tears of pain, clutching at the most delicate parts of their anatomy. She may have been barely out of childhood, but Valkia had an understanding of male physiology that was unsurpassed.

And so Merroc had let it slide. She would grow up eventually, he was advised. But still he remembered the age-old belief that his line was cursed. He feared that the line of his forefathers would end with him. After two years of her eligibility had passed and she had not borne him grandchildren, Merroc finally took the decision to remarry.

With only a little pressure from his daughter, he had considered and eventually accepted the young woman Kata into his hearth. She and Valkia had remained friends for many years, something that both of them found difficult at times. Where Valkia was feisty and masculine, Kata was quiet, subservient and as feminine as the hardships of life amongst the Schwarzvolf allowed her to be.

She had borne him two more children in the past

six years, both girls and was presently heavily pregnant with a third. Merroc had grown to love Kata deeply and was relieved that Valkia was so friendly with her. But his eldest daughter gave him cause for concern. She encouraged the two little girls, her half-sisters, to run wild around the camp in much the way she had done herself.

They argued frequently over such unbecoming behaviour. Such arguments always ended the same way: Valkia would sneer at her father and stalk from their yurt to join the young warriors of the tribe in their training. More than once she had also joined them in their drinking contests and could match them drink for drink.

She was a problem child, but in time Merroc accepted her for who she was. It was difficult not to when she proved herself on the field of battle over and over again. Wherever the fighting was at its thickest, there she would be. Valkia had no fear of death and indeed was more inclined to court its dark embrace than that of any of the young men of the tribe.

The Schwarzvolf scraped out a harsh existence in the winter months, living off what little game could be hunted in the frozen forests and vast open tracts of snow and ice. They supplemented this meagre diet with dried meat taken from kills in the spring and summer months. They ate dried fruit, and the milk of their goats was the only thing that kept most of them, particularly the young, from death by malnutrition. Although a hardy people, disease still reared its head on occasion. Theirs was a hard life, but with the turning of winter to spring came the annual journey and a cause for celebration.

Every year, when the melt came, the Schwarzvolf would break camp, dismantling their yurts with great care. They would be put onto the back of handcarts ready for transportation to the Vale.

Valkia had always loved the journey to the Vale, demonstrating a surprising love of natural aesthetic and an eye for nature that had startled her father the first time he had realised it. To see his overly-masculine daughter making a sidetrack from the main road to pick flowers and herbs was surprisingly satisfying. He learned in time that Valkia had taken it upon herself to learn the ways of the tribe's healers.

This year, the journey was different. This year, Merroc had cause for great joy. Kata had borne him his first son. Edan had been born on the night before the Schwarzvolf began the trip to the Vale and the Godspeaker had waxed lyrical about the auspicious nature of such timing.

Kata was a strong woman and there was no call to delay the journey, but Merroc insisted that she travel in one of the carts until she was strong enough to walk by herself. She had borne him three fine children and was still young enough to bear him more. He dared to believe that perhaps the Trickster had tired of his curse and given him the reward that he had worked so hard to achieve.

It was not the first foolish thought that the chieftain had entertained in his thirty-two years of life, and it would not be the last.

For her part, Valkia was indifferent to the arrival

of a brother in her life. Whilst the people of the Schwarzvolf celebrated late into the night, she set herself apart from them, a brooding expression on her exquisite face. A brother meant that the line of succession was assured. It also meant that she would be passed over in favour of Edan. Conflicting emotions raged within her. He was her brother; a part of her in a way she could never hope to explain. He was Kata's son and over the years, Valkia had come to love Kata as the mother she had never known.

He was just a baby. It would not take much to snuff out the weak, guttering flame of his existence. The thought came unbidden from nowhere and Valkia squeezed her eyes shut, deeply ashamed of it.

But yet...

'No!' She spoke the word aloud and pinched the skin on the back of her arm until it hurt. It had always been her preferred method of regaining her senses; a trick taught to her on the battlefield by the long-dead Ammon. The previous Warspeaker had fallen in battle five years ago during a skirmish that had come unannounced.

'Are you speaking to yourself again?'

The voice came from behind her and she started. Radek, the gods damn him, could walk silently when he so chose. Of all the young men in the tribe who had courted her affections, Radek had been conspicuous by his absence. It had almost infuriated Valkia. Did he think her so ugly and unimportant that he would not do as the others had done? Did he not yearn to lay his heart at her feet?

'It is none of your business, Warspeaker.' He had

taken the position with Merroc's blessing following Ammon's death and although Valkia had outwardly shown displeasure at the decision, she knew that Radek had been the perfect choice. More, Radek had taken it upon himself to offer her training with the bow, generally the weapon of choice for hunting. In times of war, the tribe preferred closer combat. He also gave her expert tuition in the use of the short, stabbing javelin sometimes wielded by the more experienced shield maidens. The bow had not suited her, but she had become extraordinarily proficient with the spear.

'We are not in council, Valkia. I have a name.'

'Then it is *still* none of your business, Radek.' She pulled her long legs into her chest and turned her face away from him. Any other man would have read that as his cue to leave, but Radek remained. The hint of a smile played at the corners of his mouth. He was only five years older than she was and had grown into a fine warrior. With the onset of adulthood, his wiry frame had become more muscled and his physique had developed until his days as a scout were behind him.

Valkia admired Radek, although she would never have openly said so. In the secret, put-away part of her psyche, she would even have admitted that she found him attractive, despite the fact that the Warspeaker was far from physically desirable.

He had left the fresh-faced boy behind after injuries sustained in battle had more or less removed the right-hand side of his face. A mass of scar tissue decorated his cheek and neck, drawing his face into a perpetual scowl. But he was strong and fearless and these were desirable qualities in a mate. His patience with her as she had learned the art of warfare had been seemingly endless and he encouraged her to wilder and wilder acts of daring and courage.

'Your welfare is always my business, chieftain's daughter,' said the Warspeaker and he dropped down onto the grass beside her. She sniffed as haughtily as she could manage and shuffled herself further down the bank. 'Congratulations on the birth of your little brother.'

'I had nothing to do with it,' she replied archly. 'All the hard work was done by Kata. I believe my father may have had something to do with it for a few seconds several months ago.' She shrugged one slender shoulder in indifference and turned her head to glance at Radek. Her eyes were as dark as her hair; so deep green that they were almost black and her pupils were large. Some people found Valkia's dark eyes unsettling, but the Warspeaker found them fascinating. There was so much going on inside the head of this young woman. From time to time, there would be a crack in their mirror-like surface, allowing him the briefest of glimpses to the heart that beat beneath the cool exterior. But they were rare and if he felt compelled to act on those moments of opportunity, he never did so.

For all their savagery and barbaric methods in war, the Schwarzvolf were respectful to one another, and Radek would never have considered suggesting any sort of feelings for Valkia if he did not expect it to be returned in kind. They had an awkward kind of friendship that was remarkably one-sided on his part and for now, at least, he was content with that arrangement.

'He will become chieftain when my father dies,' she observed and there was a note of ice in her tone. Radek noted it and frowned.

'Jealousy, Valkia? You know that is the way it must be.'

'My father is old.' She turned her head away from him again. 'He will die soon.' Matter of fact though it may have been, Radek had to concede that there was a certain truth in her words. Merroc was not as fit as he had used to be, and of late he had shown signs of slowing down. If age and infirmity did not take him, then he would be too slow on the battlefield. 'Edan is just a baby. He cannot lead our people in that event. You know that it should be me, Radek.'

'Is this what is bothering you, Valkia? Are you still clinging to this dream of leading the Schwarzvolf? I thought you gave that ambition up long ago. You are a warrior of your people now and none dispute your ability. But you are not and never will be a leader of men.'

'Do not presume to speak to me of such things, Warspeaker. What do *you* know of my dreams?' She turned around then and the full impact of her beauty struck Radek in a way it never had before. A fine-boned, almost elfin, face in which those dark eyes were the drawing feature, he had somehow missed the moment when little Valkia had become a woman. Her wild tangle of dark curls fell loosely down her back, coming to a tapered point at her narrow waist. She wore a simple tunic and leather breeches, belted in the middle; it did nothing at all to hide her all-too-feminine curves.

She was both desirable and untouchable. The two were a heady concoction that set Radek's senses to spinning.

'I only know of your dreams what you tell me and what I can work out for myself,' he replied, his eyes not leaving hers. He caught his breath as she smiled slowly.

'Tell me what you believe my dreams are, Radek. I am interested in what you think you know about me.'

If he was ever going to get an open invitation to explore more of the woman behind the warrior, this was his chance. But Radek determined then and there that he would not risk their friendship by putting his heart on the line. What he was not to know was that Valkia had already set hers at his feet. It would be the only time in her entire life that she would know what it was to truly love another person.

He considered her for a few moments, then lay back on the grass, staring up into the night sky. Winter had not yet truly fled, but the warmth of spring was in the air and he breathed it in, relishing its pure freshness. The constellations in the heavens above were simply indistinguishable patterns as the sky rearranged itself for the coming season. Everything was in flux at this moment, on this portent-laden night, and Radek felt the weight of future events on his shoulders.

'You yearn to lead the Schwarzvolf,' he said in time and she said nothing, merely watching him closely. 'You know that everyone in the tribe will be set against you from the moment you formally stake your claim.'

'Everyone? Even you, Warspeaker? And there I was thinking you were my friend and my ally.'

He turned his head sideways to consider her. 'I am both of those things, Lille Venn,' he said, absently using the pet name that her father had long since stopped using. It brought a bloom of red to her cheeks, a maidenly flush that was both becoming and extraordinarily out of place on a face that was usually only reddened by the visceral stains of war. 'But you ask too much to expect me to support you in this.'

'If Edan were to die...' Radek opened his mouth to forestall her comment, but she ploughed on regardless. 'If he were to be taken by illness, or captured by enemy warriors, then the line of succession would have to pass back to me.'

Radek felt a cold chill run through him. He believed that Valkia was not so cruel that she would slaughter an innocent child. At least until she had spoken of such a thing in that strangely indifferent tone, he had *thought* so. His eyes were held by her gaze and he could not look away. He, the Warspeaker of the Schwarzvolf, a man who had faced countless terrors, could not turn his head away from a woman.

'Indulge me, Radek.'

'I suppose... yes. That would be the case,' he acknowledged. 'But your father will stop at nothing to protect your brother.' He hoped to inject a warning into that sentence, hoped that Valkia would not do anything foolish. 'At *nothing*, Valkia. Do you understand me?'

'Of course I understand you, I am not some simpleton.' She sniffed haughtily. 'Of course, I would not wish any harm on the infant, but these are things that need to be considered.'

Was she speaking the truth with those glib words? Radek could not tell. She tipped her head to one side and wound a lock of dark hair around one finger. She smiled coquettishly at Radek and in that moment he was hopelessly, irrevocably hers. When she spoke again, she did so with such charm and guile that he would have sacrificed the other side of his face just to hear her speak to him in that tone again.

'You would be by my side if I had to fight for my rightful leadership of the tribe, wouldn't you, Radek?' She lowered her eyes demurely and peeked out at him from beneath long, sooty lashes. And he was lost.

Of course he would be by her side. He was a fool to have ever thought otherwise. A strange sense of wonder came over him as he allowed the young woman to manipulate him. For her part, she had no idea that she had already mastered the art of engaging her feminine charms to achieve her own ends.

'I pledge myself to serve you heart and soul, Valkia,' he said, drawing himself up to kneel before her. The way he had given himself over to her so wholly, just with a flutter of her eyelashes sent a thrill of power throughÈ her. She had a unique gift to bring to the potential problem of her future birthright, and she swore to herself there and then that she would never be afraid to use it. 'When your call comes, I will be there.'

'Yes,' she said and absently reached over to pat his cheek. 'Yes. I believe you will be.'

* * *

THE TRIP TO the Vale was singularly uneventful. In years gone by, the Schwarzvolf had frequently encountered other tribes; some hostile, others benign. There had even been occasions when the smaller tribes, struck down by illness or hunger, had turned themselves over to Merroc's keeping. The Schwarzvolf was now the largest tribe in the north and growing all the time.

At times, the power this gave Merroc was a curse as well as a blessing. He was a man of action, not of administration. It was not his place to consider the allocation of provisions across the people. For the most part, the people of the Schwarzvolf were left to fend for themselves and this in itself led to scuffles and disagreements.

But this year, the land had provided well. There were barrels of pickled fish and plenty of dried meat. The spring brought forth an abundance of new life in the forests and fresh game was easy to acquire. Valkia joined with the hunters daily, enjoying the thrill of the chase and engaging in games of one-upmanship with the other warriors of the tribe to see whose haul was the greatest, or who had penned down the largest deer. Everything was good for the Schwarzvolf. Everything was *too* good.

Despite his joy at the birth of his first son, Merroc heeded the words carried to him by the Godspeaker, whose dour prediction ultimately bore fruit.

The gods, he had said, give with one hand and take with the other.

From time to time, infants were born with physical defects. Sometimes these were minor and barely noticeable. Perhaps one ear was slightly smaller than the other or skin bore unsightly birthmarks. The majority of these babies were accepted into the tribe without question and though they had to bear bullying as they grew up, they thrived. Some bore the mark of the gods on their flesh however, twisted, mewling things with bestial faces and thrashing limbs.

It was the way of the Schwarzvolf to abandon these children to their fate in the woodlands. They were never slaughtered, as to murder a child of the god-touched was to invite the wrath of the divine. Alone in the wilderness they would either die, exposed to the elements or attacked by wild animals, or they would live; foundlings who were raised amongst one of the lesser tribes. Whatever became of them, it was no longer the problem of the Schwarzvolf.

More and more babies were being stillborn or stricken down with crippling defects and whilst some mothers tried their hardest to conceal a club foot, or additional digits, some mutations were harder to hide. By the time they reached the Vale, ten children had been born into the tribe – including Merroc's own son – and seven had been left behind. Two of the mothers, prime breeding stock, had died from the rigours of difficult childbirth and four more died during pregnancy. A sombre trail of funeral pyres marked the Schwarzvolf's passage across the plains, taking with them most of their spare wood, trailing greasy smoke into the clear spring skies.

It did little to ease Merroc's eternal conviction that he was somehow cursed and he sat and bemoaned his poor luck to his wife. Kata, an eternally practical woman who juggled the demands of two small children and a baby without so much as batting an eyelid, simply sat and let her husband pour out his heart. Her response at the end of his diatribe startled him.

'You say all this, my husband, and yet what is it that you do to change your stars?'

'A man cannot interfere with the path laid out before him by the gods.'

'Of course he can!' Kata shifted Edan who was nursing peacefully at her breast and fixed Merroc with a steady gaze. 'When you walk through the forests and there is a fallen tree in your path, do you stop walking and turn around?'

He did not answer at first. Her words were sensible and he felt irritated at her pragmatism. Eventually he grudgingly admitted that no, he would not turn around.

'No,' agreed Kata. 'You would climb over the tree, or find a path around it, or as a last resort, you would cut it out of your way. Your tone speaks of giving up, Merroc, and it does not become you. And others are starting to notice it.'

The chieftain stared at the young woman he had taken to wife and once again, he marvelled at her clarity of thought. He shook his head and smiled. 'Between you and my wretched daughter, you are determined to change the way I view the world, aren't you?'

'I speak as I find,' Kata replied simply. 'Sometimes I open my mouth without thinking about the words that come out. Valkia, on the other hand...' Kata shook her head. 'She does nothing without contemplating the far-reaching consequences of her words. Her every action is calculated.'

'She is cunning, aye. A quality which will serve her well.' It was rare these days to hear Merroc speak of his headstrong daughter with anything but trepidation. Kata remembered a time not so very long ago when he had doted on Valkia. How things changed... but to hear Merroc speak with such pride warmed her heart.

'Cunning, yes. And clever, too. She learns fast. I have watched her under Radek's tutelage and she has put him flat on his back on more than one occasion.' Kata smiled at the memory of it. When her stepdaughter had started training with the Warspeaker, she had learned many humiliating lessons at Radek's hands, most of which ended up with her lying in the mud, pitched face-first into a river and covered with bruises. But she had never once given up as her father had confidently predicted she would. She had persevered. She had more to prove than most and she did not let herself down.

Kata was wise beyond her years and she had also watched the unmistakable growing attraction between Valkia and the disfigured Radek with a certain fondness. Radek was not the kind of man who would ever force his attentions on an unwilling Valkia and it was strange to see the normally foulmouthed girl occasionally seem lost for words when talking about the Warspeaker.

She did not claim to be gifted with the ability to understand signs and omens like the Godspeaker, but

Kata was a woman who watched people. She could see the attraction between them and there was also a spark there that threatened something darker. She could not categorise it or even start to understand it, but she felt fear for not just her stepdaughter, but for all the Schwarzvolf.

Edan had fallen asleep in her arms and she cradled him protectively for a few moments before laying him down on the pile of furs that served as his bed. She kissed the top of his pink little ear and turned her attentions to her two sleeping daughters. Merroc had withdrawn once again into brooding, presumably on his poor luck.

Kata sighed and settled down to her work, stitching together boiled leather pieces to make new armour for her husband. Perhaps one day soon he might dispense with the need to dwell on all that he did not have and cherish what he did have.

SPRING BLOOMED INTO full summer and an unusual spate of sunny days nourished the Schwarzvolf as they maintained their summer home in the Vale. There were a few more problematic births, but several healthy children were born to the tribe and there was much cause for celebration.

Valkia continued her training under Radek's tutelage and her proficiency with the spear became unsurpassed, even by some of the older and more experienced warriors. Neither of them cared to act on the undeniable attraction they felt. Valkia was too careful not to sully the loyalty she had earned from the Warspeaker and Radek took her stand-offishness as a rejection. It worked heavily in her favour of course; every smile she threw him and every time she took his hand to get up off the floor – or more increasingly, to help *him* from the floor – he felt that old thrill all over again.

'Why do you insist on toying with him?'

Valkia had taken the conscious decision to spend a night at her father's hearth. She had missed quiet conversation with her stepmother since Edan's birth and whilst she thought highly of Kata, she bore little love for the happy infant boy who she nursed.

The young woman had simply shrugged and drawn her legs into her chest. It was a familiar gesture, one that gave away the fact that she would not care to be drawn into conversation on the matter. Kata gave it one last try.

'Radek is a fine man, Valkia. You could do far worse for yourself.'

Kata was struck into silence by the look of venom that Valkia shot at her. She physically cringed backwards. There was such anger there that Kata felt Valkia's irritation as a tangible thing. After a moment or two, the look subsided.

'Perhaps,' she said, with great ambivalence in her voice. 'But if I could do far worse for myself, by that very same argument, Kata...' A smile snaked her lips upwards and it was not a pleasant expression. 'By that very same argument, I could also do far better for myself.'

A silence, uncomfortable for the first time that Kata could recall, fell upon the two women. After a while, Valkia spoke again. She held up her long, dark hair and tugged at it. 'I have a fancy to wear my hair short, Kata. Would you cut it for me?'

Kata was shocked by this. For all her tendency to masculine behaviour, Valkia's hair had always been a rare vanity. But she did as the girl asked, partly out of a sense of awkwardness at the earlier moment that had passed between them. She took up a knife and hacked at the thick, dark curls at the length Valkia indicated. When she had finished, the hair dropped to the ground in a pile and Kata knew, somehow, that this was Valkia's final step to womanhood.

She made an effort to neaten the resulting dark cap of hair and Valkia nodded determinedly, obviously happy with what had happened. It was a solemn moment, sad even, and after her stepdaughter was long gone, leaving the yurt to spend the night in games and carousing with her warrior friends, Kata looked at the hair on the ground, sorrow lining her face.

SHE HAD ALWAYS been able to drink any of the young men under the table, but this night, Valkia was unable to hold her spirits. She felt drunk and when she was drunk, she felt angrier than usual. It left her feeling weak and vulnerable and she stalked away from the gathering early.

Unsurprisingly, Radek followed her. The Warspeaker was not drunk; he never engaged in such activities unless he was specifically ordered to stand down his vigilance over the camp.

'What do you want, Radek?' Valkia was tired and more than a little inebriated and she did not have the patience to play the Warspeaker's games tonight.

'I wanted to ensure you returned safely, Valkia. That is all.'

'Do you not think I can take care of myself?' Alcohol made her belligerent – more so than usual – and her tone was aggressive. Radek chuckled fondly, which served only to irritate her even more.

'I am more than aware of your capabilities. Nonetheless, your safety is, and always has been, part of my responsibility as your father's elected Warspeaker. So whether you like it or not, I will see you back to the chieftain's hearth.'

'I can make my own way. I absolve you of your duty.' She ran her hand over her newly-shorn hair. It still felt strange to her. Radek considered his options for a moment or two and then nodded his assent. She felt strangely grateful to him for giving her the space she needed.

Radek raised his head to the night sky and inhaled deeply. 'There are things being borne towards us on the four winds, Valkia.' He moved closer to her and she automatically backed off. 'The Godspeaker can read the passage of time like he reads the weather. Something is coming.'

She scowled at him. She liked Radek, was even prepared to acknowledge a fondness for him, but there were limits. She stood firmly, her feet planted on the ground. 'My *fist* will be coming if you take another step closer to me, Radek. What are you talking about?'

'The Godspeaker came to me earlier today. He has read the portents and wanted me to be ready.' Valkia felt a cold chill run down her spine. Despite the warmth of the night, she shivered. 'You should be ready too.'

'Ready? For what?'

'Change, Valkia.' His voice had dropped to a whisper and he held her gaze for slightly longer than she found comfortable. He inhaled deeply. 'The gaze of the Trickster turns towards us.'

Having delivered these curious words, Radek bowed deeply to Valkia and melted back into the night. She stood and watched him go, made suddenly sober.

THREE
The Black Stag

THE GOLDEN SUMMER of that year would long live in the tribe's legends. Particularly warm, which some murmured was unnatural, it nonetheless brought an abundance of food and richness to the normally hard lives of the Schwarzvolf. Nobody was surprised when Merroc made the decision to winter in the Vale.

Nobody was surprised for a number of reasons. It was foolish to move out of the Vale when everything they needed was right there. The migration of the game to the north didn't matter when there were provisions enough for months where they were. For the first time in living memory, the Schwarzvolf broke with the traditions of their people and the cost was more than anybody could ever have anticipated.

Valkia was fully supportive of Merroc's decision, an attitude which earned her a loss of respect amongst some of her peers. She poured scorn on their rebukes however. Why should she care about breaking with tradition? Her father was right. There was no point in risking the dangers of exposure and travelling the treacherous ice-fields when there was no need.

Merroc had other reasons for staying where he was, but these did not become apparent to his daughter for a while. She had spent less and less time at her father's hearth, increasingly sleeping virtually where she fell, or taking part in night patrols and sleeping during the day. The months that passed added more muscle to her slender frame until she was whipcord lean. She maintained her short hair and from the back was frequently mistaken for one of the young male warriors. Her coldly beautiful face was at incongruous odds with the leather armour and furs that she wore.

She and her father were becoming increasingly estranged from one another. He remained unhappy that despite her eighteen years, she was still without a child or a husband or even – so the whispers went – a lover. In return, she despised his lectures on propriety. Whenever they were in the same vicinity for more than an hour or two, they would degenerate into sniping and name-calling. Kata did her best to buffer the animosity between father and daughter, but to no avail.

The demands of three small children, with yet another growing in her belly, meant that Valkia's stepmother was snappish and short-tempered and when the winter set in properly, things only got worse.

Much worse.

'YOU LOOK TIRED.' Kata made the observation in a soft voice, moving to the pile of furs on which she slept with her husband. She reached out a hand to stroke his damp hair back from his face and he batted it away.

'Away with you, woman. I am fine.'

From the way he had lain awake most of the night, tossing and turning and sweating profusely, Merroc was anything but fine. For days he had been pale and listless and the weight had started to drop from him. A once strong and heavily muscled frame was becoming little more than a bone rack on which his waxy skin hung uncomfortably. The weight loss was startling and Kata knew that this was something more than just the plague.

'Let me fetch the healer for you.'

'Let me sleep. It will pass.' He coughed and raised a hand to his mouth to wipe away a trickle of blood. 'It will pass,' he repeated with a confidence that Kata did not sense he truly felt.

Merroc, proud chieftain of the Schwarzvolf people had courted the attention of the Fly Lord. He was dying.

DESPITE HIS ILLNESS, Merroc knew that he could not afford to display weakness in front of his people, particularly not when they were already unsettled due to his decision to remain in the Vale. He had to practically drag himself from his bed each morning to sit with the rest of the Circle and over the days that followed, every last one of them saw their chieftain's steady deterioration.

Stubborn as he had been throughout his entire life, he did not let up and pushed himself far harder than was sensible given his obvious illness. But there was nobody who dared suggest he might be unwell, save Valkia. The chieftain and his daughter finally came to blows on a chill morning when the days had grown shorter and it seemed as though light would never return to the sky. As was always the way with the young woman, there was nothing subtle in her attack.

'You are weak.'

The statement was blunt and came without warning. They were in the heart of the woods, hunting the day's game. They had been let alone by enemy tribes for months and the daily hunt was about the only real chance to exercise their sword and spear arms. Merroc had joined the hunt with great energy and boundless enthusiasm. He had woken that morning feeling surprisingly well. A hearty breakfast had given him more strength and he had decided that he would take to the hunt for the first time in a long while.

Kata had been somewhere between delighted to see a spark of the man she had married in this wasted stranger who shared her bed, and anxious at his ability to make it through the day without somehow shaming himself. She had watched the hunting party move out from the village with trepidation in her eyes. She caught the unmistakable sneer on Valkia's face and withdrew into the yurt, fear of the unknown projecting images of horror into her mind.

'You are weak.' Valkia repeated the words. She walked through the woods with her spine held straight and her head carried high. From time to time she cast a sidelong glance at Merroc, despising the creature he was becoming. She had been growing increasingly angry with the gossip and rumour that spread throughout the whole camp.

If she had ever loved her father, she could not remember it. Everything about him now made her so angry. He appeared to have shrunk. Once such a mountain of a man, he was thin and spare, grey streaking his mane of hair and his unkempt beard. The smell of illness hung around him and that made her angrier still. A warrior of the Schwarzvolf should not fall to illness. They should fall in battle, at the hands of an enemy. They should fall when they were defending their people, not lying in a bed and unable to move.

'I have not been well, but I am recovering,' he responded, his tone guarded and his eyes unconsciously straying to the dagger at his daughter's waist. 'Age brings with it its own new set of battles, Valkia. Be grateful that I am living still and that you are not embroiled in a battle for the leadership you so desire.'

She made no reply, but snorted softly. There was the sound of a cracking twig, soft and barely audible somewhere far to her right and she ducked down, her soft leather boots making little more than a rustle on the leaves. Merroc followed her lead. He could not help but be deeply impressed with his daughter. He had neglected her for so long and she had blossomed in his absence. She was strong and lithe, her face so like her long-dead mother's. She was confident and capable.

She was everything he would have wanted in a

son. But she had been a daughter. A thousand regrets came to plague at him.

'See! There!' Valkia hissed and grabbed at her father's arm, her long fingernails almost piercing the flesh there. Her breath ghosted in front of her and Merroc peered through the light mist at the direction in which she was pointing. His breath caught in his throat.

'The black stag...'

The Schwarzvolf, whose name literally translated as 'The Black Wolf' carried many legends about black-skinned or furred animals. They were perceived to be good omens; signs of strength and power. They were creatures to be admired and revered. This particular specimen was a magnificent sample of his species. His hindquarters were strong and well formed; the number of branches on his antlers suggesting he was in his prime. His noble head was dipped as he cropped at what little grass he could through the rime of frost. Come the end of the winter, he would lose those antlers in preparation for new growth and another year of survival would be marked.

Although the stag seemed oblivious to the presence of father and daughter, he was not. His ears twitched occasionally and from time to time he would look up and turn his head in their direction. Merroc didn't realise he was holding his breath until he unconsciously let it out.

'We are honoured to witness this, my daughter,' he whispered softly, his eyes filled with reverence. He reached out a hand to squeeze Valkia's shoul-der, hoping to build any number of bridges in the gesture, but she squirmed free from his grip and his hand fell to his side.

'Honoured? Never mind that! There is enough meat on that stag to feed several families for a number of days.' Valkia's response shocked Merroc.

'You cannot! To kill such a beast... Valkia, such an act would bring the wrath of the gods down on us.' Merroc was genuinely shocked that his daughter would willingly sacrifice an animal that was considered such a good omen. There was a bestial hunger in her eyes. She was the hunter and the black stag was her prey. She was staring at it with intensity, her eyes roaming across its glossy skin, doubtlessly considering the best place to embed her spear.

Merroc shook his head in disbelief. 'If you do this thing, Valkia, then I will no longer consider you to be any daughter of mine. I will disown you entirely.' *That* got her attention. She took her gaze from the stag and turned with aching slowness to stare at her father, the dark pools of her eyes giving away nothing of the thoughts that churned beneath the surface. When she did finally speak, it was with such hatred that Merroc felt a cold shudder run down his spine.

'If you choose to cast me out, *father*,' she said, placing heavy sarcasm on the word. Merroc had not been a father to her for many years in any sense other than that of their blood tie. 'Then you will make an enemy of me. Are you sure th...'

Whatever she was going to say was cut dead by the sudden flight of the stag. It bolted into the woods, sending up a shower of damp leaves in its wake. Immediately alert, Valkia shifted position, forgetting the argument with her father and crouching with one leg placed slightly behind the other. She was like a snake, coiled and ready to strike.

He may have been ill, but years of reflex and reaction forced Merroc's aching body into a similar stance. The only sound he could hear was that of the distant clattering of the stag's hooves as it disappeared into the forest and that of his own breathing. He was acutely aware of it rattling in his thin chest.

Valkia said nothing but her head moved imperceptibly to the right, her sharp ears picking up some movement there. A dark head of hair emerged from the woods, moving at great speed.

'Radek,' she murmured and relaxed her posture, but only slightly. The Warspeaker was repeating the same phrase over and over and it wasn't until he was a little closer that Valkia and Merroc made out what he was saying.

'Enemies coming this way!'

From all over the woods, Schwarzvolf hunters emerged from their hiding places. Some crawled out from beneath bushes whilst others dropped lightly from trees. Valkia got to her feet and jogged lightly to join Radek. Merroc also followed, although much more slowly. His heart pounded in his chest. He sensed a defining moment in his future was imminent. If an enemy attack was upon them, how he handled himself in the next few minutes could be critical.

As soon as the Schwarzvolf were assembled, Radek looked over the grouped hunters. He sent the youngest, a boy of nine, running back to the camp to sound the alarm and then elaborated on what was coming their way.

'At least forty strong, if not more,' he said breathlessly. 'I was at the far edges of the woodland stalking game and I saw them moving down the hillside. I watched for a while to see where they were heading and they are coming towards the woods.'

'Forty?' Valkia responded and there was scorn in her voice. 'We can take forty. They're on open ground and the woods favour us. We can cut them down before they even set foot in here.'

'What if they come in peace?' The voice belonged to Merroc and it was quietly reasonable and rational. 'Do not be so quick to cut down strangers, Valkia. They may only seek the protection of the Schwarzvolf.' All eyes turned to the chieftain. 'We should let them come to the edges of the woodland and demand to know their intentions.'

'But...' Valkia looked furious at being overridden by her father.

'Radek?' Merroc turned to the Warspeaker. There was a spark of his former self evident on his face, the pride and nobility that had always been etched there and which even the ravages of his illness had failed to entirely eliminate. The Warspeaker inclined his head.

'My chieftain speaks truth. It would be better to ensure this tribe comes for blood before we join them in battle.'

Merroc didn't need to look at his daughter to feel the stare that she levelled towards him. If looks could kill, as the saying went, he would not just have been dead. He would have been torn limb from limb and his intestines strung like banners from the nearest tree. There was such a hunger in Valkia's eyes that eventually Merroc had no choice but to meet her stare defiantly. The pair battled silently for a few tense moments and then Merroc made a concession. The act startled everyone present.

'We will meet them at the edge of the woods. Valkia – you are to take a group through the east side of the forest. Loop around them and remain on the right flank. Should the meeting take a turn for the worse, then you will be able to strike at them from behind and drive a wedge between their warriors.'

'My chieftain?' There was something faintly dangerous in Radek's voice, but Merroc chose to carefully ignore it. 'Are you sure this is a good course of action? If Valkia and the others are noticed, it may endanger any agreement to bring another tribe under our banner.'

'Are you questioning my ability to lead, Warspeaker?' Merroc, who had once towered imposingly over Radek, drew himself up to his full height. He may have seemed thin and wasted, his face pale and the eyes sunken hollows, but in that gesture, something of his lingering power remained.

'Never, my chieftain.' Radek bowed his head and Valkia sneered at how swiftly he had capitulated. There was no time for lengthy discourse on the matter, however. They needed to move and be swift about it if they were going to get into position before the unknown party reached the woods.

'Take twelve warriors with you, Valkia,' Radek said, his manner switching to that of the commander.

'Remain in cover until either I signal otherwise or things get out of hand swiftly.'

'As my Warspeaker commands,' she replied in a voice dripping with sarcasm. She turned and pointed at ten of the gathered men and two women and within several seconds, they had melted into the trees as though they had never been.

'Let us head out to meet these intruders then,' said Merroc after they had left.

THEY WERE LOOKING for winter sanctuary, they said. There were fifty-seven of them; all that was left of a two-hundred strong tribe who had lived in the hills for countless years. They had always kept themselves to themselves, never interfering in the politics and wars so beloved by the other tribes. They were farmers predominately, tilling the land and living from its bounty. But they were under threat from another tribe.

Their leader, a young man who had introduced himself as Eraich, had led a small deputation of five men to the edge of the woods. He was powerfully built with muscular shoulders that spoke of hours of hard toil and labour, and a ruddy complexion that he could attribute to his many hours in the sun. None of the men with him were armed other than with hunting knives worn at their waists. But there was the potential there to develop such strong men into exceptional warriors. Merroc could see it and he could tell by the appraising expression on Radek's face that the Warspeaker thought so as well.

'We have watched your people travel here and

leave again for many years,' Eraich said, breaking the moment of silence. His voice was thickly accented and difficult to understand, but he spoke slowly and earnestly. 'We have never approached you before because we have never had need to. But now...' He shook his head. 'Now, the murder that comes in the night has taken that which we hold most dear. Our families are torn apart and our crops are destroyed. Our livestock has been stolen...'

Eraich made a sweeping gesture that took in the people behind him. From a distance, it had been impossible to know that the party was made up of men, women and children. 'This is all that remains. We are... without a home. We come to seek refuge under your banner. You have not left the Vale this year and we took that as a sign.'

The young farmer hung his head in shame. Merroc felt a brief flare of compassion. It must be difficult for him, having to admit such a weakness in front of a complete stranger. The chieftain gazed over the gathered people of Eraich's tribe. They were undernourished, but still robust and healthy. There were enough young people in the assemblage to produce children for the Schwarzvolf. The Vale was fruitful and bountiful. To bring experienced farmers into the fold could be a massive benefit to the war-like Schwarzvolf. Exceptional hunters, they had no idea about agriculture, or tending crops.

'We should discuss this more, Eraich. Perhaps...'

'May I make a suggestion?'

The voice was Valkia's. Merroc started in surprise. He had not heard his daughter approaching. She was like a spectre that came from the night to startle you into an early grave. Her eyes were studying Eraich with unashamed interest. They roamed up and down his muscular frame.

For his part, the young leader studied Valkia back in return, not even making any sort of attempt to keep the admiration from his gaze. Merroc scowled, but then pointed to her.

'My daughter,' he said, with unmistakable irritation in his tone. 'Valkia.'

Eraich inclined his head. 'Chieftain's daughter,' he said, formally but she waved away the title with impatience.

'My name,' she said with steel in her tone, 'is Valkia.'

'Your suggestion?' Merroc interrupted, not wishing this to continue. Valkia took her eyes from Eraich and looked over to her father.

'Whilst you and the Circle meet with Eraich and his men, perhaps the Schwarzvolf could demonstrate kindness to the women and children of their tribe. We have food going spare and fires by which they could warm themselves.' She ran her hand through her short hair and treated Eraich to a smile that could have dazzled him into death.

'That is a most generous gesture, chi... Valkia,' replied the young farmer and looked over at Merroc. 'If your father agrees, that would be very welcome. It has been a hard journey to reach you.'

If Merroc was surprised by Valkia's uncharacteristic show of kindness, he did not let it evidence itself on his face. He merely nodded. 'As you suggest, daughter,' he affirmed. 'Take the women and children to our hearth.'

Eraich reached out a hand and caught Valkia's arm tightly. The farmer's broad hand encircled her slim forearm easily. Radek drew in a deep breath. To so lay hands upon the chieftain's daughter was considered deeply offensive, even though he knew that Valkia was more than capable of handling the situation. For her part, Valkia simply held up her free hand to forestall what she sensed were Radek's harsh words. This was an ignorant stranger who knew no better.

'Promise me you will care for them,' Eraich said. 'They have been in my charge since my father's death two passes of the moons since. I must know that you mean them no ill intent.'

'You have my word,' Valkia said, and her tone could not have been sweeter. 'The women and children of your people will receive nothing but courteous hospitality from the Schwarzvolf.'

'Thank you,' said Eraich simply and released her arm. She smiled at him again. 'I will leave you in the capable and competent hands of my *dear* father.' The smile was turned upon Merroc who felt a stirring of uncertainty. Valkia was planning something and his biggest fear was that he thought he knew well what it would be.

IT DID NOT take long for the strangers to be brought to the heart of the Schwarzvolf clan, although many of them were obviously unsettled by the sheer number of armed warriors. Nobody had yet ordered them to stand down.

Neither did they.

'Your people are fierce,' one woman confided in

Valkia. She was a matronly type, her outline soft and feminine where Valkia's was hard and masculine. Pretty? Perhaps so, but Valkia was more interested in the brood that scurried along behind her. So many children suggested that these people were prime breeding stock.

To the young woman's eyes, these newcomers were little more than a means to expand the Schwarzvolf. For years she and Radek had talked of the dream of being the greatest tribe in the north. They had the strength to do so, but they still lacked the numbers. That had begun to change in recent years, but one of the many things that the two of them had never agreed on was how precisely that change could be expedited.

'Yes,' she conceded eventually. 'The Schwarzvolf are a proud and fierce people. You will be glad enough of that when the wars begin.'

'The wars?' The matronly woman's eyes showed fear, a weakness that Valkia instantly despised. She shrugged lightly.

'Yes. The Schwarzvolf have enemies of their own. And from what Eraich was saying, it sounds as though you have some that require dealing with. It has been some time since my people went to war. They are hungry for it.' Her own hand ran lightly across the haft of the spear slung across her back. 'I hunger for the glory of battle also.'

'You fight?' Such incredulity that it was all Valkia could do not to turn around and slap the impertinent cow across the face.

'All the able women of the Schwarzvolf fight. It is our right and our honour to do so.'

'Your people are not like mine at all.' Doubt. Creeping doubt. But it was far too late. They were under the banner of the Schwarzvolf. And there they would stay.

'We *are* your people now,' retorted Valkia, dropping a low, mocking bow as she slid away from the trail of refugees back out to the woods. At little more than a crook of her finger, several of the armoured men came with her.

THE DISCUSSIONS HAD been terse since Valkia had taken the refugees to camp. Merroc sensed that Eraich knew what the inevitable outcome of their 'discussions' must be, and he had never expected to feel ashamed of who he was and what the Schwarzvolf stood for. Perhaps the illness had spread to his brain, softened him. Whatever it was, he was left feeling no better when, several minutes into the conversation, Eraich had simply sighed. He was a man defeated.

Requesting an opportunity to speak to the chieftain privately, Eraich and Merroc retreated a reasonable distance from the gathering. Radek watched like a hawk for any signs of treachery on the part of the young farmer.

But there was no hint of such behaviour in Eraich's voice as he finally found it. 'You plan to kill us and keep our women and children,' he said. It was not an accusation, merely a statement of fact. Merroc reached up to scratch at his straggly beard.

'My daughter does,' he acknowledged. 'Valkia will see no place for farmers in our war band. I have a wider-reaching vision than she does, however.'

'Do not humour me, chieftain. I have suffered more losses in this last few days than I ever thought possible. We are not cowards, but the suffering visited upon us by the mountain reavers has broken my people. There are even now plenty amongst us who would accept death as a blessing.'

'I would welcome the knowledge of those who know how best to till the land in this part of the Vale. My people are fighters, warriors. They know very little about crops. What few things we have successfully grown have been staunchly unyielding.'

'I asked your daughter to make me a promise,' said Eraich. 'And she made it. She said what I wanted to hear, but I need to hear it from you as well, chieftain. That our women and children will be cared for.'

'On that, you have my absolute word.' Merroc ran a hand over his eyes. He liked this young farmer in spite of his weakness. 'No harm will befall them.'

The sound of approaching feet caused both of them to turn. Valkia walked from the woods, at the head of several Schwarzvolf warriors. Her spear was readied and in her hand. Radek rose from where he sat, caught between the gazes of father and daughter; the one unreadable, the other mutinous. Merroc spoke eventually.

'This is not how it needs to be, Valkia.'

'It is exactly how it needs to be, chieftain.' She took a step closer to him. 'The Schwarzvolf have become soft. We have been robbed of our right to battle for so long that you entertain the notion of becoming settled, of welcoming farmers into our midst. If we are to remain strong, then it cannot be.'

'I forbid it, Valkia.' Merroc took several steps towards his daughter and she moved towards him, her face thunderous. The chieftain was acutely aware of the proximity of Radek and to his consternation, had no idea which side the Warspeaker's allegiance belonged to.

'I defy you,' she replied quietly and at a gesture, the men at her command surged forward, past both she and the chieftain, and began to slaughter the innocent refugees who had sought only succour and sanctuary within the embrace of the Schwarzvolf.

It was painfully quick and exceptionally bloody. Twenty fully armed warriors who had been deprived of warfare for months exalted in the opportunity to release their pent-up frustrations. Some of the men attempted to flee in a panic, but were brought to ground with well-aimed spear shots.

Merroc turned to Eraich who stood watching the slaughter of his men with a strange sort of resigned detachment. 'At least spare their leader,' he said to Valkia in an undertone. She spat at her father's feet and pushed him out of her way. Merroc tumbled to the floor, his head glancing off a stone with a spurt of blood.

'No, Valkia!'

With an alarming turn of speed, the chieftain made light of his illness and rose to his feet, planting himself again between Valkia and the dazed Eraich.

'Get out of my way. Let me do what needs to be done in order to preserve the name of our people.'

'There is no need for this! You have killed enough here today! Let the rest of them live.' Merroc gestured to the dozen or so men who had been corralled apart from the others. Terrified and angry by the violence, and no doubt still haunted by the attacks that had already reduced their numbers, the men stood mute with short knives clutched feebly in their hands. There had been a time, once, when Merroc would have sneered at such weakness.

Age, he thought grimly. *Age has robbed me of all reason.*

His daughter moved up to stand before him. She had grown so tall. Somehow, the little girl who had sat on his shoulders and demanded answers to questions had become a young woman; a warrior in her own right.

'You are weak,' she said to him in a soft voice. He felt the anger there; could sense how much she despised him for that weakness. 'Your time is done, old man.'

He felt his will crumble under her gaze. By the gods, but she was strong-willed. She was breaking down his resistance, tearing down the last of his fortitude like it was nothing more substantial than old hides. From somewhere, he found an inner strength that he had not known he still possessed. His death was a certainty, but then since his illness had struck, it always had been.

'So this is how it ends?' He studied her face. 'There will be no victory for you to savour, Valkia. I am dying anyway. If you kill me here today, you do me a kindness, not a dishonour.'

'You think I don't know that?' Their eyes locked and for a fleeting moment, he saw the compassion. It was deep, deep down, but it was there nonetheless. He felt a spark of hope that she would not lead his tribe to ruin with her bloodthirsty ways. He reached out a hand to stroke her cheek. For the first time in years, she did not flinch at his touch.

'Have a care, Lille Venn,' he said at a volume that only she could hear. 'After this day, after you kill me here, you will be completely on your own.'

'No,' came a voice from behind him. 'She never was on her own, Merroc.'

The chieftain was not aware of the sword that had slid in between his shoulders from behind until Radek withdrew it. Blood spurted from the chieftain's mouth and he released Valkia's face. The blade slipped easily from the old man's heart and he collapsed nervelessly to the ground. It was most assuredly a clean kill. The chieftain's daughter and the Warspeaker watched impassively as Merroc gave a last rattling sigh, their expressions unreadable. Eraich, being held fast by the arms of two of the tribesmen watched the death of Merroc with horror.

When it was over, when the body ceased twitching and lay still, his eyes staring up at nothing, Valkia looked up at Radek. There was terrible indecision in her face.

'You realise what I must do,' she said.

'I always knew it would come to this,' replied the Warspeaker. He sounded calm and in a strange echo of her father's last gesture, he reached to touch her cheek. 'I have been ready for this since the day you asked if I would stand with you. I have given you more. I have given you the reason you need to take what rightfully should be yours.' He dropped his sword and stared directly ahead.

'Radek...' Valkia stared at the Warspeaker, his scarred, ugly face more dear to her than anything else in her life. And one by one, she took the images and memories she had of him, setting fire to them in her thoughts until they were blown to ash. Any hope she might ever have had for conquering her reluctance to embark on a relationship with Radek was forever lost and she felt nothing for him.

For Valkia, detaching from her emotions had been that simple.

'You killed my father, Warspeaker,' she said, speaking in a voice loud enough to be heard by all those present. 'Such treachery can only be met with one punishment. Do you understand this?'

'I know,' Radek replied loudly and clearly. 'I know the punishment and I accept it gladly. It is a small price to pay to rid ourselves of the snivelling weakling he had become.' He lowered his eyes to Valkia who had drawn her dagger from her belt. Even now there was the faintest glimmer of uncertainty there.

'Do it, Valkia,' he hissed. 'Now.'

They would be the last words he uttered. Valkia sprang forward, putting all her strength into the movement and knocked Radek to the ground. As she knelt astride him, she raised the dagger high.

'For the crime of slaughtering my father, Radek, Warspeaker of the Schwarzvolf, I condemn you to death.'

She struck downwards and dug the knife deep into his belly, drawing a clenched grunt of agony from the former scout. With a deft slice, she split open his abdomen. That was the point at which Radek finally screamed. He thrashed wildly as glistening organs and ropey guts spilled out on to the sodden earth, mixing his blood with that of the dead chieftain. Valkia let him struggle beneath her weight for a few moments before rising once again to her feet. She cast a gaze around the assembled masses. Her face gave away nothing of what was going on inside her head. Her voice, when she spoke, was leaden.

'See this and mark it well. Such is the fate of the betrayer.'

She let the dying man squirm for a while, watching as his struggles grew weaker and then took up his sword. She turned the blade of the weapon downwards towards him. The first stroke crunched awkwardly into the bones of the traitor's neck. The second severed his head in a welter of gore and silenced his voice forever.

'Bring them both,' said Valkia, stepping back. 'My father for the rites due his position and the traitor as an example.' She turned her attention to Eraich. 'I made you a promise,' she said. 'And I keep it. But your people are no longer yours to be concerned about.' As her blade flashed from left to right across Eraich's neck and darkness rushed in to claim him, the faintest suggestion of a smile crossed his features. The last words he heard were Valkia's declaration.

'They are mine.'

FOUR
Chieftain's Daughter

SHE FELT NOTHING. Standing beside the corpse of her father, Valkia felt absolutely no grief, no sorrow or even any pleasure at her father's death. She had travelled back to the village ahead of the funeral procession to deliver the news personally to Kata. Her stepmother had nodded tersely and bitten her lip but had not shed any tears. Weakness was not an option and Valkia respected that. She held little Edan to her closely and Valkia left her alone to find her two little half-sisters.

It sickened her to hear the wail of grief that came from Kata's tent as she left, and much of the respect she had once held for her stepmother was lost in that instant.

The two little girls were only children and they cried when she told them that their father would not be coming back. She didn't spare them any details. To tell them a lie would be to do them a disservice. She told them that Radek had killed him and was mildly gratified that the elder of the two immediately demanded to know if retribution had been carried out.

She sent them back to their mother and they disappeared into the yurt scant seconds before the dead chieftain's body was borne back into camp, carried on the shoulders of the Schwarzvolf warriors. In their wake, Radek was being dragged by the ankles. His body was filthy, having picked up a light coating of leaf mould. A slimy red trail marked his passage across the ground, where what was left of his blood dribbled from the ragged stump of his neck.

Throughout the camp, whispers had already started. The newcomers, the farming community that Eraich had brought to them were huddled together, staring in fear at the horror unfolding before them.

It was her moment. Valkia hated Radek for taking this course of action, but in the end, his loyalty to her had been absolute. She owed it to that gesture to grasp the opportunity fully. Edan could not take control of the people. If she didn't stake her claim right this moment, then the entire tribe would fall to in-fighting.

She moved to stand by the central hearth in the camp. The flames were low at this hour of the day but soon the fire would be banked, to be used as a central communal cooking area. Now, though, it needed to be used for another purpose entirely.

The young woman with the close crop of dark hair took only a moment to compose herself and then she spoke in a clear voice that cut through the murmur of low, anxious whispering as cleanly as a knife.

'People of the Schwarzvolf, we have been betrayed.' Valkia pointed a finger at her dead father. 'Our Chieftain, our beloved Merroc, lies dead because of the treachery of a man he trusted. A man he loved as a brother and who we all trusted as our Warspeaker.' She turned the focus from Merroc to Radek. If anybody noticed the slight shake in her voice, they could easily put it down to the emotion of the moment rather than nerves.

'Radek the betrayer.' She levelled a finger at him. 'See him there. He lies dead by my hand. Retribution was served instantly, but not before he gave me the truth.' Now came the lie that she had carefully constructed on the journey back to the village. 'My father was going to do what was right. He planned to cull the weak from the strong, separate the brave from the cowardly and keep those who could wield their weapons with skill. But Eraich and his men conspired with Radek. They promised him the position of chieftain if he gave his aid to assassinate my father.' She looked around. She had their attention. There was a sharp intake of breath from the women of Eraich's tribe, but Valkia ignored it.

'It is no secret that Radek hungered for my father's position. He agreed to this gutless plot.' She lowered her finger as she realised just how loyal the men who had witnessed the events were to her. At least she presumed loyalty. It may have been that they were simply reluctant to speak against her. Whatever the reason, not one of them disputed her story. Their fealty gave her a swell of courage. 'Such treachery could not go unpunished. As such, the people of the hills will be taken into the Schwarzvolf conditional upon their complete, unswerving loyalty. Any of those who do not wish to accept that condition, then consider the alternative.'

A slow, exceptionally cruel smile spread across her face. 'The alternative is your own deaths. If you wish to join your menfolk as food for the animals of the woods, then my warriors will gladly aid you in meeting that desire.' Her green eyes, flat and emotionless mirrors, ranged across the women and children who were new to the hearth. Each one of them bore the same look of grief and misery as the other, but none dared defy her. Weak, Valkia thought. Come the hard months of winter, they would be the first to die.

She let the lie slide easily from her lips, feeling great pleasure at the conviction in her own voice. Every single person in the camp was hanging on her every word and that sent a delicious thrill through her. It was time for Valkia to make her final play.

'I mourn the passing of my father,' she said. 'In his time, he was a great leader. But age, sickness and a moment of weakness in trusting those traitors led to his death. I am his oldest child. As such, I take up the mantle of leadership in his place.' She stooped and unhooked her father's cloak, the symbolic outer representation of the tribe's leadership. She lay it across her arms and stood defiant, a tall, willowy figure who any of the warriors could easily have broken in two.

A silence had fallen and only ambient sounds remained. The occasional spit of the fire. A faint breeze rustling through what remained of the autumn leaves still clinging tenaciously to the trees around them. Her own heartbeat pounding in her chest. She kept stock-still, hardly daring to breathe. If there was going to be any challenge to her leadership, it would have to come sooner rather than later.

'Valkia.'

The single word came from one of the warriors who had not been present at the slaughter. Adok stepped forward and Valkia appraised him through half-lidded eyes. The man was powerfully built, a clear head and shoulders above her. His thick arms were folded across his chest and his square jaw, mostly hidden by a straggly black beard was thrust out in a pugnacious challenge. His intent was obvious to all and they held their collective breath.

Adok's next words never saw the light of day. He opened his mouth to speak and could only manage a choked torrent of blood as the tip of Valkia's spear punched through his throat and cracked his spine. The tribesman stood transfixed by the weapon for several long moments, his mouth opening and closing in a futile effort to gasp a few more moments from the air. Within seconds, the strength drained out of him. Adok toppled to the ground, his head half-severed and his life gushing away onto the cold earth.

'Do any more of you have anything to say?' She admitted a faint sense of disappointment to herself. She had been keen to prove her worth in the Circle of Blood, but she'd needed to make a swift example and Adok had amply provided. He was... he had been... a superlative warrior. But she was surrounded by those. One would not be missed. And they were all here and they were accepting her claim to leadership without question.

It did not strike her until much, much later that the reason nobody further disputed her claim was simply that many of them had all been following her command for a long time.

'I have something to say,' came a quiet voice from behind her. Valkia spun around, her gore-slicked spear levelled. Kata looked up at her stepdaughter, Edan in her arms. 'Will you spare my children? Will you let them live? It was your father's wish that Edan take the mantle when he came of age. Will you grant him life until he is old enough to challenge your leadership?'

Kata was barely recognisable from the competent shieldmaiden who had stood alongside Valkia all those years ago. Her face had aged years in barely an hour. Her eyes were red from crying and there was a dull bleakness in their dark depths. She twisted anxiously at her hair with her free hand, whilst the infant boy reached up to pull at it as well, enjoying the game.

Damn her. Damn her for asking that question in front of the entire tribe. There was only one answer to the question and Valkia felt the only stirring of guilt she had known since waking that fateful morning.

But Valkia had discovered a propensity for smooth lies that she had always known she possessed. She looked over at Kata and remembered that day, so many years ago, when the other woman had reassured her whilst standing in the shield line. She remembered the affection she bore for her. She remembered it all and she neatly compartmentalised it and put the thoughts into the back of her mind. She could almost hear Radek's whispering suggestion.

It will do you no harm to at least appear *benevolent.*

'Of course, Kata,' she replied eventually and lowered her weapon. There was no real threat, unless the traditionalists of the Schwarzvolf turned their backs on her because of her gender. And right now, that certainly didn't seem likely. No doubt it could be arranged for the infant boy to meet with an unfortunate accident once he was old enough to join the hunt.

The thought came so easily to Valkia that she was almost shocked at her own duplicity.

Almost.

Her stepmother nodded her thanks and stepped back with the child clutched tightly in her hands. She watched Valkia for a few moments longer and then returned to the comparative privacy of her tent.

Where she will no doubt howl like a dog over the death of that puny weakling.

Her lip curled in a slight sneer, Valkia's eyes roamed the assembled tribe once again. Silence had fallen and when she had waited long enough, she nodded. 'Then for my first command, I order the burning of my father's body as he would have desired. His ashes will be cast to the four winds. He wished for the Schwarzvolf to winter here in the Vale and I will respect that.'

Valkia knelt before her father's body and closed the staring, dead eyes that were boring into her accusingly. 'Members of the Circle – an immediate meeting will be necessary. I will be seeking a new Warspeaker.' She stood and cast her gaze at the mangled corpse of Radek.

'As for *that* one,' she said, and she had to work hard to keep the catch from her voice, 'let his skin be stripped from his bones by the carrion birds. Bring the bodies of the traitors from the woods and string them all up at the edges of camp so that anybody who considers betrayal can be reminded of the cost.'

At these words, the new members of the tribe began to weep; some softly and with control, others wailing hysterically. Valkia turned the full force of her stare on them.

'Stop it,' she ordered in a tone that brokered no argument. 'Stop that noise. You should be glad that I choose to show clemency at all. My own people…' It was the first time she had said that and it had been the absolute truth. It filled her with pleasure. 'My own people will go without this winter to ensure you and your squalling whelps are fed. Show some gratitude – or go back to the hills. Circle. The tent of the chieftain. Now.' The wailing dropped to a level where all that could be heard were chokes and the occasional sob.

Having made her decree – and her position very clear – Valkia strode to the yurt used for the meetings of the Circle. She passed Kata's yurt on the way and ignored the sound of sobbing from within. Without pause or respect, she pushed her way into the tent. Kata, who had been curled in a ball on the floor, looked up, deeply shamed by being found in such a manner.

No words passed between the two women but Valkia eventually spoke. 'Give him the rites due his station as chieftain, Kata,' she said. 'I put you in charge of overseeing the funeral.'

Kata's eyes were bright, but she shed no more tears. She bit her lip and nodded.

'As my chieftain wishes.' Her voice cracked on the word and she turned her head away. Valkia watched her with thoughtful eyes and then left her.

'I DISLIKE THE title "chieftain".'

If her opening statement surprised the Circle, none of them showed it. They were already in a state of wary shock from the sudden death of Merroc. She had taken her position at the head of the Circle, lounging amid the furs that until barely hours ago had belonged to her father. There was a lingering stench of him, she noticed. She would burn the furs and replace them with her own. A heavy, uncertain peace had settled over the gathering and that merely served to fan the flames of her irritation. She pointed at the Godspeaker who sat slightly behind and to the right of her.

'We need to consider the skeins of fate,' she said imperiously. The Godspeaker inclined his head graciously.

'The moment you end this gathering, my ch... my... chieftainess? The moment you do that, then we shall do so.'

'Chieftainess.' Valkia screwed up her face in distaste. 'I like that even less. Until something more appropriate comes to mind, I will be called "het-woman".' Valkia tried the word a couple of times and nodded. 'Yes. That will suffice, I think. Now, to more important matters. Firstly, we need to replace the Warspeaker.'

'With respect, Valkia,' said Hepsus, one of Merroc's most favoured warriors. He was in his early twenties, a thick-set man with wiry red hair and a curling beard. He was a vicious man and rarely spoke unless he thought that it was necessary. Valkia turned her expressionless stare on him and was gratified to see him baulk. 'With respect, hetwoman,' he said, amending his tone of address with obvious distaste, 'the chieftain is barely cold. We need to take stock of what has happened.'

'There is no need,' Valkia shot back. 'Those who were present during the hunt will tell you what happened. The treacherous fool Eraich plotted and schemed the very idea of my father's assassination with Radek.' She leaned back slightly. 'Is there any part of that which you do not understand? Perhaps if I were to speak more slowly?'

'I understand perfectly,' responded Hepsus with a faint sneer. 'None of the Circle were present for this alleged meeting. We have only your word...'

'Is that not good enough for you?' Something changed in Valkia's voice then, and the harsh snap became a thrumming purr. 'Come, Hepsus. We have known one another all our lives. Have I ever lied to you?'

'No, but...'

'Then surely my word should be all you need.' It was not a question. It was a statement and Hepsus instinctively knew that to push further would invite unpleasantness. He dropped into sullen silence and she gave him a look of approval. Her arrogance came so easily; but then it always had done.

She continued as though the interruption had not happened, drumming her long fingers against the skin of her thigh. 'Radek was an excellent Warspeaker, whatever his ultimate failing may have been. Replacing him will not be an easy task.' Her tongue ran across her lips as she considered. 'I propose that those who consider themselves suitable for the position present themselves in three days time and we will open up the Circle of Blood to them. A good Warspeaker must be a tenacious Warspeaker. The one still standing at the end of the fight will be our candidate.'

The rest of the Circle stared at her. This was unheard of. In past times, the chieftain had selected his own Warspeaker based on merit. Valkia laughed, a rich, throaty sound, at their faces.

'Oh, come now!' She practically beamed her amusement at them. 'I am not suggesting a fight to the death! Merely a trial to determine who is the most cunning and the most capable. Although, if you feel a battle to the death would be more appropriate...' She cut the sentence short and bit back the desire that this be the case. She sensed the palpable air of relief at her amendment and nodded. Fights to the death for her amusement would have to wait, it seemed.

'Secondly, the reavers mentioned by Eraich allegedly decimated their people. We should seek them out and assess whether we should consider them a threat or possible allies. Hepsus.' She turned to the warrior. 'Put together a scouting party and take them up into the hills. Report back as swiftly as you can. If Eraich's smallholdings are still standing and have not been burned to the ground, take whatever of use you can find.'

'As my hetwoman commands,' replied the warrior. *This* he understood. Direct orders. He felt relieved. Valkia nodded her pleasure at his easy compliance.

'Finally and most importantly, we need to properly inventory our supplies. We need to know what we have to see us through the winter.' This was a subject that she and her father had often come to blows over. Merroc's attitude had been that the gods would provide. Valkia, far more pragmatic, had argued that it would be the *hunters* who would provide and that every morsel of food counted. There were enough things that could kill the people of the Schwarzvolf. Starvation due to stupidity was not an option.

She looked around the group. 'Perhaps one of the women from the newcomers can tally numbers and aid with rationing. Find out. Godspeaker, that may be a task for you. You are more inclined to patience than the rest of us.'

The elderly man nodded. His eyes had not left Valkia since they had assembled and she was slightly uncomfortable under his scrutiny. She did her best not to let it bother her though. She had to demonstrate complete control and strength of purpose to maintain her position as leader. So far the fates had been on her side but she knew, without really understanding how, that one error at this stage could result in complete chaos. It was vital that she maintained her composure. There would be time to sit quietly and assess all that had happened later. Now was not that time.

Valkia chewed on her bottom lip and looked

around the assembled group. Time to deal with
the main issue. There was no point in leaving it to
be resolved later, or it would fester like an infected
wound.

When her voice came, it was clear and confident.
'I know that some of you have doubts in my ability
because I am a woman. But ask yourselves honestly:
when has that ever stopped me before?' She was
gratified that one or two of them looked faintly
embarrassed and even more pleased to see nods
of agreement. 'More than anybody else amongst
our people, I need your support. I can lead the
Schwarzvolf to greatness. All I ask for is your trust.'

She leaned forward then, her spear across her
knees. 'So tell me, my people, do I have that?' Her
finger ran down the blade of the spear tip and a
hungry look sparked in her eyes. 'Or do we need to
discuss it further?'

BY THE MEASURE of the Schwarzvolf's lifespans, Fydor
the Godspeaker was an old man. Fifty summers he
had lived and he was robust and healthy yet. Time
had not diminished his abilities or his voracious
appetite for life. He had taken three wives to his
hearth, had fathered many children, and countless
grandchildren bore his blood. Merroc had once
affectionately said that such a virile man could have
repopulated the tribe by himself. He was no great
warrior; in his youth he had lost not only his right
eye, but also most of the fingers of his left hand.
Only the thumb and part of the forefinger remained.

He could still wield a sword when the situation

demanded it, but unable to properly hold a shield he was more of a liability than an asset. At first he had struggled to cope with his loss of status but he had been young, barely an adult, and the previous God-speaker had guided him in the ways of divination.

Nobody knew whether he was genuinely able to feel the supposed will of the gods. But whether it was reading omens in the weather, predicting battle outcomes from the guts of an eviscerated animal or divining something more personal from the pieces of bone that he carried around in a pouch round his neck, Fydor was without question able to convince his people that he was speaking for the divine. The fact that his predictions came true with almost unfailing accuracy helped considerably.

When the Circle had broken, when Valkia had sent them from the tent that had once been her father's, she had turned her attention to him. Fydor had been there the day that Valkia had come into the world. Merroc's first-born. His pride when his wife had gone into labour had been so great and Fydor had never forgotten the look of disappointment when he had realised his longed-for son had been a girl. But Merroc had loved Valkia regardless.

Fydor shook the pouch around his neck, the bones within clattering together slightly. Valkia's dark eyes took in his slender form; the lined face and the bright, intelligent eyes.

'Godspeaker, you know what I must ask of you.'

'I do, hetwoman. You wish me to divine your future. A simple enough task.' She nodded and he continued. 'I will do so for you and gladly – but be warned. You must make your focus very specific.'

'What do you mean?'

'What is the answer that you seek, Valkia?' She did not berate the Godspeaker for the use of her given name. Within the tribe, Fydor was considered second only to their chieftain. The respect for him was immense and Valkia knew that she could not afford to make an enemy of him.

She leaned back on the furs and let her eyes close to half-lidded slits. She could hear the sounds of activity outside; people moving to carry out her orders. It was a heady thing to realise that she could command them so easily. The stringing up of the 'perpetrators' was a stroke of genius and she knew that it would put her mark very firmly and clearly on how she intended to rule her people.

Fydor did not hurry her. He untied the pouch from his neck and let the bones tumble to the floor. He picked through them, arranging them and generally preparing himself whilst Valkia considered the question that would shape her future.

Eventually, she sat upright again and her eyes opened. She crossed her legs beneath her and rested her chin on a hand.

'I seek to make the Schwarzvolf the most powerful tribe the people of the north have ever known. My question to the gods is this, Fydor. Will I succeed in that venture?'

The Godspeaker smiled and took the bone fragments up in his hand. He shook them in his closed fist. Their rattle sounded to Valkia like some kind of ominous overture.

'Let us find out, hetwoman.'

He opened his hand and cast the bones. Valkia could not bring herself to look down at them, but kept her focus firmly on the Godspeaker as he passed his misshapen hand across them and closed his remaining eye.

As was his way, he was mumbling under his breath, incomprehensible noises that she could not make out. She had long suspected that it was more for show than any mystical effect. But perhaps the effect of the day's events had taken her into its grip, because she felt a shiver of anticipation.

In his time, Fydor had foretold events with unerring accuracy. This was less an indication of some divine connection and more a testament to his ability to extrapolate current conditions from simple observation. He was an expert in reading the mood and shift of an army of warriors and had he been put in charge of a battle would have made a considerably lethal general. He had never experienced any kind of true holy ecstasy.

What he experienced now was far from ecstatic. Red began to seep into his mind's eye, as though a thin film of blood coated his thoughts. So real was the sensation that he actually opened his eye to be sure. He sucked in a sharp intake of breath. Valkia's eyes widened at the noise.

She looked as though she would speak, but he held up a hand to forestall her. He reached it up to his face and to his slightly detached surprise it did not come away stained with blood. Yet everything around him still bore an unmistakable tinge of deep crimson.

'Blood,' he whispered in a voice so quiet that Valkia had to lean forward to hear him. 'I see... blood in your future, Valkia.'

'Blood that I spill, or my own?'

'I cannot tell.' Even the air was charged with that unmistakably coppery scent that Fydor automatically linked in his mind to the aftermath of a battlefield. He licked his lips which had gone suddenly dry as he scrutinised Valkia. He spoke honestly, saying what he was seeing. The words given volume did not help him understand this strange phenomenon one bit, but he felt it was expected of him. 'You are falling into shadow. Darkness gathers around you. It will swallow you, consume you...' He frowned. 'Or envelop and protect you. I cannot tell which.'

The words set the hairs on the back of Valkia's neck to standing and she kept her face as impassable and neutral as she could maintain. 'Consider the question, Godspeaker. Will I succeed in my venture to bring the Schwarzvolf to greatness?'

Before Fydor could speak he experienced a terrifying vision. *Something* saw him, though he was not the focus of its attention. Its presence was vast, a fathomless thing of infinite rage. It burned with malevolence and radiated an air of sheer hatred and destruction. Against its enormity he was nothing but a speck, a tiny mote beside the furnace of an ageless fury. Heat, the acrid stink of burning metal and old blood assailed him. For a fleeting second he hungered for the glory of war once again. To wield a sword or an axe and cut down those who would dare to oppose them...

And then his thoughts exploded, shattering and raining down around him as the vision left him and the cold grip of reality drew him back into its grasp. His head was throbbing and he felt a powerful need to vomit.

Valkia's voice was coming at him from somewhere far, far away and he stared muzzily up at her. '...speaker!' She was standing above him, a look of genuine concern on her face. It was then and only then that Fydor realised he was lying flat on his back. He had no memory of falling, but it must have happened.

Her strong hand pulled him upright and without a word she handed him a cup of wine. He sipped at it gratefully and massaged his temple.

'What did you see?' Valkia pressed the matter, eager to know the outcome of his vision. She had watched the Godspeaker over the years as he had performed these rituals for her father, but she had never seen anything as convincing as what had just happened.

'The gods favour you, Valkia,' he said quietly. 'Or... a god. I cannot tell which. But their celestial eye rests firmly on you. I felt no disapproval, only...' He paused. What *had* he experienced? A bloodlust. Unable to accurately articulate something for which he had no frame of reference, he said what he believed she had to hear.

'You are strong,' he said. 'You are not afraid to take difficult decisions. I trust you will know I speak no ill of the dead when I say that towards the end, Merroc lost that ability. It will not be easy. But yes, Valkia. Yes. I believe you will succeed.'

'I knew I would,' she said, triumphant in her arrogance.

SEVERAL DAYS PASSED and the shock of Merroc's death began to lessen for the tribe. In truth, the chieftain had been so removed from the tribe's activities in the past months that most barely noticed his absence. But there was one person who felt his loss most keenly.

Valkia had graciously allowed Kata to remain in the chieftain's yurt but she had been entirely unable to settle. Edan was grizzly all the time and the two little girls were bundles of mischief who got over the shock of their father's death with the alacrity that only the innocent could manage. They were wearying and Kata felt exhausted. But she did not dare let herself sleep. She knew that Valkia's strike on her children must surely come.

More days flowed by, blurring into one. And still her children lived. Kata could not bring herself to believe that Valkia had meant her words. She could not believe that the new hetwoman would willingly allow Edan to grow to manhood and stake his claim on the tribe.

Her loyalties so torn, Kata began a slow but self-destructive descent into madness.

LIFE WENT ON regardless. Valkia's promise to open up the Circle of Blood was kept, and a pleasing number of young warriors presented themselves to her. Each one stated their intention to take on the role of the tribe's Warspeaker. It irritated the young woman that none of the shieldmaidens had chosen to present themselves, but she sensed that it was simply too much too soon.

The trial by combat commenced. From the thirty or so hopefuls, two clear potential warriors emerged. One was Hepsus, whose superior skill and years of experience gave him an edge that had seen more than one challenger carried from the circle in a daze. The other was a callow youth by the name of Pelyn, who was possessed of a considerable talent in the arena.

Valkia considered the latter thoughtfully. He was a strong-limbed young man of around her own age with hair like burnished copper and a pleasing arrogance to his stance. He would be pliable and easily manipulated to her will. Hepsus had the skill and the experience and, as Pelyn found out during the final trial, the superior cunning to lead her armies.

The two men battled for a full two hours, both sweating and panting by the end despite the bone-chilling cold. Each was covered in nicks and surface cuts from the other's practise blade.

'I can keep going as long as it takes, old man,' Pelyn had sneered, his self-assurance evident. 'You could do the honourable thing and concede defeat.'

'Were our roles reversed, boy,' panted Hepsus in return, 'would you do that?'

'I would never be in your position.'

'And that is why you will fail.' Hepsus straightened his back. 'To go into war with the belief that you are invincible will mean you fail to notice the pitfalls and snares your enemy puts in the path of your success. You are blinded to all but your own brilliance.'

Hepsus grinned suddenly. 'And so you fall victim to the oldest trick of the veteran warrior.'

'What's that?'

'Letting the old man get his breath back.'

It had been a matter of moments after that before the startled Pelyn was beaten into a daze by an invigorated Hepsus. The Schwarzvolf, who had been watching the trials eagerly, roared their approval. Valkia nodded once, curtly. But there had been no ceremony, no drinking into the night at the celebration of a new Warspeaker. Hepsus would need to fully prove himself before she formally accepted him.

She noted absently that once again, Kata had not been present. No doubt shut away in her yurt, drowning herself in floods of pathetic tears. Valkia's patience with her stepmother had worn away within days of the same reaction. She had attempted reasoning and she had resorted to shouting at Kata but neither worked. The woman was dead to the world beyond her own suffering.

'THEY CALL THEMSELVES the Bloody Hand.'

Hepsus had returned from the scouting mission after several days without a single loss. In addition, they had brought back many sacks of grain and whole haunches of dried meat that would add to their winter stores. The hills people had accepted their fate without too much difficulty, although several of them had stolen away in the middle of the night. Valkia had not bothered to seek them out. If they preferred to take their chances with the creatures of the Vale and its environs rather than remain in the protective embrace of the tribe, that was their own problem.

'The Bloody Hand,' Valkia repeated. 'Did you speak with them?'

'Aye, that we did.' Hepsus pushed a wad of dried herbs into the bowl of his pipe and lit it with a taper from the fire. The sweet, cloying smoke filled the tent with its smell and he offered the pipe to Valkia. She accepted it and inhaled the herbs, but not too deeply. They relaxed the body and it was easy to inhale too much and relax the mind as well. 'Son of their leader. Deron, his name was.'

'What led them to attack Eraich and his people?'

'They were... not forthcoming on the matter. I pressed the point as much as I dared under the pact of truce. As far as I can tell, they were simply hungry for a fight.'

'Possible threat or likely allies?'

Hepsus considered the question. 'Perhaps both,' he concluded after a while. 'They are small in number, but witnessing first-hand the damage they wrought in the farming settlement... they are also remarkably destructive. I suggest we treat them very carefully until we get a better idea of where we stand.' He took a long, slow draw on the pipe and the blue smoke clouded his face for a moment or two. 'They have asked to meet with the chieftain, of course.'

Valkia bristled slightly at the hint of amusement she detected in the other warrior's voice and shifted position until she was sitting more upright. 'And what did you tell them?'

'I said that I would speak to our leader and see what could be arranged.'

An uncomfortable pause followed. Valkia could feel her ire rising at Hepsus and his casual manner. She had always thought him flippant, but she had a distinct feeling that he was mocking her. He was baiting her, trying to draw a weakness out. Ordinarily, she would be damned if she would fall for it, but she had to ask the question. She had to ask the question and she had to ask it with confidence.

'Have you told him,' she said, her voice clear and without any hint of irritation, nervousness or indeed any emotion at all, 'that you are led by a woman?'

'No,' replied Hepsus and he took the pipe from between his teeth to grin wickedly at her. 'I thought I would let them find out for themselves.'

She could not tell from the way he spoke whether he had done this thing to weaken or strengthen her position, but a part of her was relieved. If the Bloody Hand thought that the Schwarzvolf were anything but strong, they would be attacked. She didn't doubt the capabilities of their warriors, but they were already in a difficult place. They had to have time to settle.

'Hetwoman?' Hepsus prompted her for a response. 'Do you wish to meet with them?'

She leaned back and, allowing her most imperious expression to drift idly across her face, nodded her agreement. 'I think so, Hepsus. Make the arrangements. I will speak with this – what did you say his name was?'

'Deron.'

'Yes. Deron. Invite him to accept the hospitality of the Schwarzvolf. We will discuss how we can... work together.'

'This seems... eminently sensible.' To Valkia's irritation, Hepsus was outwardly surprised at her competence. It did little to quench the flame of anger she felt towards the other warrior. She knew, deep down, that it was to be expected. He had not openly challenged her position when he had been given the chance, but he was certainly not missing any chances now. She would prove her worth to them all in time but Hepsus was a unique challenge.

He would make the perfect new Warspeaker as well, but Valkia would not grant him the satisfaction of acknowledging it. Not yet.

'I will meet with him and a deputation in four days. They are to leave their weapons with a warrior of your choosing. We will give them a feast of both food and words. They will understand that we are not like Eraich and his men.'

'As you command.' The red-haired warrior got to his feet and moved to the entrance of the yurt. She stopped him with a quiet whisper of his name. He turned and looked at her, his eyes glittering in the firelight and giving away nothing.

'Hepsus.'

'Hetwoman?'

'Do not seek to belittle me in this venture. My father may have been a forgiving, weak fool, but I am not. Play this game on my side and the rewards will be considerable. Try to push against me and the consequences will be on your own head. Do we understand one another?'

'Clearly.' A smile flickered across his face and it was filled with genuine humour.

She nodded in grim satisfaction and the warrior left her alone. After she was sure he had gone, she picked up one of the cushions and flung it the length of the yurt. She should have known that she would face this kind of problem before she started. Indeed, perhaps she *had* known and merely pushed the thought of how she would handle it to the back of her mind.

Valkia's tantrum did not last long and she composed herself within a few short seconds. She ran her finger across her dark hair and stared into the flames. Let this Deron make whatever he would of her gender. She would show him that the Schwarzvolf were not going to submit to the will of an invading tribe. She would roll over and beg for mercy from no man.

She sat alone for several minutes and then got to her feet. There was another matter that demanded immediate attention; that of the deteriorating mental well-being of Kata. In the days since Merroc's demise, the chieftain's widow had become increasingly detached. Valkia had already made the arrangements to have her two half-sisters cared for by other members of the tribe, but Kata had refused to give Edan up to anybody's care.

Valkia ducked out of the tent. Twilight had spread through the sky and the temperatures had dropped considerably. To the north, the dancing lights of the far-distant aurora could be seen as they revealed themselves to the night. A pang of long-ago memory touched Valkia momentarily as she recalled sitting atop the shoulders of a man she had once adored.

A faint flapping sound caught her attention and she turned to see what it was. The corpse of Radek, nailed to a wooden pole and placed at the edge of the camp, had already suffered badly from the unkind and merciless caress of the elements and the carrion birds that had gathered when the bodies had been mounted. What remained of his clothing fluttered in the light, chill breeze giving the body a faintly unnatural animation.

Seeing Radek there steeled Valkia's resolve and memories of her father were banished. Moving with her shoulders pulled back and her head held high, she headed for the tent where Kata had barricaded herself against the outside world.

As she approached, she sensed that something was not quite right simply from the smell that struck her. Despite the cold, which could slow down the process of death quite considerably, there was an unmistakable stench of death in the air. Her nostrils flared slightly and her pace quickened. Yes – without doubt – there was the bitter tang of blood on the wind. An almost unbearable desire to turn her back on the camp and go out in the woods to hunt swept over her, but the young woman fought it back with considerable self-control.

The entrance to the tent had been stitched together from the inside. Kata's stitches were tight but uneven; it had been an urgent act that her stepmother had performed. Scowling slightly, Valkia stood with her feet apart and her hands on her hips.

'Kata.'

She began with a soft voice, but received no reply. Her voice rose in volume until tiring of her efforts, she merely took her dagger from her hip and tore a new entrance in the thick hide of the dwelling.

The interior heat of the tent washed over her in a wave of unpleasant odour and stale air. It did not surprise her one bit to see the scene that lay before her. Kata was dead and there was no way that Valkia could start to guess how long that had been the case. She didn't know if Kata had died swiftly or had lingered for days. She was lying on the floor of the tent, her eyes open and staring upwards. Her fingers had locked around a wooden cup and Valkia prised it free. She sniffed the contents and coughed. It was one of the more potent herbs that her people used, usually to quicken the death of a warrior who had suffered a mortal wound in battle. From the number of crushed leaves still clinging to the side of the cup, Kata had taken enough to fell a mountain lion.

As if to aid the process, or perhaps simply in her madness, she had also carved gashes in each forearm and the corpse was grey. The woman was drained of all blood.

She stood up and looked around. Edan was still alive, but weak. He had no strength to cry and he lay on the ground at his dead mother's side, his eyes flowing with silent tears. He was covered in her sticky blood.

Without emotion, Valkia stared at the corpse of a woman who had always been her friend, but who had, in the end, been too weak. She felt no sorrow at this second familial bereavement, merely a faint sense of annoyance.

A choking sob pulled her attention towards the boy. Edan was almost a year old and had not yet quite mastered the art of walking unaided. The het-woman considered the infant without words for a time. It would be the easiest thing in the world to suffocate him now. Nobody would ever know.

In the years that followed, Valkia never truly knew what it was that caused her to spare the child's life that night. It was not sympathy, she knew that. It was more that she was suddenly compelled by a notion that if he lived, he would surely be of use to her in time.

She stooped and plucked the starving child up and balanced him on her hip. He clung to her, his little monkey arms around her neck and buried his face in her shoulder. Casting a final, scornful look at her dead stepmother, Valkia carried Edan from the tent and ordered it burned to the ground. In the eyes of the Schwarzvolf, Kata had committed one of the most unforgivable sins. Suicide was no way for a noble tribesman or woman to die and was never condoned.

In a short period of time, the balance of power and the very dynamic of the tribe altered. The chieftain and his wife were dead; the betrayal of a Warspeaker still haunted the conversations around camp and a woman – barely more than a girl – was taking their lives into her untried hands.

Nobody said a word as Valkia walked from Kata's tent, merely scurried to obey her commands. There was something in her manner that suggested non-compliance would not be conducive to continued good health. She pushed the traumatised Edan onto a young woman of Eraich's tribe who took the little boy gladly. Behind her, flames licked into the darkening night as the last trace of her upbringing was rendered to ash.

FIVE
The Blood God

THE MEETING WITH the Bloody Hand ran as Valkia had expected it to. The arrival of Deron and his companions had caused a certain ripple of terror amongst the farming folk who recognised those who had slaughtered their friends and family. They were dressed not unlike the Schwarzvolf in a mixture of treated leather and furs, but there the similarities ended. The Bloody Hand were of a different stock to Valkia's people: bigger, stronger and, as she found out over the course of the discussions, bordering on the insane.

The deputation had refused outright to be parted with their weapons, but had actually offered a compromise that was acceptable. Their weapons were bound tightly into their scabbards making any attempts to unsheathe them difficult and time-consuming. It was a unique solution to a long-standing problem and Valkia had taken mental note of it.

Deron was a young man of around twenty-five years old, huge and powerfully muscled, with green eyes that looked to Valkia as though they flickered between sanity and madness constantly. She found him exotic and that in itself made him strangely attractive.

Kata had spoken once of the need to bear children and it was something that Valkia had always ignored or shrugged off. She was not the maternal type, but she knew that it would fall to her at some point to bear a strong heir – male or female – to follow her. Whenever she looked at this big, powerful man with his dark hair and mad eyes, she hungered for him in a way she had never felt before. Even Radek, who she had loved in her way, had never stirred her passion in the way that Deron did.

She let none of this show during the course of their discussions however, maintaining an air of cultivated indifference to the Bloody Hand. She learned that they were small in number and that they had come down from higher in the hills several years before. They had never encountered the Schwarzvolf in that time.

They addressed every single sentence to Hepsus until Valkia finally grew annoyed.

'Speak to *me*,' she said. 'I am Valkia, hetwoman of the Schwarzvolf. You will show respect, man of the Bloody Hand, or you will answer to the tip of my spear.'

Her anger showed as two pink spots high on her cheek and Deron had studied her thoughtfully for a few moments. When he spoke, his voice was a low rumbling bass that did nothing to dispel the sense of attraction she felt for him. His accent was strange and the awkwardness of his pronunciation suggested that they either spoke very little or simply had their own language.

'Your Warspeaker tells us a woman leads the Schwarzvolf. We do not believe this to be true.'

'Do you think women weak?' Deron laughed at this.

'No,' he said, simply. 'Far from weak. We have all witnessed the pain of childbirth. My father says that no man could ever bear that. But until now, I had not met a tribe with a woman in such a position of great power.' His eyes narrowed. 'Are you imbued with the unnatural?' When she looked puzzled at his words, he corrected himself. 'Do you practise magic?'

'I am a warrior,' she retorted, affronted at such a suggestion. She took up her spear. 'I fight at the heart of every battle and I am afraid of no man.' Deron tipped his head to one side and considered the spear.

'Is that an invitation to fight?'

It was phrased as a question and Valkia instinctively understood its meaning. Deron was suggesting a challenge. Not to her position, but merely to gauge her strength. It would weaken her position considerably if she were to refuse. A smile came over her face.

'An invitation to fight? An interesting notion.' She laughed. 'Yes. We shall fight, Deron of the Bloody Hand.'

She was rewarded with a smile that exposed all of Deron's jagged, vicious-looking teeth. A handsome face? Yes, very handsome. But there was something more in that look than simple mutual attraction. There was a lust for blood. *Her* blood. And like everything else in her life, Valkia was not going to give it up easily.

* * *

THE CIRCLE OF Blood, as it was known, was little more than a cleared area of dirt on the west side of the camp with a thick post hammered rigidly into the ground that marked its centre. The arena was a churned, pockmarked landscape of mud and slush, crusted with ice and spotted with sticky, crimson pools revealing its heavy and frequent usage. The Schwarzvolf took the training of their young warriors very seriously and did not use practise weapons. A training session with the Warspeaker rarely ended in death, but it was not completely unknown.

Flakes of snow were drifting lazily down from the grey sky and Valkia raised her eyes to the heavens as she stepped into the circle, blinking away the flakes. Within days, these light flurries would turn to the endless snows of winter.

News of this trial of arms against the representative of an unknown tribe had spread throughout the camp like wildfire and a relatively large crowd had gathered. The fighting area itself was an open space but the Schwarzvolf remained at a practised distance. A length of heavy, braided rope was threaded through a hole in the central post and lay in two ends that were equidistant. The baying audience stood a few paces back from the ends of rope.

Valkia had stripped back to nothing more protective than a leather vest and a pair of heavy deerskin trousers. Her arms were bare and exposed to the cold of the day, the flesh was dimpled and the hairs raised. She did not shiver, however, either from the temperature or from fear.

Despite the chill in the air, Deron had stripped off

his heavy leathers and furs and was going to fight bare-chested. Valkia chewed on her lower lip at the sight of his physique. He was just as big beneath the clothing as he had been with it over his shoulders. His powerful arms and his broad back rippled with sinewy muscle and Valkia's eye was drawn to the curious brand in the centre of his chest. It appeared to be a strange, angular representation of a skull, and the sight of it stirred old childhood memories of a battle long past. She set them aside with easy detachment. There would be time enough to think on the discovery later.

By mutual agreement, they had decided on a knife fight and already Valkia was sizing up her opponent, working out opportunities to bring him down. She had thought that he would be big and strong, but seeing him like this, suspected that there might be a swiftness to his movements as well. Their left hands were bound with the free ends of the marker rope, creating an unbroken bond between them that must not be severed until the battle was decided. It could also be used, if so desired, to lethal effect by a canny warrior. More than one unlucky soul had met their end choked to death by its unyielding coils.

'To first blood, Valkia of the Schwarzvolf?' Deron asked the question across the arena and she confirmed her acceptance of the terms in a loud, clear and strong voice.

'To first blood. Deron of the Bloody Hand.' She readied herself, drawing the wicked, double-edged knife from the sheath on her thigh. It was a well balanced blade and one which she had used for many years. It had been her father's before hers and despite its age, the edge had never dulled. Some whispered that there was untamed magic deep at its heart. It was an unusually bright blade, not like the heavy iron that made up most of their weapons. It flashed in her hand.

The two combatants prowled around the arena, each weighing up the other and tugging at the rope experimentally. Valkia raked in the sight of the man opposite her and approved silently of his cat-like grace. These men were strong, fine warriors – that much she could tell – and that hint of madness she had seen in his eyes suggested that they were fierce.

For a time it was obvious that neither wanted to make the first move and then Valkia, perhaps tiring of the game, darted like a silverfish, quick and fast, feinting to Deron's right side and coming to a halt behind him. The move was lightning quick, but the big man spun on his heel and hunkered low in a defensive stance, the knife held out before him.

Several of Valkia's people made noises of approval as the two warriors in the arena came together. Valkia's slim, lithe body merged into the shadow of Deron's bigger one as they pressed against one another, assessing each other's strength.

'You are strong,' grunted Deron. 'Fast, too.' Another of those sharp-toothed smiles and he added the sting. 'For a woman.' He broke away from her in a movement that made her stumble slightly as the rope snapped taut. She did not fall but regained her balance quickly and dropped, rolling head-over-heels away from the downwards slash that he aimed at her arm. She got back up to a crouch and pounced, a dark-haired wildcat, towards his leg. The blade of the silvery dagger flashed in the weak winter sunlight and Deron jerked his body forward sending up a spray of mud. She missed his calf by a fraction of an inch.

She swore loudly and leaped back to her feet, only to be caught by a blow from his fist. She felt it crack across her cheekbone and her world exploded in pain. Her head whipped to the side and she turned back to glower at him in fury. There was a mad grin on his face.

'You wanted to fight, so we fight,' he said, simply. 'To first blood, yes? As we agreed? Blood for the Blood God.'

The words he spoke meant nothing to Valkia at all and yet they still stirred something deep inside her. All she knew was that this unfamiliar man who was a potential enemy of her people was taunting her and she would not let the insult go.

With a low bellow of rage, she hurled herself at the big man, not caring about form or style. She would claw out his eyes if she had to. His laughter did little to force back the anger.

'Fight!'

He said the word again as he moved easily from her attack. Her face was growing scarlet with rage. He was embarrassing her in front of her people. The thought that they were all watching this public humiliation woke something feral in her. A ululating scream left her throat and she leaped at Deron's back, winding the rope easily around his exposed neck. He was still *laughing*. And that made her even angrier.

She raised the knife, ready to plunge it into the arterial vein in his neck. She would give him blood for his Blood God, whatever that even meant. But no matter how angry she was, Deron was still bigger and stronger than she was and he threw her free quickly. She hit the ground hard and lay there for a moment, winded. The low sounds of approval from her people had swollen to cheers as she'd launched herself at Deron, but now a silence descended.

The snow was coming down more heavily and it settled on Valkia as she lay where she had fallen. Deron stretched out his shoulders in an idle way. He untangled himself from the rope and moved towards her.

'She is strong,' he said to the assembled watchers. 'But not strong enough, I think. She...'

Whatever Deron's opinion of Valkia might be was cut short as he moved within striking distance. She had been carefully waiting for him to approach, feigning injury, and the moment he was in her reach, the rope snapped taut once again, this time coiling around the big man's ankle. He flipped onto his back with a roar of surprise just as Valkia's blade flashed and stabbed deftly into the meat of his thigh. It cut through the leather trousers and bit into the powerful muscle there. He let out a growl that was somewhere between pain and outrage and put his hand to the wound.

It came away stained with red.

'First blood,' said Valkia between gritted teeth that felt slightly loosened in her jaw from his earlier blow. 'The victory is mine. Now give me one good reason why I shouldn't change the terms of this fight and gut you where you lay?'

He sat up and thrust his mud-spattered face close to hers. The next words he spoke were pitched so that she and only she could hear them. Any hint of a language deficiency was gone. He spoke clearly and with such clarity that she almost salivated.

'Because the Blood God favours you. And you want to know what that means. Kill me now and you will never know. Let me live and you will learn.'

He put out a hand to her and they stood together. He raised her arm into the air. 'Valkia of the Schwarzvolf draws first blood. Your leader, she is quite the fierce little thing.'

That awful silence that had so filled Valkia with dread was torn apart by the sound of her people – of *all* her people – bellowing her name at the top of their lungs. In that moment, she realised that she had won them over.

The Bloody Hand remained as the tribe's guest for one more day and Deron kept to his word. He told her of the god his people worshipped, an entity who in the telling was much like the god the Schwarzvolf knew as the Axefather. A dark, ancient god whose thirst for blood was engendered in the ruthlessness of his followers. He told her many things, but he did not tell her everything.

'One thing at a time, hetwoman,' he said when she had complained that he was not giving her the full truth. 'There is a truce between your people and mine and that will be honoured. We will speak more of an allied future after the winter. We must go back to our own people now, before the snows come and the hill passes are blocked.' He looked up to the dark, threatening skies and Valkia realised with a pang of annoyance that she did not want this strange warrior to leave. She had too many questions.

Deron smiled down at her. 'We will meet again in the spring,' he said. 'When we will form an official alliance of our people. Together, the Bloody Hand and the Schwarzvolf will be invincible. But when you kill, *whatever* you kill, dedicate it to the Blood God. He will reward you in kind. Of that, I am sure.'

THE BOUNTY OF the spring and summer combined with the careful rationing that was imposed on the growing tribe proved to be exceptionally effective and as such, losses of life over the hardest weeks of the dark winter were minimal. There were still a number however: the elderly, the infirm and infants who were too weak to survive the earliest days of life.

For Valkia, the long months of winter were a trial unlike anything she had ever anticipated. Juggling the demands of her people with the frequent incursions from small tribes who thought they could somehow take on the might of the Schwarzvolf was tiring. She had never realised just what leading her people would mean.

Politics.

Not all the dealings with small tribes were making short work of the more aggressive ones – and the Schwarzvolf did that with increasingly brutal style. The number of heads placed on poles around the perimeter of the camp grew almost daily. Valkia encouraged competition between her warriors; offering a prize to those who could take the most skulls in a battle. It kept them keen and eager.

Under her leadership, the Schwarzvolf were gaining a reputation as a bloodthirsty, relentless band of warriors. For some that acted as a deterrent and for others, it served as a challenge. For a handful, it opened up interesting trade possibilities. It was the latter that gave Valkia the most headaches. It was the latter that brought would-be suitors to the fore.

Valkia knew in her heart that Merroc had realised early on that he would never be able to sell his daughter off to the highest bidder – or to a worthy son of a worthy ally – and that this had inadvertently made her instantly more appealing to a wide variety of young men from across the steppes where the Schwarzvolf made their home.

She attracted the interest of a few old men as well. More than one of this seemingly endless stream of would-be consorts walked out of the camp of the Schwarzvolf having had Valkia laugh in their faces. Some walked out nursing wounds from the fiery, wicked-tempered hetwoman.

Several of these suitors had to be carried out along with the headless bodies of their entourage, having tempted the wrath of the warrior woman with their rancid breath, roving eyes and eager hands. Valkia made sure these trophies in particular adorned stakes that lined the entrance of her tent.

'You will have to form an alliance at some time, Valkia.' She was seated in the yurt that she had made hers, a cup of hot wine in her hand and a scowl on her face. She felt nothing so much as a child being on the receiving end of a lecture.

'Tell me why I "have" to do such a thing if you would, Godspeaker?' Her tone was imperious and haughty. Nearly every man who had presented themselves to her and broached the subject of an alliance had begun well enough. They had discussed ways in which they could expand the power of the Schwarzvolf. Ways in which they could strengthen the might of what was rapidly becoming acknowledged as the strongest, largest and most influential tribe in the region.

Valkia was always charming and interested up to this point. But then the tone would change and the suggested reciprocal cost would be discussed. And in four out of five negotiations, her hand in marriage was the key focus.

'You need to marry, or at least take a mate. For a start, you need to assure your line of succession.' Valkia flung a sour look at the Godspeaker, damning him silently for speaking the words that she constantly denied as truth.

'I am not yet in need of such reassurance,' she said, the scowl not leaving her face. 'I am still young.'

'Aye, hetwoman, you are young. But you know as well as I do what the gossip is throughout the camp.' Her eyebrows raised and for the briefest of moments, the scowl was replaced by something that most resembled cynical amusement.

'The rumours that I am not a woman? That I have no appetite for men? Or the one that I am barren? Which particular rumour is the favoured one of the day, Godspeaker? What do my people say of me now?' In the months since she had wrested control of the tribe, Valkia had come to treat the gossip with the contempt it deserved, but kept a very careful eye on what was said. Tongues would wag and stories would be exaggerated, but the common talk amongst the people of the camp could more effectively reflect the mood of her people.

Fydor was more than a little apologetic and as he elaborated, Valkia could see that the subject made him uncomfortable. She did nothing to interject, taking a slightly malicious pleasure from his awkwardness.

'In honesty, the current rumours are largely a combination of the two. The women say that you make yourself unwomanly; that you challenge the gods in doing so. You defend yourself with such ferocity that nothing short of the strongest man could hope to ever break down your – ah – your defences.'

Valkia stabbed the dagger she had been playing with down into the ground in front of her. 'Every man who has presented himself to me and claimed any sort of desire to bed me has not done so with passion,' she said. 'They are all weak. I am more worthy than bearing a child with nothing more aggressive than a rabbit. I want the mountain lion, Fydor.'

The Godspeaker knew who she referred to. Since Valkia had met Deron of the Bloody Hand, no other man lived up to him in her eyes. Fydor had considered suggesting to Valkia that she propose a more permanent alliance with the Bloody Hand, but the second he had mentioned Deron's name, she had screeched at him to hold his tongue. Had she been as other women, he would have gently teased her about her obvious interest in the young man. But Valkia was most assuredly not as other women.

Today, though, she was far more amenable to discussing the matter. She was playing with the dagger, her hand held splayed out as she stabbed at the ground beneath her fingers in a listless, repetitive way. Valkia was bored. And that was dangerous.

Fydor judged the best way to proceed and hit upon the perfect way forward. 'The darkest days of the winter are almost upon us,' he said. 'The Warspeaker's scouts report that a tribe has set up a camp on the far side of the Vale. They have warriors of their own, but they have not come close to our camp that we know of.'

He had struck exactly the right chord and Valkia looked up, her dark eyes flashing. 'My warriors have been idle for too long,' she said. This was a little inaccurate; only two days previously they had engaged in a small but satisfying battle against a few desperate raiders. 'Have this tribe shown any aggression towards our hunters?'

Her attention was dragged away from brooding and Fydor was grateful for that.

'Not towards us,' he said, 'but Hepsus reports that they have allegedly raided one of the small camps to which your father extended our protection just before his death.'

'Is that so?' Valkia had always quietly approved of her father's efforts to expand his leadership beyond the boundaries of the camp. It was the best way to maintain control of the smaller tribes who, as experience had shown, could easily be corrupted by other influences. They did not proclaim themselves to be Schwarzvolf, of course; Merroc had seen the sense in allowing them to keep their identities but they were more a part of the larger collective than they knew. 'Then we must address this insult with due haste.' She slid the dagger into the sheath at her waist. 'Send Hepsus. The Warspeaker and I will discuss the best way to approach this enemy.'

A wicked glint came into her eyes and she smiled, a predator's smile. 'I am sure that we can find just the right way to deliver the message clearly. Nobody threatens my people or those under my protection.' She put a finger to her chin thoughtfully. 'It would end most tragically were they not to heed such a warning.'

She was hungry for blood. It showed in her eyes, her whole face and even the restless set of her body. The legacy of the Schwarzvolf ran strongly in her veins. Merroc would have been proud. He may not, perhaps, have approved of Valkia's methods, but he would certainly have seen the sense in what she was doing. Fydor sensed she was still desperate for an acceptance that had she but looked, she would have seen she had already.

'Most tragically,' he agreed with her words and offered a rare smile of his own.

THE MESSAGE WAS delivered with typical vigour. A small party led by Valkia herself had arrived in the outlying camp at an opportune moment. The raiders had, by an uncanny chance, chosen that day to strike again. It had taken three days for the Schwarzvolf to arrive, a journey that should normally only have taken half a day. Heavy snowfall had brought down a number of trees in the forest and it had been largely impassable in places. To Valkia's initial irritation, they had to find another route through. As such, by the time they finally arrived, she was in a mood that was most certainly not one which encouraged diplomacy.

The tiny camp that Merroc had adopted into his own people barely fielded two dozen inhabitants but that did not matter one bit. As far as Valkia was concerned, a slur against these people was a slur against her personally. When she and her group of eight warriors strode from the forest, they exuded a palpable air of competence and ferocity.

The small camp's defenders, who were little more than farmers, were not doing a good job of holding back the raiders and several men lay dead on the ground. A handful of others kept the raiders at bay with primitive weapons: mostly sticks, rocks and burning fire brands. They may not have been well versed in warfare, but they were certainly tenacious.

The Schwarzvolf force charged with a single word from their leader. She prowled at their head, smaller and slighter than any of the burly warriors who had come with her, but there was murder writ large in her face. She brandished the spear that she favoured and her slender figure was clad in ornately tooled leather armour. She had hand-worked the design herself years ago and it was that of a wolf, its head thrown back as it howled towards a moon far above. It was clumsy work, but the effort she had put into it had given her great pride.

She had been offered better since taking leadership of the Schwarzvolf of course, but she had turned it all down. It had served her well enough, as had her spear and the supposedly enchanted silvery dagger.

The raiders were clearly as hungry for a fight as Valkia and her men because they charged immediately. Perhaps fourteen unkempt warriors turned away from the work of slaughtering the minimal livestock that the outlying tribe kept and turned their attentions instead to better sport. The inhabitants of the camp fell back swiftly, relieved and scared in equal measure.

One of Valkia's warriors was felled swiftly, a well placed strike from the enemy slitting open his belly. His entrails steamed as the heat of his internal organs was exposed to the cold winter air. He clutched at them as though he could hold his body together through sheer force of will and snarled a colourful array of curses as he stubbornly faced his death. His tenacity was to be admired, Valkia thought. He was doomed and yet he made no complaint about the agony. Instead, he used what remained of his strength to spit at the man who had killed him.

He sank to his knees, no longer able to keep himself upright and blood poured from his opened stomach, blossoming on the snow around him. As she leaped over him on the way to engage another enemy, Valkia drove her spear through the back of his neck, tearing off his head. Better a quick death than a lingering one in agony as the belly wound festered. She owed him that much.

Pulling her spear from the broken body, she flung herself into the heart of the battle, moving with such speed that she was little more than a dark-haired blur in battered leather.

With every blow she struck, Deron's parting words lingered in her memory. But when you kill, *whatever* you kill, dedicate it to the Blood God and he will reward you in return. It was hard, she thought, to dedicate anything to a god whose name she did not even know, but with each killing strike, she called out the words that Deron had given her.

'Blood for the Blood God!'

None of the other Schwarzvolf understood what she was calling out, but they were all hungry for the battle and after two bloody kills at her hand, they all picked up the battle-cry until they chorused it together. There was such lust in their words and such ferocity in their attack that the enemy were hugely intimidated. Of the fourteen who had begun the battle, eight were already dead and three more were grievously – if not fatally – wounded. Their leader had died early on in the proceedings and without his command, the rest of the raiders simply fell to pieces.

Valkia hacked and slashed her way through the enemies, each blow she struck filling her with a desire to land more. Deron's words perhaps had merit. Perhaps this was the reward from this blood god he had sworn by. This insatiable hunger to keep fighting until every drop of blood her enemy possessed had been spilled.

Her spear served her well until only two of the

raiders remained and then the shaft splintered, breaking in two. Even this inconvenience did nothing to stop her. She picked up the spear-tip and drew her dagger. Thus armed with twin blades, she continued to mutilate and maim, each time crying out in praise to the blood god.

'Hetwoman, stop.'

She did not hear the words of her warriors for several moments. It was only when a hand closed on her shoulder and she had almost turned and butchered one of her own men that she realised that the battle had ended. Only then did she discover that she was sat astride one of the fallen enemies, carving out his heart. The raider's severed head lay a few feet away, the ragged flesh and shattered vertebrae of its neck torn by brute force rather than parted by blade. What madness had filled her with such unholy strength?

She blinked up at the man who had disturbed her work. She could not recall his name to mind for a moment. Eilif, that was him. She knew him. She knew them all. Cold reality came crashing down around her and for a moment she felt faint. Her face and armour were smeared with blood and her beloved spear was broken. She took a deep, steadying breath.

'Hetwoman?' Eilif's brow was furrowed in concern and more than a little fear. She despised the expression. She hated the fact that one of her own people would show so much trepidation before her. 'Are you... do you need...'

'Stop babbling like a fool.' Valkia got to her feet and brushed herself down, not meeting Eilif's eyes.

He had glimpsed her in that moment of madness and it troubled her deeply. 'Are they all dispatched?'

'Almost to a man. One lives still. I am no healer, but I wouldn't think that it will be long before he joins his brethren.' Eilif nodded over his shoulder to where a single warrior lay groaning. 'We lost three of our own. These bastards put up quite a fight, but they're dealt with.' His expression became grim. 'They certainly won't be raiding again.'

'Yes,' she said, absently. Her mind was still filled with the echoing shouts and cries of the dying and, once again, that almost unquenchable thirst, that need to snuff out the spark of life from those who dared oppose her. It was the first time she had truly allowed herself to succumb to the darkness within. It was exhilarating. It was what had been lacking in her life.

Memories of what had happened were starting to break through and she remembered the moment the haft of her spear had splintered. She recalled hurling the bottom half away. She stared down at the head of the weapon, held in her hand. The iron blade was pitted and dulled from her efforts to hack through her fallen enemy's ribcage.

'I need a better weapon,' she said, more to herself than to Eilif. She shook her head to clear it of the battle haze that still permeated it and she straightened her shoulders. Looking around at the massacre that she and her men had wrought she felt a shiver of satisfaction. The raiders had been delivered a lesson, of that there was no doubt.

There was still work to be done of course and Valkia

busied herself with the rest of her warriors gathering together the corpses of both the farmers who had died attempting to defend their home and those of the dead enemy. The latter were beheaded and the trophies collected. The headless bodies were then flung together in a haphazard pile. As she put the torch to them and the stench of burning flesh filled the air, the young leader of the Schwarzvolf felt the madness finally begin to recede. It was then that the timorous voice of the camp's leader finally cut into her awareness.

'You are Merroc's daughter.' It was not a question and something in the tone annoyed Valkia. She turned to consider him haughtily.

'I am,' she confirmed. 'I am the hetwoman of the Schwarzvolf now.'

'Yes,' he said and Valkia wondered if he might be feeble-minded. He spoke slowly and carefully, each word being considered 'Thank you for your efforts here.' He took in the slaughter with a sweeping gesture of one hand. His eyes lingered briefly on the pile of bodies smouldering in the corner of his camp. 'We owe you a debt, of course.'

'Of course.' She struggled not to roll her eyes. This was usually where the offers of marriage would be put on the table. She was not in the mood to deal with that today. Still slightly dazed from her brief brush with insanity, her temper was on a hair trigger. But for once in her life, the young woman was pleasantly surprised. The villager reached over and took the broken spear from her hand. He considered the dulled blade and then looked down at her dagger.

'I forged many of the swords your people wield,' he said. 'Your father himself told me my work was excellent. That dagger you carry, that was made by my uncle who melted down weapons taken from invaders from the south long ago. The metal is an unusual one and difficult to work if you do not have the skill. I would make you a new spear if you would accept that as payment? In the same style as your blade.'

The offer actually delighted her and her response in the affirmative needed no forced enthusiasm. People spoke of her dagger as though it were an object to be feared. Imagine what they would say if she had another weapon forged in the same style.

'Accept our hospitality for a night or two,' said the man whose initial caution was wearing off. 'The weather continues to worsen and you must be weary after that battle.' Valkia would have denied the fact but she was acutely aware that the men she had brought with her were showing signs of exhaustion. The fight had been hard, as had been the trek to reach it. She became gradually aware of an ache in her own bones and with a nod, she agreed.

For two days they enjoyed the rare chance of relaxing and left with freshly sworn allegiances to the Schwarzvolf. They fell instantly for the charms of the young woman and by the time they were ready to leave, their loyalty was absolutely assured. Valkia left behind two of her party to act as a solid guard for the camp and had to practically fight off the grateful embrace of the blacksmith.

'Return in the spring, hetwoman,' he said. 'I will forge you a spear fit for a champion. It will be a weapon that will catch the attention of the gods themselves.' She had smiled perfunctorily at him, acutely and even a little uncomfortably aware that she may already have achieved that.

THE WINTER WAS not as harsh as the Godspeaker had predicted and spring came early to the Vale. But despite the comparative peace that had been theirs across the dark months, there were a never-ending stream of political issues that demanded Valkia's attention. Delegates from non-allied tribes came to speak with her. Some practically begged for the Schwarzvolf's patronage, some were more indifferent. All of them left impressed with her forthright manner, and tales of her shrewd competence and utter ruthlessness began to spread.

Her own people meanwhile were dealing with a tragedy of their own. Of six children born across the winter, only one had survived. Two had not even lived beyond their first few days and the other three had been monstrous things, warped and twisted whilst still in their mother's wombs. They had not survived the traumas of childbirth and had been left in the forest.

The mothers of these god-touched children were as pragmatic as any of the tribe's warriors and returned to their chores and daily lives without any external sign of the grief they must be enduring. There had always been babies born with physical deformities to the northern tribes, but the frequency of them was rapidly increasing.

Whispers of another curse began and Valkia

threatened to cut out the tongue of anybody she heard speaking such nonsense. There was some speculation that perhaps the tribe needed to continue expanding its borders. A basic understanding of the problems of in-breeding was explored and the solution the het-woman suggested was radical and startling.

'We have always considered the suitability of females from other tribes for breeding stock,' she observed during one of the regular Circle meetings that she found so tedious. 'Why do we not consider men from outside the tribe as well? Perhaps the reason for all these deficiencies in our young is down to the men of this tribe and not the women?' She leaned forward and studied the gathered Circle intensely. 'Perhaps it is even something in the very air we breathe?'

Centuries of tradition, a rudimentary to non-existent knowledge of bloodlines and no small level of misogynistic ignorance had left the tribe – both men and women – as to little doubt that the mothers of the deformed infants must also be in some way deficient. It was they who produced the offspring after all. Valkia's idle observation threw them into confusion and they debated the matter for what seemed like hours.

Talk. Always talk. Valkia was glad when the full thaw came. With the recession of the snows came the chance to travel up into the hills and meet with the Bloody Hand.

SIX
The Gorequeen

THE HILLS ABOVE the Vale were a breeding ground for the dire wolves and other darker things that made life in the northern steppe so harsh. When they were not hunting the same prey that the humans used for sustenance, they were hunting the humans themselves. In the early spring, the aggression was high as the animals were entering their breeding season. Those who strayed too close to a nest or to a cave den would soon meet the wrath of nature's most vicious creatures, desperate to protect their young. Other times, they would simply vanish, claimed by the denizens of the shadows.

As they travelled higher, where the air was noticeably thinner and colder than that in the Vale, Valkia found herself wondering just how robust the Bloody Hand must be to survive the harsh winters. If she had any real sense, she would have let them come to her, but something drove her up the steep hills. Curiosity. A desire to know more about this blood god whose blessings she appeared to have courted.

There had been a few small battles since the altercation in the outlying camp and every time Valkia waited... *hoped*... for another taste of that ecstatic battle-madness that had taken her in its embrace. But it had not come. Deron would certainly clarify matters for her; at least that was her reasoning. He could tell her more of the god. And if she was so inclined, she might suggest an alliance between her people and his.

Strangely, the latter idea was no longer as appealing as it might have been in the days when the two young people had first met. The first flush of attraction had worn off and whilst Valkia remembered Deron as a strong, muscular man – perhaps even an attractive one – he was more memorable as an individual who represented a tribe with whom she felt the Schwarzvolf could take a further step towards the greatness she envisioned for them.

She remembered him also as the only man who had ever dared stand up to her with any kind of courage in the arena of battle, and for that reason alone, her respect for him was high.

The cry of a distant bird of prey called her attention back to the here and now and she squinted up into the sky. Hepsus tapped her lightly on the shoulder and indicated to a point just ahead. She followed his gesture. Standing amidst a scrubby patch of green bushes was a man. He was naked from the waist up and his chest was decorated with that same strange design she had seen burned onto the flesh of Deron's body. The strange, stylised skull device stared back at her.

'Schwarzvolf, hold.' His voiced was tinged with the same guttural and slightly feral edge that she remembered. He stepped forward. On first glance he looked as though he was unarmed, but Valkia was wise enough never to make assumptions. She had seen men fall to carelessness and she would not make that same mistake herself.

'I am the hetwoman of the Schwarzvolf,' she said, needlessly. Clearly this man knew who they were, but there were courtesies and traditions that needed to be carefully observed. 'I come to seek an audience with your chieftain.'

'Deron said you would come when the snows cleared.' The man nodded. He was eyeing Valkia from head to foot, taking in her comparatively diminutive form with undisguised appreciation. She remained entirely unselfconscious under his slightly lascivious scrutiny, used to such looks. She held his gaze and adopted a faint air of boredom.

'He said you were good breeding stock,' he observed aloud. 'A little skinny for my taste, but you are strong. That much is obvious. You would bear him many fine sons. Aye, and daughters, too.'

She was furious, but did not let it show. She was not some prize mare to be shown off as an asset. That Deron saw her as nothing more than this was more than a little disappointing and a core of resentment against him hardened in her heart.

'We are here,' she said in a voice that held a cutting edge, 'to speak with your chieftain. Take us to him.' She would deal with Deron later.

'As you wish, Schwarzvolf.' The bow was more mocking than respectful and it fanned the flames of her anger a little higher. They had *no* respect for the gesture she was making in travelling up here to meet with the leader of another tribe. As she and her retinue followed the bare-chested man further up the hill, she found her hand straying to the handle of the axe that she wore in place of her spear. She felt uncomfortable without her weapon of choice, but would have felt more uncomfortable still had she come up here unarmed.

The camp of the Bloody Hand, such as it was, consisted of a number of slightly sagging tents made from a patchwork of stitched hides supported by a single pole in the centre. Their escort pulled aside the entrance to one and gestured for them to enter. Ducking her head, Valkia and her ten warriors stepped inside. There was nobody else present and their guide indicated they should wait.

The flap of the tent closed behind him letting in only a sliver of light. It was more than enough to see by and Valkia studied the interior curiously. Just as with the tents of her own people, the first thing she recognised was the nearly overpowering scent of wood smoke. Strong as it was, it did little to hide the coppery tang of blood. It was then that she noticed the faces stretched among the layered skins of the tent, and that the hides were not those of beasts, but men.

A heap of skulls at the far side of the tent caught her attention and she moved across to kneel by them. She took a few of them up and studied them. Some were animal skulls, others human skulls. Every single one was pristine, cleaned until barely any stains remained on the bone. She had encountered many tribes who used bone in construction of tools, cutlery or weapons, but had never seen such a stash of them herself.

The tent flap opened wide and a huge figure filled the entrance. Valkia, a human skull in her hand looked up once again into the eyes of Deron, the man who would redirect the course of her history and with it, the shape of the warriors of the north.

IT HAD TAKEN a long time for Valkia to ask the question. All the necessary formalities had been tedious and she had been impatient. Her manners remained impeccable however and Deron's father, Kalir, had been impressed with her. They had opened preliminary discussions about forging a possible alliance at which Deron had grinned widely.

Valkia's continued annoyance at the man's perception of her as goods and chattel was fired a little more by the look. How *dare* he be so arrogant to assume that she would offer herself as a brood sow to him. And yet... offspring from such a union could be fine and strong. There was some sense to it. The seeds of an idea formed in her mind, but she set it aside. There were other things that needed to be discussed.

When Kalir had left her and Deron to attend to other matters, the two young people had sat in comfortable silence for a while. When Valkia had dismissed her retinue, the look on Deron's face suggested that he knew what she wanted from him.

'Who is this blood god?' She demanded the answer rather than ask the question. 'You have my interest, Deron of the Bloody Hand. Now tell me why I have been dedicating my kills to a god I know nothing about.'

If he was disappointed that she wanted to talk

rather than engage in something a little more intimate, he did not let it show. Deron leaned back against the side of his father's tent and scratched his stubbled chin.

'You know,' he said, simply. 'I see it in your eyes, Valkia of the Schwarzvolf. You have touched the ecstasy of Kharneth. Once the Blood God has caught you in his embrace, he will not let you go. And you would not wish him to.'

Kharneth.

Just hearing the name sent a shudder of delight through her and she nodded eagerly, wanting to hear more.

'He thirsts for the blood of all those who oppose him or even those who follow him. Whose blood is shed is irrelevant so long as it *is* shed in his name. He demands tribute in death and skulls. His realm lies far to the north, beyond the mountains, beyond even the wild wastes. There, he sits upon a throne made from the discarded skulls of his fallen.' Deron licked his lips. 'Those he most favours he grants strength and power beyond imagining.'

Kharneth.

Valkia shivered although it was not even slightly cold. 'My people have always followed the old ways,' she said. 'My Godspeaker divines the words of the gods through prophecy and dreams. It is the way things have always been. But the way of this Kharneth is something I can reach out and touch. It feels...' She tailed off, trying to articulate that moment of intense ecstasy, the flood of excitement that had filled her entire being the day she had brutally massacred the enemy raiders. 'It feels *right*,' she said eventually. Deron nodded.

'I saw the potential in you, Valkia,' he said. 'You have what the Blood God needs.' He had moved a little closer to her. 'You have what I need also.' A hand reached up and stroked her hair away from her face. He held her gaze in his own and she gave him a dangerous smile.

He did not see the dagger until she had whipped it from her boot and had it pressed against his neck. 'Move any closer, Deron, and you will lack the parts that make you a man. Continue to press your luck and you will lack a heart. Do you understand me?' She gave him a supercilious sneer. 'When – and *if* – I choose to ally my people to yours, then we can discuss such things. But not until.' A pearl of red began to bead at the dagger's point which she had held to his throat and he swallowed, very carefully. 'Do we have an accord?'

He mouthed 'yes' and she nodded in satisfaction. With an oddly sweet smile, she then took the dagger away, sliding it back into her boot. 'Excellent,' she said. Reaching up, she wiped the blood from Deron's throat, smearing it across his neck. Taking up the cup of wine that she had been given, she took a sip from it. 'Now tell me more about this god of yours. Tell me more of Kharneth.'

TIME MOVED ONWARDS. Five years passed since the day Valkia had first demanded knowledge of the god she now devoted herself to most wholeheartedly. She found herself frequently flashing back to that conversation and particularly when she was engaged in warfare.

At times like now.

The air was filled with the sounds of battle as the two warring tribes met in combat that would determine once and for all who possessed the strongest warriors, the greatest strength. It was an intense and bloody mêlée of sweating bodies and flashing blades and the toll of life was already considerable on both sides.

Valkia fought at the head of her army as she had always done when words were no longer enough to secure the loyalty of other tribes. In the time since she had taken the mantle of the Schwarzvolf, her methods had become feared and at the same time deeply respected by the warlike northmen. It was hard not to respect a woman whose choice was simple. Pledge loyalty to the Schwarzvolf or die in a last-gasp attempt to maintain independence.

She was enforcing the second option. The tribe they fought had been given their chance. In the past year alone, the Schwarzvolf had grown to become the single largest tribe in the wastes. They moved across the steppe gathering smaller tribes into their collective as though they had simply not existed. The more their numbers grew, the larger the enemy they could approach.

Her spear held ready, Valkia turned to face the next man. Her dark hair was covered by a tight-fitting leather helmet and her once-battered armour had long since been replaced by something far more appropriate and impressive. Strong, hard leather was tooled with intricate designs by the best artificers she had found. The emblem of the Schwarzvolf, the wolf baying at the moon remained, but on the rear of the cuirass was the skull design of the Blood God.

Even the spear she held was little short of a work of art. The elderly blacksmith, true to his word, had forged her a masterpiece. She had respected his custom when he had gifted it to her and given it a name. *Slaupnir*. At her request, the smith had also forged the rune of the Blood God into its silvery blade, dedicating the weapon itself to the young woman's new-found purpose.

Slaupnir. The monster from a tale her father had told when she had been but a girl. The terrifying creature before whom the world would flee.

Two warriors were bounding towards her with murder in their eyes and she spun gracefully to meet their challenge head on. She pressed all her weight behind the spear as she held off their attack. They fought with axes, as did so many of the northmen, and she had long mastered the technique of disarming them. With a move so fluid that it was almost flawless, she thrust Slaupnir beneath the crescent blades of the axes, hooking them on the reinforced haft of the spear.

With every ounce of her strength, she lifted herself from the ground and planted a booted foot in the chest of each warrior, ripping the axes from the hands of her attackers. They staggered back, glaring in disbelief at the woman before them, but all they could see of her as she rolled to her feet were her eyes. Her mad, battle-lust filled eyes.

Lunging forward with the weapon, she speared the

first warrior through the throat. Slaupnir burst from the back of his neck and he fell to the ground gurgling his death cry in a fountain of blood. Without the time to tug her weapon free, Valkia drew her dagger and vaulted over the dying man, plunging the blade into his companion's chest. He threw his arms wide as though he would embrace her in his final moments and then pitched forward.

Swiftly reclaiming her weapons, Valkia butchered her way through the enemy to the place where their leader was surrounded by a vanguard of his elite fighters. To her extreme distaste, she saw two men standing behind him with the telltale robes of magic users. If there was one thing that Valkia found truly offensive in an opponent, it was those who invoked the mysterious powers of the unknown.

No matter. They would die at her hands soon enough. She never took the hearts of such tainted men. She had tried, once. But the taste had been unwelcome and the nightmares afterwards even more so. Killing sorcerers now gave her considerable pleasure.

With a practised eye, she glanced around what remained of the enemy. The surviving force was puny in comparison to that which had been fielded at the day's break. She must make the magic-users her first target, otherwise they would call forth the powers of the earth itself in an attempt to annihilate the Schwarzvolf. She would give them their final chance to join her. If they declined, then they would finish what they had started. Should they choose to accept, then the magic users would be executed. She could see no route to failure.

'I feel generous this day,' she called out in a slightly mocking tone. 'Swear fealty to the Schwarzvolf now and you can choose those who would live.' Her armour was streaked with gore and there were chunks of flesh and viscera hanging from the spear in bloody strings.

'We will never swear loyalty to a follower of the mad god.' The enemy leader spat on the ground. 'We would sooner die.'

'As you wish.' Valkia shrugged as though he had merely refused her offer of a drink. She threw back her head and let a mighty shout ascend to the heavens.

'Blood for the Blood God!'

The response from her own men came instantly and with it, her heart swelled almost to bursting. For five years she had dedicated every battle, every kill and every drop of blood in the name of her adopted deity.

'Skulls for his skull throne!'

The Schwarzvolf charged.

The leader of the tribe died quickly. *Too* quickly for Valkia's taste; she had been looking forward to making his screams last for a while. But he died weeping like the snivelling coward that he was. She despised weaklings. Their hearts tasted insipid and brought no pleasure when consumed on the battlefield. The hearts of the strong however... she craved that flavour.

She lived for the moments when she tore out a heart, sometimes still beating, and its explosion of flavours in her mouth when she tore the first chunk from it. After she had taken her due – her *right* as the tribe's leader – she would pass the organ to her other warriors. In such a way, the Schwarzvolf had come to believe, a measure of the strength of the enemy would be gifted to them. It was a practise that many of the northmen honoured. But since Valkia had named the Blood God as their patron, the Schwarzvolf not only honoured it, they practised it with great pleasure.

Their leader dispatched, the remaining elite guard had been granted the choice to swear their swords to her banner or die. To a man, they chose death, considering that their chance to switch allegiance had passed by the moment Valkia had taken their leader's head. Even now she held the grisly trophy in her free hand, its eyes staring sightlessly ahead, ragged strips of meat hanging from the neck.

It always disappointed her when such fearsome warriors chose death over life, but only ever for a fraction of a second. Once the bitter resentment passed, she gloried in the slaughter. They could take great strength from the fallen, she would remind herself, and Kharneth would be pleased.

It left only the sorcerers to be dealt with. Valkia had lost a handful of her warriors in the path of their unnatural methods. They had called forth fire from nowhere and her warriors, three men and two women had died screaming in agony. The moment Valkia had successfully incapacitated them she had torn out their tongues. Let them speak their words of magic now. They would be bound, taken back to the camp of the Schwarzvolf and publicly executed as the abominations they were.

* * *

THE MIGHT OF the Schwarzvolf had grown exponentially in a few short years. Valkia's ability to act diplomatically when the occasion called for it had begun to diminish proportionately. To refuse the will of the Schwarzvolf was to invite ruin. Her moods had always been mercurial but as she gained in strength and power she became ever more unpredictable. It was not unheard of for her to turn on one of her own warriors in a torrent of rage, and when she was held in the grip of such tantrums her strength was formidable.

She had installed Hepsus as her Warspeaker despite her initial dislike and distrust of the man and it had proven to be a wise move. As bloody and violent as she was, the two would always be found fighting shoulder to shoulder at the head of her army. They shared the glory of victory together and she trusted him to lead the army at times when she was otherwise unable to do so herself. He had never once let her down or tried to wrest power from her but she refused to allow complacency.

Valkia's position as leader of the Schwarzvolf had been absolutely assured when she had taken control with such affirmation. Her confidence, sense of identity and genuine desire to build on the foundations that her father had laid down, swayed her tribe to her cause in a matter of months. Those who had been gradually assimilated into the Schwarzvolf took a little longer. Some never accepted the alliance with the Bloody Hand, but they did not live long enough to raise argument.

She and Kalir had sat together for a long time

discussing the terms of their accord. It had not taken much for Deron and his father to convince her of the merits of worshipping the Blood God. She could see their strength and their might and she wanted some of that for *her* people. They had sheer, brute force – she had numbers. Together, she reasoned, they would be nigh on unstoppable. They had been simple, guileless words but Kalir had seen their worth. The Bloody Hand could never hope to achieve glory on the level they desired without the numbers to see it through. The Schwarzvolf could bring that.

Valkia had presented the solution to the biggest problem. If the two tribes were to unite, who would be the recognised leader? She had bitten back her pride and had fixed Kalir with a careful eye.

'I will marry your son,' she said. 'Together, we will represent the best of both our peoples. Such a union in the eyes of the Four will bind our tribes together by blood. And that is a message that cannot be ignored. I am the leader of my people and Deron will one day be yours.' Kalir had been set to argue the point. *He* was the leader of his people, not his son. But her reasoning was presented in a carefully moderated tone that actually made him consider the option carefully.

'I cannot answer for Deron,' he said eventually. 'My son must make his own choice in this matter. He has spoken of you often over the winter.' With those words, Valkia knew she had what she wanted. Much as she did not wish to do it, she would take Deron as a husband until it was no longer a necessity.

When he had been brought into the tent to join in the discussion, he had agreed readily. For Deron, he felt that he was getting the best of both worlds. He got to assume nominal leadership of his own people whilst at the same time marrying into the tribe that had become recognised as one of the strongest. He let his eyes linger on Valkia and her heart sank, knowing that she had been forced to give up one of her longest-standing principles. But it was for the sake of her people.

It was for the sake of her greater scheme.

She wondered, as she roamed the now-peaceful battlefield, why it was that she was letting her thoughts linger on the events of the past. She had put it all behind her and moved forward. She was no longer Valkia, hetwoman of the Schwarzvolf. She had been gifted a new name by those who opposed her and everything that she stood for. They called her the Gorequeen, an acknowledgement of her bloody, brutal methods of war. And in truth, Valkia *had* become a queen in the eyes of her people. She no longer simply led them. She *ruled* them with fairness and cruelty in equal measure.

Perhaps it was simply the fact that the fifth birthday of her twin daughters was coming up that had brought the memories forward. For all her single-minded savagery and prowess in battle, Valkia's love for the two little girls was the one thing that kept her humanity chained to her. She had fallen pregnant quickly after the marriage to Deron and had hated every moment of it. She had detested the early sickness and the later sense of being so bulky and cumbersome. Childbirth had been difficult for her; she had always been boyish in shape with a long, slim waist and narrow hips and it had not made the process easy. The Godspeaker had told her that to be born in blood was a good omen however, that Kharneth looked favourably upon the children. This appeased Valkia and drove out what lingered of the pain.

Another memory surfaced.

'They are girls.'

Deron's disappointment enraged her and had she not been so weakened by the blood loss that had come with the delivery of the twins, she would have flown at her husband in a rage. But she calmed herself. The time would come. She lay there, smouldering in barely contained fury and forced herself back to a state of comparative calmness. There was no end such wrath could bring the united tribes to but a poor one. She had to bide her time.

'But they are healthy.' She detested how weary she sounded and swore blind that as soon as she was able, Deron would pay the price for his insult – whether it had been intentional or not. The girls were perfect in every way, although a little undersized. 'Be grateful for that, *husband*.' She put such venom into the word that he had looked up from the babies at her.

Their marriage had not been an easy one. Two such strong-willed personalities in a confined space resulted in raging arguments and any early feelings they may have had for each other were quickly lost. Outside of the privacy of their own tent, they wore a united face and until her pregnancy rendered her unable to fight, they had cut a startlingly impressive duo. As hunters, they had a natural compatibility and as fighters, their styles complemented one another perfectly. By themselves, Valkia and Deron were recognised as fine, deadly warriors. Together, they were terrifying. Together, they represented the might of the Schwarzvolf and the strength of the Bloody Hand.

And yet they came to despise one another swiftly. The fact that Valkia had birthed female offspring was a deep cut to Deron's masculinity and she enjoyed his discomfort as she spoke of all the girls stood to inherit. How they would take the allied tribes forward to another generation of glory.

'Our next child will be a boy,' he said, interrupting her monologue. 'He will become my heir and it will be *he* who leads our people to the feet of the Blood God.'

'There will be no next child.' This was both a natural resistance to the suggestion and a statement of likely fact. The birth had been difficult and the damage done had left the tribe's midwife in doubt as to whether Valkia would survive another pregnancy. 'The girls are our heirs now. Look at them, Deron. They are born of a union of the finest and best our generation has to offer. They will be a force unparalleled by any other.'

Deron looked at the tiny girls, sleeping peacefully. For the briefest of brief moments, his expression softened. Both had heads covered in wispy dark hair and they had the same olive complexion of their father. Their spines were straight and strong and Valkia's main observation was that they were healthy. There were no deformities, no mutations... they were beautiful.

But they were female. Deron felt no paternal instinct towards his children. He had held out hope that he would have spent this night drinking himself comatose in celebration of the birth of his first son; the ultimate proof of his prowess. Instead, he would drink himself comatose in commiseration. The desire that Valkia would produce a male child had been the only consolation he could find in the manner in which his children had been conceived.

Valkia had propped herself up on her elbows and studied Deron wordlessly. She could see the struggle going on behind his eyes and was relishing every moment of his pain. She had got what she wanted from him. She had decided that the time to bear children was right. Deron had not agreed.

Valkia had forcibly taken from him what she needed. Enough fermented spirits and the point of a blade could be most persuasive. He had been humiliated afterwards. He had claimed theft of his masculinity, but she had simply laughed at him and barred him from her tent.

She had not cared whether the offspring she had carried for nine months had been a boy or girl. She had her heirs. That they were girls was merely a blessing as far as she was concerned.

She had what she wanted.

She *always* got what she wanted.

The phrase rolled itself around her mind. 'You should go attend to your duties, husband,' she said eventually. 'I must care for the girls. I have named them, if you have any interest at all.'

Deron looked as though he would retort, but bit

his tongue. 'What are their names?'

'Eris,' she said, pointing to the slightly smaller of the two. 'After my mother. And Bellona. After yours.'

'They will suffice,' Deron acknowledged after a moment or two. With that, he swept from the tent leaving his wife and their two children alone. In that moment, had he but realised it, he sealed his own doom. In that moment, he had invited the full wrath of a proud woman.

THE HEARTS OF the fallen had all been carved out. It had been a long, laborious process and the bale moon, swollen to a larger size than usual, threw its cold green light down on the carnage. The Schwarzvolf roamed the corpses of the dead, salvaging usable arms and armour and claiming anything of worth.

Valkia, her face smeared with the blood of all the flesh she had consumed stood apart from the others, her hand on the spear as she stared up at the moon. It was an omen, of that she was sure. She had not seen it so big or so bright for many years. She made a note to consult the Godspeaker on their return to camp. She recalled quite clearly the last time the moon had shone so strongly. It had been the night when she had finally given herself over to Kharneth fully.

She had been back on her feet the day after the girls had been born and although she was weaker than usual, her ferocity and ardour were not dampened at all. She had taken her place at the daily moot, arriving before the others so that there was no chance

Deron could usurp her position at the Circle's head. When he had arrived – late – she had given him a sweet smile that was laced with pure venom.

'Where are your children, wife?' He had the faintly sick cast of a man who had partaken of too much alcohol the night before and she took a perverse delight in his condition.

'*Our* children are safe and in the care of the women. There are matters here that need my attention. I am the leader of this tribe, husband. You would do well to remember that.' She looked around the gathered faces. 'You would *all* do well to remember that.'

There were murmured sounds of assent, although one or two of the warriors cast sidelong glances at Deron. It was as Valkia had suspected. Her husband was trying to wrest control of her people from her and the very notion filled her with bile. This matter would need to be taken care of.

'Fydor, I have need of you when this meeting is concluded,' she said to the Godspeaker. 'I require your presence in my tent to open the hearts of my daughters to the Four.'

'As the hetwoman wishes.' At least he was still fully loyal. He always would be. For a moment, Valkia felt fear for her position. It was a feeling she was entirely unaccustomed to and she disliked it. She put it down to the birth of the girls leaving her slightly addled. Forcing herself to focus, she sat through the morning's council, although her mind was not truly engaged in the discussion. After the meeting was over and everyone, including her husband, had left her in peace, she sat and chewed her lip thoughtfully for several minutes.

Her mind made up, she ducked out of the council tent and headed back to her own.

IT HAD BEEN easy, in the end. Easy enough to bring Deron out to the glade where the tribe's most fervent rituals were held. She had brought both of the girls with her and laid them naked on the grass. Eris had begun crying noisily at this treatment and Valkia had made no effort to silence her daughter. Let the Four hear how strong her voice was.

Bellona had joined in eventually, upset by her sister's discomfort and the two girls wailed into the sky. Fydor had walked around the glade several times and then had knelt by the infants.

'In the name of the Trickster, the god of lies, deceit and of change, we dedicate you. Time will change you from infants to young women of the Schwarzvolf. Life will change you from ignorant to knowledgeable. Embrace change.' He smeared their bare chests with mud from the ground and continued.

'The Fly Lord, bringer of disease, we show you these two healthy children. Their form is pleasing and it is clear that neither is god-touched. We thank you for your benevolence and ask that you leave them be.' A second smear of mud over the first left the girls with a cross marked on their chests. Valkia and Deron crossed their arms across their breast; the recognised sign of warding away illness.

'To the Reveller, god of lusts, we offer these two infants as proof of the virility and fertility of our leaders.' Another smear, this time diagonally across the other two. Finally, Fydor beckoned Valkia forward, offering her a small silver dagger.

'And the last. To the Axefather...'

'Kharneth,' Valkia interjected. 'Use his name now, Godspeaker. He is our patron god after all.' She knelt by her crying daughters and one after the other, made a small nick in the palm of their hands. She squeezed gently and the blood welled. Taking it onto her finger, she drew the final line in blood, the other diagonal that left an eight-pointed symbol on the girls' chests.

'To Kharneth, the Blood God, we ask that you turn your eye to these children and give them the strength and ferocity to build the might of the Schwarzvolf for generations to come.' The Godspeaker met Valkia's gaze and she stared back. Fydor reached out and laid his hands gently on the heads of the two babies. 'Protect our future leaders,' he said.

At these words, Deron stepped forward as though he would interrupt and Valkia closed her eyes, releasing a breath that she hadn't realised she'd been holding. It was exactly as she had hoped. His impetuous nature had caused him to violate one of the tribe's most important rituals.

'Stand back, husband,' she said. 'The ritual is not complete. Would you dare risk the wrath of the Four? Does the thought of their displeasure not fill you with dread?' They were words spoken with equal ritual severity and her voice trembled slightly. Here, in this most holy of places, he dared to defy the gods themselves.

'I fear nothing. My own god favours me beyond all else and the others are weak in his shadow. I am greater even than they.' His arrogance was unwavering and Valkia knew a moment's regret and sadness. He could have been truly great had he only learned to see her as his equal. But he had sought to control her. And for that, he would pay the ultimate price.

'As my husband says.' She bowed her head. Then, she leaped to her feet and drove her silver dagger through his eye and into his skull. 'Are you afraid yet, Deron?'

He did not answer, merely stared at her with a cyclopean gaze that became glassy and dead. He sank first to his knees, then forwards onto the hilt of the knife, pushing it further still into his brain.

Behind her, still lying in the grass, the girls stopped crying. The air itself stilled. No breeze rippled the grass or leaves in the trees above them. The only noise was that of Deron as he grunted out his last breaths. He sounded like a pig that had been taken to slaughter and the analogy delighted Valkia. She pushed him over with the toe of her boot so that he lay face upwards. She pulled the dagger from his head and spat on him.

'No man is greater than the gods,' she said. 'For the sin of such arrogance, you will meet them in their own realm and they will show you who is the greater.' She thrust the blade into his throat, the tip biting deeply into his spine. With a twist and a crackle of bone Deron's head came free, a fitting trophy to adorn this sacred place.

Above them, the bale moon had shone, eerie and insipid, but swollen to a size far larger than it had been in a long while. Just as it shone now. Valkia stared into its light for a long while as though she could divine some greater meaning from it. All she knew for sure was that the Schwarzvolf had gone from strength to strength since that night she had given herself over totally to the Blood God in name and deed.

This battle may have been over, but the new day would bring another opportunity; another threat to their supremacy. Valkia turned from the moon and walked into the night.

SEVEN
Locephax

She is unnatural.

They were words that had long been whispered about Valkia but they had gathered momentum of late. The whispers, so she had heard, originated from the most unlikely of sources and whilst she was aware of them, they did nothing to shake her unwavering sense of purpose.

Let the people gossip. Let them talk about her. At almost thirty years of age, Valkia was in her prime and at the very peak of her power. She had no interest in rumour and words that could never hope to harm her.

The Schwarzvolf had grown in power and strength without stopping until they were the undisputed tribal force of the north. At their head, always at the front of the battle line, Valkia stood; mighty and resolute.

She had taken the sobriquet 'the Gorequeen' to heart and had elected to use 'Queen' as her honorific. It was an affectation rather than an indication of any kingdom she may have ruled over, but such was the power that she wielded that very few could tell the difference. 'Queen Valkia' became the recognised and expected form of address.

She lived, as she always had, for battle. Her advance in years had not lessened her ardour for bloodshed and she was still as lithe and nimble on the battle-field as she had ever been. All that age had brought for her had been experience and skill, and a terrifying strength which ensured she could humble any man who dared to cross her.

The majority of her people adored her. Even those who initially had reservations about being con-quered by such a violent figurehead ultimately fell for her charisma and her unerring ability to lead. She could muster the entire tribe in short order and her pre-battle speeches were stirring and eloquent. Her people... yes, they loved her. There were the gossip-ing whispers that there had always been but their voices never found volume.

Her enemies – those that still remained – feared and hated her in equal measure. Valkia was an acknowledged champion of the Blood God, the god known variously as Kharneth or the Axefather and it was certain knowledge that nobody could defeat her all the time he favoured her.

She became known for her cold, dispassionate cru-elty in dealing with anybody who challenged her and those who dared to defy her never did so for long. The impressive collection of heads that she took in a few short months alone acted as a deterrent to enough people. There were still those who tried, of course.

Politically, she was ruthless. She had arranged suitable marriages for her two half-sisters, but had given her own daughters the freedom to choose for themselves what they wished to do. Now sixteen, Bellona and Eris had grown into young women who were perhaps even more beautiful than their mother had been at that age, having inherited their father's colouring which contrasted so well with their dark hair and eyes. They were identical down to the last detail and were the only people to whom Valkia ever showed any tenderness.

Her little brother Edan had ceased to be a threat to her position the day that Fydor had taken him on as an apprentice. Now a young man, he was small and undersized and had often fallen prey to winter sickness. It amazed Valkia that he still lived at all. In his position as the new Godspeaker he was still finding his way alone, following Fydor's death at the startling age of seventy-five barely six months previously.

Valkia had openly wept at the old man's funeral. The Godspeaker had been her closest ally and her dearest friend. His loyalty had been without question and his loss tore at her in a way she had not known since the day she had ended Radek's life.

The grief passed to a hollow ache of loss in time and if Valkia regretted the display of momentary weakness at Fydor's funeral, she did not let it show. Nobody dared bring the subject up with her and life resumed its usual pace. The Schwarzvolf had resumed their nomadic ways, moving between summer and winter camps that grew a little larger every year. They were in the Vale at the summer camp the day the stranger arrived amongst the Schwarzvolf.

* * *

THE AFFECTATION OF the title 'Queen' had brought with it a certain expectation and it amused Valkia that her people had practically insisted that she have a throne within the chieftain's tent. It was hand built and came apart for the need to travel.

The wooden throne was adorned with a number of skulls, a choice Valkia had made to complement the practice of displaying the corpses of traitors and betrayers around the camp. Markings denoting the manner of the deaths of these unfortunate souls were carved into the bone. It loaned an entirely unpleasant and gruesome aspect to the woman who sat surrounded by them. Although she would never have openly acknowledged it, it was the most uncomfortable thing that Valkia, a woman used to sitting on the ground, had ever had to bear. Regardless of this fact, it nonetheless earned the respect of those who came to speak with her.

And many came to speak with her. The balance of power in the north had shifted and Valkia was considered one of the most powerful warlords. As such, it became ever more desirable to ally with her. She had long since stopped going to other tribes to barter for their allegiance. Let them come to her and beg.

She had dispensed with Deron when he had no longer been necessary. She had done so without remorse and she had actively taken great pleasure from the act of murder. It had led to difficulties with Deron's father of course; Kalir had found it virtually impossible to reconcile their differences. He had openly accused her of murdering him in cold blood, but on the given witness of the Godspeaker had been forced to accept that his headstrong son had condemned himself through his heretical actions. To interrupt a ritual to the four gods was an unforgivable thing.

Still, he had openly challenged Valkia's suitability for leadership. For the first and only time, Valkia refused to meet him in the Circle of Blood.

'We need each other, remember? You agreed to this alliance and if we turn upon one another... now, when we need one another's strength, we will doom ourselves. The other tribes will ally against us and strike whilst we are weak.'

Her argument had been persuasive – and accurate – and Kalir had withdrawn the challenge. The Bloody Hand and the Schwarzvolf remained allies and it did not take too long for Kalir to meet his demise. Valkia was almost disappointed that the berserker met his end on the battlefield. She had developed many plans for dealing with dissenters. In time, the berserker-warriors of the Bloody Hand were simply absorbed into the Schwarzvolf collective.

They thrived. The gods had truly granted their blessings upon Valkia and her people. Deformities in the children disappeared almost completely. Meat was plentiful and the tribe were well fed and healthy. The fervent adulation of their patron god was worn on every face and it became common practice to behead animals or prisoners, or sometimes both on a daily basis to retain his favour.

The Bloody Hand had been secretive and almost furtive in their worship of Kharneth. Valkia denied this subterfuge, preferring instead to make sure her enemies knew where the loyalties of the Schwarzvolf lay.

Such open acknowledgement brought fear and struck terror into the hearts of their enemies… and it also drew the attention of those who Valkia had not considered.

THE VISITOR WAS tall and slender with hair that came down below his shoulders. He looked willowy, as though a strong wind could snap him in two, but there was a kind of iron strength about him that she found oddly alluring. The colour of his hair was unusual, too. She was used to seeing steel-grey or blond hair amongst the people of her tribe, but this man's hair was true silver. It glinted in the sun as he moved and wherever he walked, all heads turned towards him.

As he approached Valkia, seated upon her throne, she felt the hairs on the back of her neck rise. His eyes were of deepest amethyst, a rich, dark purple. He was one of the god-touched to be sure; one of the many deformed babies of the Wastes who were left to the hands of the gods and who had somehow survived.

The skin of his face and neck was alabaster pale with an ethereal glow about it that reminded Valkia of moonlight on the snow; one of the sights she had always found most beautiful. She stared at him as he approached. She had rarely seen such sharply defined features in a man. He was *pretty*, there was no other word for it. Where Deron had been blessed with ruggedly masculine good looks and even the scarred Radek had been attractive in his own solidly-built way, this stranger was *beautiful*.

As he took the first step up the dais towards her

throne, she saw that he wore gloves made of soft leather. He peeled one off and caught her hand in his. The skin of his hand was just as luminescent as that of his face and he raised her knuckles to his perfectly-shaped lips.

'I feared that the many tales of your beauty were grossly untrue,' he said in a musical lilt. 'Yet you are quite lovely, Queen Valkia.' The bold approach took her by surprise and she stared hard into his eyes, allowing him to hold her hand a moment longer before she snatched it away and forced an imperious glower onto her face.

'Who are you?' The words came out tinged with wonder rather than with the usual barked impatience.

The smile he gave her was devastating. 'My name is Locephax,' he said. 'And I am here to make you an offer.'

EVERYTHING ABOUT LOCEPHAX fascinated Valkia. The way he moved with such easy, fluid grace. The manner in which he held himself. There was a confidence to his stance, and his bearing was almost regal; at first, Valkia had wondered if he was some southern lordling. Over the course of the evening's conversation, it transpired that Locephax was a northman.

She had told him to present his offer, but he had laughed gently. 'There will be time enough later, my lovely warrior queen,' he had said. 'For now, why don't we take advantage of one another's company? I have brought you gifts.'

He had brought fine wine the like of which Valkia had never tasted. It was fermented, so Locephax explained, from fruit that grew freely in his domain. It was sweet; nothing like the bitter berries and blood that Valkia had grown accustomed to over the years and she savoured each drop. The wine was deep claret in colour and she swirled it around in the stone cup as she considered him over the top of it.

Locephax's charm was insidious. He had won over every single person to whom he had spoken – even Valkia. And yet the warrior queen felt an uncertain hesitation about him. She considered him as he flirted shamelessly with Eris and Bellona. Her daughters were enchanted by the man and from the look on their faces as he whispered to them, he was making suggestions that were probably lewd. The tether on her patience ran out.

'Eris, Bellona – leave us.' Both the girls scowled their disapproval, but neither was bold enough to refuse a direct order from their mother. Perhaps when they had been younger, yes – but she considered them as grown women now. They pouted prettily at Locephax who watched them leave, devouring their shapely figures with eyes that did nothing to hide the lascivious thoughts he clearly had.

'I would remind you that you are a guest in my presence, Locephax,' Valkia said when they had gone. 'You would do well to treat my daughters with the same respect you would afford me.' Was she jealous? She was rather startled and a little embarrassed to realise that yes, she was. She was envious that her beautiful daughters were attracting the attentions of this captivating stranger.

Angrily, she tossed the stone cup away from her. The

wine was affecting her judgement and she had always sworn blind that she would not succumb to such a weakness. The drinking vessel hit the ground with a dull thud, the wine spilling out in a crimson stain on the furs that were strewn on the floor of the tent. 'Now speak of this offer you have come to make me.'

'I mean no offence, Queen Valkia,' he said, leaning back on the floor, his arms behind him and his head bent backwards so that his long fall of silver hair brushed the earth. Not quite understanding why, Valkia wondered how his hair might feel if he was leaning over her. Locephax was stunningly attractive. His words of flattery seemed genuine and designed to strike true and yet there was something in the way he spoke that genuinely repulsed her.

'I have taken none,' she said. 'Not yet, anyway. But Eris and Bellona are my children. I have a vested interest in what happens to them. I know nothing of you. I will not have my daughters whoring themselves out to you in such a way.'

'A pity,' came the unexpected response. 'I had such grand plans for them both. But since you have forced my hand in this matter...' He sat up straight and smiled winningly over the distance that separated them. 'I am here at the behest of my own lord and master, although the rumours of your beauty would have drawn me to you eventually anyway.'

'Stop it,' she said, her fingers curling briefly into a fist. 'I am not a gullible child. Your words may be pretty, but you are not fooling me. Stop it and tell me what it is that you want.'

The smile he gave her this time was far from

winning or even remotely charming. It was chilling. A faint shock of understanding ran through Valkia, but she couldn't comprehend why or what it was. She let her fingers slowly unfurl and then gripped them tightly once again. 'I asked you this question before. Answer me truthfully. Who are you?'

'Beautiful *and* clever.' Locephax ran a hungry tongue across his perfectly-shaped lips. 'What an exquisitely charming combination. Very well then, Valkia of the Schwarzvolf, I will tell you precisely who I am and why you will see that what I offer you is far beyond anything you have ever known.'

Rising to his feet, Locephax stretched out his shoulders and took a contented breath of air. Valkia watched him like a hawk, her hand straying to the hilt of the dagger in her boot.

'For most of your life you have sworn allegiance to the Four, favouring the – what is your people's name for him again?'

'The Axefather, we used to call him,' she responded warily. 'We know him as Kharneth now.'

'Closer, admittedly,' sneered Locephax. 'Crude names at best, but fitting for a god whose only driving desire is that of death and bloody destruction. Now, my lord and master…'

'You are a creature of the Reveller.' So much was obvious. The flirtatious behaviour, the perfectly groomed appearance… everything about the man spoke of a life of debauchery. Valkia knew little of the other gods, only that Deron had once mentioned Kharneth's abiding hatred of the followers of the frivolous Reveller. Instinctively, she went on her guard.

'That is not the name by which I know him,' acknowledged Locephax. 'But he feels that a woman with your unique...' The man's eyes rested on Valkia's hips, moving slowly up to drink in the swell of her breasts. '*Talents*, shall we say, is wasted in the service of a warrior-god. If you would only reconsider, give yourself over to me, then you will reap the ultimate reward.'

She felt physically sick at the suggestion and rose from her throne. 'Get out of my camp right now,' she said, 'and I may spare your life – if you run fast enough.'

'Oh come, Valkia. How long is it since you last bedded down with a lover? I can give you what you yearn for deep in your darkest, put-away heart...' His voice was poison. Dripping blades that were coated in honey and it sickened her that she felt part of herself responding to him, the part of her that was still a woman with a woman's needs and desires...

I belong to Kharneth.

She spoke the words over and over inside her head and it helped quash the heat of the rising desire for Locephax.

'There is no reward your god could offer me that...' Locephax had somehow sidled right up to her until he was virtually nose-to-nose with her. His breath was sweet and yet made slightly sour by the wine; a potent combination that made her dizzy.

She had not even seen him move.

'Life eternal, Valkia? Come now. Even a woman of your strength and power cannot last forever. Would you not welcome the opportunity to rule over your tribe for *ever*?'

'We live as long as we are meant to,' she responded. She had learned that from Fydor, a near-mythical figure who had lived almost twice as long as most of the Schwarzvolf. 'If I die in battle tomorrow, it is because that is what *my* god has set down for me. I will march at his side in the ever-after and reap skulls for his throne in the realms beyond.'

'You deny yourself the pleasures of the flesh, Valkia.' Locephax's voice was the low purr of a predator. He reached out his hand and stroked her face with his long, delicate fingers. She turned her head to the side, but he caught her chin in his hand, pulling her back to look at him. 'Why do you think it is that your own most trusted whisper against you?'

She was caught in his grip and his amethyst stare, unable to turn away and not truly *wanting* to turn away. 'My people do not...'

'They speak that you cannot be a true woman. That you have become so mired in bloodshed and death that you have forgotten how to truly live your own life.' She wanted to shut out his words, to push him away and tear out his lying tongue but she was frozen to the spot. Whoever this Locephax was, he possessed true power. 'You are a dead and barren husk of a woman, Valkia daughter of Merroc. But I can breathe life back into you. With the power of my master flowing through you, you will learn to experience pleasure like you have never known.'

Locephax leaned down and placed his lips on hers in a long, sensuous kiss. She shivered violently and to her horror, it was not with cold. It was with pure, unfettered lust. A thousand images raced through her mind; all of them suggestive and lewd. It took every ounce of willpower she possessed, but she somehow reconnected with her senses. Her hands came up and grabbed at his wrists, tugging him away from her. She turned her head from his kiss and he laughed lightly.

'Relax, Valkia. You have earned a little pleasure. Let me show you how it could be. When you are in your rightful place amongst my harem, you will yearn for the nights I choose you to keep me warm.' He crooned the words softly, hypnotically, and for a heartbeat Valkia felt her resolve waver. But then her earlier mantra pierced through the haze of glamour that Locephax had woven around her.

I belong to Kharneth.

'You *dare* imply that I am destined to be nothing more than a slave girl? To cater to your lusts and whims for an eternity? Death is preferable by far.' She stepped back, her face aflame with shame and confusion. She whipped the dagger from her boot and sprang forward, the tip aimed at his heart. He roared with laughter.

'Kill me if you can, Valkia. This form is merely a vessel for my greater will. I could stop your heart where you stand, before your little knife even scratched me. Know that I will not give up until you succumb to my desires. My powers are beyond anything your mortal mind can start to comprehend. You will yield before me, Valkia. And do you know why? Because you are weak. Your mortality *lessens* you. Become mine and you will be granted something more.'

With a scream of rage, she flung herself at him. Locephax snorted and made a dismissive movement with his hand, flinging Valkia to one side without so much as touching her. She crashed down to the ground, dazed.

'Magic,' she said through gritted teeth. 'You have the nerve to imply that *I* am unnatural? You would use the tools of a *coward*? What kind of god must your Reveller be to resort to sorcery to win his battles?'

'The kind of god who delights in all the pleasures the world can give,' came the immediate response. 'The kind of god who sees the pleasure you get from murdering and butchering your way through the Northern Wastes and who sees in you the potential for greatness.'

His words brought Valkia up short. She had been about to deny that she found battle pleasurable, but what was it if not? For the second time, her will began to waver but she forced herself to clarity.

'No,' she said. 'No. Your words are as twisted and as meaningless as you. Your perverse lusts and desires do not compare to the purity of battle.'

'I do not *need* my magic to crush you Valkia. What if I were to defeat you in your own so-called Circle of Blood?'

'To fight to the death? What would be the point? You have told me yourself that you cannot be killed, if I am to believe such a thing.'

'As you say. However, I can be...' He considered for a moment, then smiled. '*Inconvenienced*. I would consider it a victory for you and in the unlikely event you defeat me, I will leave you and your people and not return. Should I win, then your soul will belong to my lord and master.' Locephax shrugged his slender shoulders. 'I will of course petition for you, but as you have not agreed to my terms... I cannot say what will happen.'

Valkia ground her teeth furiously. Locephax could not have struck a more vicious blow to her pride by challenging her to a duel. She was a mistress in the arena. She could destroy this prancing interloper, she was sure of it.

But she was not *completely* sure and it was that uncertainty that made her angry enough to agree.

'I accept your challenge, Locephax.'

'Tomorrow, then?'

'No,' she said. 'No. I want you out of my camp now, and if I have to cut out your heart to do it then so be it.' She moved to the entrance of the tent. 'Now is as good a time as any to accomplish that task.'

Locephax sneered unpleasantly and for a moment his fine-featured face became a thing of nightmares, twisted and distorted beyond humanity. 'You would fight me now? Without your precious armour?'

She returned his sneer with a look of outright contempt. 'I would fight you naked to prove the point, Locephax. Except that given what you have told me, I suspect you would enjoy that too much. Yes, I will fight you without armour. I have my spear and my shield and I have my god's blessing. I need nothing else.'

She held the tent flap up.

'Get out.'

* * *

EIGHT
To The Victor The Spoils

It was a chill night and Valkia felt the kiss of the cold northerly wind raise goose bumps on the exposed flesh of her arms and neck. Above her, the twin moons were hazy and indistinct, their faces veiled behind the heavy clouds. They shed very little light on the camp of the Schwarzvolf. There was no problem with visibility however; flaming torches burned brightly and the warrior queen moved with purpose towards the muddy arena.

As she exited the tent, a warrior came up and walked beside her. She didn't need to look around to know that it was Hepsus and she felt a moment's gratitude that he was there.

'Our guest has not endeared himself to me, Warspeaker,' she said, her coiled rage turning the words into a snarl. 'He has demonstrated either courage or stupidity in throwing down a challenge. He has invoked the Circle of Blood and I have accepted. I intend to humble him.'

Behind her, Locephax snickered like a child laughing at an inappropriate comment. She ignored him staunchly and pointed at a young boy. 'You! Fetch me my shield and my spear.' The boy bowed his head and scurried off immediately.

'Your armour, Valkia...'

'I do not need it. This will be brief. When I have taken this decadent, snivelling bastard's head, I expect you to throw his carcass to the wolves. Is that understood?'

'I...'

'Is that understood, Hepsus?' The snap in her voice caused even the solid, unyielding warrior to start slightly.

'Yes, hetwoman. I could remove him now if you prefer.' In response to his words, he saw a raging glimmer of madness in Valkia's eyes that he had never seen before, even during the heat of battle. It unsettled him in a way he could put no word to.

'When my honour is called into question, Hepsus, I would rather settle the dispute swiftly and with finality. Leadership is about never being afraid to do the things you would order your own people to do.' They had reached the arena and Valkia stepped confidently into the churned circle of bloody mud.

'We will need more light here,' she conceded quietly to Hepsus. 'And I suppose in the interests of fairness, we should give him back his weapons. I presume he surrendered them on entrance into the camp.'

'He did,' confirmed Hepsus and raised his hand, bringing one of the gate guards across. 'Fetch the visitor's sword.' The Warspeaker turned his attentions once again to Valkia, noting the determined set of her jaw and the growing fire in her eyes. He glanced

over at Locephax who had also entered the arena and
was strutting around on the opposite side with what
could only be described as a swagger. Both of Valkia's
daughters had come out to see what the commotion
was about and were watching him admiringly.

'Keep them away from him,' she said to Hepsus
in an undertone. 'He claims to be a chosen of the
Reveller.'

Her words drew a sharp intake of breath from Hepsus and a look of hatred flashed into his eyes. Valkia
knew that her people felt much the same as she did.
There was a time for the Reveller: rites of spring and
fertility and the celebration of birth – but a hardy
people like the Schwarzvolf had little need for such
decadence in their lives. They had just enough and
that was adequate.

Valkia could not bear the way her daughters stood
together, their eyes fixed on Locephax. She could
understand it however; he had shrugged off the tunic
he had worn over a light shirt with long, wide sleeves
gathered at the wrist. The shirt too was removed,
revealing a smooth, alabaster white and entirely hair-
less torso. The abdominal muscles were well defined
and Valkia's eyes narrowed. Locephax was not just
slim, he was strong as well.

'Your spear, hetwoman.' The boy had returned with
Slaupnir and the large round wooden shield that she
tended to favour in battle. She did not thank him,
but took up the weapons, garnering comfort from
their familiar weight and feel. Her eyes had not left
Locephax. She was gauging his speed and potential
weaknesses. The guard brought him a rapier sword

with a basket hilt; a delicate weapon that to Valkia's eyes looked insubstantial and almost hair-thin and nothing like the sturdy weapon she herself wielded.

'There is still time to change your mind about this, Valkia,' Locephax called across the arena. He made a deliberate show of making a fancy display with his sword, cutting the air before him in a series of intricate movements designed to catch the eye. Valkia did not watch. She was looking straight into his face.

She slid her arm through the back of the shield. 'The choice was made the moment you told me who you serve, Locephax,' she said. 'Now stop your childish mewling and let us bring an end to this.'

'It will give me no pleasure in killing you, Valkia.' Locephax sounded as though he actually meant those words with all his heart. 'My master saw such potential in you. He will be greatly disappointed.'

'You can explain it to him yourself when I send you screaming back to his realm. Now fight, Locephax.'

Valkia surged forward, the shield held up in her left hand, Slaupnir in her right. The arena was not particularly large and she moved with the killing speed of a hunting cat. Within a few seconds, she was in striking range of Locephax, who stood idly, his sword resting against his shoulder. His insolence infuriated the warrior queen and she pointed the spear towards him.

'Fight,' she roared in a curious echo of the altercation she had had with Deron all those years before. 'Or at the very least kneel and accept your death like the coward you are.'

'Oh, very well,' Locephax said with a theatrical sigh.

He tipped his head to one side for a moment. 'But I should warn you. I will not hold anything back. My master has granted me powers beyond your understanding and I *will* use them.'

'Try using them without a head.' Valkia tired of the endless discussion and lunged forward, the tip of her spear flickering toward Locephax's unprotected throat.

With a casual step, he moved slightly to the right so that her thrust missed him completely. She did not hesitate to consider the speed of his movement, and merely spun to attack him where he stood. Again, he moved idly out of the way.

'Is that the best you have, Valkia?' His voice took on a mocking, taunting tone and he held his sword out in front of him, closing one eye and studying her down its full length. Before she could retort, his form blurred and was behind her. In less than a heartbeat he had closed the distance between them and was bringing down the hilt of his sword on her shield arm. The pain was immediate, but passed swiftly as the muscle deadened. Her shield arm was numb for now, but she had experienced enough to know that it would recover.

With grim determination, she forced her muscles to retain their position so that she didn't lower her guard and twisted her body around so that she was standing virtually toe-to-toe with Locephax. His smile was sardonic and superior.

'Slow,' he said. 'Like an old, weary farm horse. An interesting comparison, don't you think?'

The insult to her person was startling. She was used

to being called many things – not all of them flatter-
ing – but a spiteful swipe of this nature was entirely
new. A snarl of primal rage began somewhere in
her chest and boiled its way past her lips, spraying
Locephax with flying spittle.

'Charming …' He sniffed.

*Control your temper as far as you are able in battle, Lille
Venn. If your temper takes hold of you, it becomes your
master and your sense of reason is lost. But always remember to ride the wave of fury. Let it carry you through the
hardships and trials of battle, but never let it control you.*

The words of her father came back to her in an
unexpected rush. She had always heeded his quiet
wisdom, having witnessed warriors lose themselves
to the red berserker-like rages that claimed so many.
Their power was undeniable, but their ferocity was
wild, undirected and inevitably ended in their death
as they plunged into the enemy. Consumed by her
swelling hatred for her foppish foe, the furnace of her
rage rose up, filling her limbs with killing strength.

Locephax finally tired of exchanging light verbal
blows and actually moved in with his sword. She
deflected the first three attacks with the haft of Slaupnir but the fourth caught her across the shoulder
blade. It cut through the leather of her jerkin, leaving a red trail as the blood welled from the wound.
Her opponent's sword was impossibly sharp. The
injury registered on some level of her awareness, but
it did not seem to matter. With a cry she launched
herself fully into the attack, the spear flashing in the
torchlight.

The fight began in earnest after that. Valkia's

psychotic rage burst forth in a berserker fury and she lunged at Locephax over and over. Her attack was met with languid ease as the silver-haired man parried everything she had to throw at him. His amethyst eyes glowed in the blazing torchlight and taunted her, stoking her temper ever higher.

Whenever Valkia took the field of battle, she always reached a point where perception of the world around her faded into the mists of insignificance. Within the boundaries of the Circle of Blood, the same thing was happening. A red mist at the very periphery of her vision was clouding everything but the sight of her hated enemy. Locephax was in sharp focus and her every effort was concentrated on bringing him down. Thus it was that she did not notice the slow but sure effect of the man's presence on her tribe.

Locephax's depravity and ambient aura of decadence was seeping from him in an invisible trickle, taking root in the hearts and minds of those who were closest. It brought with it an insatiable desire to satisfy appetites for whatever excess the individual desired.

Valkia did not notice, therefore, when fights broke out around the arena as one warrior turned on another. She did not notice those of her people who were overcome with lustful desires for the person they stood beside. She noticed none of it. All she could see was his face, hateful and abhorrent and all she wanted was to end him in the most violent and bloody way she could manage. In such a way, had she but known it, his influence had taken her as well.

He was speaking to her; his voice a muffled buzz

breaking through the veil. It took several moments before she could comprehend what he was saying. He was taunting her which did little to improve the rage.

'You are weak, Valkia. Your mortality gives you only so much strength. You will tire of this battle long before I do. And when you are at your weakest, I will strike.'

She did not respond, physically unable to get words out past teeth that were clenched so very hard that her jaw was already aching. Her athletic body spun gracefully, the spear in her hand a living thing that had been known as a bringer of death and terror to the people of the north for many years. Now it was useless, nothing more than wood and metal. Her rage briefly directed away from Locephax and turned inward.

Why could she not kill this man? She had fought in countless battles and slaughtered her way without compunction across the north. She had ruined all before her with blade and spear, casting down chieftains and warriors alike. Some had claimed to bear the favour of the Four, sporting marks and tokens of the gods upon their flesh. All lies and trickery for they had died to a man, their sundered skulls added to the racks of trophies that lined the entrance to her tent.

Why could she not kill this preening fool?

Locephax danced in, his sword pliant and an extension of his own body. He sliced through the air and she felt warm wetness on her face. He had cut her across the cheek and drawn her blood. She howled in inarticulate rage and lunged after him again, her vision filling with blood and focused utterly on the retreating form of Locephax.

Time ceased to have any meaning as Valkia pursued her foe beyond the boundary of the circle and into the camp. She was oblivious to her people as they struggled with one another, overcome by their base desires. They traded blows again and again, Locephax staying just beyond her reach, but closing in to nip and cut at her, inflicting dozens of tiny wounds until her body ran red with her own blood.

Flames spread among the camp as cook-fires were trampled and kicked over, trapping heaving, sweating people in the burning confines of their tents as they gorged themselves in the pleasures of the flesh or feasted on any meat they could lay their hands on. It was an orgy of excess, but here and there a warrior of iron will held back the madness, fighting off or executing those that had given way to their own weakness of spirit.

It was only when the fiery stain of sunrise creased the horizon that Valkia became aware of her own leaden movements. She was caked in blood, soot and filth and the camp had grown eerily silent, as though the Schwarzvolf had abandoned their mad revelry and fled to the hills. She glanced around, gasping for breath and saw shadowy figures moving furtively through the detritus. Her people were there, but they were keeping their distance and in that moment the fires of her rage began to gutter and die. Valkia glared at Locephax through eyes dull with fatigue and to her disgust saw that not only was he unharmed, but that there was not a trace of dirt upon him. Her skin prickled and burned in humiliation and frustration.

Why could she not kill this man?

'You could concede defeat to me now, girl.' Locephax, by the light of cold day, was nowhere near the mysterious creature he had been by torch-light. The silvery hair sapped all of the colour from him and he seemed, to Valkia's eyes, almost insipid. 'Admit that I am your better and take your place at my side. Your days will be filled with all you desire and your nights will be spent in pleasurable ecstasy.' His eyes narrowed to slits, the purple glow of them disappearing beneath his lids and long lashes. 'I am offering you so much more than the snows of the north and the ingratitude of these barbarous peo-ple. If you come with me now, you will be a true queen.'

'I will be your slave. That was what you said.' She finally found her voice. 'And that will not come to pass. Ever. Now still your tongue and fight me.'

'I admire your courage and tenacity, Valkia,' Locephax said with a cruel sneer on his face. 'But I think you should know that I can maintain this for as long as necessary. And I can use many of my master's gifts to help me. For instance...'

The man turned slightly and cast an expert eye around the carnage. Over the sound of her wheez-ing lungs, Valkia could hear that there were still struggles going on amidst the chaos as her people sought to master themselves once again. Bodies lay everywhere, some clearly unconscious from their exertions while others lay in bloody disarray, their limbs and heads hacked away by frenzied hands. The

Schwarzvolf were broken. The thought sent a new shock of anger through the exhausted queen. Her people, the tribe she had lifted from the dust and forged into the mightiest power of the steppe were broken. In the space of a single night this foppish stranger had undone the work of years.

Locephax was talking again and gesturing to the figures slinking through the shadows, but Valkia could no longer hear him. A fury was filling her, stiffening her tired muscles with a strength she did not know she possessed. She blinked the blood from her eyes and stared with naked hatred at the creature that had invaded her home. The man, if he truly was a man, was beckoning to someone. He still wore that disgusting grin on his face, clearly enjoying the destruction he wrought. She *needed* to kill him. It felt as though there was a colossal pressure building behind her eyes. It crackled along her limbs and filled her heart to bursting.

A voice in the distance roared in defiance and a detached part of her recognised Hepsus as he bellowed in denial. Every bone, every muscle, every sinew, every part of Valkia filled with the terrible need to tear Locephax apart, to cut the head from his shoulders and bathe in his blood. Nothing could stop her. A flurry of cinders gusted past her on the breeze, the dancing motes of ash and sparks seeming to crawl past in slow motion.

'Blood...' Valkia growled, though it was the voice of a stranger.

Locephax's perfect, violet eyes widened fractionally in surprise and he started to turn. He moved so slowly she wondered how she had been unable to strike him before.

'Blood... for the Blood God.'

The tension broke and Valkia exploded into violent action, her berserker fury raining down on Locephax like a storm. She was a whirling, screaming cyclone of destruction, her spear weaving a lethal design through the air that cut and stabbed at her enemy again and again. Someone or something rushed at her from the side, but their attack seemed ridiculously slow. She knocked the blow aside with contempt and struck the assailant's head from his shoulders before continuing her pursuit of the retreating Locephax.

Though pressed, the Reveller's chosen defended himself with surprising skill, though he no longer wore his self-assured smile. All trace of smirking superiority had vanished in the face of Valkia's renewed assault, but she was too consumed by her fury to take any satisfaction from his discomfort.

From the outside the battle was a blur of blades and violence. Hepsus cradled the broken, headless body of Aric, his eldest son, in his arms and groaned in anguish. The boy had stood firm throughout the long night despite the desire etched clearly on his face, yet when Locephax had called, he had answered. The man had simply beckoned and the boy had come, blade ready to strike his queen down.

Hepsus watched the raging duel through dulled eyes and saw the same madness repeated again and again as the pair fought across the camp. Loyal men and women snatching up weapons and charging to the aid of the silver-haired stranger. One after the other, they died. It was hypnotic. Valkia never so much as broke her stride as former friends and allies assailed her. They would run screaming into the mêlée, there would be a flash of silver, a gout of blood and their bodies would tumble headless to the ground.

The Warspeaker wondered if they could recover from this. Even if Valkia triumphed over this hellish interloper, the Schwarzvolf were badly wounded. Of the thousands that had filled the valley of the Vale, maybe a third lay dead or dying and another third had fallen victim to other wild vices. There would be punishment for such weakness, though the tribe could ill afford more deaths. So the Schwarzvolf waited as their queen fought. They waited and they saw to their wounded and they kept their distance from the raging battle.

For Valkia time had long since ceased to have any meaning. She was sustained by her rage which burned like liquid fire in her veins. It was a rage that could only be satisfied through violence and the death of the hated enemy before her. Locephax was sporting dozens of cuts on his naked torso, but where Valkia was drenched in a mantle of gore, he did not bleed. He gazed at the warrior woman through hate-filled amethyst eyes.

'Was the boy a little too easy? Yes, I think so, too.' He taunted. His silver hair streamed out behind him as he spun and parried. 'Still, it was an amusing diversion. And your Warspeaker is most displeased.'

Valkia managed nothing more than a snarl and pressed her attack. Had she killed Aric? She did not know. She had killed so many people in the past few hours that it was impossible to tell one from the next. Lost in the purity of her rage, she also realised that she didn't care. If he was dead it was because he had been weak, and there was no place for weakness in battle.

Almost as though he could pick up on her thoughts, Locephax grinned. 'Do you yield to me yet, Valkia? I can carry on throwing your own people at you for days if necessary. What will it take to make you surrender to me? Another headstrong youth? Your daughters, perhaps?' His tongue ran lasciviously across his lips. 'Such beauties. They would be a delightful addition to my harem.' He glanced over at the tribespeople who still lingered cautiously near the battle, but neither Eris nor Bellona were to be seen. The mention of her daughters sent a shock of recognition through Valkia's rage-clouded mind and a scream of unfettered fury erupted from her lips. The tip of her spear smashed Locephax's slim sword aside and impaled him through the gut.

Locephax looked down at the blade puncturing his perfect flesh and back up at Valkia. There was no gush of arterial blood or wail of agony, he simply sniffed in annoyance and grabbed the haft of the weapon.

'As I told you, you cannot best me with your little spears and knives. You know nothing of real power. And to think you came so close...'

'Reveal yourself, daemon.' Valkia barked. Cords of muscle bulged from her shoulders and arms as she attempted to push the spear deeper into Locephax's body while the creature held fast to the weapon, holding it in place.

'You should be careful what you wish for woman, I could... '

'I said reveal yourself!' Valkia cut him off with a bellowed curse and the rune etched into the spearhead flared a terrible, fiery red.

For the first time since their battle began, Locephax screamed.

He tore the spear from his body and flung it and Valkia away with hideous strength. She tumbled across the muddy ground, managed to get her feet under her and sprang up in time to see the form of the silver-haired man bulge and split.

The fabric of his breeches stretched to bursting point and Valkia could do nothing but stare as every seam on his meticulous outfit split simultaneously. The man who was her sole focus was swelling and stretching; all dimensions filling out at the same time. He grew taller, wider and more monstrous in appearance by the second.

Those few tribesmen who still lingered, those whose hearts were not as hard or whose stomachs were not strong as others were fleeing, screaming in terror at the horrifying creature that was taking shape before them. And yet... even in his true form, there was something oddly *exquisite* about Locephax, Daemon Prince of Slaanesh.

He was clearly inhuman although his body had a humanoid shape to it. There was a discernible head, a face and long, powerfully muscled legs. Arms – yes, there were those too – indeed, they were one of the more obvious things about him. The creature possessed at least six of them, two of which ended in cruel-looking pincers that snapped hungrily at the air.

His skin was a uniform shade of silver – the same colour as his hair had been in human form – the only hints of colour about him were the iridescent purple scales that flowed over his back. He was reptilian. He was human. He was both and he was neither.

The warrior queen stared at the thing before her. Repulsive... attractive... how could something so freakish in appearance be so strangely beautiful? Snakes had always held a fascination for Valkia and this, she reasoned, was no different. That something which moved with such sinuous grace and ease could kill a man with a single bite... this was no different.

She took Slaupnir in hand and steadied herself on the ground, rooting herself to the spot.

'I am Locephax,' the creature hissed in a sibilant voice. 'And I will be your undoing.' His face elongated slightly; the eyes lost their amethyst shine and became completely black. Horns sprouted from his head, curling forwards and as he opened his mouth to speak, she saw the needle-pointed, razor sharp teeth that lined his jaws. Locephax might once have been human, but that day was long since past.

She raised the smouldering spear to the heavens and screamed out her god's name. And this time, he heard her and acknowledged her cries. Unholy strength flooded her battered frame, filling her with killing rage and a singular determination to destroy the abomination that had violated the Schwarzvolf.

SHE WAS A dervish; a maelstrom of violence. Slaupnir flashed wickedly in the afternoon sunlight. The sun had passed its zenith and she had never even noticed.

Valkia landed blow after blow on Locephax and the daemon returned the attack with equal ferocity. She was bloodied and wounded, but if she felt any pain from the countless lacerations on her body, she gave no sign that they impaired or inconvenienced her in any way.

The daemon was covered in similar wounds, a lattice-work of injuries that had been sketched across his body by the sharp point of the spear. Every time the blade made contact with his flesh, there was a searing flash of light and the smell of burning meat. The rune of the Blood God etched into its depth was more damaging than the weapon itself – but the two combined had the potential to bite deeply into pale, daemonic flesh.

Concentrating on the battle, the fug of glamour that he had projected cleared. All around the camp, those who could still stand were watching the battle in silence. Even Hepsus, whose grief at the death of his son was great, could do nothing but stare as the warrior queen battled the inhuman creature.

They fought on, neither seeming to gain the upper hand. Two perfectly matched opponents and neither of them could defeat the other. It didn't seem possible; Locephax had the size and speed advantage. He had long since abandoned any pretence at keeping his form remotely human and his lower torso had warped into a snake's body, silver and purple scales gleaming. He moved across the arena floor on the looping coils, a terrible, beautiful thing from another world.

He was superior in every respect – but Valkia had

determination and the wild abandon of the Blood God on her side. She thrust Slaupnir repeatedly towards Locephax, but the scales on the daemon's body were as hard as any armour she had ever fought against. Penetrating his hide was nigh on impossible. Her eyes roamed the creature in an effort to locate any obvious weakness, but she could see none.

Every bone in her body was aching as she pushed herself further, screaming for the chance to rest. Adrenaline kept her going but the fury that had sustained her through the gruelling battle was beginning to ebb, her mortal frame stressed beyond its limits. She knew that realistically she could not sustain this for very much longer. She needed an opportunity and she needed one to present itself soon.

'You look tired, Valkia,' said the Locephax-thing, smirking his inhuman smile at her. The needle points of his teeth were bared and the daemon's forked tongue darted in and out. The eyes were filled with hunger. 'I can help you rest... eternal rest. Wouldn't you like that?'

His tone was hypnotic and tired as she was, Valkia almost fell under his spell. With a scream to the Blood God, she jumped back, hurling a torrent of abuse at him in the guttural language of her people. Locephax threw back his head and screeched with laughter. And it was then that she saw her moment; the golden opportunity that she had waited for.

It all happened between one heartbeat and the next, a flash of silver faster than the eye could see. With his head thrown back the way it was, the soft part of his lower jaw was exposed. If she got the strike right...

She sprinted the short distance that separated them and leaped upwards, jabbing Slaupnir up towards the daemon. The spear tip entered the unprotected flesh of his throat and passed through his neck. His six arms flailed wildly as he reached out to return the attack, the pincers snapping furiously and two of his other arms struggling to pull the spear free.

'I cannot die, Valkia!' His voice was a bubbling gurgle, but she could see that her strike had mortally wounded him. 'I am a champion of my master and he will not confine me to his domain! I will return, he will grant me a new body...'

The creature slumped, its head against its torso and the arms went limp. The coils on which it sat sagged and crumpled until Locephax was no longer towering over the warrior queen. She reached up and wiped a hand across her face, smearing blood and soot over it. Leaning forward, she snatched the sword from Locephax's hand.

'I know nothing of the ways of the Four, creature,' she said. Her voice was strong and powerful despite her bone-aching weariness. 'But I am going to carry your head as a trophy to the very feet of Kharneth, and all who look upon it will know the weakness of the Reveller and his pawns.'

With those words, she spun around with deadly accuracy. Locephax's blade was keen; she knew it well. The lacerations on her body were testament to that fact. She wielded it with enough strength and swing to cleave straight through his neck, just below the spear that still protruded from it and sever the head from the body.

Just as she had promised she would.

The head fell to the arena floor, rolling several times before coming to a stop. The body wavered a moment or two and then collapsed, blood flowing unchecked from the gaping stump of a neck and pooling on the ground.

Hoping that her shaking hand did not give away her exhaustion too much, Valkia reached down and snatched up the severed head of the daemon.

'Thus all followers of the Reveller end,' she said. The head in her grip writhed and twisted, taking on a life of its own. It was a grisly thing to witness, particularly when it spoke with a voice it should no longer have had.

'You cannot kill me, warrior bitch,' it snarled, trying its utmost to bite at Valkia. 'All you will do is infuriate my master. He will not let this transgression go unanswered...'

Kneeling down in the dirt, Valkia dipped her finger in the blood from one of the many injuries on her body. She daubed the rune of the Blood God on the daemon's forehead.

Locephax screamed. A terrible, shivering sound that caused more than one of the remaining tribesman to lose control of their bladder. Most turned and fled from the sound, but Valkia did not move.

'Does that hurt, daemon prince?' She leaned close and whispered the words to Locephax's head. 'Does it *hurt*?'

Did it hurt like Hepsus must do? Did it hurt like she did knowing that she had been duped into this position? She would make this creature pay for the damage it had done. For now, she could keep it under her control with the torment of the rune on its face, but she already had an idea what she would do. She had witnessed Locephax's power, even as a head.

'Burn the body,' she ordered, still staring down at the head. 'And fetch me some nails. I'll keep this thing from fleeing my grasp.'

Nobody moved for several long moments, mesmerised by the sight of their blood-spattered queen and the still-screaming head.

'I said *move!*'

The few warriors who had slunk close enough to hear her did as they were commanded, except Hepsus who lingered. He still cradled the broken body of his son. Valkia could not meet his gaze, but she could feel his rage and grief even as the killing frenzy that had sustained her flowed from her bones and muscles.

'You understand what happened?'

There was a hesitation and Hepsus finally replied.

'I understand. I do not forgive, but... yes. I understand.'

'He will receive a warrior's burial, Warspeaker.'

Hepsus crossed back through the rope and paused, Aric across his shoulder. He turned and looked at his leader.

'I will bury my son as *I* see fit, hetwoman. I do not need your kind of intervention.'

'See how they start to turn on you!' The head of Locephax was still loquacious, even having been severed from its body. She shook it violently – she could no longer think of it as a he – and it sputtered its rage.

She may have won this battle, but she knew she had lost something vital.

NINE
Promises

WITHIN MINUTES VALKIA had what she had asked for. A pale-faced boy presented her with eight heavy, square-headed nails. Despite her crushing weariness she drew her knife and carefully etched the symbol of the Blood God into the top of each one. She had trailed the head of the daemon across the camp, leaving a virulent scarlet trail in its wake and she stood whilst the smith finished his work.

The head of Locephax had fallen silent for the time being, its eyes closed but from time to time, the eyelids would flutter. If anything, it appeared to be in a state of deep slumber. Valkia did not pretend to even begin understanding the deep sorcery that kept it alive, but she instinctively knew what she had to do.

Taking the eight nails in hand, she lay down her shield on the ground. Kneeling, she reached a hand up for a heavy hammer. Setting the daemon's head in the centre of her shield, she drove the first of the nails through Locephax's forehead.

The eyes flared open and the mouth opened in a silent scream of agony. Sound rushed in eventually and the cry of anguish was heard across the camp of the Schwarzvolf. It resonated around the Vale, but Valkia did not even flinch. She hammered in the other nails, securing the head to the front of her shield. When her work was complete, she rose to her feet and held the grisly article aloft.

'With this trophy, this demonstration of my strength, the enemy will surely flee before us. And they will clear the way for the journey I must make.'

The boy, looking decidedly uneasy at the proximity of the daemon's remains, furrowed his brow.

'Journey, hetwoman?'

'To the far north,' she replied, looking over at him. Her eyes shone as though she was feverish. 'I must present this trophy to my lord and master. Imagine the reward.'

The young man stared at her. The warrior queen had clearly lost her senses. But he was not going to tell her that. He did not envy the person who did.

'She has crossed the line into madness.'

Valkia had finally retired to her tent in order to rest. As soon as the adrenaline had left her system, the exhaustion of the fight with Locephax had finally caught up with her. Her injuries had been tended to; mostly superficial cuts and scrapes, but there had been one gash on her upper arm that had needed stitching closed. She had not even so much as flinched during the process, her eyes fixed hatefully on the daemon's head. Restoring order to the devastated camp would be a much more arduous task and they were still discovering the true extent of the damage wrought by the daemon's insidious will.

In her absence, Hepsus had called a clandestine meeting of the Circle. Every member had come at the summons, including the hetwoman's younger brother. Edan, now Godspeaker, sat quietly to one side, his head hooded, his thoughts contained. Occasionally, his glittering eyes would pass across the assembled warriors.

'With respect, Hepsus, you are angry...'

'You are right I am angry. She killed my boy.'

'He attacked her. And besides, Hepsus, you must admit that he displayed a terrible weakness.' The Warspeaker turned a furious stare on the man who had said this, but the other warrior didn't back down. 'He was weak-willed. I understand your grief at his loss, but would you have been able to live with the knowledge that he was weak?'

It was strange. Had circumstances been different, Hepsus would have sneered at another man whose child had been weak. But Aric had been *his* son. His pride and joy. His *future*. And now the boy was stone cold dead. Hepsus was struggling to accept it.

The Warspeaker controlled his rising temper. He could not afford to lose the backing of the Circle in this matter.

'You are right,' he repeated. 'Yes, of course I am angry. But regardless... her choice in this matter put the whole tribe at risk. She accepted the creature's challenge. Had she lost, who knows what further havoc it would have wreaked?'

'But she did not lose, Warspeaker.' The voice belonged to Edan. The boy pushed back his hood.

He bore a startling resemblance to his older half-sister; the same dark hair and well-chiselled features. Intelligence oozed from every pore. 'She defeated a daemonic emissary. Her power is unmatched. We should surely be praising her name, not trying to plant the insidious suggestion that she is mad.'

Hepsus looked over at Edan. He was well aware of the relationship that existed between the Godspeaker and his warrior sister. She despised what she perceived as Edan's weaknesses and kept him very much at arm's length. For his part, the boy idolised her. He had been spun the tale as to how she had saved his life from a mother with murder in her heart and his loyalty was total.

It suited Valkia's purposes to have him on her side, but she spared little time for him and rarely openly acknowledged their blood ties.

'Did you see the thing after she had torn it from the body? It still speaks. Still has some sort of unnatural life about it. It is sorcery of the very worst kind and she has brought it amongst us.'

Edan's dark brows feathered together. 'There are those of the other tribes who say that my position within the tribe is one that smacks of sorcery, Warspeaker. Would you say the same of me?'

Damn the boy and his silvery tongue. Hepsus kept his temper under control and forced a polite bow of the head. 'Of course not, Godspeaker. What you have is a gift. A talent. But were your head to part company from your shoulders, your voice would be forever stilled. It does not bode well. Surely even you must agree with that?'

'It is an omen, granted,' conceded Edan thoughtfully. 'I should perhaps spend some time in meditation on the subject. But all of you know my sister as well as I do. She will entertain a notion for a while and if it does not come to pass swiftly, she will grow bored with it.' It was an extraordinarily honest appraisal of Valkia's behaviour. Having conquered so many of the smaller tribes and absorbed them into her own, the warrior queen frequently grew restless. Without war, she felt imprisoned. She had been building her strength and her forces to take on the other large tribes of the north. That time was approaching, they all knew it.

She had made a clear and concise statement. She planned to abandon the war on the tribes and head to the far north, to the place where they said the gods dwelt.

The Circle gradually broke up after this, with no sense of resolution. The Warspeaker stared into the fire in the centre of the tent, lost in the flames and lost in his own thoughts. He did not notice that there was another presence until the voice cut through his ponderings.

'Would you follow her?'

Startled, Hepsus looked up. Edan had remained, still sitting in the shadows. The boy was too fond of mystery and for a moment, Hepsus was angered. 'What?'

'If she turned to you tomorrow and ordered you north, would you follow her?'

'Of course I would! Are you calling my loyalty into question?'

'The truth, Warspeaker?' Edan stood up. He was slim, like his sister and taller. Just as she had seemed as a young woman, he looked as insubstantial as a reed. But Hepsus had seen the young man swing a great axe with ease. He knew that the wiry body hid a core of strength. 'The truth... yes. I *am* calling your loyalty into question. You doubt my sister. You doubt her motives because you do not understand them.'

The easy manner in which Edan said the words made Hepsus uncomfortable. The feeling came from knowing that the Godspeaker was absolutely right.

'I am her right hand,' he replied eventually. 'I can see no end to this venture north but a poor one. I would not see the prosperity of the Schwarzvolf fall in the wake of one person's whim – be that person the youngest child in the tribe or our queen. Does that put a question against my loyalty?'

'Not to your people, no.' Edan tipped his head on one side. 'You have served your tribe well for many years, Hepsus. I would suggest that you may have to endure a little longer.' His eyes glittered dangerously. 'Because there is a way forward, if you are prepared to listen to me.'

Sensing something he couldn't quite articulate, Hepsus stared at the boy in an attempt to gauge something, *anything* from his closed expression. But Edan was outstandingly good at giving away nothing in his body language. Eventually, the Warspeaker nodded.

'I'm listening,' he said. 'Tell me what you will.'

* * *

She was running. Always running forwards; never running away. She was not fleeing from danger, but heading directly into it. There were sounds… inhuman sounds at her back, but they were not chasing her. They were running with her. A distant howl. She ran on.

The sky ran red with blood. Her father… her father had told her once that when the Blood God was pleased, the skies would run scarlet. She stared up at the sky and stumbled, falling forwards.

She put her hands out to stop herself landing on her face. Her fingernails had grown; curled like talons. They were the hands of a beast, of a daemon. Unable to rise, she stared at her unnatural talons as the army at her back continued to charge forwards. A terrible, searing pain tore through her and she arched her back in agony. She was changing. Becoming something else. Something… better? Something more?

Her agony burst forth in a terrible scream that was half feral, half terror.

She woke up.

HER DREAMS HAD long been troubled, but since the death of Locephax, Valkia had begun to suffer true nightmares. Repeated visions of her elongated nails; her clawed hands swam before her eyes constantly and she had not managed a full night's sleep in days. When she was not having the dream in which an army flowed at her back, she was reliving the battle with the daemon. Usually those ones resolved themselves as events had played out, with her victory.

But sometimes...

Shuddering, she would wake in a cold sweat, the

fading vestige of the dream and the overwhelming memory that of the daemon tearing out her liver and feasting upon it. All her life she had been exposed to grotesque acts of wanton violence and never once had she had such nightmares. They weakened her, startled her, *frightened* her. And that fear, like many other things in her life, made her angry.

She had thought of removing Locephax's head from her shield, convincing herself that the unholy thing must be the source of all her sleep disturbances, but she could not. She had sworn to deliver the prize to the very foot of the Blood God's throne and she would not go back on that promise. Over the days following the daemon's demise, Valkia became increasingly driven and single-minded about the quest north until she lost her ability to see objectively.

But Valkia was not so foolish as to think that she could travel such a distance alone and when she finally stood before the tribe, her eyes shadowed and her cheeks hollow from lack of sleep and sustenance, there was an immediate cadre of followers who instantly moved to stand beside her.

Their loyalty filled her heart with a swell of pride. Winter was closing fast and the journey would be long and arduous. But still these men and women of her tribe showed their steadfast allegiance.

But during the darkest watches of the night, a soft voice whispered words of treachery. *They think you weak. They think you insane. They would let you die, Valkia of the Schwarzvolf. You are* nothing *to them but a hindrance.* The whispers filled her with paranoid suspicion and she began watching her closest followers very carefully whilst at the same time drawing up her great plan.

Within the week, she had promised. Within the week, they would begin their journey. She was filled with purpose unlike anything she had ever known and yet it was such a familiar sensation that she could have always felt this way.

Her people were hardy and they were robust. A number of the outlying camps had been brought into the main fold of the Vale to bolster the numbers lost during the battle with Locephax. Despite such terrible, aching loss the Schwarzvolf thrived. Despite the countless deaths, they continued to dominate the tribes of the north. It was a testament to her tenacity and superlative leadership that her tribe had grown so large. Yet as she sat staring out across the Vale, she did not see the growth and richness of her people. She did not absorb the changes.

Where once tents made from the skins of animals had stood, there were now semi-permanent wooden structures growing up in ever-increasing numbers. In the wake of the battle, an agreement had been reached that something more permanent was required and there were workers willing and able to perform the tasks necessary. As well as warriors, the Schwarzvolf had absorbed artisans into their number. Her people prospered and she resented it.

She resented the stability of it all. She was born of a proud, noble warrior race and they had become a generation of peace-time farmers and hunters. It was demeaning. The Schwarzvolf had always been nomadic. This settlement was becoming permanent.

Her fingers idly drummed on the arm of the wooden throne upon which she sat. Slaupnir rested across her lap and the daemon-headed shield was by her side. Locephax's eyes were shut as it engaged in whatever passed for its slumber.

Valkia let her eyes narrow as she scanned the activity that went on. A faint swirl of snow was blowing in the air, huge, fluffy flakes that drifted lazily on the fitful breeze. It was still too warm for them to do much more than coat things in a white powder before melting to nothing. The flakes rested on the various structures that had been built, but where they fell on the forge, they melted immediately. From within that large building, she could hear the sound of metal ringing on metal as the smith and his apprentice followed her orders to produce as much armour and weaponry as they were able.

Warriors were seated in small groups, sharpening their blades and stitching tears in leather, or standing within the arena engaging in training exercises. Their swords clashed almost in harmony with the sounds of the forge.

Others were busy at the central cookfire, skinning and salting meat for drying, or stirring seemingly endlessly at the huge, communal iron pot that served the entire tribe on a daily basis. Their staple diet consisted of stews made from the plentiful meat that they caught, supplemented by flat-baked, dark bread and fruit. The smell of a roasting haunch of venison, spit-turning over the fire wafted across her nostrils and she inhaled deeply, feeling her mouth water.

All of these sights, sounds and smells were achingly familiar to her and, for a while, she had taken great pleasure in the ongoing prosperity of her people. But now she feared that she had tamed them. The wolf that was the symbol of her people was tamed and little more than a dog.

Her fingers curled around the arm of the throne and she chewed on her lip. When she returned from her expedition to the seat of the Blood God, when she returned bearing his favour, she would rectify this domesticity. She would tear down the buildings and her people would rise again, instilled with fresh vigour.

As if hearing her thoughts, the eyes of the head nailed to her shield fluttered open. A cruel smile touched its lips.

'When you return, Valkia? *If.* My master is enraged still. He waits for you in the realm of the gods just as much as the savage you worship...' The voice cut off as Valkia delivered a swift kick to its face.

'Be *silent*, worm,' she hissed. Locephax snorted in derision but did as she commanded. For good measure, she kicked the daemon again. It had little effect but it made her feel better.

And yet his words, designed to fan the flames of her fear, had the effect of lighting a spark of determination. She cast another glance around her camp. She would put together her war party and leave before nightfall the following day.

Before she changed her mind.

* * *

'You sweep too low.'

She was sparring in the arena with her half-brother. He had come to her barely an hour hence and asked if she would give him some training. She had never been approached by Edan for such a reason before and had treated him to a look of suspicion.

He laughed. 'If I am to accompany you on this venture, sister, then I should be as well prepared as I can be. Hepsus and the other warriors have given me much training, but I would consider it an honour if you would train me.'

She had agreed, pleased that Edan had pledged his allegiance so openly, and was relieved to have something to occupy her thoughts. The two had entered the arena with training swords and buckler-sized shields, as this was Edan's preference. They had been fighting for a while and she had repeatedly put her brother onto his back, the tip of the training sword at his throat.

He got to his feet again, looking slightly ruffled at the continued humiliation he was undergoing. But he had his reasons for what he was doing. All the time he was keeping Valkia thus occupied, her attention was removed from anything else that was going on. Hepsus had listened to the young Godspeaker and had seen the wisdom in what he proposed.

'Again?' Valkia's grin was surprising and also infectious. He grinned ruefully back at her, feeling one of the occasionally twinges of regret that they had not been closer over the years. Perhaps if she had let him in, she would not have taken the route of folly.

There was no time to dwell on what might have

been. Edan had the best interests of his people at heart and that steeled his resolve.

'Again,' he acknowledged.

Still grinning at her younger brother, Valkia took up her position, the shield close to her chest, the training sword ready.

'Begin,' she said. 'And this time, aim for me as though you mean it. Don't be afraid of hurting me, Edan.'

'I'm not,' he said, and they began to fight. Valkia had retained every bit of speed and strength that had marked her across the years and age had not weakened her at all. Whenever she fought now, she reached for that moment of true glory she had touched when fighting the daemon. She *strove* for it. Hungered for it. Burned for it.

For the most part, it eluded her. But every so often, she would touch the ecstasy of the blood rage and come out desperate for more.

Edan had the advantage of youth, but he found it hard to keep pace with the older woman. He was already regretting in part his decision to occupy Valkia's attention in this way. He would come out of this with bruises from head to toe – but he would also benefit from her training.

His sword came up to deflect an overhead blow and she thrust forward with the buckler, catching him just under the jaw. His head snapped back and he stumbled, dazed. Valkia gave him no respite, following up immediately with a blow from the flat of the practise blade that left his arm aching. He almost dropped the sword, but with grim determination, kept a grip.

'Good,' she approved, noting his efforts. 'That's good, Edan. Now give me everything you have. Come at me like you *really* want to kill me.'

There was a pause of barely a heartbeat and Edan found the same core of strength that had served his sister so well for her entire life. With a feral roar, he charged towards her and she thought, for an unlikely second, that she saw bloodlust in his eyes.

She moved position as he lunged and he went wide of the mark. She stepped nimbly to the right, the leather skirt that she wore flaring out with the movement. Slit either side to allow for ease of movement, it whipped back as she steadied herself. Bringing the hilt of the blade down hard between his shoulder blades, he sank to his knees, Valkia standing over him.

'And down you go again, brother. How long is it since you stepped away from your role and actually practised in the Circle of Blood?' It was something she had noticed for a while; the fact that there were fewer fights amongst her own people. They were growing lazy, she reasserted. It would all change soon.

He didn't reply. He felt humiliation flushing his cheeks, despite the knowledge that he could never have beaten her. From the corner of his eye, he saw Hepsus crossing the camp and turned his head to look at the Warspeaker. The red-haired warrior had an amused smirk on his face as he watched Edan's humiliation. It was enough of a sign that his business was concluded and for that at least, Edan was grateful.

'Again?' Valkia was addressing him.

'By your leave, sister, I will take a break for now. You are correct of course. I have been lax in my training. But I promise you that when the situation arises... I will not fail you.' Edan accepted her help up and gave her a slightly pained smile. Valkia squinted against the late afternoon sunlight. For just a moment, he had looked so much like her father as a young man that she felt a dull, long-forgotten ache of loss.

'Very well,' she said and clapped him on the shoulder. He winced as pain stabbed through him. 'The journey north will be a long and difficult one, Edan. I am glad that you will be with us. You will learn a great deal.'

'And I am glad to be coming with you,' he lied smoothly.

She called another Circle meeting that night. Her cheeks were still flushed from the practice bout with Edan and there was such life and enthusiasm in her face, her eyes, her every gesture that every warrior who sat in her tent could not help but be swept up by the magnitude of her vision.

'We will leave in two days from now,' she declared. 'Those who wish to remain here may do so. Those who wish to come with me will understand the risks. They are Schwarzvolf. They will bear such uncertainty with grace and honour.'

She had brought the shield into the meeting with her and set it down face upwards so that Locephax's foul head was clearly on display.

'I took this trophy by my own hand,' she declared. 'This... *creature* was a servant of the Reveller. We all know, as our Godspeaker teaches – and as his predecessors taught before him – that there is a time and place for worship of his bounty. In his aspect of fertility, we thank him for giving us babes who are not god-touched. In his aspect of lust, we thank him for providing us with the ability to bring new lives into the world. But this... Locephax... was *perverse*. He took the ideals we understand and distorted them beyond recognition.'

She kicked the shield, but the eyes remained firmly closed. Sneering slightly at the daemon, Valkia continued.

'This thing's master is the exact opposite of all we have come to believe in. We believe that power lies in strength and the conquering of others. Locephax was slovenly, lustful and lazy. Such a creature deserved death. And by presenting the head of an enemy to the Blood God...'

Her eyes shone with mania and for the first time, even those who had supported her most closely over the years wondered if she was quite sane. There was something unstoppable in that expression. Something that would not be denied.

'By presenting this trophy, our patron god will reward me. More!' She stood up and paced around the gathered Circle, her hands animate and her voice filled with deep, abiding passion. 'He will reward our *people*! We will be stronger than ever before! Look at all we have accomplished. Think of what remains to be done.'

'The larger tribes...' Hepsus began to speak, but she bounded to stand behind him, her hands on his shoulder.

'Don't worry yourself about them any more, Hepsus! When we return from our trip north, the power we will hold will be beyond anything they can ever hope to resist! The Schwarzvolf will sweep across the steppes and take everything for themselves. And then, when our force is great beyond imagining...'

She released Hepsus and stood back from him. Every pair of eyes turned to stare at her, captivated by her words, mesmerised by her sheer beauty and passion.

'Then we will take the south.'

An immediate ripple ran around the tent. To suggest such a thing was madness itself. Everyone knew that all who had dared venture south were thwarted by the mountain-dwelling dwarf folk. Fierce fighters who would give no ground and gave back just as violently as they received; several raiding parties had headed into the warm-lands only to never return.

Valkia stood backwards, in the shadows where she knew they could see nothing of her except her glittering eyes and the even whiteness of her teeth as she smiled. Words such as 'preposterous', 'suicidal' and 'mad' were flung around easily and she listened with pleasure to the arguing that broke out.

For too long, this Circle had sat like sacks of straw, dutifully nodding and agreeing with everything she had suggested. For too long they had forgotten what it was to think for themselves. She had now given them much to consider.

'We should remember,' Valkia said eventually, finally cutting across the squabbling with a cool, clear voice. 'We should remember that such a thing will not happen for many years. We must take the north first. We must leave no doubt in the minds of the soft southerners that we are a force united. They will lay down their weapons and flee from us. Just uttering the name of the Schwarzvolf will send them running, piss trickling down their legs.'

The words raised a hearty laugh or two from the group. Hepsus, she noted, looked troubled, but she did not single him out. He would see. She knew that he would see. They would *all* see. Once they stood in the presence of Kharneth...

Khorne.

There it was again. That whispered thought; a breath of an idea that the name she had known her master by for all these years was nothing more than a lie.

Khorne. Kharneth, it matters little what you call the Blood God. The truth remains that the followers of Slaanesh will be waiting for you, Gorequeen.

It was Locephax. The daemon's eyes remained closed and his words were *felt* inside her mind rather than spoken. The smile slid slowly off her face and she stared at the shield.

You will cross the ice. You will enter the Wastes and there... there, your people will be slaughtered. One after the other, they will fall. Their blood will stain the snows crimson. And then, when only you remain...

The daemon's eyes flared open and those sitting closest leaped backwards in alarm.

'*Then* I will claim you,' he said.

Quick as lightning, without ever missing a beat, Valkia drew the dagger from her boot and hurled it across the room. It embedded itself in the wood of the shield just to the right of Locephax's face with a loud *thud*. The daemon fell silent again, but not before a serene smile had played across its dead lips.

It was a look that would return to Valkia in her nightmares that night.

TEN
The Breath Before the Plunge

IT WAS THE nature of the northern weather to turn like a savage animal and this year was no exception to that rule. Within hours the occasional snow flurry had become a steady precipitation. As it had always done, the arrival of the winter brought a strange silence to the camp of the Schwarzvolf. It muffled the tread of people's feet, killed what little birdsong filled the air and even the people lowered their voices. By the time Valkia stepped from her tent, the entire camp was covered in a blanket of white.

It was early and whilst the weak winter sun shone, it did little to alleviate the chill in the air. Valkia reached back into the tent for her furs and shrugged them on across her shoulders. She felt calm and in control despite the horrific visions that had plagued her in the night. There was something about the first true snows of winter that made her feel... *comfortable*. This was her heritage.

The communal fire which was always kept burning was barely more than glowing embers at the moment, but there were several children working on banking it. This was one of the many chores that were given to the young people of the tribe and she watched them with a slightly indulgent air for a few minutes. Finally, she crossed the camp and accepted a cup of a hot beverage from one of them. It was a delicious drink, made from the leaves of various herbs that grew in the area. The aromatic scent belied a preparation that was in truth, quite bitter; honey was added to sweeten it. Sipping at the beverage, Valkia welcomed the warmth it brought even as it burned down her throat.

A sound overhead caught her attention and she looked upwards. A dark shadow moved across her face and far above her, a mountain bird of prey screamed as it rode the thermals. The bird was enormous, its wings fully stretched as it glided free, revelling in the thrill of the hunt and rejoicing in its simple existence. Valkia watched it for a moment, fascinated as she always was by the efficacy of creatures who lived their lives on the wing.

With a cry of triumph, the bird dived downwards, having spied its unfortunate prey and disappeared briefly over the crest of a hill. Scant seconds later it was aloft again, a dead rodent hanging from its talons. It was quite wonderful to watch and Valkia, child of a deeply superstitious people, saw it as an omen.

Today, she and her assembled party of warriors would begin their pilgrimage. The sighting of the raptor, revered almost as much as the black wolves of the hills by her people, filled her with great confidence and there was a definite swagger in her stride as she moved back across the camp towards the tent shared by her daughters.

* * *

THEIR RELATIONSHIP HAD never been particularly close but as Eris and Bellona had grown, Valkia had seen herself reflected in them. The girls had always shared the same appearance, but personality-wise they were extraordinarily opposite. Eris was like a younger Valkia; fierce, angry, resistant to just about anything whilst Bellona was cool-headed and able to offer a diplomatic solution to any situation. Both had received – with their mother's blessing – proposals of marriage. They would be well provided for and it was well known that on Valkia's death, the throne would pass to one of the twins. It was her stated preference that they share leadership of the tribe, but whether that would happen or not she would never know.

She had denied them the opportunity to travel to the realm of the gods. Bellona had accepted her mother's judgement without question, but Eris had raged for hours, throwing a tantrum not unlike those Valkia herself had once demonstrated. In the end, Valkia had backhanded her across the face. It had been the first time she had physically remonstrated either of her daughters and all three of them had been startled by the fading echo of the slap.

It had achieved the desired effect nonetheless. Eris had been shocked into listening to her mother's reasoning and with Bellona's help, had accepted the decision. Neither was surprised when Valkia ducked into their tent that morning.

There was no emotional goodbye for the three women. They came from hardy, pragmatic people who rarely expressed any sort of heartfelt feelings for one another. Valkia felt a little sorrow that they would not be with her to experience the glories of the realm of the gods, but little more than that. In part, she fully anticipated returning and so the thought she may never see them again never even crossed her mind.

'In my absence,' she said, accepting another cup of the aromatic drink, 'I have arranged for Olan to over-see the activities of the tribe's warriors. In the unlikely event you are attacked, he will ensure the safety of the Schwarzvolf.' Olan was the tribe's current head scout; young, but entirely capable and extremely competent. Already he had been earmarked as Hep-sus's ultimate replacement should anything happen to the Warspeaker.

Eris looked as though she would comment, but stilled her tongue at a glance from her mother.

'In terms of the rest of the tribe's welfare, how-ever…' Valkia sipped at her drink, her dark eyes going from Eris to Bellona and back again. 'I have every faith in both of you.'

'Your faith is well placed, mother,' Bellona smiled. Valkia's expression hardened slightly.

'Don't make me regret the decision. Either of you.' The words were directed at both, but Eris knew they were meant for her. Both girls shook their heads.

Finishing off her drink, Valkia rose. 'Be well,' she said to her daughters. 'We will speak again soon. On that you have my word.'

'THE PARTY IS almost assembled,' reported the Warspeaker. 'We will be ready to leave straight away when the last of them are here.'

'Your gift for organising such matters has always impressed me, Hepsus,' Valkia said admiringly. There were almost a thousand warriors leaving from the main Schwarzvolf camp in the Vale and Valkia had sent runners ahead to muster warriors from the outlying tribes. Word received back had been optimistic to say the very least.

'It is my honour to serve,' said the Warspeaker, bowing before her. 'That, and they are all eager for a fight. You were right with that assumption. I barely had to snap my fingers and they were armoured and ready.'

Valkia cast an expert eye over the assembled group. Consisting predominately of young males, there were nonetheless several female warriors standing amongst their number. Ages ranged from her own age group right down to youths barely into their late teens. Every face she saw was filled with open enthusiasm and fierce determination. Her heart swelled.

'I should say a few words,' she murmured. Hepsus nodded, his face strangely closed and expressionless. Valkia did not notice; instead she moved to stand upon the dais where her throne sat.

'My people,' she began and was startled to realise that there was a catch in her voice. The emotion of the moment had caught her far more than bidding her own daughters farewell. She coughed to clear her throat.

'My people,' she repeated. This time there was no weakness in her voice. This time her words were clear and strong, filled with the honest passion of the moment. 'We embark today on a war unlike anything any of us have ever known. I have never lied to you and I will not start now.' Her dark eyes skimmed over the faces. Youthful or older, they were all fixed on her in rapt attention. She saw no fear in the upturned faces. These were her people and how they loved her.

'We will not all return here,' she continued. 'But know this, brothers and sisters. Those of us who do will bear the blessing of the Blood God back to our people, and will ensure that your noble deeds will live forevermore in the stories of the Schwarzvolf. The dead are never forgotten when they live with courage and honour.'

She jumped down from the dais and moved amongst the warriors. 'We face the unknown and that in itself is enough to cow the most stout-hearted. But none of you have refused this chance. Our tribe is strong. We seek to make it stronger still.'

A ripple of approval ran through the army. Valkia smiled her devastatingly charming smile.

'I am more proud of you right now than I have ever been. In the days, weeks, maybe even months ahead I may not always have the chance to remind you of that. But never forget it. When darkness comes and enemies surround you – and they will – remember the legacy of the Schwarzvolf. Look at all we have accomplished. We will go on to great things and it will be because of you all.'

The ripple rose to a cheer and Valkia felt the thrill of power that she got from knowing her words had incited such reaction. She stood once again upon her dais.

'We head north. We gather the rest of our army and

then we will keep following the God Light until we reach the realm of the Blood God. Everything that we kill on the way, we dedicate to him.' She raised Slaupnir high above her head and screamed at the top of her voice.

'Blood for the Blood God!'

'Skulls for his skull throne!'

It took a good ten minutes for the roaring cheers to die down enough for Valkia to be heard again. When she spoke this time, it was softly and yet they all heard.

'We leave. Now.'

The army marched out, the Gorequeen at their head, their voices raised in song. Most of those voices were gruff and tuneless, but it was heartening.

THE INITIAL MARCH was accompanied by high spirits and as the ranks of the Schwarzvolf swelled, so did the mood. The warriors walked companionably, encountering nothing more threatening than a few mountain lions which were swiftly dispatched. Each such encounter was turned into a trial of bravery ,with the showdown between hunter and prey always ending in a lethally close knife fight. Valkia herself fought down one animal, a huge alpha male, and received barely a scratch.

One warrior did not fare so well. His arm was torn from his shoulder by a lioness before she was run through by Hepsus. The man was gravely wounded, but not dead; a hardy testament to the strength of those born to the Schwarzvolf. The blood loss left him weak but as soon as he regained his senses he had taken himself straight to Valkia at the head of the army. He had insisted on still coming with them.

'I still have my axe arm,' he had stated pragmatically. 'I can still fight.'

'Indeed,' Valkia responded, narrowing her eyes and assessing the warrior. He was fine and strong and if his injuries did not get infected there was a chance he might yet survive the hardships of the journey. He could and clearly *was* willing to serve her for as long as he was able and that was acceptable. She had fixed the young warrior with a hard stare. 'Understand that if you fall behind, we will not wait for you. You will be left as carrion for the predators of the mountains.'

His gratitude had been almost embarrassing, but Valkia had let the feeling slide in favour of the pleasure of the young man's unswerving loyalty.

'Nobody will watch your back,' she told him. 'If you are strong enough to survive this, the Blood God will look favourably upon you as well.' She had smiled inwardly at the zealous glow on his face and as he had strode away to the back of the army where he walked with the other youths, she had called after him.

'What is your name?'

'Kormak, my lady.'

'I will remember this bravery, Kormak. Be assured that your reward will come in time.'

THE FLURRIES SOON became blizzards and in due course, the blizzards became white-outs. The snow blanketed razor-sharp rocks, pitfalls and deep fissures and its uniform surface sparkled with curious green striations. Upon closer inspection, the discoloured snow contained flecks of glowing emerald dust that warmed the flesh and hurt the eye. The difficulties of traversing the mountain passes were made even more treacherous by the sheer depth of some of the drifts. The army trudged ever onwards. They did not complain. They were men and women of war and the thought of the battles to come sustained them through the difficulties.

The mountains in the harsh of mid-winter were every bit as spectacular to look upon as they were deadly, and many of the Schwarzvolf found that the sheer majesty of the range quashed their grumbles. A rough but clear path through the peaks had once been marked out by ancestors of many different tribes, huge, crumbling black monoliths lining the route. Although the snow piled up against their obsidian faces, sometimes in drifts four or five feet high, it was easy enough to spot their jagged tips above the surface. Steep and difficult, it took them a full two weeks to reach the highest point.

They encountered no other human life in these early parts of the journey other than the warriors they collected from the outlying tribes and, keen to conserve her army's strength, Valkia ensured that the army broke off their march from time to time to get some rest. Food was in plentiful supply; they had wisely kept much of the meat taken from the mountain lions. There were animals in the mountains too, but after they had killed several, a sense of revulsion kept the Schwarzvolf from eating them, at least at first. Misshapen and grotesque creatures that had too many eyes or in some cases, too many legs. In time hunger took over and the creatures were skinned and eaten. Most of them were covered in white fur and they blended in perfectly to their surroundings. It took a sharp eye and excellent sling arm to take one down.

Once they had been caught and killed, the hares were skinned and stewed with handfuls of edible herbs and eaten alongside flat-baked bread that cooked in the embers of the campfires. It was meagre sustenance; the animals were lean themselves, but the meals were more than adequate for the army to march on.

At some point, without any of them really noticing it, they began to eat the flesh raw. It was just the first of many such physical changes that started happening to Valkia's army as they headed further north and as the leaking tendrils of Chaos began to wrap them in its warping embrace.

On the eighteenth day of the march, they had crested the mountains and were making their way down the other side. The contrast could not have been greater. Greenish snow still dappled the rocks and crags but thick grey dust and crushed bone lined the pass. It spilled down the jagged valleys and carpeted the shattered plains that stretched away as far as the eye could see. Heavy, tumultuous cloud churned overhead, the colour of bruised flesh, and wild lightning creased the air almost constantly. For all its savage, alien nature, the path was wider and easier on the north face of the mountain and a brief respite in the seemingly endless winter snows gave them additional energy.

It also brought with it the army's first true skirmish of the journey.

* * *

A PARTY OF five young scouts had moved at the head of the army since they had left the Vale, reporting back regularly. Until now the news had always been the same. The way ahead was clear.

But Valkia could tell long before they reached the army that this time they had something more to tell. They were approaching at a flat run; determination in their youthful faces. And one of them was missing.

'Hepsus.' Valkia only had to speak the single word and the Warspeaker was already amongst the troops, readying them for potential battle. The Schwarzvolf had not survived and prevailed for as long as they had by being disorganised. The Gorequeen took her daemon-headed shield from her back, strapping it to her arm in readiness as the four scouts reached them.

'Make it fast,' she said, giving them a moment or two to catch their breaths. Their eyes were wide, more with shock than fear and when they spoke, they did so at the same time, their words jumbling together incoherently.

Scowling, Valkia nodded towards one of them. 'Speak,' she demanded.

Still desperately out of breath, the young man's words came out in a gasp. 'Monsters,' was the word he used and it drew Valkia's brows together in confused irritation. She passed Slaupnir to the warrior on her right and caught the scout up by the neck of his fur tunic, dragging him towards her.

'What *kind* of monsters,' she hissed, her eyes searching his face for some clue as to what he had seen that could have induced such levels of cowardice. 'Answer me!'

The scout swallowed hard and made an admirable effort to compose himself. Eventually, Valkia released her grip on him and he stumbled backwards. Despite the cold of the day, there was a faint patina of sweat across his forehead.

'Troll-kin,' he finally managed to get out. 'But not like I have ever seen before. Many of them. Ten. Twelve. Maybe more. And they...'

He broke off and Valkia caught him again, shaking him slightly.

'Control yourself,' she said. 'Or I swear that I will cut your tongue from your head.'

'They killed Farand.'

'You engaged them in battle?' Valkia was dismissive. If five untried boys had thought themselves a match for the massive trolls, then they were lucky that any of them had survived. The boy was shaking his head though and now he was speaking far more coherently.

'We smelled them first but didn't know what to make of it. Then we turned a bend on the mountain path and they were just... *there*. We kept our distance. They had not noticed us, or at least gave no sign that they had. So we watched them. As we have been taught to do.'

Hepsus had rejoined them by now and nodded at the boy's words. 'Keep your calm, Garvin,' he said. Valkia glanced at her Warspeaker and knew a moment's irritation that she had not known the scout's name. 'Tell us what happened.'

'It all happened so fast.' Garvin ran his hands through sweat-soaked hair. Accepting a sip of water

from the water skin that Hepsus offered him, he
stammered out the story.

THE SCOUTS HAD remained crouched, simply observing this new potential threat. The Schwarzvolf had
encountered trolls in the past, although altercations
between the two had been thin on the ground. The
monstrous, scaly creatures that they had periodically
fought with dwelt close to the western banks of the
river that ran through the Vale. They were mostly
solitary things; rarely had they had to deal with more
than two or three at any time.

The creatures they watched were clearly of the same
base stock; the same huge size and abnormally dis-
proportionate bodies. The similarities ended there.
The stench of rot rising from their distended bodies
brutalised the senses and stung the eyes. Their skin
was mottled and sickly and hung in tattered strips
from their chests and bellies, exposing diseased bone
and glistening, wasted organs. A morass of flies surrounded them like a veil and tiny, vestigial horns split
the flesh above their milky eyes. The rugged trolls of
the Vale were notoriously stupid and whilst none of
the scouts had ever personally encountered one, they
were aware of the implicit dangers. The story of the
warrior who had disembowelled a fallen troll, only
to be burned to death by the acid that had bubbled
forth from the thing's guts, was well-told around the
Schwarzvolf fires.

The large group of trolls were interested in nothing but each other. They were grunting and evidently
squabbling amongst themselves as they shambled

around the mountain path. The scouts could not determine if they were actually planning on heading further up into the mountains or if they had a lair nearby.

For several more minutes, they had watched and then picked what they felt was the opportune moment to make their move and return to the army to report. The sudden movement of the five young men had alerted the closest troll. It had grunted its displeasure at the sight of the boys and had begun lumbering towards them, its crude club swinging. Barely more than a thick, rotten tree branch, it would nonetheless do considerable damage when introduced with force to the side of a hapless victim's head.

Garvin had been at the head of the group as they had run at full pelt up the mountain path, but Farand had stumbled and fallen.

'Keep going! Warn the queen!'

They had been the last words that Farand would ever speak. A few moments later, the troll was virtually on top of him. Garvin, following Farand's desperate demand that they keep going had paused briefly and what he had seen would haunt his nightmares for the rest of his days.

'The beast retched,' he said to Hepsus, staring up at the Warspeaker. He switched his gaze to Valkia and the boy's face was filled with horror. 'It made itself vomit. And it hit Farand square in the face.'

'Acid?' Valkia virtually spat the word. From experience, she knew that two trolls were hard enough to kill. To fight them in such greater numbers would be... bloody.

Garvin shook his head. 'No,' he said. 'Far worse.'

The acrid-smelling, foul bile that had spattered itself across Farand's head and neck was disgusting enough and Garvin had watched as his fellow scout had done his utmost to stand and wipe the vomit from his face. But then the screaming had started.

'There were... white *things* all over him,' said Garvin. 'Worms or something like that. They were writhing and crawling all over his face... and they were eating his flesh. Whilst he was still living.'

The troll had simply stood there, not attacking, but just watching as the carnivorous worms that it spewed forth caused the most excruciating pain to its victim. Farand had only managed to rise as far as his knees and Garvin had watched helplessly as his fellow scout had clutched at his rapidly disintegrating face. The agonised screaming had lasted right up to the moment the worms had rushed into his mouth and begun eating away at him from the inside. When the troll, finally bored with its crude entertainment, had caved in the scout's head with its club, it had been a mercy in Garvin's eyes.

'And we ran,' finished Garvin. 'We ran back to you.'

'Did they follow you?' Hepsus looked up at the path down which the boys had raced towards them and Garvin shook his head.

'No,' he responded. 'I think they are too big, they would have found the gaps in the rocks impassable.'

'So they are just beyond the ridge,' interjected Valkia. 'Waiting for us.'

Garvin nodded, miserably. The Warspeaker put a hand out and touched the scout's shoulder lightly.

'Go and get some food, boy. You will need your strength back.' The scout heeded Hepsus's words immediately and walked away. Turning his gaze to his leader, the big Warspeaker raised a questioning eyebrow.

'Your thoughts, Valkia?'

She pursed her lips as she considered her response. 'Trolls are never easy to kill,' she observed. 'But they are standing between me and my goal.'

'Indeed,' he responded with a wry smile. That alone would be enough to fire her into action.

'My concern is their numbers,' she continued. 'They are stubborn beasts to take down when they are alone. So many of them in a narrow valley... and with abilities like Garvin described...' It was rare that Valkia shuddered, but the thought of carnivorous worms eating at her flesh was a far from pleasant one. She considered for a few moments longer and resolve straightened her spine.

'I will take a hunting party and we will get them out of our way.' She snatched her spear back from the warrior who had been holding it for her. 'There was advice given to the hunting parties when I was a girl. The animal grease we use in battle offers some small protection against the acid of the trolls in the Vale. It may work here. Cover any exposed flesh with it. Also, it may be worthwhile tying cloth around our faces. If these enemy are as pungent as we have been told... it may reduce any need to be sick ourselves.'

Hepsus agreed. They had face coverings that they all used from time to time during the driving bliz-zards; thin fabric that came from one of the river traders and was virtually transparent. It was not thick, but would prevent immediate skin contact. It was a good plan and Valkia's swiftness in thinking of it was commendable.

They were big creatures though and if Garvin's estimate was even halfway accurate, it would be a long, arduous battle. The Warspeaker exchanged a glance with Valkia and without words even passing between them, he knew what she wanted. The strongest, fastest and best warriors that the Schwarzvolf could field. They would put on a show of force that would make these monsters regret their defiance.

In the end, they formed a party of fifty consisting largely of older, more experienced fighters. Valkia also formed a part of the group; whilst this was going to undoubtedly cost lives, both she and all those around her knew she was a superlative warrior. The shield bearing Locephax's head was strapped to her arm. She had yet to determine how to invoke the daemon's will; it seemed that for now at least, she had no control over whether the thing was asleep or awake. She was willing to bet that if she could bring it to awareness, it would count heavily in their favour.

She had tried a few things. Shaking it, prodding it, screaming into its face... none of these things had the desired effect. She knew it still lived. Or existed. Or whatever it was the vile thing did and she knew that its reluctance to cooperate was to be expected. But soon, she would unlock the secret of mastering Locephax. And then... she would be *invincible*.

Slaupnir held aloft, Valkia led the group of warriors along the mountain path until they reached the gap in the rocks that Garvin had described. Even through the crude face cloths the stench of spoiled meat and rancid guts was almost overpowering, and Valkia struggled to accept that anything that reeked so badly could possibly still be alive. They could hear the sounds of the trolls beyond; evidently closer than they must have originally been. They were grunting to one another in their thick, bubbling voices and a careful listen suggested several distinct individuals.

The gap in the rocks was going to prove difficult. Barely wide enough to allow the passage of two people at a time, it would have the effect of funnelling Valkia's warriors so that they could not easily ambush the trolls.

'We need to move them further way from the rocks,' she whispered to Hepsus. 'Drive them backwards so that we can get more of our party through to face them.' If they tried to attack in pairs, they would be obliterated almost immediately.

'Fire?' Hepsus's suggestion was simple and not too dissimilar to the thoughts that the warrior queen was having herself. They might be huge, powerful and exceptionally dangerous, but like most beasts the trolls were wary of fire, often more so since their robust flesh never healed as rapidly from its touch. In such a confined and narrow corridor as offered by the mountain path however, there were dangers to them as well.

'We could use that to drive them further down the path,' she conceded in the end. 'If we can push them back to a more open area, the fight will tilt in our favour.'

She squinted through the gap in the rocks. 'If we could drive them over the edge, that would be even better. Tough as they are, a fall from this height will kill them just as it would you or me.' She glanced over at Hepsus. 'It'd rob us of a fine battle, but I am in no mood to linger in these infernal mountains.'

It was difficult. They had several eager warriors ready to fight, but the narrow passageway was going to prove hard to deal with. Things the size of trolls – and these monsters were *huge* from what Valkia could see of them – were not easily startled and whilst they might initially retreat from the fire, they would swiftly overcome such fear.

I could help you, you know.

The tone of the cold, dry voice in her mind was sardonic and amused. *All you need do is call on my power and you could deal with this problem immediately.*

Valkia shook the shield and glowered down at the daemon's head, a thing so still and without animation that she genuinely wondered if the voice she kept hearing was nothing more than her imagination. When the eyes flared open, a rush of green, malevolent light bathed her face briefly.

The expressions on the faces of her fellow warriors suggested that her mind was perfectly sound. She stared down into Locephax's evil eyes and spoke in a strained whisper.

'Do not think to trick me, daemon. My people are not so weak that we cannot handle this problem. I will not succumb to your fiendish whisperings. So still your tongue before I rip it from your foul mouth.'

I am merely offering assistance, Locephax retorted lazily. *On the one hand, I could let you walk through that passage and die at the hands of the trolls. On the other... my master lies in wait for you in the far north. And I would hate for you to miss that meeting.*

The dead lips drew upwards in a smirk. *So, I can help you, Valkia. All you need do is ask.*

'It will not happen,' she retorted. 'Cease your prattling and leave me be.'

A pity.

The words in her mind faded and Valkia became aware that her companions were giving her strange looks. It seemed that only she could hear the voice of the daemon and that the one-sided conversation had startled them. She drew her features into a scowl and the staring stopped immediately.

'We press on,' she said and pushed the moment of temptation away. She would not be tricked by Locephax again.

VALKIA AND HEPSUS pushed through the rocks first and within a few short seconds, the trolls had spied them. With heavy tread, they lumbered up the mountain path, grinning viciously with mouths filled with rancid, yellow teeth. Some dragged rotting clubs while others clutched massive, corroded blades, though it was more than obvious that the creatures could pull them limb from limb with sheer strength alone. Even Hepsus, the most stalwart of warriors, tensed slightly at the sight of the massive trolls coming their way.

'Trust me, Hepsus,' she said softly and shifted her

arm so that the shield was in front of her. She steadied herself, her soft leather boots planted firmly on the rock. Her face was a grim picture of determination.

'I have always trusted you, Valkia,' came the snapped reply. 'It's that *thing* on your arm that gives me doubts.'

She glanced up at her Warspeaker. 'I have refused its offer of help,' she reassured him. 'This fight is ours.' She stepped forward to join with the other shield users who had formed as big a line as they could manage on the mountain path.

'Step!'

They inched forward towards the enemy and had taken barely four steps before a searing flash of pain pierced through Valkia's head. She let out a brief cry and unleashed a torrent of expletives. Driven by some compulsion she could never satisfactorily explain, she forged in front of the other warriors and held her shield up high.

One moment she was standing, the shield raised slightly aloft and pressed forward. The next, she felt a thrill of delicious power course through her veins. She threw back her head and screamed in fury; partly at the trolls, but also at the daemonic head that had taken control of her senses. The horror of being used as a conduit for the one thing she despised more than any other left her feeling as though she needed to vomit. Eventually her scream dwindled, her eyes bulging and her mouth giving silent voice to her combined feelings of disgust, agony and ecstasy.

Much better. I find that such a noise is unnecessary. Now watch and learn the meaning of true *power.*

The head of Locephax came to terrible animated life. The eyes flared open, the unnatural green daemon-light seeping from it like a poisonous mist. The face drew into an expression that mimicked Valkia's own and the silent scream that the warrior woman emitted erupted from the daemon's maw. It was amplified and distorted and Hepsus clamped his hands over his ears. The sense of absolute terror that ran through him was something unlike anything he had ever known before.

Every instinct in his body told him to turn and run. And he was standing *behind* the shield, which was the only protection from this dark magic. He hardly dared imagine how he would have reacted had he been on the receiving end.

The trolls stumbled to a halt, crashing together in a tangle of festering limbs, their shabby forms seemingly frozen to the spot and their eyes fixed on the daemon's hypnotic gaze. They were simple creatures, barely more than a bundle of nerves and thoughts that worked together to create the basic need for survival. Kill, eat, and sleep when needed. Such was the cycle of a troll's life. They had little requirement for sophisticated thought and as such, they fell prey to Locephax's hypnotic suggestion instantly.

The scream stopped abruptly and a voice emerged from the daemon's mouth.

'Die,' was all it said, but the voice curdled the air with its menace. It said the word with such implicit urgency and underlying cruelty that three of the trolls immediately flung themselves from the narrow mountain path. A fourth paused briefly. It had been behind the three who had just flung themselves to their doom and had not received the full brunt of the daemon's will. A repeat of the one-word command, however, and the troll joined its brethren, crashing down the mountainside and slicing itself open on the snow-covered rocks on the way.

The majority of those that remained had already turned on their brethren in a furious rage and begun battling, tearing one another limb from limb. For long moments the mountain pass resounded with the noise of trolls grunting and screaming. Valkia and her army moved back as far as the daemonic shield allowed before it snapped she would go out of range. She could feel Locephax drawing power from her own body as she used his ability but she held firm.

She could not keep control of it indefinitely though and eventually she lowered the shield. The green eyes closed and the last of the power drained from Valkia. She staggered, almost falling off the cliff herself, but Hepsus caught her before she fell.

'Valkia!'

'Hepsus.' Her voice sounded weak and drained. Two of the repellent creatures remained standing, their weapons readied for the attack. All around them was carnage of the kind that usually only appeared in nightmares. Limbs were ripped from bodies and more than one of the trolls had been picked to the bone by the flesh worms.

Valkia swayed slightly and then tore the shield from her arm. She dropped it as though it were on fire. Although Locephax had once more fallen silent, as inanimate and rigid as it had been before the bond to the shield had been forged, the expression on its face had altered

It looked satisfied.

Hepsus continued to support the unsteady Valkia who bent over double, retching violently. Locephax had used her to perform the sort of sorcerous act that she had always found so abhorrent. It was a violation of her mind and spirit that made her feel desperate to bathe in a river of blood to clean off the feelings it had left her with and to prove to her beloved god that she had not betrayed him. Magic was the tool of the weak.

And the tool of the hopeless. Admit it, Valkia. Without me, the trolls would have slaughtered you and your army of fools like they were children. I would say that if nothing else, you should at least be pleased I evened the odds.

'Do not speak to me, daemon. Never speak to me!'

A simple thank-you would be more than sufficient. Nonetheless...

Whatever it was that kept life in the head of Locephax drained from the face and it was once again nothing more than a gruesome ornament mounted on the front of Valkia's shield. She stared at it for long moments, loathe to admit that Locephax was possibly right and even more reluctant to take it up once again. But neither would she leave such an object here.

She leaned down and took the shield back up, strapping it to her arm again. 'Schwarzvolf,' she said, and Hepsus noted the steel that had returned to her tone. 'Recover anything of use from the dead.'

Valkia shifted the shield back into its comfortable position and gave it a brief glance. 'We move on.'

ELEVEN
The Edge of Oblivion

AFTER THAT, THE slaughter of the remaining trolls was almost laughably simple. Not that the defeat of such massive creatures, easily seven feet tall apiece was simple, but they were outnumbered as the rest of Valkia's warriors squeezed through the rocks. At the sound of the daemon's scream, those who had been farthest back had moved still further, desperate to get away from the terrible noise, but not goaded into hurling themselves to their death.

Hepsus had taken the lead and Valkia brought up the rear. She was feeling slightly light-headed although not weak, as though she had downed slightly too much alcohol. The shield had fallen silent to her relief. Whilst she had relished the moment of power, it had nonetheless left her a little shaken. Ultimately, Locephax was her enemy and to allow him to channel power through her like a conduit had been a difficult decision to make.

She remembered words her father had spoken once many years back. *The ends justify the means.* She had a specific goal in mind and she would use any tools or weapons to achieve that goal, no matter the cost. It was something she would have to consider more carefully later. Right now, the pressing need was to slaughter the remaining monsters.

The twenty warriors who formed the advance guard had pushed the massive creatures down the mountain path, backing them up against the mountain itself and had already engaged. Glossy, black flies filled the air around the creatures, their tiny bodies creeping into clothes and nipping at exposed skin. The bites left itching, red welts that infuriated the tribesmen as they swatted at the insects.

Just as Garvin had described, one of the trolls was already making retching noises. Seconds later, a plume of bilious liquid spewed forth from its mouth, splattering against the three closest warriors. Having heeded Valkia's suggestion, they were all saved the fate of the unfortunate scout by being covered from head to foot. The white, wriggling creatures that were borne in the troll vomit were easily brushed to the ground and crushed underfoot.

Angered that its preliminary defence was ineffective, one of the two trolls rushed forward to confront the group, its club swinging steadily. It grunted and snorted furiously at the Schwarzvolf warriors who lunged towards it. Its rotted flesh was alive with parasites and already split with running sores and open wounds. The blades of the Schwarzvolf punctured it again and again, but the beast did not seem to feel the damage as it swung ponderously at its assailants.

Whilst they were thus engaged with the first of the trolls, the second wave of warriors was battling the other. One lucky strike by a young woman armed with a short sword opened the troll across its distended midriff, evidently a weak point given the way it opened up. Milky, sizzling pus sprayed from the wound, pitting the nearby rock-face and rapidly corroding the offending weapon.

'Flesh-eating worms and acidic ichor? This just gets better by the moment,' said Hepsus as he ducked to avoid another blow from the swinging club. He bellowed a warning to the others, but not before one of them had discovered first-hand the effects of the pestilent fluid. A trail of the gooey substance had splattered across his shirt sleeve when the wound had been opened and already the material had been eaten away. He dropped to the ground, rolling in the dust in an effort to wash the muck away, but in so doing, brought his body into contact with the few surviving fleshworms still writhing on the floor.

His screams were agonising and Valkia chewed at her lip in an effort to block out the sound. There was nothing that could be done for him any longer and she brought her spear down between his shoulders as he twisted and contorted on the ground. It was a mercy stroke.

Her senses regained, she hefted the weight of Slaupnir in her hand. It had been wrought from the same exotic metal that her dagger had been fashioned from and she worked on it diligently, keeping the edge razor-sharp. It was likely one of the few things that could finish the trolls.

Squaring her shoulders, she lunged towards the first of the two monsters, the blade of the weapon aimed at its chest. Hepsus screamed a warning to the others to stand clear to avoid the inevitable spray of ichor. The length of the spear's haft meant that Valkia had enough distance between herself and the creature as the spearhead pierced through the troll's festering flesh, breaking yellow bones and rupturing organs. Its bubbling shriek of rage increased in volume until Valkia, crackling with bloodlust, heaved on the spear and lifted it from its feet. Muscles bulged like knotted ropes beneath her skin, dwarfing some of the male warriors of the tribe. With a cry of rage, she bodily picked the troll up, still impaled on the end of her spear and flung it from her. Its limp form struck a jutting rock and it crashed to the valley below.

The tip of the spear was coated with the disgusting pus of the creature and Valkia used this to her advantage as she thrust it at the other one. Its flesh parted like parchment and Slaupnir drove through its filthy guts and pinned it to the slab of black rock at its back. The troll hooted in anger, its arms flailing and its considerable bulk pressing back toward Valkia, but she held it fast.

'Finish it,' she said. Her voice sounded strained. 'It is weakened. Finish it. Hepsus...'

The Warspeaker had already led the charge towards the monster which was scrabbling with the haft of the weapon fixing it in place. Nothing in its minuscule mind had prepared it for the concept of defeat against tiny humans and it fell to its knees beneath a flurry of blades. Hepsus's own blade was the last to strike, finding a weak point just below the ear. It pierced through the troll's skull and into its brain. It died instantly, crashing to the floor.

The echoes of battle resounded around the mountain pass until finally it silenced. Valkia was leaning heavily on Slaupnir, her eyes unfocused and her limbs shaking with the exertion of the past few minutes. She had just achieved an impossible feat. There was no way that she could have lifted that troll by herself unless she had been granted a blessing. Unconsciously, the rest of the warriors kept a distance from her.

'Send back for the others,' she said in a voice that sounded on the edge of exhaustion. 'We move on.'

THEY TRAVELLED SEVERAL more miles before nightfall. The light of the moons was hidden behind the bank of perpetual cloud that continued to churn above them, but there was a thickening of the gloom. The winter chill of the mountains had given way as they descended from the peaks, but now it returned with a vengeance, though some warriors complained of feverish heat while still more claimed to feel a pleasant noon day sun. The wind drove at them from every direction, whimsically rushing at them from the north, redolent with the scent of ashes, before billowing in from the south carrying the scent of fresh snow.

Broken obelisks dotted the plain ahead, some sharp and new, as though they had been carved mere moments before, while others were worn smooth by the passage of aeons. Many were surrounded by obscene trophies, desiccated bodies, bestial heads and bowls of foul-smelling slime scattered around their base. Those stained with blood and adorned with skulls Valkia raised her spear to in salute.

Valkia called a halt to the march, sensing that even she needed rest. Her body was still suffering the after-effects of so much adrenaline and the strange strength that had graced her felt as though it had left, taking all her reserves with it. They set up several lean-to style shelters against the wild weather and huddled together in small groups for the additional warmth. Out in the gloom, beyond the fires of the Schwarzvolf, things gibbered and screeched. Men lay with weapons held close and slept uneasily, plagued by nameless fears that woke them with a start. Those few that dared the darkness to relieve themselves did not return, and warriors took to digging holes with their bare hands, scooping fists of dry dust out with their hands for makeshift latrines.

Curled beneath the thick woollen blankets that were the only protection between her and the elements, Valkia slept fitfully. The daemon voice of Locephax whispered constantly to her, promising her everything her heart desired. She had felt, for the first time, what it truly meant to be blessed by the gods she so desperately sought. Locephax's whispers were words of carefully constructed temptation, luring her, appealing to her innate lust for power.

What you felt today was a fraction of what you could become if you give yourself over to me and my master, Valkia. Beautiful, strong Valkia! How I would treasure you! You would be the crowning jewel in my harem. Nobody else could boast such a prize.

The daemon filled her waking hours with words

such as these and projected lustful, arousing thoughts into her dreams. She would wake, sweating in spite of the freezing temperatures and fight the memory of the dream down. The voice promised her repeatedly that in time she would give in to her desires. She insisted, equally repeatedly, that she would not.

The army marched on for several more days. Each morning took longer in coming around as the nights seemed to extend forever and each feeble dawn found a few more warriors missing from the camp. Bitter cold and hardship was something that the Schwarzvolf were long used to, but it did not make it any easier when they were expected to march on meagre rations. Tempers began to fray and some among the host became sick, their bodies stippled with pustules and their flesh pale. The easy mood they had known at the beginning of the campaign was replaced by an air of hostility amongst brothers-in-arms. Squabbles and bickering broke out regularly and more than once Hepsus had to step in to stop the warriors from actually killing one another.

The further north they travelled, the more intense these feelings became. Anger, rage and in particular paranoia magnified and spread amongst the army. The formerly organised group were starting to splinter and break apart. But Valkia didn't care. Not any more. Her heart and mind were too firmly fixed on achieving the goal she had set.

Although the crazed weather never settled into any kind of recognisable pattern, the wastes were almost uniformly flat. Drifts of grey dust would sometimes give way to unyielding black rock or thickly veined green marble. At other times they crossed fields of crushed bone littered with the remains of countless dead. Those hunting parties that returned invariably came back empty handed and supplies continued to dwindle. More than one man suggested slaughtering the sick to ease the pressure on the rations until Hepsus silenced them with a furious retort. But always... *always...* that underlying sense that the man walking next to you was looking for an opportunity to stick a dagger between your shoulders.

Three days came when rain drummed down from the skies in a seemingly endless flow. It dampened the spirits of the Schwarzvolf and even Valkia had to concede to the need to find shelter. They had found abandoned caves that bore no obvious signs of recent habitation and they had taken a break from their journey within their dank walls. They were small and with so many bodies inside became quickly crowded, but the army was able to manage some small reprieve from the elements.

Valkia, always curious about such things, had explored deeper into the caves, discovering an intricate network of tunnels that linked them to one another. Lighting her way with nothing more than a burning torch, she walked deep into the heart of the barrow.

At the heart, she found a huge chamber that sported a number of human skeletons and countless skulls. Aged and crumbling, they had clearly been here for a long time. Valkia's heart had pounded to the realisation that the iconic representation of her god was drawn in faded sigils upon the cave walls. She traced a finger over the barely visible sign. Close examination had led her to discover further images and runic scrawlings upon the walls. The writings she could not even begin to understand, but one image stood out beyond all.

A winged beast of some sort, with a human shape and curling, bestial horns was depicted soaring above a straight line that symbolised the earth. It was a poorly rendered piece of artwork to be sure, but it was repeated so many times within the heart of the cave system that Valkia could not ignore its obvious importance.

It would be many years before she came to truly understand what it stood for.

After the trolls, they had seen nothing living for days, though the fearful cries and ever-growing numbers of missing men suggested that something roamed here and called the wastes home. This did little to disperse the anger that was running at a high throughout the army and it came almost as a relief when, after they had crossed a seemingly endless plain of blue ice, they were set upon by an army of wild beasts.

'THERE IS AN army of creatures approaching from the... west!'

The report had come back from the forward scouts and despite their low mood, Valkia's army were prepared and ready to face anything that came their way. There was a hunger; an eagerness in their eyes that filled the Gorequeen's heart with a swell of pride. All the bitterness and jealousy, all the sneering disdain she had felt for them over the past few days melted away in the anticipation of a battle to come.

The scouts had not lingered when they had spotted the approaching force moving with some speed towards them and so had been unable to give exact numbers. The best they had to go on was that the unknown army were perhaps equal in size to that of Valkia's.

When they finally came into sight, Valkia was unsure of what to make of them. The northlands were riddled with small tribes of beastmen, but they had never mustered in anything approaching the number that bore down upon the Schwarzvolf. From a distance, they looked human. They were wearing furs not unlike those of the Schwarzvolf, but they were not moving along in a manner she was used to seeing. Some loped on all fours, like animals as they raced eagerly towards the huge travelling army. Many sported huge, curling horns and several towered over their companions, thickly muscled, bull-headed beasts. Across their backs were slung crude weapons, clubs for the most part, but here and there Valkia spied longbows and quivers filled with arrows.

'Ready yourselves,' roared Hepsus. 'Shields to the fore!' It was unnecessary; the army had already deployed themselves into formation. As a shield bearer herself, Valkia slotted into the front line, the daemon-head of Locephax raised and locked with those either side of her. If her neighbours were made uncomfortable by the proximity of the monstrous trophy, they had the good grace not to let it show.

Now that the approaching group were close

enough, Valkia was assured that they were not here to offer friendly greetings. Their faces were twisted and inhuman and some were warped beyond recognition. The one at the head of the pack was crowned with a colossal pair of twisted rams horns and covered in a thick mane of coppery hair, matted with gore. It clutched a pair of massive, notched cleavers and its bulky muscles attested all too clearly to its ability to use them. Those either side of him were similarly bestial, though not nearly as threatening.

'Their leader,' Valkia hypothesised aloud. She received a terse nod from the warrior next to her. The beastmen thundered toward them, their wild charge entirely committed and the one in the front barked out an unintelligible few words. They were obviously a command of some kind, because several of the smaller beasts rose up on their hind legs and reached for their bows.

'Watch for arrows,' shouted Hepsus who was somewhere off to the right. Valkia bit back the scathing retort about not being blind and merely focused her attention on the creatures. The arrows were loosed in a flurry, although there were only a handful of archers, and they either fell short of their target or thudded into shields.

'They have made their intentions clear,' Valkia called out in a commanding tone that rivalled the red-haired beastman's own. 'They are the enemy. Schwarzvolf, in the name of the Blood God – attack!' Her spear arm, which had been raised, came down in a sweep and the shield line marched relentlessly towards their attackers.

Their bestial enemies crashed into the shield line with thunderous cracks of splintering wood, the ring of metal upon metal and the unfettered screams of the dying. The beastmen clearly had no concept of organisation and fought as a wild, savage mob. The Schwarzvolf fought back with equal tenacity and a grim unity that eclipsed the mistrust that had so recently blighted them. Axes, cleavers and clubs rose and fell with murderous repetition, splitting skulls and reaping bloody ruin among both sides, but after the initial shock of impact the tribesmen began to push back.

One of the beasts, small and wiry and practically naked but for a loincloth, hurled itself onto the back of one of Valkia's warriors. With a snarl, it opened its mouth wide and tore off the unfortunate man's ear. Valkia caught a glimpse of razor-like teeth and hands tipped with wicked-looking nails that were curled under like talons.

The warrior fell to the ground, blood gushing from his head and almost instantly, his attacker was on him, tearing chunks of flesh from his face and scratching viciously at his throat. It took four swords through the torso to put the thing down, such was its determination. Valkia's warrior lay in screaming agony beneath its corpse, his blood pooling beneath him, but there was no time to lend assistance as the other creatures were similarly hurling themselves bodily at their prey.

It was a blur of violent activity. The careful formation of the shield line had long since fallen apart as the Schwarzvolf defended themselves desperately from the attacks of these feral monsters. Swords clashed against their heavy clubs and everywhere, men and beasts grappled with each other. Valkia was engaged with facing down the army's obvious leader. His face was a blunt snout, leonine with amber-coloured eyes that gave little to no hint of any intelligence. But he was quick and dodged her spear-thrusts with ease.

She brought up her shield again and again to deflect him and if he was daunted by the appearance of Locephax, he gave no sign of it. He came at her relentlessly, mouth open to reveal his filed teeth as his cleavers rang against her spear and shield. She twisted Slaupnir beneath one of the weapons and deftly wrenched the blade from the creature's grasp, the cleaver tumbling away into the raging battle. Undaunted, the beastman seized the haft of her spear and pulled it from Valkia's hand. It cast the beloved weapon contemptuously aside and drove forward once more, its remaining cleaver hammering at her daemonic shield. On the third stroke, the snarling mouth of Locephax snapped shut around the offending blade and held it fast.

The beastman actually managed to look momentarily surprised. Valkia seized the opportunity and let the shield slip from her arm. Mustering every ounce of rage she possessed, she physically launched herself at her attacker.

He was bigger and stronger than she was, but she was more determined to survive than the creature gave her credit for. She kicked and punched, grabbing at great handfuls of his thick, red hair. Once her grip tightened around the hanks of fur, she pulled in a way she had not done since she had been a child. Saliva dripped from the beastman's open mouth, warm and foul-smelling and she slapped out at it. Her palm met the flesh of his face in a stinging blow and he turned his head, startled by her strength.

It was enough to give her the moment's advantage and, putting all her effort into the move, she lunged forward and grabbed the creature by the jaws. It let out a snarl of indignation, the sound more human than she would have thought possible from such a twisted throat and it thrashed in her grip. It flailed at her with its claws and hooves, gnarled knuckles pounding at her back and shoulders, but she would not relent. Fire filled her veins with a killing frenzy and she could feel unholy strength swelling within her once again.

The nearby members of his wild army, seeing their leader about to die, broke off from their own engagements and began to swarm towards Valkia. Charging after them, the rest of the Schwarzvolf defended their queen with everything they had.

Valkia was unaware of what was going on around her. Everything had narrowed to just her and the red-haired beastman struggling beneath her. She was going to tear it apart with her bare hands. Muscles like cords bulged from its neck as it attempted to snap its mouth shut and shear off Valkia's hands, but by agonising inches it was losing the battle. Unnatural vitality pulsed through her limbs, swelling her arms and shoulders with power; allowing her to shrug off the beast's increasingly frantic struggles. As soon as she ended the life of this foe, she would drink deeply. A hunger, a desperate *need* to taste the life's blood of her enemy filled her and she could not deny it.

'Blood for the Blood God!'

With a guttural, animal cry, she redoubled her efforts, splitting the skin of the beastman's shaggy cheeks and wrenching an agonised wail from its throat. Red welled up instantly, running down its face in thick streams and pooling on the ice. Behind her, seven of the wild-eyed creatures readied their clubs, their aim to smash the skull of this woman who was about to take their leader's life.

Valkia remained supernaturally unaware of their presence and then of the arrival of Hepsus and the rest of her warriors as they cannoned into the enemy with violent force. All that mattered was the blood of her victim.

Beneath her, the beastman bucked and heaved as though trying to steal his final chance to escape. She stopped him immediately with a final, terrible surge of strength that tore the top of his head off. Dark blood fountained from the useless lower jaw and ragged neck and Valkia let the hot blood gush over her, drinking her fill of his rich vitae. The shorn top half of the skull lay discarded, its empty, golden eyes staring glassily past Valkia to the warriors that stood behind, watching their queen gorge herself.

Around her, the fading sounds of battle dwindled to silence. When she had finally satisfied her fury, she raised her blood-stained face to observe several other Schwarzvolf warriors copying her actions, gulping down the blood of the fallen. Others stood to the side, their faces varying from expressionless to disgust.

Valkia ran the back of her hand across her bloodied face and got to her feet. Without meeting Hepsus's oddly accusatory stare, she picked up her spear and shield and dusted herself down. When he spoke, there was a strange straining in his voice.

'We lost more than a hundred of our men in that battle, Valkia.'

The Warspeaker's voice sounded as though it came from a long way away; tinny and distant. She looked up at him and blinked away the red haze of battle.

'So many?'

'Look around you.' Hepsus gestured. There were warriors with their skulls caved in by clubs or hacked with blades. 'Some were practically eaten alive before we could pull those things off them. The rest are not yet dead. But they will be soon. More than a hundred men, Valkia.'

Valkia felt nothing. No regret that her people had died, no satisfaction that the enemy was defeated... she felt *nothing*. Her heart was not motivated to feeling at all. All that had mattered was the kill.

'Our army still numbers in the hundreds,' she said eventually with casual indifference in her voice. 'Salvage their weapons and armour. Leave the bodies. Then we move on.'

Hepsus did not bother to tell her that in the wake of the battle, whilst she had been feasting like an animal on the warrior, a large contingent had slunk away into the gloom with Edan at their head. Her army had once numbered more than a thousand and now barely a few hundred sick and wounded men and women remained.

THEY MOVED ON. Ever northwards.

The plains of dust and ash and crushed stone were apparently endless. The air was tinged with that crisp, clear scent that suggested the weather was forever on the cusp of frost and ice, but laced with the copper stink of blood and the acrid smell of burning metal. What remained of the Schwarzvolf army that had not turned back in fear – earning Valkia's venomous sworn oath that she would hunt each one down on her return and kill them – or had not died of the wasting sickness, marched in silence.

There was no camaraderie amongst brothers and sisters. No idle banter. None of the easy talk and gentle squabbling that had marked their earlier steps. Now they did not speak to one another.

Valkia had grown increasingly withdrawn and short-tempered as they travelled, her thoughts turned inward as she dealt with the constant whispers of Locephax. The daemon's delighted anticipation grew by the day. Her head ached from dealing with his promised whispers of revenge and satisfaction.

The army had been on the march for an interminable period of time. It felt like years but could have been only months. Valkia did not know when she had stopped counting the passage of the days. Time had become meaningless, particularly when the days had grown so short that at times, the wan light that marked the arrival of morning lasted barely a few hours before the oppressive darkness closed in once again.

Further encounters had been brief and surprisingly easy. They had fought against more of the beastmen, each one more twisted and warped than the previous. Feral savages and packs of drooling god-touched with writhing limbs and sucking maws. Distorted, mutated and disfigured creatures that may once have been as human as the Schwarzvolf were hacked down like saplings if they put themselves into the dwindling army's path.

And still they headed north.

The God Lights were strong in the skies here; illuminating the bleak and desolate wasteland with their ever-shifting yellow and green hues. Yellow and green. Occasionally tinges of blue. But never *red*. Valkia stared into the skies night after night willing a sign from her god. Some indication that he was waiting for her. Some sign that he was pleased with her progress.

When the red finally came, so did the end of the world for the queen of the Schwarzvolf. When the God Lights finally burned like flame with the colour of the Blood God, Valkia the Bloody stepped into darkness unending.

THIS WAS NOT the gloom of night to which they had become accustomed. This darkness was all-encompassing. It had shape, volume and an almost tangible feel. To step into it was to turn your face forever more from the light of day. And the Schwarzvolf stepped willingly. Such a shroud of darkness was a thing that invited fear and horror, but the remaining members of the army bore it stoically. They had little choice.

All around them could be heard whispers. The voices of the damned, Hepsus suggested in a flat, emotionless monotone. The voices of those who had stepped this way before. Warning them. Threatening them. Trying to turn them away at the last.

But they were made of stronger stuff, or at least some of them were.

In many ways, the mental hardships of battling invisible enemies were more complex and difficult than anything that the Schwarzvolf had accomplished during the course of their epic journey. For each warrior, there was a personal daemon. For each man or woman, there were torments that were designed to strike fear and doubt into their hearts. A few weaker-willed warriors succumbed to the creeping madness. They were killed without compassion or without hesitation by their stronger fellows, while the fastest vanished without a trace, their mad laughter echoing in the heads of their companions.

The further into the blackness they walked, the harder the passage became. The darkness thickened until every step was a struggle. It was like wading through a frozen river and every bit as bone-marrow chilling. A pressure was exerted on them, pressing them backwards. But heads bent low, on they marched.

Whispers became words. Words became laughter, low and sinister. Rotting, half seen cyclopean creatures plucked the sick and the weary from their number. There were *sensations*; eerie and terrifying. The brush of invisible feathers across the face, or the grip of strong hands clutching at ankles and legs, trying to pull their would-be victims to the ground. Some simply lay down and let the sensuous, grasping fingers pull them out of sight. But there was nothing they could physically beat off. Nothing they could actually *fight*. Nothing they could even see.

Until they saw the steps. Vast, uneven slabs of glossy green stone that could not have been cut by mortal hand piled atop one another, reaching toward the fractured heavens.

Valkia, walking at the front of the diminishing army saw the flight of stone stairs first and her heart leaped into her mouth at the sight of it and what waited at the top.

The portal was vast, seeming far too huge for the span of the stairs themselves. It stood out from the velvet blackness in a way that could not be expressed; it was something *beyond* darkness and veined with crackling streamers of arcane light. And Valkia felt its irrefutable draw. It pulled her onwards even as the things beyond her understanding attempted to push her back.

'I come, my master,' she screamed into the darkness. Her voice sounded dead and lifeless, swallowed by the sucking emptiness.

He does not care. He never cared.

It was the first time since she had stepped across the point of no return that Locephax had spoken. The daemon's voice in her mind was crystal clear and somehow stronger than it had been until now.

You are in my realm, the space between worlds. And soon, Valkia, very soon there will be the exacting of my revenge. It will taste sweet, my love. Even as you draw your last breath, I will savour your doom. My master already senses my presence. Already he sends his children to avenge me. Your life is marked in minutes, Valkia. Your god, the idiot-thing that he is, does not hear you.

She would not listen to his words.

You have one final chance, Valkia. Be mine for eternity and my master will show you mercy. Prostrate yourself at his feet and swear allegiance to his banner and your reward will be eternal. Continue this search for a god who does not care for you and die.

Valkia's entire body was shaking with a mixture of emotions that she could not describe. There was no fear, of that she was certain. But she was here at the foot of a staircase that would bring her to the realm of the gods. She had made that journey she had promised her father so long ago.

If anybody could make that journey, it would be you. That had been his reply. Would he have been proud of her, had he lived? Valkia hardened her resolve. She had long ago given up the right to wonder what could have been. She had manipulated her own destiny and she would continue to do so.

They come, Valkia. I sense them. This is your last chance. Lay one foot on those steps and your life is forfeit. Lay down your pride now and become a child of Slaanesh. There was something oddly pleading, almost regretful about the offer, but she shook her head.

'Blood,' she said to the shield. It hurt to speak; the darkness was pressing against her ribs, crushing her and just getting words out took an age. 'Blood... for the... Blood God!'

So be it.

The daemon-head mounted on her shield twisted

into life and let out a shrill scream that caused several of the warriors to wail in madness as their minds finally snapped. Valkia was aware that blood was running from her ears and nose as well. Her head felt as though it would explode with the pressure, but she took one further step, placing her foot on the bottom-most stair. There were eight stairs in all. Eight between Valkia and her ultimate goal.

Hepsus raised a hand to stop the handful of survivors, holding them back. This was the moment that Edan had foreseen. This was the sign that he had told Hepsus to spread around the camp. *This* was the boy's proclamation. That when Valkia defied the gods themselves, then – and only then – would her reign end. Hepsus had sworn his loyalty to Edan that he would get her there. Standing here, at the edge of creation, staring into the abyss, the Warspeaker could feel himself unravelling. But in the corner of his mind's vision he could still see the dead eyes of his son, and they anchored him to life like nothing else. They were his rock, his salvation and his deliverance. He stood there, his hollow gaze fixed on the woman who would damn them and he held the Schwarzvolf back. Edan had promised him he would live to see it done. And so he had.

Valkia's interest in her half-brother had been so light that she had never even noticed the moment at which he had stopped following her. She had not noticed the moment at which all those men who had switched allegiance during the journey had stayed with him. Her arrogance, her need to succeed, had prevented her from turning back and now it would cost her.

Behind her, before her, around her... the entire swathe of absolute night suddenly came to grim, chilling life. She felt the press of invisible force lift suddenly, only to be replaced by an onslaught of daemonic creatures like she had never seen before. They poured from the portal at the top of the staircase like a tide. They came in their tens, their hundreds, maybe even their thousands. They came at Locephax's call and finally she turned, to give the order to her army to attack.

Nobody stood by her side. Only one man, the one-armed Kormak who had pledged to fight at her right hand until he fell doing so remained with her. His face was lined with determination mingled with stark terror at the legion boiling toward them, but he would not relent. He was the only one of barely a hundred who had remained with her to the very end.

She knew. It was as if she had *always* known that they would betray her at the last. Hepsus stood, some distance away, his arm still raised. Their eyes met for a final time and she watched, unable to vocalise the pure hatred that rose within her as he fled and left her to die.

The daemon tide that had gushed out of the portal was holding back. Waiting for her to come to them as they knew she must. Her foot was upon the stair. She could not turn back now even had she wanted to. Not when she had come so far. Not when she had given up so much.

'Kormak.'

'My queen.'

'Leave. Leave me now. You can do no good here.

You may as well live. Go and take the heads of those traitors in my name.' Hepsus and his followers – she could no longer think of them as hers – were gone, swallowed by the dark. She had no idea if they would live or die and she frankly did not care. This betrayal could spell the end of her people, but she was finally able to acknowledge that she had ceased caring about them years ago.

'Go, Kormak. You can do nothing. This fight is mine alone.' She raised her head and lifted her shield high. 'You see this?' The last was addressed to the daemon horde. 'This is what became of the last creature of the Reveller who tried to stop me from reaching my goal.'

Locephax's laughter was a terrible thing to listen to and behind her, Kormak trembled. He was not much more than a boy, she realised, and she reached out to touch him on the shoulder, once.

'The prize will be ours, Kormak,' was all she said. She paused, realising that here, at the end of all things, how angry she was with the lies. All those who had feigned loyalty to her and to her cause. Cowards, every last one of them. Kormak was the only truly loyal warrior and it was right and just that he should stand by her side. But there was no time to linger on the matter.

With a concerted effort, fighting valiantly against every instinct that was telling her to turn and flee, Valkia took another step upwards. Kormak stood at the foot of the stairs, gazing upwards into the depths of infinity. He was mesmerised; rooted to the spot and completely unable to move.

He never went further than the lowest step. Without Valkia's iron will and determination, he was easy prey for the daemons. They flowed past Valkia, who struck out with her spear, viciously hacking and slashing at them, but they did not stop for her. They went straight for Kormak.

At that moment, she learned the final truth of what she had committed to. She could not turn back. She physically could not retreat down the steps. She would reach the realm of the gods or she would die. There was no third option. She had to watch, helpless and enraged as the daemons swarmed around the most loyal of all her people and hacked him down.

Blood flowed from countless wounds as Kormak fell, but she noted with some small satisfaction that he died with a curse on his lips and his axe buried in the skull of a clawed fiend.

You see how it ends, Valkia. Locephax laughed aloud, the sound echoing across the blighted nightmare landscape.

She took a third step upwards and stared up at the abyss. Five more such stairs, each one as wide as a cart track, stood between her and the gateway to her master's side.

Five.

Behind her, Kormak's terrible dying screams; the gurgling of his final, furious cry to the Blood God. Ahead of her, the very portal where she knew her destiny lay.

Another step.

Kormak died in agony; alone at the foot of the steps. She hardened her heart against the sounds of

the daemons feasting upon his mortal flesh. He had
been the bravest and the best of all her people, but
she had been unable, at the last, to save him. She
could not afford to feel remorse. In seconds, the daemons would be upon her as well. She had to take
advantage of Kormak's death... of the distraction it
offered...

Another step.

Three to go.

Welcome to the hereafter, Valkia, said Locephax and
once again, he voiced the scream that had caused her
ears and nose to bleed. The daemons currently sating
their hunger on Kormak's body raised their heads at
the sound and returned the cry.

She was subsumed by them. Within moments, their
physical forms were on top of her. Sickening musk,
cloying and sweet drifted like mist, a living thing that
coiled about her with lewd tendrils. It filled her nostrils, her throat. She sank to her knees, clawing at her
face as though she could tear them from her in that
manner. All the while, she kept a tight hold of Slaupnir. She thrashed helplessly against the insubstantial
embrace; the suffocating fog was choking her, dulling
her senses, tempering her killing rage. Her eyes met
those of one of the daemons, a bizarre, two-headed
creature with one head that was like that of an ivory
woman whilst the other was some kind of pale rep-
tile. A forked tongue flickered from its mouth and
stroked against her cheek in the parody of a kiss.

*These are my brothers and sisters, Valkia. They are
angry with you.*

Still she struggled against her inevitable demise.

Hardly able to breathe, she crawled up another step, dropping both Slaupnir and the shield so that she could better grab at the step. She tried to call out, but nothing more than a gurgle left her throat.

Her master. Her god. He had abandoned her at the last. She had come all this way. She was...

...angry.

Her god had not abandoned her. He was with her. He had *always* been with her. He was calling to her.

Come to me.

I come, my master!

Rage filled her to bursting point and with what would prove to be a final, inhuman surge of strength, she rose to her feet one last time and hurled the daemonic host back far enough to climb one last stair.

She felt no pain as the slithering claw pierced her back and exited through her belly. She merely stared down at it before falling once more to her knees. She threw out her arms and held her head back.

'Khorne!'

Blood welled up in her mouth as claws and talons tore at her skin, silencing her. But she did not scream or beg for mercy. She took her death with stoic pride. As the final bubble of blood burst on her crimson-stained lips, it carried with it the final whisper to a god she had come so close to reaching.

'Khor...'

Valkia fell forward on the steps, her left arm outstretched towards the portal. Her broken body twitched a few times and then she was motionless, her heart forever stilled in sight of her destiny.

And the world was shaken by the wrath of a god.

TWELVE
Rebirth

THE WORLD TREMBLED in the wake of the bellow of rage that thundered from the realm of Chaos. A catastrophic shockwave of fury erupted from the roof of the world and expanded outwards, laying waste to all in its path. Exposed to the terrible force of such rage, the daemons swarming around the body of Valkia were vaporised instantly, the stuff of their bodies dissolving into insubstantial mist and sent screaming back into the abyss. The few survivors were flung in all directions, howling and wailing in their unnatural voices.

Most of them crashed to the ground beyond the steps, stunned by the Blood God's wrath, but the ripple of intense ire continued to spread outwards, flattening anything it encountered. It crushed the black rocks that lined the route to the portal into nothing more than fine powder, which was thrown up as a billowing cloud of grit and dust.

Already some distance from the maw of Chaos, Hepsus and the remainder of Valkia's army were thrown off their feet as the very ground beneath them was torn asunder by the sheer force of Khorne's anger. Cracks and fissures split the earth's surface as the land shook. With desperate yells of panic and terror, the betrayers picked up speed, running in an effort to get ahead of the unseen wave of destruction.

A second roar of fury burst forth, this one perhaps even more terrible than the first. The few remaining daemons, which had crawled with determination back onto the steps in a concerted effort to seize the body of the fallen queen, were obliterated. The head of Locephax, still mounted on Valkia's shield, writhed and contorted in terrible agony. It was unable to block out the awful sound of the Blood God's fury and it was suffering.

The ruptures that had been torn in the plain split further, the ground shaking beneath the feet of the Schwarzvolf as they fled. Many fell, unable to maintain their balance and the slowest of them were swallowed by the earth, falling without hope of rescue into the bowels of the world.

Above them, the God Lights bled. A spreading corona of baleful crimson the colour of blood, the colour of anger, flooded the sky. Across the Northern Wastes, far beyond the epicentre of the furious shock wave, tribesmen stared up at the shifting lights that finally burned scarlet and spoke of omens and horrors beyond imagining.

As far away as the dwarf strongholds, the ground was felt to shake as Khorne, the Blood God, made his primal anger known. The countless daemons, both visible and invisible who had previously swarmed over Valkia's body dared not approach.

The figures that spilled from the abyss were also moving towards the still corpse, but they did so with a curious reverence, their black blades held low in their bloody claws. Regardless of this fact, the daemon servants of Slaanesh who slunk from the darkness in the wake of Khorne's fury dared not approach. They hissed and howled, screeching their displeasure at being denied their feast, but even the urgent promises of Locephax would not call them forth.

One of the new arrivals, a creature with the obvious physical form of a woman, but with scarlet flesh and the cloven hooves of a beast stooped to pick up the shield that had Locephax's head nailed to it. The herald studied the nails, each one worked with the symbol of Khorne and a smile flickered onto her terrible face.

'Do not touch me, child of Khorne!'

Had Valkia lived, she would have been forgiven for mistaking the tone in Locephax's voice for that of fear. The daemonic head was not afraid. He was terrified.

Without speaking, the bloodletter slid the shield onto her arm and held it aloft, letting out a cry of triumph. Locephax's voice rose in a scream of terrible anguish and then nothing but silence reigned across the Chaos Wastes. The daemons of Slaanesh watched sullenly as the legion of bloodletters took up Valkia's body, hoisting her on their knotted shoulders with reverence.

The leader, the one bearing the shield of Locephax, nodded in satisfaction. She glanced at the bottom step where the unrecognisable, half-chewed body of

Kormak lay and then bellowed a command. Without further hesitation, the line of bloodletters walked their burden up the remaining steps and moved through the portal.

The herald was the last to step through and when she had gone, the skies once again shifted to the ever-changing colours of the north. The creatures and people of the Chaos Wastes and beyond released their collective breath and the world continued to turn.

She had heard from the elders of the tribe that no single person could recall the precise moment of their birth. The shock would kill them, it was said. The sheer memory of the trauma of being brought into the world was something that the mind blanked out.

Strange then that it was this very thought that jolted her to wakefulness.

Valkia opened her eyes with a gasp, her heart hammering in her chest and terrible, agonising pain wracking her body without forgiveness. She was struggling to draw breath, as though she were drowning, or if a great weight was on top of her and she clawed desperately, trying to gain purchase on whatever it was that was crushing her.

There was nothing to hold and her fingers closed on empty air.

Awareness, such as it was, slowly began to take control of the sheer horror that she had felt on opening her eyes. Her entire body was in pain. Her head, her chest, her limbs... all ached and throbbed. She had fought a battle. An *epic* battle that...

...she remembered the sensation of the claw that had eviscerated her and she put a hand to her belly, half-expecting her bowels to slither out through her fingers. Sure enough, she felt the gaping wound there, the cleaving gash where her intestines threatened to spill. Blood ran freely from countless injuries and she lay still, knowing that if she moved too much, whatever life she had remaining in her would be forfeit. She was blind in one eye and she felt more of her own life running down her cheek. She had lost one eye. Her face was lacerated; her beauty rendered into a visage of horror and shredded flesh that hung in strips from her skull. With each drawing of breath, there was a single thought that ran around her mind.

I died.

She was in so much pain from her terrible injuries that she did not notice at first that she had been stripped of her armour and lay naked in the insubstantial gloom of this non-place. Some part of her insisted that she should be freezing, but the void of sensations made mockery of her instincts. Her hand rested against the bare flesh of her stomach, again feeling the slimy presence of her internal organs. She had watched countless hundreds die slowly from such injuries.

But I *died.*

'I do not understand,' she said. Her voice sounded cracked and broken, and was harsh in the silence that permeated everything. 'I died. Is this the beyond?'

The emptiness swallowed her words and gave nothing back. She shivered involuntarily and shifted position slightly. The pain this brought extracted a cry of agony from her lips and she lay flat again, closing her eyes against it.

The moment her eyes closed, images assailed her consciousness. She saw herself, broken and bloodied on a table of green rock. Even as she threw back the monsters that assailed her, she knew that she was dying, saw the terrible wounds that laced her body, but she refused to fall. She saw the claw pierce her and her muscles clenched in sympathetic agony. She saw herself fall. Valkia's brow furrowed. She suddenly became aware of the fact that she was not alone, but that she shared her featureless afterlife with a presence that cradled her like an infant. It was a thing of pure malevolence, but somehow she knew that it was not directed at her, that this thing, whatever it was, held her in this insubstantial prison. It was not close by. Neither was it distant. It was everywhere around her and it was nowhere but inside her mind.

She saw herself die again, the event unfolding in her mind's eye, but this time she did not jerk at the killing blow, instead bearing witness to her demise and the events that followed. A legion of crimson-skinned daemons sported night-black blades and followed a terrible, bestial herald. She watched them take up her spear and shield and bear her body into...

In an instant, she knew who had gifted her this vision and tears sprang to her eyes. 'My master,' she said through sobs that threatened to rip her body apart. 'My master.' They were not tears of sorrow or misery, but tears of joy and devotion at the realisation. They ran down her face from beneath her closed lids, salty and very real. This was no dream. This was where she was. The pain in her belly, the dull throb of her torn face paled into insignificance and she no longer cared if she spilled her innards on the ground. She tried to drag herself up, but lacked the ability to move more than a few inches.

A shock of strength ran through her, filling her limbs with heat and power and searing away her uncertainties. There was no kindness in the action, but there was a sliver of understanding that cut through her emotions and brought equilibrium to her tangled thoughts. She opened her eyes for the second time and this time she *saw*. A dry wind rushed across a plain of crushed bones that stretched as far as the eye could see. Ash and cinders fell from a bloody sky stained with bands of sooty cloud. Screams, wordless cries of fury and the clash of weapons filled the air and a charnel house reek assailed her senses laced with the acrid stink of hot metal. And on the horizon, a mountain of skulls so vast it swelled until it filled her vision, an impossible monument to the glory of endless slaughter.

'I failed at the last, my master.' Valkia remained where she was, lying on her back with her hands clasped over her stomach. But her voice bore the strength of the woman she had been. She called the words out into the boundless, barren plains that surrounded her. She did not purport to understand anything the god was showing her, but she realised that she existed in a limbo of sorts. A place where if she moved too far forwards, she would fall into eternal sleep. Or a place, perhaps, where the potential for other things existed. 'I failed you.' She whispered the confession into the void, hot tears prickling at her eyes again. 'I did not climb the steps. I did not reach you.'

A torrent of images assailed her, one after another like pages of her life being turned by an invisible hand. A girl pushing a spear into the heart of a defeated barbarian. A young woman shearing the head from a man who lay squirming in a pool of his own spilled guts. A bitter mother burying her knife in the throat of a hulking brute. A raging warrior queen screaming across a hundred battlefields, her spear falling again and again, piling stained skulls at her feet in an endless war of devotion. A blazing, bloody berserker dancing an achingly perfect duel with an obscene monster. And finally, an unholy warrior casting down beastmen and daemons on a bleak, dusty plain.

She lifted a hand from her abdomen to wipe across her face, ashamed of the womanly tears that she was still weeping. She felt a ghostly brush across her face in the darkness and courage returned to her.

'So what happens now?'

The towering presence that she had felt flowing about her suddenly withdrew and its raw, unchained force fell upon her like a suffocating shroud. It laid the very fabric of her being bare, stripping away doubts and fears. It erased any last vestiges of pity, mercy or remorse and discarded those parts of her that did not serve its insatiable thirst for slaughter. The experience lasted no longer than the blink of an eye, but scoured her nerves like liquid fire and filled her mind with torment. When it was done, its absence felt like a soothing wellspring on seared skin.

The flesh of her torso had begun to knit together, wounds sealing themselves closed. Beneath her hands, the ends of the ragged tear that had claimed her life stretched together, sealing closed the fatal injury that had ultimately slain her. It felt peculiar to her touch; the skin itself writhed as though it were alive. Cautiously she let go of the wound and her intestines remained where they should be. She put her hands to her face in wonderment, discovering that those injuries too were sealing closed as though they had never been.

She ran her hands over her naked body, feeling the ridges of invisible scars that could not be seen on the surface. Her god had wrought a wonder. His power was phenomenal to behold.

It took everything she had to battle past the remaining pain and get to her feet. Even then, she swayed and wavered for a while, unable to keep herself steady. She felt as though the unseen presence was studying her, watching everything that she did and judging her.

Her eyes glowed like coals and she turned her burning gaze on the towering monument of skulls, its ivory flanks reaching up into the blighted clouds. Rivers of molten brass carved dark channels down the mountain of bone and howled with every dying scream that had echoed from every battlefield since the birth of time. Valkia looked up and up, feeling the pull of the colossal entity that rested at its summit.

'What my master desires...'

She never completed the sentence. It transpired that Khorne had only just begun the task of moulding his chosen. What Valkia had thought of as pain a few moments before was suddenly replaced by the realisation of true agony. It began as a pulsating throb across her shoulders as the skin twitched and distorted under the guiding hand of the god as he reshaped her body into something that pleased him even more than her natural form. The repair to her mortal frame had been a prelude to his true intentions.

The throb dulled down to an almost manageable level and then her skin tore open. In a detached way it reminded her of the day she had given birth to her daughters, the sense of being torn apart so that Eris and Bellona could rend their way into the world. She screamed, unable to bear the anguish any longer and dropped back down onto her knees. She fell forward onto all fours and squirmed in agony as the wings tore through the skin of her shoulders. Blood flowed and her nose was filled with the coppery scent of it. Her mouth remained open in a long, silent scream as the leathery pinions grew, unfolding themselves wetly from where they sprouted, bones crackling as they grew and distended.

They opened out in full, a wingspan of several feet and slowly, she got back to her feet. She reached a hand out to them in wonder, her fingers running their length. They twitched under her touch and instinctively, she flapped them experimentally. She felt their sheer power. These were no ornamental limbs. These were instruments that she could use.

A cruel laugh burst forth from her throat. Once, she

had marvelled at the swiftness of the avian raptors who hunted the stark tundra. The irony of this transformation was not lost on her.

While she writhed in the throes of transformation, creatures emerged from the ash haze, their clawed feet crunching splintered bones beneath them. A host of sinuous, crimson-skinned daemons with vile, midnight blades surrounded her, their blazing, hateful eyes fixed on the changing woman.

More pain thrummed through her body, but this time she threw out her arms and cried out in sheer ecstasy, welcoming the agony that the change brought with it. Her beloved god was rewarding her beyond anything that she could ever have dreamed. The bat-like wings that arced gracefully from her back moved imperceptibly as her thighs lengthened, changing shape and form. Her feet were contracting and reshaping into the cloven hooves of an animal. There was a bow to her legs that matched those of the monsters that surrounded her and a pair of curling horns, tiny and vestigial, crowned her pale brow.

The snarling daemons fell silent and as one they bent their knees to their new queen, pressing their bloody snouts to the ground in a gesture of servitude. They were bent to her will and would serve her in slaughter like no other. Valkia opened her clawed hands and revelled in her raw power.

'What of my weapons? My spear, my shield?'

The twisted visage of Locephax flashed briefly in her mind, its screaming face still nailed firmly to her battered shield.

'Yes,' she acknowledged. 'But the shield... fell upon

the steps beyond the abyss.'

Images assailed her once again. She watched as the herald bore the severed head of Locephax into the Blood God's realm and ascended the mountain of skulls. The creature of Slaanesh had screamed and gibbered throughout the ascent, its usually malignant gaze wild with the horror of its situation. She saw darkness close about it and heard its final wail of despair as Valkia's long promised doom came to pass.

The shield had not been within her line of sight before and yet now it appeared, shimmering into being before her. It had been remade, trimmed in etched brass and fused with the severed neck of the creature. The head of the daemon was scowling up at her, motionless and seemingly without the animate life that it had possessed.

She took up the gift and strapped it to her arm and she could feel the cowed will of Locephax shrink at her touch. Where once the daemon had taunted her with its promises and false words, in this place it held no power.

'By your will, my lord, it is so.'

Her spear appeared before her, its haft cast in hell-forged obsidian and its silver head etched with brass and black iron. The angular skull design throbbed with a crimson, infernal light and her mind came alive with images of slaughter that dwarfed anything that had come before. She would return to the world of men and she would reap the souls of the living.

'In your name, my lord, it will be so.' Her eyes were bright with zealous fury.

The vast, black will atop the mountain withdrew and the daemons parted before her, opening a path to the foot of the monument. She could feel the unquenchable fury that burned atop that bleak summit and sensed its expectation. It called to her in a visceral way that promised an eternity of death, rage and relentless carnage.

She gave a little sigh of sheer adoration. 'I have never forgotten my promise, my lord. It matters not how the blood flows. It matters only that it *does* flow.'

The throne of brass and skulls beckoned and clothed in her new daemonic flesh she approached the impossible edifice. Opening wings of fathomless night, Valkia spread her pinions and was borne upward into the windblown ash. Torrential rains of blood lashed at her and screeching, fanged monstrosities tumbled about her gleefully. Past the skulls of a million dead that buried a million more she ascended until at last she passed beyond sight of the plain of bones and the eternal battlefields, until at last she hung before the throne of brass and iron. Until at last *she saw*.

Valkia the Bloody stepped beyond the woman she had been and became something greater. Something eternal.

Something terrible.

AND THE WORLD continued to turn.

In the realm of the gods, the passage of the aeons moved differently to the time in the land of mortal man. To all intents and purposes, it stopped altogether. After all, time itself was a concept invented by the living to count down the moments until their inevitable demise.

They broke their fleeting lives down into years,

months, days, hours. They came and went, rarely registering as little more in the eyes of the gods than a pattern of lights against the dark canvas of the universe. But once in a generation, one would burn with more fury than those around them.

Valkia had caught the attention of the Blood God early in her life. Had she not met Deron, the man who had brought the god's name with him, then Khorne would have found another way to bring the remarkable young woman to his side. He had watched her over the years as she had honed and sharpened her considerable talent for slaughter. He had watched. He had waited. And in his way, he had guided.

Here in the realm of the gods, time ceased to have any sort of meaning. In the world beyond, it continued to flow. Uninterrupted, ceaseless and relenting. In the wink of an eye a year had passed. Before Valkia had even begun to understand the sheer magnitude of the power she had been gifted, three more had gone by.

Not that she cared. Not that she retained any interest at all in the world of men. Not whilst she was enjoying the pleasures of all that her immortality had to offer her.

Far beyond the mountains over which she and her army had laboured throughout the cold winter, the Schwarzvolf were learning the ways of a new master themselves. But for them, things were not quite so pleasurable.

* * *

OF THE THOUSAND or so warriors who had left at Valkia's call, less than a few hundred returned. They struggled to the far outposts of the Schwarzvolf, bloodied and broken. Some were on the very cusp of madness itself with all they had witnessed and raved endlessly. Others retained a stoic, taciturn silence, refusing to discuss the journey at all.

One thing was abundantly clear: the army was no longer headed by Valkia. Instead, Hepsus the Warspeaker and the Godspeaker Edan walked at the army's fore. The former looked like an old man, his hair greyer than it had been when he had left and his eyes reduced to sunken hollows that had seen too much. The younger man, the brother of the former queen of the Schwarzvolf, had grown in stature and confidence. Finally allowed to step beyond his sister's considerable shadow, Edan's sheer arrogance was palpable.

There was a considerable outpouring of grief in the wake of Valkia's loss. Her lengthy rule had been sometimes difficult to bear, always controversial... but at least she *had* ruled them. She had never left them to fend for themselves and she had always ensured that the smaller tribes she conquered into submission were provided for.

Her daughters bore the news of her death with a calm acceptance that they knew would have made their mother proud. Edan delivered the news to them in an uncanny echo of the day, years ago, when Valkia had told her two little half-sisters that their father had died.

Bellona nodded, tight-lipped. She had never truly

expected her mother to return from the journey. She also suspected Edan without reserve. Her uncle had always projected an air of self-satisfied smugness that had made her uncomfortable.

Eris on the other hand demanded full details. The entire time she questioned Edan about her mother's death, her hand rested easily on the pommel of her sword. From time to time, Edan's eyes flicked down at the weapon and an air of unspoken tension crackled between them. Eris trusted her uncle about as far as she could comfortably throw him. She didn't care about his rank and status within the tribe. She had seen the way he would always sit and watch Valkia, cold, calculating shrewdness in his eyes.

'She fell under the daemonic might on the steps leading to the great beyond,' relayed Edan. He only had Hepsus's word for that fact of course, having ducked out of the journey when Valkia had been too obsessed with her destination to even notice. But Edan knew his sister well enough to know what she was likely to have attempted. That she had even made it as far as she had still surprised him.

If she had taken but a few more steps, his entire plan would have come crashing down around his ears. And it had taken him so long to carefully piece the whole thing together. He had spent so long cultivating the right attitude, that air of seriousness and just a little aloofness. A tendency to speak softly so that people had to strain to hear him. It was a simple trick that gave the impression he thought carefully about everything he said. He had learned it from his predecessor and he had learned it *well*.

He let his eyes move from one girl to the other. They were virtually identical in appearance, although Eris was more prone to sporting bruises and cuts from her more eager forays into battle. Bellona had ever been more cautious. He let his gaze linger on the former. There was almost visible rage smouldering in her eyes.

'She fought bravely if that is what is worrying you,' he said. His tone was soothing, perhaps even a little condescending. Eris bit immediately.

'And you witnessed this fall with your own eyes?' Eris's hand closed around the weapon at her side. Her uncle met her accusing stare without flinching and he told the lie.

'Yes, Eris. I did. Your mother attempted to lead our people to their death, but although she fought with the strength of a mountain lion, ultimately she failed.' Seeing the flash of anger in Eris's expression, he gently laid a hand upon her arm. 'Listen to me. Upon my sworn oath, her dying words were that until a decision is reached by the great Circle to determine her successor... The future of the Schwarzvolf is in the hands of the Warspeaker.'

'Our mother said...' Eris began to protest, but Bellona put out a hand to forestall her argument. Edan's normally benign expression flashed into a moment of anger that gave him more than a passing resemblance to his sister. It was such a rare thing to see Edan riled that Eris took a physical step backwards, startled by his temper.

'Your mother said a lot of things, girl. I merely suggest that if you have even a trace of lingering respect for her at all, you would do well to honour those last wishes.'

'Don't you ever *dare* say such a thing again. Or so help me, uncle, I will slay you where you stand.'

'Did you not respect her, Eris?' The taunt was obvious and got exactly the response the Godspeaker sought. For a girl who was usually so reticent about demonstrating any sort of affection, Edan had pushed her just one step too far.

'Never presume to tell me whether or not I respected my mother.' Eris drew the sword this time, but she was not fast enough for Edan. The slightly built Godspeaker had unhooked his battle-axe from the belt at his waist and stopped the killing strike.

He was imbued with a strength that Eris had never realised and as she withdrew her attack, she found herself for the first time truly frightened. She had never known fear in her life, but something in Edan's eyes scared her.

'And thus did your mother die,' he sneered. 'Filled to bursting with arrogance. Not caring whether her people lived or died. Seeking to fulfil an ambition she could never hope to realise.'

'Enough!' Bellona stepped forward again and this time, she put her hand forcibly on her twin's shoulder. 'Uncle, I implore you to forgive my sister's impetuous nature, but similarly, beg you to consider your words. You may be travel-weary and tired, but you have brought us sad news.' Eris shrugged herself free from Bellona's grip and strode from the tent. Bellona watched her go and sighed inwardly.

'Of course we will respect Mother's wishes in this

matter – on the condition that we are allowed to sit on the Circle in her place.' It was a diplomatic question, well-posed and pitched completely without rancour. The anger drained from Edan in an instant. He hooked his axe back on his belt and bowed to his niece courteously. *This* was the Edan she knew. The man who demurred to everyone. But she had momentarily caught a glimpse of his other side and she was on her guard.

His voice, when he spoke, was laden with carefully pitched weariness. 'You are correct, of course. It has not been an easy journey. I will make my apologies to Eris later. But I heartily suggest that you keep your sister under control, Bellona. She is in danger of following too closely in her mother's footsteps. It is hard enough that we have lost Valkia.' He looked in the direction of the tent's exit. 'It would be tragic to lose either of you as well, unless it is with honour and glory attached.'

'Yes, uncle.' Bellona lowered her eyes in respect. It was the right thing to do and she knew it; Edan nodded in satisfaction before turning and leaving. Bellona sat down and stared blankly at the tent wall. She should seek out her hot-headed sister and offer some sort of comfort but for now, she grieved alone. She grieved for the wasted time, for the lack of real love that had existed between them. She grieved for the future, for the difficulties she could predict without any skills for foresight that lay ahead of them. She knew that she and her sister faced a challenge unlike anything else they had ever known, but she was clever enough to know that caution would pay far more than any other reaction.

Bellona held her head high and stood, dusting her hands down the front of her tunic. She would go and find Eris and talk sense into her. They both had the blood of chieftains flowing through their veins and if they were to continue the line, there would need to be a lot of politicking.

With Bellona's guiding hand and clever mind, coupled with Eris's strength and fire, they would prevail through the hardships ahead.

THIRTEEN
The Long Game

THE RIVER OF time flowed ever onwards, heedless of
the betrayal of a warrior queen in the northernmost
reaches of the world. Time flowed onwards into
weeks, months and finally years.

Edan had been unhappy with simply betraying his
sister on the field of battle and within weeks of the
party's return to the Vale, had also turned the tide of
favouritism against Hepsus. It had not taken much
more than a carefully placed whisper and gentle re-
working of the truth to ensure that everyone believed
that the Warspeaker had been responsible for Valkia's
death.

Whispers grew to murmurs, which in turn became
angry rumours. Hepsus, revelling in the fact that the
tribe was finally under his command, was oblivious to any of it. He had already instigated a number
of startling changes that did not sit well with many
of Valkia's more staunch supporters and there were
obvious fractures starting to appear across the scattered tribes that had united beneath the queen's
banner.

'War does not have to last forever,' had been the Warspeaker's message. 'We are plentiful in number. Let us spend time carving out a solid, permanent existence. Let us stop the ceaseless wandering. The Schwarzvolf are acknowledged as the greatest tribe of the north. Let us revel in that for a time.'

Days after giving this speech, he dropped the title of Warspeaker, firmly stating that it did nothing to support the message of unity he wanted to promote amongst the people. It had been this act which had led to a further splintering of the tribe.

The Circle had gathered for the first time since the appropriate observance of Valkia's death. The tribe had been in mourning – some genuine, some not – and despite their inherent ferocity, to appear as anything other than united in their grief would expose them as vulnerable.

These had been Hepsus's words and Eris had not reacted well to them.

She stood up and faced him, her elfin-like features contorted with suppressed rage. Bellona stared up at her twin helplessly. The moment Hepsus had spoken, the final line was crossed as far as Eris had been concerned.

'You are promoting nothing but cowardice, Hepsus. You sit there, full of your own self-importance and boast about how you will lead our people forward. But this is an act of foolishness. We are a tribe of warriors. We honour the Blood God...'

'The Blood God? Where was the Blood God when we were fighting for our lives in the far north?' Hepsus responded in kind, his own face furious. 'It was because of a misplaced belief in a mad god that your mother died. Do not forget that.' The former Warspeaker rose from his own place and stood before her. He had the advantage of height, strength and age but Eris did not move. She faced him with as much courage as her own mother had always shown.

'Eris…' Bellona spoke softly. She was not blinded by rage and she could see no end to this discussion but a poor one. She tried without success to appeal to her sister's better nature.

'No, Bellona! This needs to be said.' Eris acknowledged her twin with nothing more than a brief glance. 'Hepsus, give us the truth of it. You never forgave my mother for the death of your son…' She ploughed on despite seeing how much the reminder stung the man. 'You abandoned her to her fate at the last. I have heard many people say the same thing. Her belief in Kharneth was strong and it was pure. A misplaced trust in her own Warspeaker was the thing that cost my mother her life.'

'I did not kill your mother.' Hepsus's hand strayed unconsciously to his scabbard, but he had ceased wearing his sword openly in an effort to prove he was serious about a more settled way of life. 'Do not make such accusations unless you have proof to bring before this Circle. Your mind is addled with grief, girl. Now take your place and shut your mouth until you have something useful to bring to this meeting.'

Nobody had ever spoken to Eris in such a manner and her face went beet-red.

'Eris, please.' There was something commanding in Bellona's soft voice and Hepsus sneered.

'Listen to your sister,' he said, moving so that his face was barely a hair's-breadth from Eris. 'There speaks a *proper* woman.'

Eris didn't miss her stride at all.

'Once,' she said in a low, passionate tone, 'you may have been a worthy successor to my mother's throne, Hepsus. But now? Now you are a broken old man who has lost his edge for battle. I will not stand by whilst you dishonour the tribe further.'

'And what,' said Hepsus, 'do you plan to do about it?' He leaned still closer, almost as though he would kiss her. She gave him a charming, crooked smile.

'This.'

Her hand moved alarmingly fast, and the serrated blade of her dagger cut upwards with a soft displacement of air. It entered Hepsus's face just below his chin, exiting between his eyes. Red blood surged and covered Eris's hand. Hepsus gagged and tried to push Eris from him, but her grip on the blade was firm. He struggled to free himself, even as the crushing inevitability of his certain death pressed him to his knees. Eris watched dispassionately as he suffered, enjoying every second of her hot-headed and impetuous revenge. Then she moved the dagger ever so subtly and pierced the meat of the Warspeaker's brain. The light died from his eyes and she finally released her grip on the dagger. She watched with emotional detachment as Hepsus expired and then moved back as he toppled like a falling tree, his powerful bulk crashing heavily to the ground.

And not one member of the Circle moved to help him.

Hepsus bled out on the floor in front of every member of the Circle, gore soaking the ground around him. Finally, when there was no further drop left in him, he lay still. Eris bent and retrieved her dagger. She forced open the jaws, not yet stiffened through death and cut out what remained of the old warrior's tongue. She held the grisly trophy aloft.

'So will end all liars and traitors,' she said. 'My mother brought the Schwarzvolf to greatness. This man snuffed out that light and has paid the ultimate price. My sister and I are the rightful successors to her leadership and we will take our place accordingly. Is that not right, Bellona?'

Bellona's face was set like stone, demonstrating neither disapproval nor pleasure at her sister's unprecedented actions. She rose to her feet in an almost prim manner.

'It was our mother's wish that we stand together when she was gone,' she affirmed in her quiet voice. 'I am with Eris on this.'

Eris flushed with delight at her sister's concurrence and, responding to a cough of attention, moved her glance to Edan. Her uncle had sat motionless, concentrating on hiding his delight that his little scheme had worked out so well.

'Godspeaker?'

'You speak words of wisdom for one so young, my niece,' he said in his quiet voice. 'I merely wish to affirm my loyalty to you and offer my services as advisor to you and your sister. If you will take me, of course.'

The last was said with such humility that all the

anger Eris had felt towards him for bearing the news of her mother's death flowed out of her in a rush.

'Of course, Godspeaker.' Eris gave him a tight, controlled smile. Beside her, her sister's eyes were as cold as ice. 'The Schwarzvolf belongs to the three of us by birth. Your guidance will be welcomed.'

'I will not disappoint,' said Edan with a low bow from the waist. He told the lie without any difficulty.

CHANGE WAS INEVITABLE, and in the turbulent years since Eris had taken the Warspeaker's life, many things had altered within the tribe of the Schwarzvolf. Some of these changes had been very hotly contested by a certain contingent of the tribe, but their arguments had been quickly resolved. In the worst cases, their arguments had been silenced with the careful application of a dagger blade to the throat.

In the wake of Hepsus's death, the tribe had looked ready to revolt. But under Bellona's careful guidance and Eris's impressive temper, the daughters of Queen Valkia demonstrated the ability to control the people of the Schwarzvolf.

Both girls matured into stunning replicas of their dead mother and both drew exactly the same amount of attention from neighbouring tribes. They discussed the situation with the Godspeaker and he very cleverly left the decision in their own hands. He made it clear in carefully phrased words that if they remained childless, then the line of succession would once again fall to uncertainty. This was more than enough to convince even Eris, who had long since sworn never to take a man to husband, to begin to view the situation in a different light.

They had little time to concern themselves with such things however; within six months of Valkia's death a civil war broke out amongst the united tribes. The work of years in bringing them together under the Schwarzvolf banner slowly unravelled and the twins found themselves leading the loyal of their tribe in bloody battles of retribution against those who had once called themselves allies.

Eris proved herself to be an able front-line warrior, leading the Schwarzvolf at the head of the warriors, flashing through the line with twin battle-axes that cleaved skulls and took lives. Bellona was less skilled but no less fearless and when the twins fought together, although they still possessed but a fraction of the skill their mother had displayed, they were nonetheless formidable.

But fight though they may, they could not convince many of the rebellious tribes to come back under the yoke of the Schwarzvolf. Valkia's death had fractured the alliance held together by the fear and respect that had initially brought them together and no amount of diplomacy or warfare could convince them otherwise.

From being the mightiest tribe in the north, the Schwarzvolf's numbers were dwindling. It brought the matter of inter-tribe marriage to the table once again and Valkia's daughters – forever doomed to walk in their mother's shadow – eventually conceded that the inevitable had to happen.

'I will find the best I can for you both,' Edan had promised. 'Allow me to handle this matter and I promise that you will be pleased with the results.'

Neither young woman wished to marry outside of the Schwarzvolf, but they could both see the necessity. If they did not begin the arduous task of reinforcing alliances, their tribe's numbers would once more dwindle to nothing. They agreed that the Godspeaker should make the necessary arrangements whilst they concentrated on the more important issues of survival against constant raids from formerly allied tribes and other, opportunistic enemies who had come out of the hills once the mighty Schwarzvolf were visibly vulnerable.

War raged endlessly across the snowfields and valleys of the north. Within five years of Valkia's death, Edan felt considerable pressure lift from his shoulders when without his intervention, Bellona coupled with another young Schwarzvolf, a warrior who had courted her vigorously from the start. Eris, who was perhaps a little bitter if not jealous of her sister, cheerfully circulated the rumour that Bellona had only given into the young man's endless demands for a little peace and quiet. Whatever the reason, they seemed content with one another and within a short time of their joining, Bellona was pregnant.

Keen to marry off his other niece and get her removed from his long-term plans, the sly and insidious Godspeaker found a willing suitor for the other of Valkia's daughters. He instigated the first step of his scheme for the tribe's future during the ceremony that had joined Eris with a young warrior of a small, nameless tribe. The people of the Schwarzvolf had always had great respect for the 'visions' that the

Godspeaker experienced and so it was easy enough to take them in.

Halfway through the ceremony, he had faked a sudden fit, followed by a trance. He spoke gibberish for several minutes, flailing and lashing out so violently that two of the tribesmen had to hold him down in case he hurt himself. Then he had feigned unconsciousness for a day.

Eris had postponed the ceremony, earning the ire of both her intended husband and his tribe, but she had not cared in the slightest. The health and well-being of her tribe's chief adviser was far more important to her than some pointless ceremony binding her to a man she cared nothing for. Bellona had dealt with the raging leader of the tribe and had mollified him, promising that the ceremony would take place as soon as the Godspeaker had revived from his trance.

Edan had waited. There was little point in spoiling the dramatic effect of what he was trying to achieve. When he finally decided that enough was enough, he had allowed his eyes to slowly open and had arched his back on the bed, crying out as though in pain.

'Uncle, be calm.' It was Bellona's voice. Edan felt her slide a hand beneath his head and lift a water skin to his lips. 'Drink.'

He complied meekly and then turned his head to look at her. 'How long?' The question was soft and hesitant. 'How long was I in the hands of the gods?'

'Some considerable hours have passed since you fell into the trance,' said his niece, taking back the water skin. Edan groaned softly and she lifted a damp strip of cloth to his forehead. It was easy to fool her.

She was soft-hearted and it would be her downfall in time. Her belly had swollen with the child she bore and there was a maturity to her that had blossomed even more of late. She was now five months into her pregnancy and the condition suited her. Like her mother before her, she had stepped back from the battlefield until the infant was born.

'Eris's marriage? The ceremony?'

'It has been stopped. Your health is our concern.' He groaned again, and put a hand to his head.

'I have ruined her chances... I...' Edan was genuinely startled into silence by the snap of Bellona's harsh tongue. It was so rare to hear her speak in such a way that he was taken aback.

'Enough. What did you see? Is Kharneth... are the Four displeased?' Over the years, Edan had carefully steered the beliefs of the tribe to what he called a 'greater understanding' of the interlocking majesty of the Four gods. Devotion to just one lessened them, he said. It weakened them. In this way, he was able to pursue his own interests without damaging external appearances. When the moment suited him, he would invoke the practise of specific worship.

'I... I need time,' said Edan in a trembling voice that he had spent so long practising and perfecting. 'I need time to gather my thoughts and try to extract the meaning of the visions. All the gods are angry though, Bellona.'

Edan had seen the power of the daemon that his sister had fought so long ago. He had seen the strength in the creature and when he had learned that it was an emissary from another of the Four, he had started thinking. What power could he wield if he were to earn the favour of all the gods?

And so his plan had been born. The first part had been alarmingly simple. Removing the fanatical Valkia from the picture had been much easier than he could have anticipated. Then removing Hepsus, the one man in whom he had confided... well. When Eris had rammed her dagger through his throat, he could have laughed.

This dramatic 'vision' was to form the last part of his plan. Through this, he would lead the Schwarzvolf away from the endless, unrewarding devotion to bloodshed and into something greater.

Edan never once stopped to consider that Kharneth would be enraged. He didn't consider it because he simply didn't care. Of all the people within the tribe, the Godspeaker was the only one who could connect directly with the gods; or so the Schwarzvolf were taught. The word of the Godspeaker was the command of the Four themselves and they would obey his every whim without question.

'How much time?' Bellona interrupted his thoughts and he waved a hand at her irritably, briefly forgetting he was supposed to be weak after his 'episode'.

'It will soon be nightfall. I will bring you my thoughts to tonight's Circle,' he said. 'Let me rest, girl.'

Bellona got up from his side and moved to the tent. Her condition caused her to move awkwardly, the growing baby adding a rolling gait to her movement. She paused in the entrance of the dwelling, her hand resting easily on her stomach and spoke the words that would ultimately spell her own fate. Her intelligence was outstanding and the trap she had laid for him was sprung.

'You seem very sure of the hour of the day, Uncle,' she said, quietly. 'I did not share that information with you. I am very pleased to see that you are so quick to recover your senses.'

She left the tent and left Edan to dark thoughts of further treachery.

AFFRONTED AND INSULTED by the matter, Eris's would-be husband had left the camp of the Schwarzvolf and not sealed the marriage. It had put the God-speaker right back at the beginning of his plans and he silently raged at his own lack of foresight in the matter. Nonetheless, finding other suitors had not been terribly difficult. Whilst all the neighbouring tribes treated the daughters of the dead queen with tentative distrust, they were nonetheless desirable. Not only for their positions as the heirs to Valkia's leadership, but for their physical appearance.

To Edan's irritation, Eris had announced that clearly the postponement of her marriage had been a sign from the Four themselves that she would not marry. Angered by this, but unable to let it show, Edan turned his attentions to dealing with Bellona instead. It had been the hardest thing for him to feign grief when Bellona's husband had died during a border skirmish with would-be invaders. By then she was nearly seven months pregnant and it seemed unlikely he would be able to deal with her without bringing attention to the matter.

He had plotted and schemed and eventually, had negotiated with one of the bigger tribes. He could not leave his poor niece to bear a child with no husband, he had said. Promises of elevated status within the tribal hierarchy were made and a variety of valuable goods exchanged hands.

It was more than a month before the seeds of his multi-layered and conniving scheme could germinate and finally come to fruition.

The man who came to seek Bellona's hand in marriage arrived at the tent of the Godspeaker more than three months after he had set the wheels in motion. Hrafi was young and arrogant and at first both girls dismissed him as another empty-minded fool. But once he engaged the pair of them in conversation they discovered that behind his exterior lay a mind as sharp as any they had encountered.

Eris soon tired of his company, but could tell that her sister was infatuated with the man. She had taken the death of her husband well, but Eris knew that Bellona had missed the presence of a man in her bed. At first, Eris could not hide her disappointment. She had hoped that Bellona would follow her example and eschew marriage with an external tribe. But she loved her twin and would not stand in the way of her happiness.

For five days, Hrafi was entertained by the Schwarzvolf. Along with his small retinue, he was granted space to stay within the host camp, and every morning he emerged from the tent in which he had slept with a new gift for the apparent object of his desire. Once it was an exquisitely hand-tooled amulet that he told her would protect her from any evil spirits. On another day he had sat by her side and carved her a fertility statue from a piece of wood. The humour of such a gift, given Bellona's advanced state of pregnancy, had made her laugh; the first time she had done so in an age. Hrafi was strong, thoughtful, and talented and seemed to be not in the least perturbed by taking on another man's child as his own.

Edan watched carefully from a safe distance. He had performed the duty expected of him as both Godspeaker and relative of Bellona. For three of the five days he had been confident that his plan would play out as it was meant to. Throughout the fourth day, when he saw the looks that his niece and the young, dark-skinned warrior shared, he began to wonder.

On the fifth day, he considered staging another fit as he had done at Eris's nuptials. Hrafi and Bellona looked entirely too happy for his liking. But he had underestimated the slyness and competence of those he had hired.

Amongst Hrafi's retinue was a youth. A slave boy, he had been introduced as. Barely more than a child and of no consequence. He fetched and carried at Hrafi's bidding and was seldom seen more than three feet behind his master. He was a scrawny, puling thing whose ribs could clearly be seen through the paper-thin skin of his bare chest. His head had been shorn of all hair and his dark eyes seemed huge in a drawn face that looked perpetually afraid. His tongue had been cut out long ago and he seldom made any sort of sound.

Hrafi initially offered to make a gift of the boy to Bellona, but she declined. The Schwarzvolf were not the type to enslave others. So the youth trailed along behind his master like a dejected wolfhound. Hrafi occasionally threw him a strip of meat or some other treat and he would wolf it down hungrily. Bellona requested Hrafi's permission to ensure that the boy was given a proper meal instead of scraps and despite pouting at this idea, her suitor eventually agreed. The slave-boy had given Bellona a grateful look as he had eaten a full plate of food for what was perhaps the first time in his young life.

He frequently arrived at Bellona's tent ahead of Hrafi, heralding his master's arrival, so on the fifth day, nobody looked twice when the scrawny slave-boy made his way inside.

She looked up as he entered the tent and treated him to a smile. Discussions and negotiations with Hrafi were going better than she could have hoped. Unlike her sister, Bellona was not averse to the idea of marriage and children borne through union with those not of Schwarzvolf blood. Her sense of duty and loyalty to her people was strong and she knew that there were many who hoped to see the Schwarzvolf regain the strength and power they had once wielded.

'Does your master come to see me this morning, boy?' Bellona asked him the same question she had asked for the last few mornings and he had nodded. His eyes were huge and agitated and she felt uncomfortable looking at him. She sighed and rose from her seat, no easy task given her advanced condition.

The lack of a tongue meant that she could not easily expect him to tell her what had given him cause for a look of such fear. She had little patience for attempting to extract anything from him and was preparing to send him from the tent when he gripped her arms with his bony fingers.

'Let go of me!' The boy gripped tighter and looked up at Bellona desperately. He made abrupt motions with his head as though indicating she should leave the tent and her brow furrowed.

'Unhand me, slave, or your master will...'

'He should not be here.'

The voice belonged to Hrafi who had come into the tent whilst she had been distracted with the slave boy. The youth continued to cling to Bellona and made a strange moaning sound that sounded like sheer desperation.

'Remove your slave from my presence, Hrafi.' Bellona's voice contained all the haughty surety of her breeding and Hrafi's brow arched at her tone. 'Then explain why you allowed him to treat me this way.'

'Of course, my lovely.' Hrafi moved across and caught the slave by the shoulder, dragging him backwards with considerable force. He leaned in close and whispered something inaudible. The fear on the boy's face was enough to send him running instantly from the tent. Hrafi smirked and turned to his would-be bride.

'We would not want him to disturb us now, would we?' He gave her a seductive smile that was almost lecherous in its intensity and he caught her in his arms, pulling her to him for a kiss. It was nothing

he had not done already, but Bellona felt uncomfortable with his closeness and tried to pull herself free
from his grasp.

'Let go of me, Hrafi.'

'You do not enjoy this?'

'Let *go* of me.' She tugged harder to free herself
from him, but his strength far exceeded hers and this,
coupled with her delicate condition, meant that she
simply stumbled slightly. He seemed to come to his
senses and released her. She sat down on the end of
her sleeping pallet looking dazed and pale.

'My love, I am sorry. I got over-eager.' At that
moment, the slave boy returned, looking timid and
uncertain. 'His timing is superb! Give me what I sent
you for, brat.' He snatched a soft bag from the slave
boy and opened it. 'Let me mix this for you.' From the
pouch he wore at his waist, he took a little pinch of
herbs which he mixed with some water. 'The healers
of my tribe use this all the time for women expecting
children. It helps settle an upset stomach and relaxes
the mother.'

'I don't...'

'Bellona, please. Let me do this thing for you.' He
smiled his charming, winning smile and the young
woman stared up at him. Everything screamed out
not to trust him given the way he had just treated her,
but she saw in that smile the echo of his charm; the
pleasant, caring young man who had won her heart.
She gave him an uncertain smile back and Hrafi positively beamed. He dropped the herbs into a cup of
water and stirred them around. He immediately gave
the bag back to the slave boy and the child hopped

from foot to foot nervously.

The smell of the concoction drifted across to her and she wrinkled her nose. It was acrid and more than a little bitter. There was an earthy undertone to it, some herb that she did not recognise.

'I am told that it tastes better than it smells,' he promised her, kneeling down beside her and offering her the cup. 'Take a sip. See what you think.'

Dubiously, she raised the cup to her lips and took a tentative sip. The suspicion on her face disappeared almost immediately and she nodded. It tasted quite lovely.

'Drink,' he urged her and his apparently concerned expression was the last thing she ever saw in the seconds before the poison, fast-acting and lethal, began to take hold. In a few seconds she had dropped into a deep sleep. It would take perhaps half an hour before she drew her last breath, but she would not suffer.

Hrafi watched the young woman as she slept, her chest rising and falling gently. There were many barbarous ways he could have taken her life, but he had decided on the poison for reasons of his own – and it was not kindness.

He had agreed to commit this murder on the promise of greatness, but he was also no fool. He had seen through Edan's plan quickly enough. The Godspeaker of the Schwarzvolf had never intended to honour his word and Hrafi was about to turn the tables on him.

'Slave,' he called aloud. He drew his dagger from his belt. 'Come in here. I have need of you.'

He had very little time. He intended to make sure it was well-spent. She would stay alive long enough for him to carry out the rest of his plan.

AN HOUR LATER, Eris found the body of her twin sister.

Suspicious at the length of time Hrafi had taken paying his respects, she had attended Bellona's dwelling and called for her sister to come outside. There had been no response so she had leaned forward and listened very carefully. She could hear soft sobbing.

Tearing the entrance open, Eris darted inside and found the most grisly of scenes before her. Her sister, her beautiful, vivacious and courageous sister was most certainly dead. Her body was laid on the floor and her eyes were closed. There was a look of oddly peaceful contentment about her which suggested that she had not been aware of what had been done to her.

The sobbing came from the slave boy who had Bellona's head in his lap. He was stroking her hair and weeping. He looked up at Eris in fear and made his peculiar grunting noise. Eris paid him no heed. Her eyes were fixed on her sister's belly. Her tunic had been torn apart and the infant that she had carried almost to term had been cut from her, and she had been left to bleed out whatever of her life had remained. For a wild moment, Eris realised she had gotten so used to seeing Bellona looking so engorged with her baby that the woman lying before her seemed to have burst like an overripe fruit. Glistening strands of her intestines were visible and the contents of her abdomen and uterus had spilled everywhere.

Eris had fought on the field of battle countless times. She had seen evisceration, decapitation and any number of grisly deaths. But for the first time in her life, bile rose and she turned away from the scene, retching violently. The contents of her stomach removed, she dropped to her knees beside the scene, shoving the slave boy away violently and grasping her sister's body in her arms.

As an adult woman, she had never cried. But she did now. She screamed at the slave boy to fetch a blanket so that she could at least cover Bellona's dignity and the boy did as he was told. Eris's scream of rage brought others and eventually Edan appeared as well. He took in the scene and realised instantly that Hrafi had played him for a fool.

'We must find him,' he said at once. Eris, almost inconsolable with grief felt wildly grateful and did not stop for a second to think that Edan wanted Hrafi for his own purposes. 'His crime must not go unpunished.'

'He has been gone some time judging by how much blood she has lost,' said one of the healers who had rushed to inspect her body. 'None of us know where he has gone.'

Many pairs of eyes turned to the slave boy who let out a wail and shook his head vigorously. Edan stared at him coldly.

'Put him in the Pit,' he said in a tone that was unlike his usual affable manner. 'He will pay the price for serving a traitor. And get together a party to travel to Hrafi's tribe. We will get answers. I promise you that.'

But Hrafi was not there.

His tribe denied all knowledge of what he had done. A prince amongst their people, Hrafi had announced his intention to marry into the Schwarzvolf and his people had disowned him. They would not have let him come back.

Despite his best efforts, Edan realised that he would not easily track down the barbarian who had betrayed him. He had planned Bellona's death, that was true enough. But he had also planned to take the infant for himself, to raise the child in a manner fit for a future leader. Valkia's grandchild would be a valuable commodity. As a girl, she would have been a fine prize to tout. As a boy...

But he would never even know. The humiliation was great and Edan took a spiteful revenge by having the slave boy publicly executed as a traitor. In an act of generosity, he fought down his urge to carry out the process himself and let Eris do it. She had done so gladly, needing to feel that justice had somehow been served. And unknowingly following the pattern of her mother so many years before her, she performed the ritual disembowelling on a traitor who had been party to the death of one of the ruling family.

The innocent slave boy, who had been too frightened to refuse his master's order and unable to warn Bellona as he would have liked, welcomed death with a calm stare. No sound left his mouth when Eris tore out his guts. He dropped to his knees and stared straight ahead. Eris had thrown her dagger to one side and snatched a battle=axe up in one hand. She did not make a clean job of beheading the boy and it took four blows before his head parted company with his shoulders. Indulging her need for revenge, Eris was in no mood to care about such niceties.

From his vantage point beside the scene of execution, Edan smiled. He had all but declared war on Hrafi's former tribe, but that was fine. The Schwarzvolf needed to keep their blades honed and their battle-senses sharp. It had been an elaborate, intricate plan and Edan had never once been outsmarted. He glowered at the dead slave boy as though it had all been his fault.

'Hang him out with the others,' he said, waving a casual hand at the body. 'And bring me more wine.'

FOURTEEN
Emergence

IN THE REALM of man, time moved on. Ten years passed and yet in the place between worlds, that realm wherein dwelt the gods themselves, time had no meaning. For the consort of Khorne, a year could pass in less than an hour. She had no concept of the passage of the years beyond her realm. Neither did she care.

For a long while, Valkia had lost herself in the eternal battle, her sense of purpose having been swallowed up in the glory of Khorne's gift. She was no longer a human warrior queen, but a creature of destruction. Her wings gave her a freedom she had never had in life and her ferocity was unsurpassed. From the moment she stood in the presence of her lord and master, she was totally lost in his service.

He had been satisfied with her new appearance, completing her new form with additional gifts: a mane of spines sprouted where once she had sported her raven black hair. They gave her a fearsome appearance, but somewhere beneath it all, somewhere beneath the new, feral creature that she had become, Valkia was still an astoundingly beautiful woman. She was clothed in a suit of baroque armour wrought from brass and black iron in the hell-forges of the infernal realm. The overlapping plates fit snugly to her lithe form and accentuated every curve of her powerful, slender body while living chains bound themselves to her collar and belt, laden with the skulls of the favoured.

The flayed hides of defeated daemons were draped over its burning, black plates. The ruddy flesh hissed and hardened, its unnatural fortitude turning aside sword and axe while it writhed with shackled power and unholy runes.

Blood oozed from the armour as soon as she was buckled into it and within moments thick ropes of gore trailed to her ankles. If she stood in one place for too long, the seeping fluid would pool beneath her, reflecting half-formed faces of the slain. The blood of the eternally tormented was a weapon in its own right, adding to the palpable aura of terror that emanated from the daemon princess.

So armoured, wielding her beloved Slaupnir and bearing the daemon-shield, Valkia looked upon herself. She gazed upon the terrible, wonderful changes that had been wrought upon her and she was pleased. She was her master's servant, his beloved and his consort, but she was treated by the other daemonic entities that fought the eternal battle with fear and loathing in equal measure. Her will was absolute, her wrath terrible to behold and her vengeance swift.

But she had lived her life as a warrior and although she thrilled to the ultimate gift of standing at Khorne's right hand, she soon yearned to spill the blood of the living once again.

Her daemonic form needed no sleep, no rest and no respite. But she would sometimes remember shards of what had been before, like half-remembered dreams. Those fragments unsettled her, teasing her with thoughts of tasks not yet done. She remembered a time before she had stepped into the flesh and armour she wore and had been something less, but that others had taken that from her.

The memories of the great betrayal on the riven steps at the heart of the great wastes slowly filtered back into her thoughts and Valkia the Bloody remembered.

She remembered and she burned with an unholy desire for revenge upon those who had failed her. She would stalk the lands of the north and she would visit her terrible rage upon them. She would spill rivers of blood in the name of Khorne and he would revel in the carnage. She would tear the limbs from the bodies of the treacherous cowards and feast on their lying tongues which she would pluck from their screaming mouths.

A vision unfolded in her mind's eye as her fury grew. She saw a village surrounded by a sprawling camp alive with activity. Tokens and offerings to the Four adorned every dwelling and a shrine housing roughly carved totems stood in a square at the heart of the settlement. They were nomads no more. Warriors still prowled the lanes and sparred together in a small arena, but they were not the wild men she had once known. The sight of their complacence sickened her.

Worse, they had cast aside all that she had brought them in her long, bloody reign and had turned from the path of blood to something lesser.

Valkia threw back her head and screamed her fury to the crimson sky, and the creatures of the eternal battle responded in kind. Monstrous throats roared in wordless, primal rage and clawed hands raised ebony blades in salute to the call to arms. The daemonic horde swelled and heaved at the promise of slaughter, their burning eyes following the sinuous, winged form as she parted the veil and stepped back into the world of men.

Hell followed with her.

AT FIRST, THE cold, bloodless reality of the world hurt Valkia's senses and she turned her face from the feeble light that broke through the banks of ashen cloud which churned endlessly above the blighted wastes. She had spent so long in the twilight of Khorne's realm that the cruel sun brought a stabbing pain to her daemonic eyes.

The host at her back hissed and spat in disdain for the world, but the promise of the bloodbath to come kept their thirst alive and their rage thrumming through their limbs. They would need to kill soon.

She forced herself to look up at the storm-wracked sky and pushed the weakness from her with a force of will. Her eyes slowly adjusted to the constant lines of reality and what had been little more than a blur of colours resolved into the monolithic steps that led down to the plain.

She sprang down three of the massive slabs and

then stopped. Throwing back her head, she laughed at her own foolishness. Why should she walk? She had the power of flight now. She unfurled her wings and rejoiced at the magnificence of their sheer power. With barely an effort, she beat them gently, raising herself with ease from the cold stone of the steps. Borne aloft by the chaotic winds that poured from the abyss, Valkia descended to the plain like a fallen angel. Where her hooves settled, the grey dust parted and beads of blood welled up from the ground as if the land itself was wounded by her tread.

The air here was charged with unfettered sorcery and it coloured the winds like oil on water, sticking to the tongue like the taste of metal. The glossy steps were still stained with old blood and marked from the countless deaths that occurred upon them and Valkia could easily identify the spot where she herself had fallen.

A thought came to her. A hazy thread of memory formed in her mind and she grasped desperately for a name. A youth. A warrior who had been the only truly loyal follower. The only one who had possessed courage enough to follow her to the edge of the world.

Kormak.

At the foot of the steps a corpse lay face-down in the dust. Its flesh was shrunken and grey, mummified by the passage of years and the writhing magic that permeated everything. Tattered strips of skin hung like ribbons from the body, evidence of the dreadful wounds that had finally brought the tenacious young warrior down. For ten years it had lain on the very cusp of creation, in sight of the realms of madness but denied the promised glory.

Valkia nudged the corpse over with her foot and it rolled onto its back. Ragged wounds lined Kormak's face where the creatures of Slaanesh had torn him down, exposing desiccated muscle and bone beneath. His furs and clothing were stained and shredded and across his body were the multiple lacerations which had ultimately killed him. She fixed her gaze on the stump where his arm had once been and it filled her with pure, murderous anger. So many great, powerful warriors at her command and in the end, just the one who had believed in her vision.

Hunkering down beside the remains of her most loyal follower, Valkia stroked a long-fingered nail across his ruined face. 'Such a waste,' she murmured. A low moan escaped from the ruined hollow of Kormak's mouth and a pale wisp emerged from between its cracked lips.

The misty exhalation expanded above the body, shimmering and bloating until it formed the outline of a man. Even incorporeal as it was, one arm still clutched a spectral axe with grim determination. The wraith's features were set in a look of abject fury, its insubstantial form unable to vent its hatred on the flesh of the living.

'Kormak.'

Valkia marvelled at the raw tenacity of her one-armed devotee. He had been a decade dead but the heady combination of a violent death, the energies that coursed on the wind and his own thirst for vengeance had kept his spirit shackled to his sundered flesh. The spectre gave a reedy howl of impotent fury and locked its pale eyes with Valkia's burning gaze.

'You served me well in life, Kormak, and by extension you served Khorne. For long years you have prowled this place, denied your just reward – and your rightful vengeance. I go now to spill the blood of those that fled when they should have stood beside us.' She reached out and caressed the ghostly cheek of the man before her. 'Will you join me?'

The shade let out a long, mournful wail that echoed across the desolate plain and the crimson daemons hissed in agitation. The host was eager for blood and they would not long be denied. Valkia gave the daemons a baleful glare and returned her attention to the soul of Kormak.

'You swore to me that you would not fall behind and I do not yet consider your oath fulfilled. Khorne calls to your blood and must be answered in kind. Rise now and revel in the roar of battle once again.' Valkia sunk her claws into the old flesh of Kormak's corpse and the shade let out another moan, its maw distending into a snarl of bestial rage.

With a crack of dry sinew and yellowed bone the cadaver's jaw shuddered into unnatural life, matching its ethereal counterpart. Valkia moved her hands across the flesh of the corpse, cutting obscene runes that glowed with a fell inner light. As each burst into life, the wraith diminished, its spectral form shrinking back into its frame of skin and bones. Valkia completed her work by inscribing the angular rune of the Blood God on the bone of Kormak's exposed skull. She continued to cradle his head in her hands, crooning soft words to him as though he were a baby. Barely a few minutes had passed before the half-dismembered warrior sat bolt upright, a yell of terrible anguish on his lips. His soul was once again shackled to his broken flesh. The rest was his decision.

'Be calm, Kormak. Be calm.' He stared straight ahead as long-dead memories cascaded uncontrollably into his mind. Visions of battle. Recollection of terrible fear and a moment of great calm. And darkness. He could remember the darkness.

He tried to speak, but his half-destroyed face was only good for allowing him to make dry, hollow sounds. His desperate words came out as barely more than a grunt. It did not matter, his congealing mind told him. If you can grunt and scream, you can give voice to your rage.

'Be calm. I have given you life enough to make a choice.'

He could hear a voice. A female voice. It was both alluring and terrifying. He *knew* that voice. Another memory burst the surface of confusion.

Another grunt left his mouth. He could not form the shape to say her name and it came out as a drawn-out 'a'. The three syllables of his one-time queen's name were clear in that sound. He reached out his remaining hand towards her and the daemon princess nodded. She caught his hand tightly and clutched it to her armoured breast.

'Yes, Kormak. Yes, it is your queen. You have a choice to make. You can serve me again and in so doing become a warrior without peer, a champion of slaughter and a taker of skulls. If you do not choose this destiny then you can accept the embrace of oblivion and the eternal darkness of what lies beyond.'

He shook his head and his twisted, distorted face moved imperceptibly as though he would smile. He mustered everything he had and managed to form a sound.

'...ay, a.'

'You wish to stay?'

He nodded and there was such devotion in his eyes that Valkia's hatred for those who had led to their mutual downfall grew even more. 'So be it,' she said. She released him from her grip and got to her feet. Raising her spear and shield to the sky she cried out to Khorne.

A wind began to rise, whipping at the daemon princess's mane and blowing up clouds of dust and debris from the plain. Kormak's eyes widened in startlement at a gathering cyclonic vortex that moved towards him. Valkia watched the approaching phenomenon with a glitter of delight on her face.

'Rise, my champion,' she said. 'Rise up from the long sleep and do the bidding of your queen and your lord.' She watched as the broken, malformed Kormak was caught up by the twisting energies and lifted high into the air. His entire body stiffened, his limbs thrusting outwards and his head thrown back. No sound left him but that same long, low moaning that was all he could manage.

The storm grew violent and Valkia had to unfurl her wings simply in order to maintain her balance. She caught the updraft and rose gracefully into the air where she could watch the changes that were being wrought upon her first champion.

Already Kormak was unrecognisable. Molten brass
and fire spewed from the stump of his severed arm
and knotted itself into a new limb that throbbed
with hateful life. A horned helm in deepest arterial
crimson now covered his face and even as the Blood
Queen watched, more armour plates were encasing
his body. All the same deep, dark red hue, the suit
was chased with brass edging and detailing. The stylised skull symbol of Khorne adorned his chest and
the eight-pointed star of Chaos was repeated in black
iron decals everywhere on the armour.

The grunting had stopped and for a few moments,
the armoured champion made no sound at all. Then
a bestial roar emanated from within the helmet. The
wind dropped abruptly and the warrior plunged to
the ground heavily with a crash of metal. He was
back on his feet almost instantly. The armour loaned
bulk and height to his muscled form, but even so,
Valkia was certain that were she to strip the armour
from his back, the man beneath would be far bigger
than he had been in life.

Her eyes ranged over his impressive figure and she
laughed in delight. With a warrior of this calibre at
her side, the armies of the north would flee before
her. She would scythe through them as though they
were blades of grass and she would reap the skulls of
the fallen.

'I have gifts for you my champion, first among my
warriors.'

Valkia beckoned to the slavering daemons and five
of the creatures approached, lashed by her black will.

With a twist of power she seized their monstrous forms and crushed the stuff of their existence into something altogether more fitting. They shrieked and howled as their unnatural flesh twisted and bent, running together into a mass of bone, horn and teeth. The daemonic matter seethed and bubbled until, at last, it resembled a barbed axe, the huge smile of its blade a jagged line of snapping daemonic maws.

'You will slake their thirst for slaughter, even as you feed your own.' Valkia purred as the horrific weapon settled into Kormak's eager grasp.

Another curt gesture brought a steaming, iron-skinned beast thundering from the mob of daemonic minions. It lumbered obediently up to the waiting warrior and glared at him with hateful red eyes set deep within its massive, armoured head. The juggernaut pawed eagerly at the ground and Kormak stepped up into the broad saddle without hesitation.

'Perfect,' Valkia hissed.

She allowed her wings to lower her to the ground so that she was standing before the mounted Kormak. His formidable bulk towered over her and in a former life she would have felt a tremor of uncertainty faced with such a warrior. He was bound to her more profoundly now than he ever had been in life however, and she was his queen.

'You are my champion now,' she said in a commanding tone. 'You will serve my lord first and you will serve me second. You will bind yourself to this oath and you will not falter. You will spill much blood in Khorne's name, Kormak.'

The juggernaut reared up on its hind legs, a tower of

burnished flesh and unstoppable killing might, and Kormak bellowed his bloodlust to the broken skies. The beast crashed to the ground and bent its knee to Valkia, presenting its rider. She laid the tip of Slaupnir against Kormak's shoulder. 'Rise, my brother,' she said. 'There is much to be done.'

THE CONSORT OF Khorne and her champion did not have an easy journey across the wastes, but the challenges were nothing that the warrior queen could not handle. Once she stepped outside of her lord's realm, the daemon princess was what could only be called fair game. Every minion in service to the other gods of Chaos prowled the blasted plains, waiting for her.

In life, nothing had frightened Valkia. She had known hesitation when facing enemies who called for a different strategy, but she had never been afraid beyond a glimmer of uncertainty. Her belief in her own ability and the devout faith in the Blood God had seen to that. Now, though, she was utterly fearless. Kormak, who was little more than an unstoppable golem marched wordlessly at her side, a loyal minion beyond a death that had come too soon.

Valkia did not engage Kormak in conversation beyond commands to attack. Neither of them needed rest and the only sustenance that was required was the spilling of blood and the desperate attacks of lesser daemons and warped creatures provided that in plentiful supply.

With a growing band of wild daemons, bloodthirsty beastmen and gibbering mutants at her back, the number of warbands choosing to oppose her slowly dwindled until only the most crazed, foolhardy or insane dared to meet her in battle. Blood and skulls marked their passing, a road of carnage that crossed and re-crossed the wastes as Valkia gathered ever more followers to her banner.

The warriors of Khorne walked with purpose and focus. Occasionally, Valkia would take flight, spreading her wings and relishing the glory of soaring in the skies. The first time she swooped to slaughter an enemy, she did so with a ululating scream. Like an eagle, she drove downwards, Slaupnir at the ready. Her victim never stood a chance. She soon adapted to this method of attack, delighting in the gore that was inevitably spilled.

She exulted in her new-found power and strength and as she and Kormak reached the mountains that bordered the plains, the trail of death that lay like scattered trees in her wake stood as testament to that.

In the dusty hills at the feet of the bleak mountains the war band found its first tribe.

THEY HAD NEVER bothered with a collective name beyond 'Chosen'. Worship of the Blood God was instilled in them from birth and the Blood Let, the first rites of a young warrior, happened at the age of four. They were savage and violent, given very much to fighting amongst themselves when there were no enemies to make war upon. Animalistic and vicious, they spoke few words.

Like the Schwarzvolf, they put great store in the visions of their shamanic leaders, although these shamen were as far removed from the Godspeakers of the Schwarzvolf as could be. These men – and women – foretold the future and read omens through bloody sacrifice. They would slaughter whatever unfortunate creature happened into their path first. Rats, hunting dogs, sometimes one of the tribe. The guts of the victim would be spilled and the shaman would read the signs in their entrails.

They were quite mad, driven beyond sanity by the endless killing and slaughter and the mutations that blighted any who spent too long near the dusty green stone. It thrust up from the earth like rotten teeth, great, lambent shards that the tribe claimed hailed from what they called God's Realm. It was not uncommon for them to be born with extra eyes, twisted limbs and bestial features. Some were so warped that they bore little resemblance to anything remotely human.

This isolated tribe ran amok, slaughtering their way through the few others who settled on the north face of the mountain. But they never killed them all and they would leave many years between raids. Long enough for them to grow, even if just a little.

The tribe never abandoned any but the weakest to their fate, however. For them, the ability to hold a weapon and butcher anything that opposed them was all that was needed in order to please their master and to live well. And by this token, by this self-imposed ideology, they lived *exceptionally* well.

When the daemon princess descended from the heavens on wings of darkest night, her armour running with blood and with a warrior wearing the symbol-chased imagery of their god, they flung themselves to the ground at her feet, wailing and swearing allegiance to her before she even opened her mouth.

Her coming had been foretold many years before by one of their shamen. The iconic and primitive etchings of the winged warrior queen adorned the walls of the mountain caves in which they made their homes. Long before Valkia had even died and been reborn, long before she had stepped beyond the mortal realm, they had worshipped her as a goddess. For them, her arrival heralded a new dawn.

She did not recall the cave drawings that had held her fascination so many years before. The iconography of the winged creature that had appeared countless times in the poorly-drawn images.

Delighting in this unconditional devotion, Valkia accepted their service freely and without reserve. They were scrappy fighters; many of them were like wild animals who fought with their fingers and teeth. The many and varied weapons that they sometimes wielded however, were curious works of stone and iron. Their maker was a man of no words, his tongue having been cut out many years before during a particularly heated argument with one of his brethren. But he was also a man out of place among an unruly mob of savages. He had been born with an ability to work metals and stone and fashion the most magnificently balanced weapons, a fact that had undoubtedly given the mutant tribe it superiority over its neighbours.

'My army needs weapons and armour worthy of Khorne,' Valkia decreed to the smith after declaring his work far superior to any that she had seen since setting foot in the wastes. The tribesman glowed briefly under her praise and grunted his acknowledgement of her command.

Wordlessly, he took one look at the seething horde already snapping at each other in agitation. In that single glance, he took in the scale and needs of the army with the skill that those so highly practised in the art of weapon making possessed. He nodded in satisfaction and turned to his forge to begin work. Kormak glanced at Valkia and clanked after him.

The two warriors took a certain comfort in their mutual silent state, and whilst Valkia set the tribesmen upon one another in an orgy of bloodshed to earn her favour, the champion would stand motionless for long hours in the corner of the smith's forge. Were it not for the occasional shift of position, he might simply have been a display of armour.

Within days, a steady stream of raw iron armour and cruel stone weapons began to stream from the forge, the beast-kin and twisted humans of her army revelling in the killing power it granted them. The clash of arms, the scream and howl of daemons and the agonised cries of the dying surrounded the growing horde and while blood flowed daily to appease their queen, word of the coming slaughter brought fresh warriors to her banner.

What the lone smith had begun soon became the work of many as arms and armour poured from the forge-fires and were spread amongst the war bands that now sprawled across the hills. Hundreds of skulls adorned lines of stakes that spread from the heart of the camp in eight-pointed stars. At the centre of it all Valkia sat on a throne of green stone, watching men and beasts butcher each other for her amusement while Kormak and his towering mount stood at her right hand.

Far, far away from the energy and rising hunger of Valkia's growing army, what remained of the Schwarzvolf lived on in ignorant bliss. Reduced to endless in-fighting and squabbling, the once mighty barbarian tribe was a paltry shadow of its former self.

Soon, it would no longer matter.

FIFTEEN
Death or Glory

'We are weak.'

'What? I apologise, Eris. I was lost in thought.'

'You were ignoring me.'

Edan had long trained his ear to tune out his niece's continual complaints. For so many years he had worked hard to turn a friendly, kindly, even *paternal* face towards the twins. But since Bellona's death, Eris had become unbearably difficult.

'I was not ignoring you.' Edan shifted position on the throne – Valkia's throne – and gave her his most charming smile. Eris scowled in return. 'You were discussing our strategic position.'

'I said we were weak,' she retorted, folding her arms across her chest. She despised it when Edan sat upon the throne of the Schwarzvolf in a casual, idle manner. His legs were resting over the arm of the seat and his indolence infuriated her. As far as she could tell, it was an open challenge on her unofficial position.

'The same thing,' replied Edan, still with that same smile on his face. 'Only worded differently.' He enjoyed watching the flare of anger that flickered across her eyes. For ten years he had played her like a finely tuned instrument, inciting her anger with a carefully placed word and sending her to war on a whim. Not as skilled a leader as her mother had been, Eris made bad decisions that had seen many good warriors lose their lives. When Bellona had no longer been present on the battlefield, it had gotten worse.

Eris returned from campaigns with fewer and fewer warriors at her back, but rarely took more than superficial injury herself. She continued to live and thrive.

More was the pity.

Still, Edan thought, a sigh on his lips, she was probably right this time. The last raid had been unexpected and for the first time the Schwarzvolf had faced the very real risk of total defeat. Fortune had favoured them however and an abrupt turn in the weather had given them the final advantage. Eris still bore the fresh wounds and bruises from the fight and she was evidently in no mood for word games.

'Edan!'

It was serious this time. Eris only ever called him by name when she was ready to launch into him with one of her barbed and frequently violent temper tantrums.

'Eris, calm yourself.' Swinging himself round, Edan rose with unexpectedly lithe grace from the throne. He stood head and shoulders above her, but she did not even flinch at his proximity. She took in his form with a sneer on her face. In the past two years, the Godspeaker had run to fat. Inactivity and gluttony had padded him out considerably. He had not wielded a weapon in those two years, claiming that he had been visited in a vision. He had been told to step away from the battlefield by the gods themselves. He was too important to the people of the Schwarzvolf to be lost in the fires of war.

They had not dared question the words of the gods. The last person who had done that had been Bellona. Murdered by a man who had arrived at the camp claiming he sought her hand in marriage, Bellona's life had bled out on the floor of the tent, her infant child stolen away from the tribe. Despite having delivered justice herself, Eris had never really gotten over her sister's death and had always strongly suspected Edan's hand in the matter.

'I will not *calm myself.*' She may have said the words, but Edan could tell by the way that her shoulders shook that she was doing her very best to do just that. 'The next raid that comes will see the end of our people. Can't you see it?'

'They got lucky. There will be no next raid.' Edan moved away from his wildcat of a niece and moved to a small wooden table on which stood a flagon of wine. He poured a generous measure and took a long drink. He recalled his manners and waved the flagon at Eris. She stormed across behind him and swept the remaining goblets off the table. They tumbled to the ground with a loud clatter.

Placing her palms down on the surface, she leaned in towards him, her eyes flashing with those same fires as before.

'There *will* be another raid, you fool. And another. And another. And our forces are dwindling. Do you *want* to lose everything that my mother fought for all her life?' She saw immediately by his expression that she had hit the mark with her first shot. She stood up straight, triumphant.

'I'm right, aren't I?'

'Don't be such an idiot, girl. Of course I do not want to see the Schwarzvolf fall. But... well...' The hesitation was carefully studied; a master stroke. Whatever else he may have been, Edan was a superlative dissembler.

'Well?' Eris prompted the rest of his sentence and he raised his head to look at her sadly. His eyes were sunken in slightly yellowing skin, a by-product of failing organs that were accustomed to too much food and wine.

'I do not wish our people to be defeated. But it is not me who leads the warriors, is it? You are the one who is failing your mother's dream, Eris. Not I.'

She was incandescent at his words and as her hands clenched into fists, he wondered if perhaps he should have ensured he had a bodyguard detail whenever she came to see him. He let his moment of concern show as little more than a slight twitch under the right eye, which Eris was too angry to care about.

'I can't help it if the men under my command are weak and spineless. It is your feeble suggestion that we learn to till the land and harvest its bounty. It is *you* who is turning us into a weak tribe of wasted grass-eaters. I should lead my own army against your beloved farmers.'

That was it. That was the moment he had been waiting for. He pounced on it eagerly, his fat jowls wobbling with affected anger.

'You speak of open rebellion, Eris. You would rise up against your own uncle? I have always been the better choice to lead this tribe and you know it. You are impetuous, like your mother before you, but you are not gifted with her quick mind. That was your sister's gift, may the gods protect her in the hereafter.'

'Never mention her in front of me.' Eris clenched and unclenched her hands until they ached. 'And in whose eyes are you the better choice, Edan?' Eris fingered the hilt of her dagger. 'I'll tell you. Yours. That's whose. There are none within this camp who would follow your call to battle and even if there were, they would be the farmers and the fools. And my warriors would slaughter them where they stood.'

'Are you challenging me?' He raised his voice slightly. It would not take much to alert others to any potential predicament he found himself in.

She thought about it. She thought about it seriously. If the fat old bastard would not let her take control, she could simple reach out and snatch it away from him. But before Bellona had been taken away, she had always told Eris to wait. She heard her sister's voice in her head as clearly as though her beloved twin stood beside her once again.

A fool like Edan will eventually dig his own grave, my sister. All we have to do is wait until he stands at its edge… and then we push him in.

How easy it would be to push right now.

The two of them stood there in silence, both too stubborn to back away from the brewing argument. In the end, it was Eris who capitulated.

'I hope when you die, Edan, that I am there to witness it. I will savour every moment of your demise.'

'Are you threatening to murder me?'

Her eyes narrowed. 'No,' she said. 'Because then, I wouldn't be able to watch and enjoy it. You are safe from death at my hands, *Godspeaker*.'

With that, she spun on her heel, marching out of the tent and leaving the Godspeaker to dark thoughts.

RUMOURS OF A gathering army in the north had already begun to cross the mountains. This pleased Valkia greatly, for she had ensured it was the case. It had been easy enough for her to fly beyond the borders of the frozen peaks, allow herself to be seen.

It was a glorious thing to ride the winds and soar with the creatures of the sky. She invariably chose night time to make her appearance, understanding with intuitive malevolence that terrifying as she may be to the soft-bellied people of the south during the day, her true terrible beauty was only enhanced by the velvet cloak of night. Those who saw her read the omens and spread the word of the monster in the north. The monster, they said, that was coming for them.

She built the effect gradually and when she allowed herself to scream that she would seek and slaughter the Schwarzvolf, the rumours became frenzied. Soon, word of Valkia's existence would spread further to the south. Soon, her former people would be aware that the daemon princess was seeking them. She knew that there were those amongst the tribe who would have wisdom enough to fathom out who the monster might be. The thought filled her with warm, spiteful pleasure. That feeling swiftly became an all-consuming hunger to spill their blood.

It would be a wondrous thing to tear them apart, limb from limb.

She *wanted* the Schwarzvolf to know that they were being hunted. She *wanted* them to live in constant fear of the retribution that blew with untempered force from the roof of the world. She would hunt them down until the tribe was wiped from existence.

Such thoughts of revenge occupied her almost constantly and during battles with the warped marauders of the wastes, she killed more than one unfortunate she imagined wore the face of the cowards who had left her to die.

By day she sat upon her graven throne and watched as ever more followers flocked to her banner, eager to spill blood for Khorne and gather skulls in his name. It was not a harmonious existence as rival war bands drew together in the sprawling camp and came to blows, warring for supremacy amongst the horde and dragging the defeated before Valkia to offer her their heads. Grisly trophies adorned every tent and banner pole.

This woman-creature was idolised by the marauders who were harbouring her and she revelled in their adulation to the point of decadence. There was one individual who took pleasure in observing this.

Such indulgence, Valkia. What a disappointing bride you must be for the Lord of Blood. I will always maintain that you made the wrong choice of patron, no matter what you say.

The voice had come into her mind, dusty, dry and deeply sarcastic whilst she had been enjoying the battles of her new subjects.

'Locephax!'

She spat the daemon prince's name and snatched up her shield. Since Khorne had taken his hand to it, the crude nails that had held his head rigid had been removed. Now, Locephax was an integral feature of the shield, which had grown in size and stature. The face of the monster stared out from its eternal prison, locked in swathes of the same daemon leather that covered the plates of Valkia's armour.

The cruel mouth turned upwards in a smile at the warrior queen's attention and Locephax spoke aloud.

'You look different,' he observed. 'Did you change your hair?'

'Still your tongue, slave,' she countered, her eyes blazing with red fury. 'You are mine to command. You would do well to remember that before you speak. It would take but a stitch to close your mouth permanently.'

But I can always speak to you, Valkia. I may be enslaved by your child-god, but I am not without power of my own.

She was quiet for a long period as she gathered her thoughts together. She had all but forgotten the infuriating nature of the Slaaneshi daemon that she held in thrall, but was quietly grateful that he had spoken up. He was right. Caught up in the wave of fanatical worship, she had forgotten herself. But not any longer.

'Enough,' she said. 'Speak no more. I have an army to raise.'

With a smirk, Locephax closed his eyes and was still

once more. He may be forever bound to the consort of Khorne, but he had been considerably powerful in his own right. Just because he had to serve her, he did not have to do so willingly.

NONE COULD AGREE on a description. Some said that the airborne daemon that flew on wings of night from the realm of the gods was a faceless creature. Others swore that the monster possessed a very definite feminine shape. No single person claimed to have looked upon its visage and lived.

She – he – *it* – appeared only at night, a silhouette against the light of the moons and these sightings were rarely corroborated. From the whispered rumours, exaggerated stories evolved with an alacrity that defied belief.

Without solid facts, the story of the winged beast became something uncontrollable. It grew in size, picking up speed as grave tales were told around camp fires. Within days, it had spread to neighbouring tribes, growing and becoming more terrible with each retelling. Small children believed that if they were punished, the 'crimson daemon' would come for them and feast on their flesh or make off with their soul.

Within days, the tale had a life of its own.

Within a few more, they would stop being stories and start to become harsh, terrifying realities. After Valkia and her army surged from the north, there would be no more stories. There would only be bloody slaughter.

* * *

THERE HAD NEVER been any doubt at all that the marauders would follow her into battle and as Valkia had watched them stream up the pass, wearing an assortment of crude armour made by their own mad smiths and that which they had scavenged over the years, she felt a swell of pride. These were warriors who may not have possessed the sense of unity of a disciplined fighting force like she had groomed the Schwarzvolf to be, but who were wild and savage in their ferocity and bloodlust.

In the course of a few short days, barely two weeks, she had wrought them from a manic force of disparate tribes and war bands into something entirely more terrible. The most formidable warriors she set as squad commanders and they embraced the role with eagerness, frequently doling out surprisingly creative punishments to their less intelligent underlings.

They fought viciously and were entirely without fear. More than one of the influx had seen fit to challenge Kormak's position at the head of the army. All of them, man, woman or beast, had died without coming remotely close to making so much as a dent in the warrior's armour, but their efforts had been pleasing.

Valkia found herself fascinated by her champion. Her memories of Kormak as a human were fragmented and disjointed by the inconstant passage of time. She knew that he could not have been as imposing as he was now. That she had created something so physically impressive and intimidating was testament to her sheer potency. When Kormak took his place at the head of the horde, ready to lead the march south, he struck an impressive figure.

Valkia rose into the air, her wings barely moving, and gazed down on the serpentine, irregular line. It was a formidable gathering of warriors and she knew that there would be many battles on the way. She also knew that some of the beings and creatures that called the storm-lashed mountains home would instantly give her their allegiance, recognising in her the same thing that the Chosen had done.

Many of these warriors, mutated and warped into monstrous things that could barely pass as human, would die on the journey south. The fact they not only didn't care but were eager to do so was more than satisfactory.

It matters not whose blood is spilled. Only that it is spilled.

'Your wish is my command, my lord and master,' she murmured aloud before screaming the order to march. They would gather allies and numbers as they travelled. Everything else would be incidental.

THE FIRST THING they encountered was glorious battle. Within hours of breaking camp and beginning their ascent, the first of the Chosen's rival tribes struck at them.

They came through the dry, petrified forest that clung to the mountainside above the cave system that the Chosen called home and they struck with a force that took the armoured vanguard completely by surprise.

Valkia grudgingly gave them a modicum of respect when one of the first to attack went straight for

Kormak. She gave no order, preferring instead to drop into the main battle. Her champion was more than capable of dealing with his own situation.

The threat was greeted joyfully and the Chosen threw themselves at their enemy with a vigour that demonstrated their fearlessness perfectly. Engaged in a battle with a burly warrior who was naked but for the fur loincloth that covered his groin, Valkia's attention flitted around the battlefield. This was the first time she had been in true battle since she had been reborn and everything was so different, so alive and filled with the promise of glory.

Whenever blood was spilled, her senses fired. She could scent the opening of every wound as though it had happened on her own body. The pervading odour of copper and salty vitae that swiftly dominated her olfactory senses drove her into a frenzy. She needed to spill blood in a way she had never needed before.

The very thought of it sent every part of her body into a wild frenzy. She began to salivate in anticipation and her tensed muscles sang with the sheer thrill of carrying out her grisly duty. She raised Slaupnir high above her head and screamed out *his* name. It rang out in the still, winter air and then the clash of weapons overrode everything.

The berserker rage took hold of not only Valkia, but many of her army as well, and they threw themselves into the fray with frenzied madness. What ensued could not be described as a clean or ordered fight in any way. The opposing sides were unbalanced from the beginning, the attackers relying on their advantage of surprise, but Valkia's army were entirely more bloodthirsty and threw caution completely to the wind.

Kormak thundered through the throng of fighting bodies, his massive daemonic axe swinging in powerful overhead strokes that split more than one of the enemy from throat to hip, spilling their innards in a glistening pile. One blow landed with such brutal force that an entire top quarter of the unfortunate man's body was sheared away and slid messily to the ground. The remainder of the ruined corpse stood for a second or two, gore and bile spewing forth in fountains before it was crushed to paste beneath the bulk of the rampaging juggernaut. The champion stooped in the saddle and delivered a blow to his next target that opened his ribcage in a welter of ragged flesh and shattered ribs. The frenzied daemonic jaws chewed hungrily at the meat, consuming the barbarian's throbbing heart with a keening wail of pleasure.

Valkia noticed very little of this. For her, the entire fight passed in a semi-conscious haze of red. All that mattered was the total and utter annihilation of those who stood between her and her revenge. Perhaps it was this thought that dragged her from the maddened state of bloodlust and brought her up sharply.

Spreading her wings, the warrior queen rose into the air above the battlefield.

'Warriors of the north!' Her voice rang out loud and clear, audible to all. 'Warriors of the north, I give you a choice.' Her wings beat gently, a hypnotic rhythm and the sound of her voice was compelling. Slowly, very slowly, the battle force on the ground beneath her slowed until all, Chosen and enemy alike, were staring up at the beautiful, blood-spattered woman who gazed down on them.

'The choice is simple. You can lay your weapons at my feet. Follow me and the host of the Blood God and know reward like you have never known.'

She gave them a smile, slow, sensuous and winning. Her beautiful, alabaster-pale face positively glowed with a feigned benevolence that was at odds with the ribbons of scarlet that marred her skin. The blood that had been spilled on her armour went unnoticed, absorbed into the plates forever. 'I promise you this. My lord is a generous one. Those who serve him well do not go unnoticed. Join me now and you will revel in conquest and bloodshed.'

'And if we do not?' One voice rose above the hushed awe that had spread around the remainder of the battlefield.

'Are you so foolish that you do not know our creed? It is a simple thing to decide, barbarian. Death... or glory. But I suggest you decide quickly.' Gangly, crimson-skinned creatures were prowling through the throng toward the enemy tribe, their wicked blades still hungry for blood. Valkia dropped to the battlefield and walked towards the man who had spoken. Despite the hoofed feet in which her long, slender legs now ended, she walked with easy grace and with an exaggerated feminine sway to her hips which may have been intentional.

The Chosen watched her with sheer adoration evident in their eyes as she stood before the barbarian. She cupped his chin in her hand and gave him a smile.

'Which will it be, sweet one?' Her lips parted slightly in a pout and she closed her eyes briefly. It was an almost demure gesture. Her long lashes brushed her cheekbones. When they opened again, he saw the truth of her words. He stared into those daemonic, burning eyes and was hopelessly lost.

'Glory,' he whispered brokenly, and was rewarded with a dazzling smile that made him fall eternally in love with the Blood Queen. 'Give me glory.'

'As you wish,' she said and drove Slaupnir through his gut. He did not cry out, but spread his arms wide, welcoming the death that had to come before he received his reward.

All around the battlefield, voices rang out in indignation at what was seen as a blatant betrayal of one of their own and for a moment or two, it looked as though the fight would recommence. As the body of the half-naked barbarian slid gracelessly to the ground, Valkia tugged Slaupnir free and drew her wings tightly around herself momentarily like a leathery cocoon. She raised one hoofed foot and placed it squarely on the dead man's chest.

'Thus does my master reward the loyal,' she whispered down into his unseeing eyes. She stooped down and with one delicately clawed finger carved the angular rune of Khorne into the dead man's forehead. Blood welled up from the cuts and spilled down his face in thick, scarlet streams. With a rush of air, her wings stretched out to their full span and she threw back her head. Her arms reached for the skies above and she felt the gift of her consort's power thrum through her.

'I give you glory,' she said loudly. 'Rise up, my loyal subject. Live once more in service of the Blood God. You see this?' She gestured to the body, her eyes raking the warriors on the field. 'Witness this. *This* is true glory. The moment you understand.' The corpse spasmed under her foot and she stepped off him, reaching down a hand to aid him to his feet.

He staggered slightly as he retained his balance, but then took his place at Valkia's side and brandished his sword in triumph. There was a wild, fey light in his eyes, devoid of any trace of humanity and a feral snarl of bloodlust distorted his features into something monstrous.

A silence lingered, but then across the battlefield, the former enemy fell to their knees one by one, awed at such a display of power. Their voices rose in a swell, repeating the one word over and over until it was all that could be heard.

'Glory!'

Valkia's lips drew back in a hungry and eager smile. 'Deliver them to my side,' she said to her newest subject. 'Bring them everlasting glory.'

SHE HAD STORMED from her uncle's presence and her angry feet had taken her far from home. Eris was not alarmed to realise how long she had been walking. She often came out to the hunting grounds by herself. It had been a habit borne from years of losing her temper. Walking calmed her, she had always found.

Once, Bellona would have come after her.

Eris could still not quite articulate just how much

she missed her sister. Ever since her twin's violent death, her world had become a darker place. She had grieved for the loss of her mother in an almost detached way. Valkia had never really shown much in the way of affection towards her children. But Bellona had been her twin. Her *other* half. To lose that was as agonising as losing a limb.

Bereft of her twin's calming influence, Eris had thrown herself into the skirmishes and battles that occupied the Schwarzvolf. It had not been until a number of years had passed that the young woman had realised that they were no longer fighting to conquer. Now, they were fighting simply to survive. Tribes who had once rallied to Valkia's call had turned against them.

From being the greatest, most powerful tribe, the Schwarzvolf were little more than a pale shadow of their former selves.

Eris dropped down beneath the ancient tree that marked the very edge of the Schwarzvolf territorial boundaries. Sited halfway up a small hill, it had always afforded a superb view of not only the Vale, but of the surrounding lands. Usually, there were lookouts stationed up here. Eris noted with a sour face, that nobody was here. She would have to speak to her uncle about that.

Since Hepsus had died at her hands, there had been no long-term Warspeaker, although Eris herself had offered to take on the role. She had been humiliated in front of the Circle when Edan had said that she was too immature, too inexperienced to lead the Schwarzvolf's armies into battle. A succession of young men had taken the position only to fall in the endless struggles for supremacy.

Staring down over the Vale, Eris's eyes narrowed as she thought. For too long now she had put up with her uncle's self-destructive ways. For the first few years, Bellona's hand had stayed her from simply slotting a knife into his gut. After her sister's death, a sense of duty to her dead sibling had held her back. But his words this morning had finally pushed Eris to a place where there was only one thing on her mind.

Edan must die. His continued existence threatened the continued survival of the tribe. His gluttony was unbearable to watch and above anything else, she detested him. Blood-related he may be, but she had never liked him. Once so softly spoken and confident, he now oozed arrogance from every pore that stank almost as much as the rest of his unwashed body.

Staring across the Vale, the sprawling settlement of the Schwarzvolf was vast and industrious. The insipid farmers were gathering in the last of the year's crops, ready for the winter and there were children running everywhere. But there was no clash of steel. There were no shouts that had always accompanied the endless combat in the Circle of Blood that had once marked the warrior tribe.

They were soft-bellied and vulnerable. The Schwarzvolf would die if something did not happen soon. And it was up to her to salvage whatever she could of her mother's legacy.

Leaning back, her eyes closed, Eris allowed herself to meditate quietly. She had never been very good at the practise; clearing her mind had never come easily. She could rarely concentrate on any one thing for long enough to keep her mind focused. But today was different. Today, she had something to focus on.

The faintest of smiles crept onto her lips as she envisioned how much pleasure she would glean from taking her uncle's life.

THE SCOUT ARRIVED back in the Vale three days later. Despite his desire to live a 'peaceful life' as he put it, Edan ensured that scouts were regularly dispatched to keep abreast of occurrences in the lands beyond his immediate remit, a world that was getting smaller and smaller by the day.

'Rumours,' said the scout when pressed for news. 'Rumours and wild tales are circulating. An army marches from the far north, from the realm of the gods themselves. If the rumours are to be believed, this horde is heading southwards.' He took a long drink of water. He was looking flustered and anxious.

'We have handled would-be invaders before.' Edan shrugged off the news with indifference. The scout reached up a tentative hand and gripped the other man's arm.

'I only have the stories I was told to go by,' he said, his eyes wide and more than a little afraid. 'But this is no rogue war band of mindless wildmen! The army is swelling in size as it travels. They are led by a winged daemon in blood-red armour.'

'Myths, legends and campfire tales,' sneered Edan and with that, he dismissed the threat as ridiculous.

'How can you be so sure?' Eris asked the question.

Startled, Edan turned. He had not even heard her approach. 'We are surrounded by enemies. From what you and Hepsus said, my mother may have angered countless others on her journey north. Perhaps they have merely been biding their time. Waiting for…' Her eyes glittered and her top lip drew back in a sneer. 'Waiting for just the *right* moment to strike.'

Edan sensed, without knowing how, that there was something more than just a warning about a potential attacking army implicit in Eris's voice. For the first time, he suddenly saw his niece as a genuinely serious threat.

She needs to be dealt with.

The thought swept through him and he returned her sneer with a friendly smile.

'It has been many years, child,' he said in his most condescending tone. Eris, who had long since grown to womanhood, always found it irritating and well he knew it. 'If some paltry tribe in the north was offended by our victories over their feeble warriors, they have had many long years to strike back. Why now?' He waved a dismissive hand and poured himself more wine. 'It is ridiculous to believe such talk.'

'And the rumours of the daemon at the head of the army? You think that is something that can easily be dismissed? Surely you do not so swiftly forget the creature who challenged my mother?' Eris spat on the ground. 'Was that ridiculous?'

She had found a weak spot in Edan's armour of self-confidence. Memories of the daemonic thing that had battled Valkia and laid waste to the Schwarzvolf frequently returned in his dreams. He had never been

able to truly reconcile its existence. The sheer power
the thing had possessed, even when decapitated and
mounted on his sister's shield, had fed his curiosity
and in turn had given him a lust for power.

Eris ran her fingers through her hair, then stood
firm, her hands planted squarely on her hips.

'I suggest that we heed these rumours of coming
war. I believe we should send scouts into the mountains to watch the peaks and passes. Such an army
could not move unnoticed and we need to know if
there is a real threat. Because perhaps it may not even
be a threat at all.'

'I do not think…'

'That much is evident, Uncle.'

It was a swift reply that took Edan completely by
surprise. His jaw dropped slightly and Eris took the
immediate opportunity to assert her authority.

'Our numbers are declining. Our ability to defend
ourselves is becoming weak at best. If there is a legion
of warriors travelling this way, then perhaps we could
approach them. Consider an alliance.' Eris gave the
scout a winning smile. 'We could regain some of the
strength that made us the greatest, most feared tribe
for so long. The Schwarzvolf *will* be great again.'

The scout nodded eagerly. Like many of the tribe's
younger warriors, his memories of their time under
Valkia's leadership were broken and vague. He had
been little more than a child when Valkia had led her
army north. His memory, when forced to recall his
former leader, remembered a beautiful face, a strong
soul and a leader who knew every man, woman and
child under her leadership by name.

Those same memories never recalled the cruelty, the harsh punishments that she would mete out to those who disappointed her, or the screams that came from the tortured souls who dared try to take Schwarzvolf land.

How easy it was to forget.

The scout's heart swelled with eager pride at Eris's words and the young woman turned to her uncle with a look of vindictive triumph on her face.

'You see, Uncle? Not all of us have lost faith in our heritage.'

Determined not to let the little witch get the better of him, Edan regained his composure swiftly. He nodded, putting what he hoped was a sincere expression on his face. 'You speak true words, my child,' he said in an imperious tone. 'And you are quite, quite right. We will send out scouts as you suggest.'

'An excellent plan, Uncle,' Eris treated him to a rare smile of genuine pleasure. He had acted just as she had anticipated.

'Perhaps you might want to lead them?' It was an immediate counter. And Eris agreed readily. Just as Edan had known she would. Whatever it was she was scheming was as nothing next to the plan he was formulating himself.

VALKIA SAT PERCHED on a rocky outcrop, the full moons bright behind her. Her slender form was perfectly silhouetted. To anyone looking up into the night sky, she seemed so still as to be a statue. Her head was raised slightly, the curving horns sweeping gracefully from her head. The wings that bore her aloft and gave her such mastery of the skies were partially opened as she retained her balance.

The shield bearing the head of Locephax was strapped to her arm and Slaupnir lay at rest beside her. Far beneath her, the army of men, beasts and fell creatures was gathered in near silence. There was none of the laughter and camaraderie that the tribal war parties enjoyed, but this was in part due to the nature of Valkia's followers.

They sat in disparate groups, each eyeing the other with wary respect. Through half-lidded eyes, Valkia considered them. They were violent berserkers for the most part. Some were barely even still human. In the space of a few short days, they had killed so many and slaughtered so willingly in Khorne's name that it took every mote of self-control to stop themselves tearing each other limb from limb.

A winged creature of the night, a bat, perhaps, flew past the daemon princess and she sniffed the air in its wake. The creature smelled of the high, pine woods. Valkia's army had travelled far enough to reach the vast forest that hugged the southern slopes of the mountains. The next few days would take them beyond its borders and into the bleak troll country.

She knew she would not struggle to bind them to her will. Already a number of other misshapen, twisted monsters who roamed the rim of the blighted wastes stalked the shadows surrounding the horde. Chimerae, great wolves and slinking reptilian things clung to the darkness, drawn to the promise of blood. The trolls would seem almost mundane next to some of the monstrosities who loped behind the army, not wishing to get close to the warriors, but desperate to serve their queen. She tipped her head imperceptibly to peer into the gloom. She could see these malefic creatures, moving about in the hard shadows cast by the light of such bright moonlight.

The gathering force beneath her was a tool. It would break upon the Schwarzvolf with the name of Khorne raised in adulation. Both sides would die in droves, but that was all she craved; blood and skulls and endless slaughter. Her army, those who followed and served her, would receive their reward when they reached the red plains of the Blood God.

Those who had betrayed her...

Valkia's fingers, each topped with curved talon-like nails closed tightly around the rock she was gripping. It crumbled beneath her touch and tiny fragments fell to the ground below in a shower of particulate dust.

She unfurled her wings and rose into the night sky. In a matter of days, battle would be joined. There was little time to spend planning the revenge she so sought, but there would be an eternity in which to relish it.

SIXTEEN
Nightmares and Dreamscapes

HIS DREAMS WERE getting worse with each passing day, but Edan could not let anybody see the state in which he woke. Sweat bathed his night garments, soaking into the rough blanket under which he slept. His thinning hair was plastered to his skull and his breath came in shallow gulps when he jolted awake.

At one time, Edan had entertained the company of his pick of the young women of the tribe. Ten years ago, he had been desirable. No issue ever came forth from him, despite his best efforts to produce children. It had been a constant thorn in his side. If he had been able to produce an heir, his stake on the Schwarzvolf throne would be that much stronger.

Now he was not a desirable or coveted man. His decadent lifestyle had padded out his once-slender frame grotesquely. He rarely bathed and he had a reputation for violent rages that meant the women of the tribe largely avoided him. He was still reluctantly afforded the respect due the tribe's Godspeaker however.

Edan could not pinpoint the exact moment that his

life had gone out of his immediate control. Perhaps it had been in the darkest reaches of the north, when the head of Locephax the daemon prince of Slaanesh had whispered promises of great reward...

Pushing himself up from the pallet upon which he slept, Edan crossed to the bowl of ice water and splashed it on his face, trying to shed the clinging vestiges of the nightmare. He pinched the bridge of his nose between thumb and forefinger as though that could somehow chase away the headache that throbbed at the base of his skull.

He picked up a piece of clothing, one of the out-size tunics that were all that fit his rotund frame any more. He drew it on over his head and dragged fingers through his still-damp hair. An appalling stink of alcohol hit him and he realised with alarm that it was him. Not the tunic, although that was reasonably pungent in its own right, but Edan himself. The sweat had chased all the lingering alcohol from the previous night's excess from his pores.

'I should bathe,' he mused, then immediately discounted the idea when his stomach growled in hunger. For Edan, the path to decadence had not come at the price of lust and sexual perversion. For him, it had been an entirely different route. But the touch of Locephax on his weak mind had been irreversible. The damage had been done and he was a slave of the god he knew as the Reveller.

It was, perhaps, a mercy that his corruption was entirely contained. The majority of the tribe had retained such strong warrior urges that his attempts to seduce them to what he called the finer things of

life mostly fell on deaf ears. So he kept his gluttony
and sloth to himself and enjoyed every moment he
spent forcing food and wine down his throat. He
was lazy and indifferent to the problems that the
Schwarzvolf were suffering.

The nightmares were most likely a byproduct of all
the rich food and alcohol that he was consuming. He
told himself that on a regular basis in the hope that it
might explain the sheer horror of his sleeping hours.

His head was pounding and he sat down on the
hard, carved wooden seat at the end of his pallet-
bed. Leaning back, he scratched at the wild, unkempt
beard on his chin and closed his eyes.

The horror of the dream slammed back into his
skull with an intensity that set his fat body quivering.
He gripped the arms of the chair as though he were
pitching into a fit and fell headlong into the terror
that welled up in him.

'Where am I'?

His voice echoed around the landscape. Everything
was tinged with a hint of red as though his pupils
bled. He felt a tremendous urge to reach up and rub
vigorously at them to clear his vision, but he could
not move anything but his head.

No answer came to his question, so he called out
once again. He felt the faintest of brushes against his
cheek as though something flew past him and tried
to move away. Whatever was holding him rigid...

He glanced down. Ropes lashed around his body,
holding him firmly against a wooden pole that was
driven into the ground. The thick coils bound around

him like a serpent, holding him tightly. He could not feel them, but surely they must be biting into his flesh.

'This is not real,' he called into the emptiness. 'I am not really here. I am dreaming.'

'That's as maybe,' came a whispering voice. It was barely a voice at all, more a low purr. Edan was immediately reminded of the mountain lions that had plagued their trip to the Northern Wastes. There had been one foolish boy who had tried fighting one and lost his arm. 'You may be dreaming this, Edan, son of Merroc, but this is as real as I want it to be.'

He felt that same brush against his face and flinched. There was nobody here with him, unless they stood directly behind the stake, just out of his extreme peripheral vision. The thought made his bowels twist with anxiety.

The touch on his cheek ended abruptly and he heard a new sound. Wings, beating slowly. A faint breeze that lifted his thin hair from his head. His breathing came in low rasps, his chest restricted by his bonds.

'Who are you? What is this?' His voice was rising in pitch and urgency and it was all he could do not to scream his terror into the darkness. The reply came to him in multiple voices, from different directions, and still no sign of the speaker.

'I am the guilt that has hunted you all these years, Edan.'

'I am the harbinger of your demise.'

'I am the nightmare in all mortals. I am the thing you fear the most.'

'I am death.'

Edan began to cry like a babe. Huge tears formed in the corners of his eyes and rolled unchecked down his cheeks. 'I am dreaming,' he said.

'Dreaming? Yes.' Finally, the voice resolved into something much clearer. It was a female voice. 'But not for much longer. Soon, this dream will become your reality, Edan.'

He said nothing in response, merely hiccuped his misery as the tears continued to fall. The unseen enemy laughed spitefully.

'The great and powerful Edan. See him weeping like a child.'

'What do you want?' He wept the sentence out through his shameful tears. The silence following the question was aching in its length. Then he felt a clawed hand grab at his hair and pull his head back against the stake.

'Revenge.'

He could clearly feel the point of the blade as it entered his throat just below the left ear.

Then a sudden, terrible pain.

Then...

'GODSPEAKER? ARE YOU well?'

Edan's hand flew to his throat and he blinked rapidly to clear the haze of blood. He was sitting in the main council tent. The Circle were absent and try as he might, Edan could not recall at all the moment he had left his own tent and made his way there.

'What?' He stared around at the owner of the voice. It belonged to a young man who was vaguely familiar. He knew the boy. One of the tribe's scouts. The name escaped him and he did nothing to recall it. 'What do you mean? Of course I am well.' He hesitated. 'Why would I not be?'

'You were just sitting, staring off into space. As though you were having some sort of vision. Are the gods trying to send you a vision of what is to come?' The young scout was eager that this be the case. He had witnessed Edan's incoherent babblings before and always found it a thrilling thing to be in the presence of the gods themselves. That was how Edan explained it. He was merely a conduit through which the Four could communicate with their loyal followers.

'The gods? No. I...' Edan slowly removed his hand from his throat and gave a short laugh. 'I was, shame upon my soul, daydreaming. My attention drifted. I slept poorly last night and I am not as young as I used to be. Perhaps a cup of wine...' He let the sentence trail off. The young scout stared at him in fascination for a moment before realising it was an order rather than a suggestion.

'Of course, Godspeaker.' Without a further word, the youth disappeared from the tent to fetch Edan's wine, leaving the man alone. Groaning softly, Edan let his head drop into his hands.

'I am going mad,' he muttered to himself. He genuinely had no recall of the time spent between waking and moving to the tent of the Circle. Had there even been a meeting? Had he sat through it like some sort of fool?

Perhaps you are *mad,* came that female purr in the

back of his mind. It was a horrible sensation, as though the inside of his skull was itching. *Perhaps you are still asleep. Perhaps this is all still a part of your dream.*

'No,' he said aloud. 'No. This is real.' He lifted his arm. He was not restrained or tied in any way. There was no blood on his body and he could feel the bite of the air outside the thick hide tent. 'This is who I am. I am Edan, son of Merroc. I am the rightful chieftain of the Schwarzvolf tribe. I am...'

'You are talking to yourself.'

Eris stood in the entrance of the tent, that infuriating sneer on her face. In her hand, she held the cup that the scout had fetched. She had intercepted him on his way back to the tent and informed him that she would deliver it herself. She had come into the tent to find Edan with his face in his hands, muttering to himself.

The Godspeaker straightened his back. The girl had caught him at a disadvantage, something she had a disturbing habit of doing. But he would not give her any satisfaction.

'And what of it?' His response was haughty. 'It is the only way to be sure of a truly intelligent conversation at the best of times.'

'Best not let the Circle hear you say that,' she said in a conversational tone that infuriated him. 'They already think you are on the path to madness.' She moved across and set the cup of wine down next to him.

'They do not,' he replied. 'Watch your tone, Eris.'

'You are so sure? Very well.' She shrugged one

slender shoulder. 'I will leave you to your ranting. I have things to be doing. She cast a brief, telling glance at the wine. 'Enjoy that, won't you?'

With that, she left the tent. Edan scowled after her back and leaned back in the chair. He mopped at his sweating brow and took up the cup of wine. He raised it to his lips.

Revenge comes in many forms, Edan.

The thought came unbidden and he stared at the cup. He would not have put it past Eris to poison him. Perhaps that was where these hallucinations were coming from.

With a bellow of fury, Edan threw the cup across the tent, the blood-red wine spilling as it went.

THEIR NUMBERS WERE swollen beyond anything Valkia had anticipated. It was as though their mere passage through the hills and mountains created a vortex that drew more to their bloodthirsty cause. The recruitment of the trolls had been a remarkably easy matter. On seeing Valkia descend from the skies, they had immediately grunted their acknowledgement of her rightful leadership and begun shambling along behind the marching army.

The faintest of memories tickled the back of Valkia's mind as she remembered the battle against them on their journey north. How the wheel turned.

Daily, they edged closer to the borders of Schwarzvolf lands. Daily, she invaded her brother's dreams with increasingly terrifying images and thoughts. The closer they were to Edan's location, the easier it became to torment her betrayer.

The army travelled mostly by night, when the wild and damned things of the darkness would crawl from their holes and slither in among the horde. Sometimes, Valkia would descend from the heavens and prowl among her devoted legion of killers. Her tread stained the earth with fresh blood and a hissing mob of daemons followed in her wake, butchering any that dared stray too close to their unholy queen. A pair of huge, carmine hounds stalked at her flanks, their jaws dripping fiery spittle and their broad necks adorned with tendrils of daemonic flesh that fanned out like blades.

They were her hunters, Khorne's peerless killers of men, and each night they would range far and wide around the marching army and sniff out barbarian scouts who thought themselves hidden from prying eyes. The tribes would not know of the doom that descended upon them until the axe was at their neck and their blood already stained the thirsty earth.

Her army needed no training, for they themselves were the weapon. They needed no food, for they feasted on the flesh of the fallen, and they needed no rest as Valkia drove them on with her iron will and inflamed their own insatiable lust for battle.

Their passage through the forest was met with no resistance. Everything that dwelt there either had sense enough to go into hiding or was eager to join with the daemon princess. By the time the land was levelling out, the slopes of the mountains falling behind them and the weather becoming bitingly cold, the hunger and thirst for the spilling of blood could no longer be contained and neither did Valkia attempt to contain it.

They were legion, out for war and out for revenge. But there were also bloody appetites that needed to be sated. And once they cleared the reaches of the far north, hunger for war became the ultimate driving force.

BY THE LIGHT of the setting moons, Valkia's army spilled into the settlement. Their approach had not gone undetected and the resident warriors were ready for an attack. The settlement belonged to a tribe who had once proudly flocked to the banner of the Schwarzvolf, but had long since broken away to resume their prior independence. They had been one of the many.

The Queen of Skulls was not to know that they no longer swore allegiance to her former tribe. As far as she was concerned, they had arrived at the doorstep of her enemy and she unleashed her horde upon them without compunction.

The arrival of Valkia's army had not been anticipated for several days, but the force that surged across the steppe had become vast and the earth shook beneath their tread, heralding their approach. The tribes of the north were always prepared for battle however. Within minutes of catching sight of the foe bearing down on them, they had ensured that their young and vulnerable were already on their way to the nearby cave system where they took shelter when absolutely necessary.

When the first cries of 'enemy approaching' were heard, they stood ready. But for all their experience and ferocity, they were ill-equipped and totally underprepared for the reality that followed.

A preliminary wave of warriors led the charge, their feet thundering as they gained momentum in their eagerness to slaughter. They were met with fierce but entirely inadequate resistance.

Starved of battle during the trek through the mountains, Valkia's army ripped their way through the helpless barbarians without mercy, killing every living thing that stood in their way. When the last of the people had been slain, they started on the livestock. As the last of the creatures fell beneath a battle-axe they turned upon each other.

Valkia herself did not join in until it reached the closing stages. When her own warriors fell on one another like the animals they were, she merely watched for a while, enjoying the slaughter. There was something maternal about seeing these beasts and warriors turn on one another. Each understood clearly the basic tenet of the Blood God.

'It matters not from whence the blood flows,' she intoned as she stalked through the battle. In her wake, the fighting gradually ceased. Those who still lived and were able to drop to their knee, or incline their heads in a respectful bow, did so. 'So long as it flows.' At her side rode the ever-silent Kormak, his mighty blade sheathed across his back.

The camp had been rendered into little more than a charnel house, an occasionally twitching mound of corpses that had been torn apart. Blood, gore and faecal matter loaned a foul stench to the air that, for Valkia, merely added an olfactory highlight to the sweet taste of murderous revenge.

'Where are your women and children?' Valkia reached down and easily hauled up a mortally wounded warrior. The man was a pitiful wreck. One eye had been burst by troll-vomit and ran in a jelly down his bloodied cheek. His tunic was soaked through with red and his life was measured in minutes.

'Safe,' came the croaked reply. 'Where you will never find them.'

'Never is a long time, mortal,' Valkia crooned softly. 'And unlike you, time is something I have plenty of. You may be on the verge of death, but I have ways of keeping you here for as long as I wish. Why suffer the torments of the flesh that will be visited upon you? Tell me what I want to know and you earn yourself a swift end.'

'I will not betray...'

'Betrayal?' Valkia threw the man to the ground and he lay still. He was not quite yet dead, but something told him that he may stand a better chance of survival if he feigned otherwise. 'You *dare* speak to me of betrayal? When I was betrayed by those I led to greatness? It is my sworn vow that the tribes of the Schwarzvolf will *burn!*' Her voice rose in pitch until she was screaming her fury at the dying warrior.

'I will tear them down one man at a time if I must. There will be no mercy.' She had already determined not to give them the choice of death or glory. For the betrayers, there would be only the long darkness of oblivion. She put her cloven-hoofed foot on the neck of the unfortunate barbarian. 'Now tell me what I want to know. Where are the rest of your people?

Or should I have my pets hunt them down in their craven holes?'

One of the immense beasts lowered its drooling muzzle to sniff at the wounded warrior and a tectonic rumble sounded deep in its cavernous chest. Crimson lips peeled back to expose fangs as long as a man's arm and its tiny eyes glittered with undisguised malice.

'My attentions will be... swifter, to say the least,' Valkia purred.

'I will... never...' He began to speak, and with a faintly bored expression, Valkia exerted extra weight on her foot. The villager heard the bone at the top of his spine crack loudly. The pain, which followed a split second later, was excruciating. He had so little strength that he could not even scream and a gasp of agony left his mouth. Moments later, a barely comprehensible stream of words was uttered.

'Caves. They're in the caves.'

'Of course they are.' With a nonchalant movement, Valkia stamped down on the man's spine. His back broke in two instantly and the body arched backwards at an unnatural angle. The light in his eyes died out slowly and she savoured it. After a few moments, she stood clear of the corpse.

'Kormak.' She beckoned her champion close. 'There are matters I must attend to in preparation for the slaughter that awaits us. Therefore, I leave this hunt to you. Find the caves. It should not be too difficult given the stench of weakness that seeps from these soft creatures.' She indicated some of the more feral amongst her army. More beast than man, they were burying their snouts in the gore and viscera that was on offer. 'Find the survivors and spill their blood in my name.' She gave him a radiant smile. 'Spare none.'

The champion nodded his understanding and set off to carry out his mistress's bidding. The daemon princess looked around at the camp, its tents and layout so reminiscent of things that she had pressed far into her memory, and a sneer marred her features.

'Burn it,' she said. 'Burn it all.'

THE RUMOURS BECAME reality in a far shorter space of time than Edan could ever have feared. The initial claims that a daemonic army was moving south had been shrugged off as overreaction. But the scout currently standing before the Circle brought different news.

'Speak.' Edan waved a hand in an indifferent manner towards the young man who was noticeably pink in the face from his exertions. The youth inclined his head respectfully.

'The Red Hawks are no more,' he said. Edan sat up a little straighter at this news. The Red Hawk tribe had been one of their former allies, in times past. They had been one of the first to break their ties following Valkia's death and had resumed their own independence. They had never been opposed to the Schwarzvolf, but there had always been a faint suspicion that they could turn at any time.

'When you say "no more",' Edan asked, voicing the question with obvious care, 'do you mean that they have been driven off their lands?'

'No, Godspeaker.' The scout accepted a cup of water gratefully and downed it. 'Two of our fastest runners have been sent to check over their camp. But word is that they have been slaughtered to a man. None have been left alive.'

'We will wait to hear from our men then,' declared Edan. 'This could be a trap on their part to draw us in.' Eris, sitting beside him, nodded her agreement at this.

'Foolish rumours can get out of hand too quickly,' she acknowledged, reaching an accord with her uncle for once. 'The question we should be addressing now is what we should do if these tales have any truth to them? We must track whoever carried out such an attack.'

Edan did not reply. If the Red Hawks, a fierce war band in their own right had truly been obliterated, then the Schwarzvolf faced a deadly enemy. But for now, these were unsubstantiated claims. He said nothing in response to Eris's rhetorical question and she answered it for him.

'I do not think that it would harm us to prepare for war. Just in case.' Around the tent, the other members of the Circle nodded eagerly. Eris glanced at the Godspeaker, but Edan was lost in his own thoughts. His dreams had come to haunt him again, only this time it seemed that the whispered promise that his death was imminent was moving uncomfortably towards reality.

'I... do not feel well,' said Edan, rising from Valkia's throne. 'I must go and rest.' Indeed, he suddenly felt sick to his stomach. An army was moving south, an army that showed no mercy. And if his dreams held any truth, he had a terrible suspicion that he knew who marched at their head.

It wasn't possible, he told himself repeatedly. She was dead. Hepsus had watched her die. She was gone. She could not hurt him.

Nonetheless, Edan did not sleep that night, afraid of what dreams may come to torment his darkest hours.

But the dreams came anyway.

'RELEASE ME, VALKIA.'

She ignored the whispering voice that tickled the very edges of thought and focused instead on the way ahead. Her army travelled with speed and purpose. The slaughter of the Red Hawks had slaked their thirst for blood for a short time, but it was a desire that could never truly be satisfied.

The warrior queen flew through the air above her surging army, although to call them an army was something of a misnomer. Somewhere in the dark recesses of her memory, she recalled organisation, ranks of warriors arranged according to their skills. The mob that crossed the snowy wastes beneath her was haphazard at best. There was little cohesion but for their shared desire to kill.

Other than the human warriors, the berserkers who stood as her vanguard, none of the creatures of Chaos served *her*. Not truly. They served Khorne without hesitation and to Valkia it mattered little. Blood would flow and more skulls would pile at the foot of the brass throne. The god would be pleased and his power would swell still further.

'Release me.'

The whisper came again and she glanced down at Locephax. The daemon prince was awake, his ethereal eyes glowing a virulent green.

'You keep asking me to do that, slave. And yet I have not done it. You are *mine* now. And you will do my bidding.' Her leathery wings flapped, bearing her further aloft. 'You offered me a reward and I refused then as I refuse you now. It is time to accept that I am greater in all things, Locephax. Your eternity will be much more sanguine.'

'Followers of the idiot-god will *never* be greater,' came the retort. 'You are creatures of reflex. Simple and thoughtless. Where is the pleasure in such mindless slaughter? To kill with a purpose, to savour the suffering of your victims, though? That is precisely what you are doing, my love.'

'Do not speak to me.'

'Are you afraid I tell you the truth? That your lust for revenge brings you pleasure? Ask yourself which god you truly serve, Valkia. It is not too late for you…'

'I said be *silent*!' Valkia unstrapped the shield from her arm and raised it before her so that her burning red gaze met that of the daemon prince. 'I am my master's consort. You may court me all you wish, Locephax, but I know my own way. Hold your tongue until I have need of your power.'

'What will you do to me otherwise, Valkia?' Locephax's sneering tone angered the warrior queen beyond measure. 'Kill me? Take my skull? I believe you have already done all you can. All I have left to torment you with is the truth. Grant me that much at least.'

She secured the shield to her back so that she could no longer see Locephax's face and beat her wings harder, driving the pace below to something much faster. The disembodied voice continued to taunt and complain behind her, but she lashed it with her fury and it dwindled into bitter silence. She had made her choice a long time ago.

Why, then, did the daemon continue to try to tempt her? She shook her head, scowling.

'I am Valkia,' she said, her tone strong and her voice clear. 'I am Valkia, known as the Bloody. The Gore-queen. I am the Bringer of Glory and I serve Khorne. Your words are meaningless, Locephax. So hold your tongue.'

As she flew onwards, leading the horde towards the Vale, she could hear the cruel laughter of the daemon prince behind her. Locephax was her gift, her reward, and she could bend the creature to her purpose when she so desired. But he was also her eternal curse.

She hated him.

So close to her goal, she channelled that hatred into a single bolt of rage that she hurled with supernatural might at her desired target.

'I know you are not real. You do not frighten me.'

Edan was back once more against the wooden stake, held rigid and immobile by invisible bonds. He could sense rather than see the presence of his tormentor.

'You should be terrified, Edan, son of Merroc. Why are you not afraid?'

'I know this cannot be real. I know that you cannot be real.'

'You seem very sure of yourself.' The creature of darkness moved around him and he tried with every ounce of strength in his body to turn his head to look at her. *Face your fears head on and they will no longer frighten you.* His own sister had taught him that when, as a mewling child, he had been afraid of his own dreams. But he could not move.

'Hepsus watched you die, Valkia.'

There was a laugh and a shifting in the darkness. The creature that shimmered into being in front of him began to take form and substance, ethereal tendrils of mist coalescing into a more tangible shape.

'So you acknowledge who I am, at least.'

Edan swallowed although it was difficult. The rope that was lashed around his neck was drawn excruciatingly tightly. 'I think I always knew,' he said after a period of silence. 'I think I always knew but did not accept the truth.'

'But you have said yourself, you know none of this is real.' The shape before him was now more than just air, but somehow distorted. The face was too blank, devoid of not just expression but of defining features. The shape, although clearly female, was also something he was not familiar with. It had been ten long years since Valkia's death... or at least her alleged death... and although time lessened the memory, Edan was almost entirely certain that his sister had possessed neither horns nor wings the last time he had seen her.

As if she sensed his thoughts, the female shape emitted a low chuckle. There was no amusement in the sound. 'Time,' she said, 'changes all things.'

'Indeed.' It was a useless response and Edan knew it was

nothing more than a verbal placeholder whilst he struggled to organise his thoughts.

'You are right, of course. None of this real.' His captor broke the lengthy pause. 'You are... how shall I put this delicately... a prisoner within your own mind. I have brought you here so that you understand why it is that you have to die.'

'We all die,' he countered, but his voice held none of the conviction of his words.

'Indeed,' she said sneeringly, mocking his feeble response of earlier. 'But most of us die gloriously. Some of us die well before our allotted time. Your death, Edan, will be neither glorious nor noble. You will die on your knees, screaming for mercy. And for you, my dear brother...'

She leaned forward and he could smell her breath. It was not unpleasant; it put him in mind of autumnal leaf mould. The earthy scents of the decay that permeated the air at the end of a Vale summer.

'For you, there will be none. Enjoy the last hours of your life, Edan, for that is what it has become measured in. Soon, it will end.'

With an effort he had not thought himself capable of, Edan pulled back his head and spat at the Valkia-thing. He awoke seconds later to the ringing sound of her derisory laughter.

SHE WAS CLOSE, of that there was no doubt. Edan had woken from the most recent dream in abject terror. Perhaps he could run. Perhaps he could gather up what mattered to him and flee from the oncoming storm of his sister's rage.

But where would he go?

The sheer inevitability of what was going to happen filled him with a strange kind of calm acceptance. If he could not flee, then he would stand his ground. He would show courage until the moment he died. The irony of the fact that he had spent his entire life seeking the easy way out was not lost on the Godspeaker. When Eris came to his tent, alerted by the sounds emanating from within, she found her uncle barely able to stand, laughing so hard that he was vomiting. Several empty wine bottles littered the floor at his feet and his intoxication was without doubt.

'Uncle, control yourself.' Eris put steel into her tone and that served only to make Edan laugh harder. The man was quite deranged, broken by the terrifying visions he had been suffering.

'Send out your warriors if you wish, Eris,' he said between choking gales of laughter. 'The Schwarzvolf are doomed either way. Stay here and be slaughtered. Head out to face the maelstrom and be destroyed in the effort.' He reached over and patted Eris on the cheek in a fond way. 'The ogre's choice, my dear. Die quickly or die slowly. Our death is assured.' He nodded solemnly, although the effect was somewhat spoiled by the thin trickle of drool that oozed from the corner of his mouth.

'Then if the gods have seen our end,' said Eris, her back straightening and defiance coming into her expression, 'then we will make it a glorious one.' With those words, she turned and strode to the tent's entrance. 'It is what my mother would have done.'

After she had said that, Edan stopped laughing.

'Your mother,' he whispered and then passed out

in a dead faint, inebriated beyond capacity to even stand any longer. With a disdainful sniff, Eris left her uncle face-down in a puddle of his own waste and began the task of preparing the Schwarzvolf for war.

SEVENTEEN
From Whence the Blood Flows

THE ARMY OF Valkia moved south like a roiling wave of devastation. Behind them they left nothing but ruin and death. They fed well and they did so with startling regularity. Those who needed blood to survive indulged their gluttonous appetites with every kill.

Increasingly suspicious of her uncle's erratic and unpredictable behaviour, Eris had decided to remain behind rather than accompany the scouts from the camp. It had proven to be a wise choice as not one of them had returned. That in itself had been warning enough. The warriors of the Schwarzvolf would not sit idle and wait for their enemy to invade the Vale. Eris gathered them together, delivering a rousing speech that put many of the tribe elders in mind of her mother. They would not wait to die at the hands of this unseen foe, she had cried with feeling. They would meet the threat head on.

Edan had been insensible after she had found him laughing in the tent and she had turned away from him in disgust. Her uncle's mind was lost and she had no time to give him any kindness or sympathy.

She bore such hatred for the man that she would have been hard pushed to spare him a kind word anyway. She had planned to leave him in the charge of the young and the infirm, those who could not take to the field of battle. He would be of no use to them once the fighting started. But he came anyway, spouting some incomprehensible nonsense about facing his destiny as the gods intended.

In this situation, Eris finally came into her birth-right. She had always been her mother's daughter but now she was able to move out of Valkia's considerable shadow. It didn't matter that her grasp of strategy was nowhere near the calibre of her mother's. It mattered only that she could lead the Schwarzvolf into war and that she could conduct herself with due deadly force at their head.

So the army of the Schwarzvolf marched north, their remaining scouts sent ahead of them. Better by far to be prepared for what they faced, even if they had barely any concept of the horror that approached.

The horde of Valkia moved steadily south. They had no need to send runners ahead of their force. Valkia had no need to prepare for what they faced at the end of the march. Moreover, she did not care. The ultimate battle would be but a formality, its details consigned to the vagaries of history. Her victory was assured. Her success was never in question.

The Schwarzvolf would die.

'It's too quiet.'

Night had fallen, bringing a chill that promised the first snowfall by dawn. The army of the Schwarzvolf, not gifted with the same unnatural strength and resilience of a daemon host, had paused in their march. It was a time to gather their strength, a time for reflection and preparation.

For Eris, it was also a time to look upon the heavily diminished numbers of the warriors. With so many of the former allied tribes breaking their ties to the Schwarzvolf, the host had been decimated. A head count had put their numbers at several hundred still, so it was still a force to be reckoned with. But at Valkia's zenith, her army had numbered well over a thousand.

The first party of runners still had not returned and Eris was beginning to wonder if their enemy had some breed of war-dog to sniff them out. Had she known the nature of the hounds stalking the darkness ahead of Valkia's monstrous legion she would have kept every man as close as possible.

'It's too quiet.'

Eris made the observation again, but she was speaking to herself. She had dismissed her battle commanders and had taken a walk away from the ribald laughter and conversation of the resting army. To her mind, such high spirits were inappropriate when their doom was coming towards them with relentless certainty.

And it *was* quiet, even given that it was the dead of night. Usually, there would be distant sounds of howling wolves, or the flitter of bat wings. But there was nothing. No night-time insects or any other ambient noise that Eris had always associated with the evening. Even the air was still, as though the world held its breath before the bloodshed to come.

Nothing but the dark and the cold and the chill of anticipation.

Eris stroked the whetstone down the length of her blade, comforted by both the motion and the sound. The soft *sching* of the stone on the steel brought confidence and familiarity. Readying the blade she wielded reminded her who she was; what her purpose was.

'I am Eris of the Schwarzvolf,' she said, raising her head to the moonlight that shone down on the chill plains of the north. 'I am the daughter of a warrior queen and I will lead my people to their victory or to their death. Either way...'

Sching.

'Either way, I will lead them. In the name of the Four, I do this thing.'

The words left her mouth, but they were mechanical and without any true feeling. They were words that she had learned from an early age and which she had repeated over and over in her life. She had prayed to gods she had once truly believed in, but in whom she had ultimately lost faith. Her uncle had fallen to the lure of the Reveller, that much was clear to her. Where her mother had walked the path of blood, her uncle had stumbled down the path of excess.

Edan *disgusted* her. His idle manner, his weak will and his pathetic attempts to play politics. That the people of the tribe still put stock in the words of nonsense he spouted infuriated her. Out of respect for them, she kept her tongue stilled when she really wanted to shout that he was nothing more than a charlatan. But he claimed, as he always had, to be the mouth of the gods and without proof otherwise the Schwarzvolf did not dispute the matter.

She had always suspected his hand in her sister's untimely death. Had she been able to prove it, she would have executed him publicly. His head would have made a delightful addition to the front gate of the camp.

Eris lightened her darker thoughts with this image for a while, her hand still stroking the whetstone down her sword edge. She was snapped out of her reverie, the moment broken by the shout of a single word.

'Enemy!'

THE SCHWARZVOLF FELL easy prey to the charge. So much so that Valkia was almost embarrassed for them.

Almost. She would have been embarrassed had she cared about the fate of her former people, but their laxity and idleness fatally revealed their flaws and weaknesses. And those were all she cared about.

She had dispatched a group of the berserker warriors to act as a herald for the arrival of the rest of her bloodthirsty horde and had taken the decision to fly at their back. A group of no less than fifty battle-hardened Chaos warriors charged at the Schwarzvolf line with screams on their lips and murder in their eyes.

The numbers were not great, but what the berserkers lacked in quantity they more than made up for with their insane ferocity. For them, all that mattered was the kill. They flung themselves at the Schwarzvolf without any care for their own safety or survival. Armed for the most part with battleaxes, some pitted and rusty with age, the berserkers fell upon the outermost group of Schwarzvolf before they could even get to their feet.

Three of Eris's warriors were cut down immediately, the enemy's axes buried in the soft meat of their brains. Those who were not hacked apart instantly retaliated by closing ranks around the rampaging wild men. The clash of weapons broke the eerie silence that Eris had noted and from her vantage point atop the hill, she could see the unfolding mêlée. She watched without emotion as the berserkers tore some of her people limb from limb and watched as her own people answered the call to battle in kind.

The enemy was attacking in small numbers, she noted, and knew that this was nothing more than a vanguard, a swift thrust driven in to test their defences. This mob was nowhere near the size of army she had been anticipating. This was just the tip of the blade. Behind it would come the mailed fist.

'Eris!' The voice calling her name was high pitched and she didn't recognise it at first. She ran lightly down the hill to join the rest of the army and make ready for the inevitable second wave.

'Eris!'

The call came again and she turned in irritation to see who demanded her attention at such a time. Her uncle stood a few feet away from her, practically weeping in terror as he pointed towards the fight.

'Eris, see there. She comes for me. For you. For *us*!'

The young woman turned to follow the line of

Edan's finger and her eyes widened in disbelief. Descending from the skies on leathery wings of darkest night was a monster clad in red armour.

From such a distance, Eris could not make out the monster's features, but could tell from the form-fitting armour that it was female in gender. Edan was on his knees, repeating the same words over and over.

'She comes for me... she comes for me...'

'Who is it? Edan! Damn you, you fat fool, answer me! Who *is* it? What do you know of such daemons, Godspeaker? Who is it?'

The Godspeaker, once so proud and arrogant, raised his tear-streaked face to his niece.

'Your mother,' he wept. 'Valkia comes!'

THE WARM COPPER smell of fresh blood was attracting the attention of the rest of Valkia's army, who were still perhaps half a mile away from the slaughter below. The warrior queen, from her vantage point in the skies above the battlefield, could see them creeping forward, defying her order to hold. She could not restrain them much longer, neither did she truly want to.

Her own lust for bloodshed was stoked to bursting with the scent of death that rose from below her. Holding aloft Slaupnir and her daemonic shield, she began the descent to join her warriors. She felt eyes upon her: eyes of both the Schwarzvolf and the eyes of her own army. She basked in the attention.

'I am the Blood Queen,' she screamed. 'I am the Bringer of Glory! I am the avatar of my beloved on the field of battle and I am here for the prize of your skulls. I am vengeance and I am death!' Her wings were spread wide as she plunged towards the battle. 'Fear my presence. I strike terror into the darkest recesses of your treacherous hearts and drive you from me like vermin.' She held up the shield of Locephax.

'Fear me!' The two words rang out clearly and echoed around the foothills. There was a fraction of a pause and then the eyes of the daemon flared open as Locephax awoke. Compelled by the arcane shackles of his bondage to Valkia, he responded to her bellowed command without question. The twisted mouth distorted in a scream that was so high-pitched as to be almost inaudible and the Schwarzvolf warriors who still stood turned tail and fled in all directions. Valkia's feet touched down on the icy-cold ground and she held Locephax before her.

Green, virulent light spilled from the daemon prince's eyes and she laughed spitefully.

'Run, Schwarzvolf,' she called after the terrified warriors. 'Flee before me so that I might better hunt you down and tear your hearts from your bodies for my lord's pleasure!'

From the scramble of feet and the shrieks of abject terror, they were heeding her words in earnest.

'Be silent, slave.' Valkia addressed this to the shield. Locephax's mouth snapped shut and the wailing scream died away. He looked as though he would speak again, but Valkia cut in. 'Say nothing. I will not listen to your words this night.'

She strode amongst the mangled bodies, a tangled mass of limbs and corpses made up from her own warriors and those of the Schwarzvolf who had already fallen. She stooped to grasp the hair of one of her own dead warriors. With no more difficulty than tearing a piece of parchment, Valkia tugged hard. The berserker's head parted company with his body instantly and Valkia held it up, the ragged strips of flesh hanging from the still-warm neck. Blood oozed and dribbled onto her armour, where it was absorbed instantly.

'This warrior died well, serving the will of the Blood God,' she said, holding the grisly trophy aloft so that the remaining berserkers could see it. They were barely keeping themselves in check, obviously desperate to resume the battle. 'His skull will adorn Khorne's throne. Fight well… die well… and you too will earn this honour.' She attached the berserker's head to her belt, its eyes wide in the moment of death.

'Will you fight and die for my master here this night?' There was a roar of assent. Valkia's berserkers were fired up and ready to pursue the retreating tribesmen. She spread her wings and rose once again from the battlefield. She pointed Slaupnir at the warriors who gazed up at her in adoration.

'Will you fight and die for *me* here this night?'

There was a brief hesitation and then one of the warriors began repeating her name over and over like a mantra. Others picked up the rhythm of the war chant and it increased in volume until they cried out their queen's name so loudly that, had there been any doubt in the Schwarzvolf's mind as to the identity of their nemesis, it was resolved.

'Valkia!'

* * *

'WHAT DO YOU mean, my mother?'

Eris had crossed quickly to the quivering God-speaker and smacked him around the face in an effort to bring sense to his babblings. It had not been a delicate slap, but a punch so hard that at least one tooth was loosened in Edan's gums. He staggered backwards with a cry of pain, his hand going to his mouth.

'Answer me, and make it swift!' Eris's temper was incandescent and his ears still ringing from the blow, Edan could do little more than just stare at her. His jaw moved as though he would speak, but no sound came out.

She went to strike him again and he shook his head. Eris scowled and drew her weapon.

'My mother is dead, you bastard. How can she be leading this attack? Unless you lied to me. Unless you *lied to me!*' She sprang at him in absolute fury, ready to take his life there and then, but Edan demonstrated a surprising show of agility, dodging her attack nimbly. He squeaked a few times and then finally found his voice.

'She *was* dead,' he said, the tears still running unchecked down his cheeks. His voice was choked with fear and emotion. 'There was no way she could have lived through the horrors... Hepsus saw...'

What it was that Hepsus saw was lost in the distant battle-cry that reached Eris's ears. Her blood ran cold.

'Valkia! Valkia! Valkia!'

Every last drop of blood drained from Eris's face and she gave Edan one last, vicious look. 'If I somehow live through this battle,' she said between clenched teeth, 'then I will tear your throat out. Do you understand me? There is nowhere you can run that I will not find you!'

She did not wait for his response, but sprinted lightly towards the bulk of her own warriors in an effort to corral them and prepare them for what could only be the true horror that lay ahead.

How could she tell them that the enemy they faced were led by their former queen? How could she even hope to explain that to them? As it happened, she didn't need to. They had heard the enthusiastic battle chant raised in adulation as the daemonic legion approached.

They stared at her as she approached and she felt shame for their obvious fear. Several of them were visibly shaking in terror at the echoing cry of Valkia's name. Eris turned her eyes from the younger warriors to some of those who she knew had gone with the party north over ten years previously. Most of Valkia's chosen entourage were long dead, but a few survived.

One of them met her gaze directly but could not maintain it. The challenge and accusation in Eris's eyes was too much. The way he turned from her gave silent reply to the unspoken question.

The resounding chant of Valkia's name was still audible as Eris raised her voice to be heard over it. She had planned to give a rousing speech, an encouraging last-minute bolster, but she could not find positive words. Eventually, she spoke from her heart.

'The Schwarzvolf are dead,' she said with harsh bitterness in her voice. 'Whether or not we are victorious here today, the heart of this tribe has been torn from us. There are traitors amongst us. Liars. Cowards. Weaklings. We fight for the survival of a people who died ten years ago far to the north in Gods' Home.'

She gave a humourless smile. 'But for all that... for all the Schwarzvolf are ended, we fight today for the chance to be reborn. The chance to carve out our own existence and start again. We fight for glory. Above all else, we fight for victory!'

Her words were a spark in a powder keg of tension. Despite the negativity of what she was saying, the passion with which she spoke her piece ignited the energy and battle lust that had long marked the violent Schwarzvolf. They roared their defiance, brandished their weapons and bar one or two who shot looks of venomous hatred at the young woman, they all shouted her name. It created a curious counterpoint to the words being bellowed elsewhere. An unholy chorus that was a prelude to the coming slaughter.

For a fleeting, wonderful and uplifting moment, Eris truly believed that they might actually stand a chance. Thoughts of her deceitful uncle and the revenge she would take on him were pushed to the back of her mind. Right now, her only concern was the battle and surviving the next few minutes.

'To arms! Warriors of the Vale... we attack!'

The army swarmed together and began to advance in surprisingly even formation with Eris, Valkia's daughter, at their head.

VALKIA'S ARMY MOVED with a surging, unnatural life that reached for their enemy with hungry jaws.

The moment the daemon princess heard her victims voices raised, she brought Slaupnir down in a sweeping stroke, indicating that the butchery should commence.

They rushed forward in their countless numbers. The second wave of crazed berserkers were bolstered by horrors of a kind that the Schwarzvolf had never before witnessed. Bloodletters, their cloven hooves thundering across the cold ground as they ran, brandished rune-encrusted swords of ebony. Flesh hounds tore along at their heels, slavering rivulets of drool and blood in equal measure.

At the rear and flanks of the army lumbered the warped and distorted creatures of the mountains: a throng of towering trolls, packs of ravening wolves and screeching monsters of every stripe.

Valkia waited until the last of the beasts had passed her and beat her wings vigorously, rising into the air and exalting her consort's name to the night sky.

The horde was finally unleashed and Valkia's bloody army did not hesitate.

THE TWO SIDES struck one another with a force that shook the very ground beneath their feet. The strong, rigid line of Eris's warriors was practised and tempered by countless battles, but softened by the latter years of idleness. They stood their ground with grim determination however, the shield bearers at the front bearing the brunt of the enemy's initial charge.

Long gone were the days when only women bore the shields of the Schwarzvolf. Now men and women fought alongside one another as equals. And now they died as equals, falling beneath the serrated blades, axes and teeth of the inhuman enemy with alacrity.

At the fore of the army, the beastmen and berserkers rampaged without thought, pity or mercy. Already whipped into a frenzy by the act of battle alone, their eyes were wild and staring as they hacked and set about themselves. To step into the path of one of these killers was to die. The cover of night did not help. Eris's army had no blessings of a god of war. Their vision had adjusted reasonably, but they still fought against ill-defined shapes. More than one Schwarzvolf turned on one of his own in the mêlée.

Each of the berserkers took countless wounds to be felled, hacking and maiming long past the point at which any mortal warrior should have fallen. Even with the loss of limbs, and wounds so deep that white bone was visible, grisly and wet with blood and caught in the paltry light cast by the torch bearers, they fought on.

Everywhere there was carnage. Death cries and howls of rage filled the air and the clash of weapons resonated throughout the night. The berserker contingent began to steadily thin as they lapped around the stubborn tribe, the Schwarzvolf line holding firm and resolute in the face of their insanity – but they too were losing their warriors at an alarming rate. Bodies began to pile up underfoot, causing men to stumble and fall easy prey to the keen blades of the encroaching enemy.

'Drive them back!' Eris, in the front line with

the shield bearers screamed the order. 'Drive them back over their dead!' It would mean treading on the corpses of their fallen, but they were dead or soon would be and it no longer mattered. 'Shields! Advance!'

On Eris's command, the Schwarzvolf found a thread of strength and pulled it taut. Their expressions grim, their resolve set, they stepped forward one pace at a time. The remaining berserkers flung themselves bodily into the shield line but were driven back.

They threw themselves at the shieldbearers again and again, determined to break through and cause as much mayhem as they could manage. Some had already peeled away from the pack and tore around the flanks of the tribesmen, striking from the side. The Schwarzvolf shield line, however, was well-practised and whilst they were slower to react than they may have been in their prime, they bowed the line to deal with the peripheral threat.

Their casualties were not as heavy as Eris had feared, but many of those who stood beside her were already bloody and wounded. She had fought in many battles against ferocious rival tribes, but nothing like the enemy that presently swarmed about them. In mere minutes they had suffered more than any engagement over the last decade. When the last beastman was dispatched, bleating the name of his god to the last, Valkia's daughter dared to feel a glimmer of hope, that maybe they had weathered the storm. Nothing could have prepared them for what was to come however. And what came next was a waking nightmare.

The earth shook at the tread of something vast and terrible that thundered toward the Schwarzvolf. Warriors stood pale and fearful in the moonlight as the titanic form of Kormak, astride his daemonic mount, charged the ragged line. At his back a host of unholy abominations with eyes of hellfire surged like a tide, their ruddy flesh alive with blasphemous runes and slick with mortal blood.

At first, the Schwarzvolf front line could do nothing but stare at this new, terrifying enemy in horror. More than one of them turned and tried to flee back through the press, but they could not. The tribe was encircled, their line forced around until the men at either end stood side by side against the night.

Raging at their cowardice, Eris ordered them thrown to the enemy. 'Fight them!' Every word came out as a scream. 'Stand your ground and fight, or die by *my* blade!'

Many of her warriors were crying openly at the sight of their unnatural foe. The bloodletters were tall and wiry and their eyes glowed with insatiable hunger. They remained desperate to feed, despite having gorged their voracious appetites on the journey to this battle. Most were the same height as the men, but others were taller, slim and wiry. Crests ran the length of their spines and across their heads, and thin, serpentine tongues flickered in and out.

Kormak struck the line like the fist of a god, the blunt head of the juggernaut lowered into a killing ram that shattered shields and crushed men like frail saplings. The formation of the Schwarzvolf broke apart instantly, any sense of unity lost under the unstoppable assault of the murderous champion in their midst. His axe rose and fell with swift and terrible rhythm, cleaving heads and limbs and leaving a wake of gory ruin.

In the half-light cast by the flickering torches, the daemons cast eerie, intimidating shapes, moving with lithe grace as they bounded from enemy to enemy. Their hellblades pierced and cut, sowing injury and death wherever they struck. The blades, encrusted with runes that glowed viciously in the darkness, moved with such speed that those unfortunates who got caught in their arc were torn apart instantly.

'Steel yourselves,' Eris shrieked at the top of her voice. She had already dodged and weaved her way through the onslaught. The blades of the bloodletters had, thus far, not found her body which was already streaked with blood from the wounds she had taken whilst facing the berserkers. 'Muster all the courage you have. We are the people of the Vale. We are *strong!*'

So many of them, she thought desperately. So many of the daemonic creatures. Just when she had resigned herself to the likelihood that they were far outnumbered, things got worse still.

The first of the flesh hounds, which was easily half a length longer again than the tallest of the Schwarzvolf warriors, sprang on one of the shield bearers to Eris's right. Razor-sharp teeth within the snapping jaws caught a hold of the unfortunate woman's exposed neck and within seconds, tore her throat out. The hound threw back its head and bayed its pleasure before burying its snout in the woman's body and taking its fill. It was evidently some kind of pack alpha as the sound of its victory summoned others. Four, five, six... perhaps more. They hurtled into the maelstrom, their milk-white eyes intimidating and horrific.

The moonlight glinted off the collars they wore around their thick necks and their hides took flurries of blows without so much causing a yelp. Not a nick appeared in their unnatural flesh, but Eris turned on the closest animal with fury, her own weapons flashing.

Whether the monster's hide had been weakened by the blows it had withstood or not, it did not matter. Seconds after she launched her attack, Eris's blade sank in through muscle and sinew and she sliced the tendons in the animal's rear leg. She gave the thing a cursory glance, not even sure that it *was* an animal at all.

It gave an unearthly howl of pain and rage and turned to face this new attacker, its jaws slavering and snapping as it tried to crouch ready to pounce on Eris. The young woman feinted with her blade and struck forward with the shield she carried. The daemon hound was thrown off balance.

'Now!' Her cry came and her people obeyed. They turned on the stricken daemon hound and pierced its body, running it through a dozen times. It twitched and stopped moving and then with barely a pause, simply ceased to be. It did not even leave behind a puff of smoke. It simply... was not.

'We can't hope to defeat this enemy, Eris.' She

didn't know who spoke the words, but they brought forth a blaze of fury. 'We should retreat. Now.' Raging, she struck out with her shield again and knocked the speaker away from her.

'Do *not* say such things! Where is the fire? Where is the passion? We will fight until the last breath leaves our bodies! We cannot retreat, you *fool*. Where would we go? Now *fight!*'

And despite the futility of it, they fought. There was nothing more that they could do

VALKIA COULD NOT help but admire the sheer determination of the enemy she faced. They could not have a hope of defeating the daemonic host and already their warriors were dying by the score. The trolls and other beasts were lumbering into the thick of the battle and as soon as they began employing their unique methods of self-defence, the battle would be all but over.

Her original plan to simply enjoy watching the slaughter of the tribe she had once called her own had not lasted beyond the first skirmish. The sheer lust for battle drove her down from the skies. She tossed Slaupnir up into the air and caught it so that the spear was pointing from above, ready to impale its next victim.

Whilst the Schwarzvolf were dealing with the threat of the flesh hounds, Valkia indulged her own need to spill the blood from her enemies. The first warrior whose life she took screamed like a child at the sight of her.

'You know who I am.' It was a statement, not a

question and Valkia caught the warrior by the throat, her long-taloned fingers wrapping around his neck. She pulled him up and towards her so that they were nose to nose. The warrior lost control of his bladder and warm urine ran down his leg. He squeezed his eyes closed, too afraid and too ashamed to look his former queen in the eye.

'Say my name, Schwarzvolf.' The words came out as a sultry purr, oddly seductive and compelling, and his eyes slowly opened again. 'Say my name.'

'V... Valkia.'

'Say it properly. It will be the last word that crosses your lips. Make it strong. Make your death count for something. Who am I?'

He found strength from somewhere and his voice rose, strengthening and increasing in volume.

'Valkia!'

'And I am your doom.' The last thing the warrior saw were Valkia's eyes, suffused with a crimson glow. The last thing he felt was the sharp stab of pain as Slaupnir slid into his gut and Valkia slowly eviscerated him. She enjoyed every second of the process, savouring the look of undisguised anguish on her former comrade's face as she twisted the spear around in his bowels, tearing them out through the gash in his abdomen.

Then she just dropped him and trod on his skull as she passed by. The man's head caved immediately and she rejoined the battle. She took personal death to many of those who she had once called friend. Each one died in a similar way. She would single out those who had travelled with her into the north and she wreaked slow, bloody revenge upon them. Most were methodically butchered, much like the first, their guts spilled in glistening ropes on the ground. One had his tongue torn from his mouth by her bare hands. She had thrown the still-twitching organ to one of the flesh hounds and the doomed warrior had watched the animal devour it whole before Slaupnir had punctured his chest and stilled his heart forever.

She felt Locephax's desperation, the daemon's desire to be a part of such slaughter tied to his perverse nature and insatiable lusts, but she did not unleash his brand of terror again. She would not sully these perfect moments with the disgusting touch of the prince of pleasure. She blocked out his endless pleading and she strode through the battlefield, her eyes raking the dead and the still-standing.

But she could not find her brother.

'Edan!' Valkia howled his name to the moon. 'Come and face me!'

Spreading her wings, Valkia rose above the battlefield, her daemonic eyesight perfect in the darkness. She scoured the landscape for the telltale scamper of the rodent she sought.

Her attention was torn from her task by the sound of a voice below her. A voice that stirred memories she had put away.

'Valkia!'

Glancing down, the winged warrior's face spread in a slow, cruel smile and she allowed herself to descend once again. The young woman she faced bore a visage that was almost the double of her own; or at least how her own had been before Khorne had so gloriously re-shaped her in his desired image.

'This must end,' Eris said, staring at the mother she had once known. She was at once disgusted and in awe of what Valkia had become. She knew no grief for the loss of a parent but she felt fury at the death and destruction wrought by the creature's hand.

Valkia considered her daughter carefully. If she knew her, or recognised her, she gave no acknowledgement of the fact. She hefted Slaupnir in her right hand and steadied Locephax on her left arm.

'And who will end it, mortal? You?'

'If I must.'

Without pausing to speak any further, Eris threw herself at Valkia.

EDAN HAD FLED the moment battle had been joined. Too cowardly to engage with the daemonic forces that were sure to destroy his niece and her army, he had turned tail and run away. It had been the only option left to the corpulent Godspeaker.

Branches whipped pitilessly against him as he stumbled blindly through the darkness, skirting the edges of the grove of trees that led eventually to the Vale. In his tumbling, breathless panic, they were like grasping fingers trying to take hold of him and haul him backwards to the battlefield. He plunged through bramble and bracken, never once daring to pause and look behind him. The hungry, avaricious branches caught in his clothes and his hair, lacerating the skin of his face. Stinging pain came and went almost unnoticed. He felt warm blood trickle down his cheek, dribbling its unmistakable coppery tang into his mouth, but he didn't stop to wipe it away. Stopping was not an option. He had to run.

So he ran.

His breath was ragged, his heart pounding like a battle drum against his ribs. It had been many years since he had exerted so much energy and the tight, burning pain across his chest was excruciating.

Even as he fled, his jowls and belly flapping with the exertion, he knew that it was an exercise in futility. There was nowhere he could hide from his sister. There was nowhere he could ever call safe again. Even in his dreams she tormented him. The rational side of his brain mocked him ceaselessly and as he ran, propelled by the desire to live, he clamped his hands to his ears as though he could drown out the sound of his thoughts.

He had not gone far before his sprint slowed to a brisk walk and even that petered out after another half a mile or so. Behind him, even through his hands which were still tight against his head, he could hear the sounds of death as his people were torn apart.

He cried. He cried for the murder of his people. He cried for all that had gone wrong. He even cried for the sister in whom he had once believed without question and who he had ultimately betrayed for his own selfish reasons. But mostly, he cried for himself. The thought of his imminent death brought Edan no pleasure.

Pleasure…

Years ago, he had put his faith into the Reveller. He had listened to the whispers of the decadent god and had given his soul over willingly. His gluttony had been his chosen method of showing his devotion to his chosen deity. Death would rob him of all the pleasures in life he had come to expect and revel in.

For just a moment, Edan saw himself as he must appear to others. A pathetic shadow of his former self, bloated and warped into something almost unrecognisable and he felt deep shame.

A second burst of energy suffused his limbs and he began to run again, fleeing from the seeds of his own destruction.

EIGHTEEN
Bringer of Glory

As a battling pair, Eris and Valkia were poorly matched. Eris was a creature of rage and fury who attacked on impulse, hacking and slashing at her opponent blindly. She was also obviously, painfully mortal. Valkia dodged every thrust and avoided every blow her daughter attempted to bring down on her with ease. The Blood Queen knew that she could take down Eris with a single stroke if she so desired, and yet the final ember of humanity that glowed somewhere in her daemonic soul could not bear the thought of ending such sport so quickly.

So she toyed with the mortal for a while, her own movements with Slaupnir fluid and graceful. The two female warriors remained locked together in a mesmerising and deadly dance. Where Eris had to duck and weave, expending energy rapidly, Valkia's movements were languid and lazy. She pre-empted every thrust and every attack was defended with hardly any effort.

The two warring women broke off for a moment.

'I do not know what it was that happened to you,'

panted Eris, withdrawing from the fray briefly. Sweat trickled down her face, smearing the blood and the dirt that she had gathered during the course of the battle. In the moonlight, she was pale and her expression was one of pain. The wounds she had taken during the course of conflict were beginning to take their toll on her. 'I do not know, nor do I care. You seek to destroy my people and I cannot let you do that.'

'You cannot deny me,' Valkia replied, her eyes fixed on the slender form of the warrior daughter before her. 'The price of weakness and betrayal is death. When these cowards turned their back on me they turned their back on all they could have been. Now vengeance comes, and when I have claimed the skulls of every living Schwarzvolf warrior, I will raze the Vale.'

'You would slaughter the infirm and our infants?' Eris was shocked by the words. 'You have no compassion at all?'

'It matters not from whence the blood flows, Eris,' Valkia said, leaning in close, her voice low so that Eris had to lean in to hear her. 'So long as it *does* flow. Thus it must ever be.'

Before Eris could assimilate the words, Valkia's skull met hers in a savage head-butt and she reeled backwards, stunned by the blow. The daemon princess spread her wings and stood straight, a truly awesome sight to behold and she lowered Slaupnir at her child.

'Thus it *will* be!'

The spear lunged forward, its razor-sharp blade

aimed directly at Eris's heart. With a resounding *clang*, the young woman found a reserve of strength and brought her shield up to block the killing stroke. Her ability to hold her ground was fading rapidly and her breath came in ragged, pained gasps.

'Not whilst I still live,' she said and Valkia's smile was one of pride.

'You truly are my daughter,' she said, and drew Slaupnir back for another strike. Her clawed hand slid down the weapon's haft so that she was holding it just above the tip, as though she held a long dagger.

'Yes,' said Eris, struggling to draw breath. Her mouth was filled with the coppery taste of blood. Her ribs had broken against her lungs and if she continued to fight, she would not need to concern herself with her mother's weapon. She would die anyway. 'I am.'

'Then in recognition of that fact, your death will be...'

The movement was so fast that Eris never even saw it coming. One of Valkia's talons pierced her chest and drove through her heart. Pain, agonising and yet exquisite, shot through her and she dropped her sword and shield to the cold earth. She fell to her knees, blood dribbling from the corners of her mouth and stared stupidly down at the hand embedded in her chest.

'Blood,' she managed to eke out around her final gulps of life. 'Blood for the...'

For a few moments after the light of life left Eris's eyes, Valkia considered her. Then she withdrew her hand and let her daughter's body slump face-down onto the ground. She considered the girl's corpse without emotion and eventually gave a terse nod of acknowledgement.

'You died well, Eris,' she said. 'I will bring you your reward in due course. But for now...'

Once again, the Blood Queen spread her wings and soared into the skies above the waning battle, raking the horizon for her brother. Like a bird of prey, she scoured the landscape and, when she saw what she was looking for, she swooped in for the kill. She crossed the distance between the battlefield and the small copse of trees with alarming haste.

Beneath her, the massed army of daemons and the handful of berserkers who still lived pressed onwards, moving ever-closer to the Vale. Kormak charged at their head, his massive armoured bulk little more than a huge silhouette in the moonlight.

EDAN HAD FALLEN to the ground, his sweating body unable to keep him running any longer. He had simply dropped to his hands and knees, panting and gasping to get breath into his heaving chest. It was never meant to have ended this way. He had always had plans... great plans... and he would eventually have gotten around to carrying them out.

The sound of Valkia's wings was soft and almost soothing up ahead and when their rhythmic beat ceased, he knew that she plunged towards him. Edan did not even have the strength to raise his head so remained where he was, on all fours with his eyes downcast. He remained there and waited for his death.

It did not come.

Slowly, he looked up to discover that a daemon who wore his dead sister's face stood before him. She was staring at him with a look of hateful incredulity. The last time she had seen her half-brother, he had been a lean, tautly muscled young man. Now he was barely recognisable, his once-pleasant features lost in rolls of sallow skin. The redolent stench of alcohol and stale sweat that steamed from him was noxious. She put out one hoofed foot and kicked him on to his back. Unresisting, Edan slumped over weakly.

'Get up,' she said.

'Why?' His response was weary and bitter. 'Strike me down whilst I am kneeling or when I am standing. What difference does it make to me, Valkia? We both know that this cannot end any other way. Just take my head and end it.'

This was more like the Edan she remembered, even if only in part. The man who could play with words and turn them into weapons if he felt so inclined. In the face of death he lost none of his eloquence.

'Get up,' she repeated. 'If you have any courage at all in that blubbery frame, you will face me like the warrior you once pretended to be.'

'Why would I give you such satisfaction?'

Valkia hesitated no longer and reached down to drag the quivering mass of blubber to his feet. A soft chuckle started somewhere behind her and she realised that Locephax was laughing.

'His mind was weak,' said the disembodied daemon. 'I put the seeds of suggestion into the minds of all your people, Valkia. At least one found fertile ground it seems. Congratulations, *Godspeaker*. My master will be pleased that you devoted yourself to him so fully.'

The heavy sarcasm that he placed on Edan's title did not go unnoticed and Valkia scowled as her half-brother inclined his head in deep respect.

'You have always been my enemy, Edan,' she said eventually. 'You wove the web of deceit that led my own people to turn from the glory that I offered them. For that alone I will have my vengeance. But you declare yourself a follower of the prince of excess and for that there can never be any mercy.'

'I expect none,' countered Edan. His composure in the face of his doom was boiling her blood.

'To kill one of my master's servants could be considered a feat of strength, Valkia.' Locephax sounded deeply amused. 'To kill two may draw his attention in a way you would not like.'

'Be silent, creature. This worm is favoured by none, least of all the gods. You are nothing more than a slave to my will and you will do as I command.' Valkia silenced Locephax with a sharp word, but the daemon continue to chortle softly. She turned her attention back to Edan whose face was oddly beatific.

'I am ready for my death now, Valkia.' He sounded calm and at peace with the world. He flung out his arms, exposing the vast expanse of his torso so that she could slay him.

But still she did not.

'I am not yet ready to spill your worthless blood,' she retorted, though the need crackled through every fibre of her being. 'First, you will answer me one question.' She stepped closer to him, much as it disgusted her to do so. 'Why? Why did you lead the Schwarzvolf astray? The power our people could have had. The strength they could have wielded if they had laid themselves at the feet of Khorne. You were their Godspeaker and yet you turned them from the path with lies and poisoned words and in so doing, you damned them to this end. Why, Edan?'

He considered her, fascinated by her new form. She was still very clearly the woman he had known in life. The sister he had once clung to as an infant. The sister he had once looked up to. The sister he had watched descend slowly into madness. The sister he had betrayed.

A thousand flash images shot through his mind. So many memories. So many mixed feelings towards the woman... the *thing* in front of him. But he could not find the words to answer her question. Instead, he just shook his head.

'Because it should have been me, Valkia. No more to it than that.'

She had tired of his conversation long ago and he could see that in her eyes. He did not fully understand why she had not simply killed him on sight. A wild thought struck him. Perhaps there was something of his sister still inside the daemon woman clad in bleeding armour. He put out a hand towards her.

'Valkia...'

'I do not wish to hear your mewling any longer, Edan.' She stepped forward and gave her half-brother a contemptuous sneer. 'When your blighted soul reaches the feet of the Reveller, be sure to tell the lord of pleasures who has sent you before him. Perhaps, as he slowly tortures your frail spirit, he will consider the folly of bringing his weakling creatures to my attention.'

Edan could do nothing but wait for her to run him through with her spear, but she didn't. She planted the weapon in the earth and took hold of his head with both her hands. She pulled him closer to her as if she was going to touch her head to his in benediction.

Then with the supernatural strength with which she had been blessed, she pulled.

A series of sharp cracks sounded as the bones in his neck stretched in protest and Edan was dragged upwards onto his toes. He could not even cry out in pain as the thick flesh of his throat constricted under the mounting pressure. The last thing he ever saw was the cruel half-smile on Valkia's face as she tore his head from his shoulders. A glistening tail of vertebrae followed, meat and gristle still attached but snapping as she pulled her trophy free.

Edan's headless corpse stood motionless for a few seconds, hot blood spraying explosively from the ragged stump of its neck, and then it toppled with a meaty thump to the ground. Valkia held up her gruesome prize to the skies.

'Khorne!' Her voice rose to a scream. Somewhere in the distance she heard the sound of her own army returning the cry and she knew that they advanced on the Vale. Within minutes, what remained of the Schwarzvolf would face the daemon horde. She had her prize. She had taken her revenge on the figure that had orchestrated her demise more than a decade ago.

She stared into the dead eyes of Edan. In death, his face was locked in a rictus grin that she felt mocked her. She had done what she had come here to do. With a word, she could prevent the obliteration of an entire people.

She could.

But she would not.

Valkia had fulfilled the obligation that had tied her to life, and even as she attached the head and spine of Edan to her armour, she forgot the idea of ever having considered leniency. Taking up her shield and spear, she once again spread her wings and took to the skies.

Throwing her head back, she gave voice to the cry that would echo across countless battlefields through the ages.

'Blood for the Blood God!'

The answering roar of the army roared into the night and the Chaos horde swarmed into the Vale.

THEY WERE RUTHLESS and they were swift. The latter was out of necessity rather than compassion. Dawn was fast approaching and, released from Valkia's will, many of the daemonic creatures who stalked among the army would return to the eternal realm once the first rays of daylight crept through the grey skies.

Those in camp who had not taken to the battlefield were largely children and the infirm, although there were a few heavily pregnant women. Every last one of them did all they could to defend their home from the horrific invaders. They died in their droves.

The flesh hounds, weakening with the coming of day, prowled the camp, burying their muzzles in the bodies of the slain, closing powerful jaws around the heads of the fallen and feasting on the slaughter.

There were a handful of berserker warriors remaining who looted the camp for anything they considered useful; weapons for the most part, but they also indulged themselves with the wine and food they found. Now that the carnage was all but over, Valkia turned a blind eye to their antics. They had served her well. They faced a hard journey back north and there was a good chance that they would not survive the mountain crossing. The daemon princess cared nothing for their fate.

Striding through the camp, Valkia glanced this way and that, finding nothing that stirred any meaningful memories. Her life here was truly over and it held no sentimentality for her. The sight of the slaughter had only one effect on her and that was satisfaction at the appropriate sacrifice to strengthen her lord and master.

A few paces behind her, Kormak rode, his massive, gore-soaked axe resting easily across his armoured shoulder. Forever bound to his armour and the service of his mistress, he could not speak to voice his opinion. But the set of his massive shoulders and the straightness in his spine spoke of his own quiet satisfaction.

'Kormak, first among my warriors.' Valkia turned and beckoned her champion to her. 'I must depart this place soon. I leave you to spread the bloody word. Carve a path of death and glory and bury the land in skulls.' The armoured warrior inclined his head in acknowledgement. Valkia stared up at the sky. The pink tinge to the edges of the clouds suggested that dawn was minutes away. It would not cause her any bother, but she could feel her distant lord calling her, ordering her to return to his side and she would not defy him.

Around her, flesh hounds and bloodletters were dissipating into the morning mists, drawn back to the eternal battle from whence they had come. Whilst they had marched at Valkia's side, their mistress's inherent power had bled into them, giving them form and purpose. They had always been weakest by day, but now that their task was complete, they simply returned to their twilight existence.

Valkia was aware of the way they responded to her, the deference they showed to her, and she soaked up the glory with hungry pleasure. The slow but certain knowledge of the power she wielded had gradually eroded any doubts she may have harboured.

'Before you leave this place,' she ordered her champion, laying a hand on his shoulder, 'ensure that everything is burned to the ground. Leave nothing of the Schwarzvolf but a vague and terrible memory.'

Her champion nodded again and turned to walk from her and begin the task of rounding up the warriors ready for the task ahead. As the sun's weak winter rays began to poke through the mist, Valkia inhaled deeply. The day would be cold and fresh. The first snows of winter would settle on the ravaged Vale before nightfall.

Leave nothing of the Schwarzvolf but a vague and

terrible memory. That was all she had herself. Memories that she could somehow neither fully reconcile nor care to linger on. What she had been... who she had been... all was the stuff of legend. If any still lived who remembered her, then her name and deeds she performed in life might continue to live on.

She did not bother to dwell on the thought. Instead, she closed her eyes. Taking another long, slow breath of the ice-tinged morning air, she noted with pleasure that the scent of death and blood had seeped through and permeated the morning.

There was one final task she needed to perform before she returned to her lord's side. Valkia stalked the Vale and the battlefield where the majority of the Schwarzvolf had fallen. With care, she selected the most loyal of her own warriors, taking their heads. Kormak and his warriors would deal with taking the skulls of the enemy, but Valkia's choices were personal. She took maybe three or four; skulls of those who had battled with particular valour.

With the exception of her personal prize, the head and spine of Edan, there was only one other Schwarzvolf head that she had taken.

'You fought well, my daughter,' she said to Eris's corpse as she knelt by the dead woman's side. 'And your skull will be added to our lord's throne by me personally. There is no greater reward.'

She brought Slaupnir down and severed Eris's head, cutting through the final lingering tie to her past. Without another thought, the daemon princess vanished just as the first shafts of pale sunlight broke over the distant mountains. Thick, black pillars of smoke were already climbing into the cold air, filling the sky with ash as Valkia abandoned the Vale to its ultimate fate.

SHE HAD BEEN here before.

Valkia stood once again at the edge of the abyss, the crackling maelstrom that would take her back to her lord and master's side. The last time she had stood here, she had faced the horrors of the wastes alone, but for the eternally loyal Kormak. Now, she was able to command those horrors to do whatever she desired. The irony entertained her.

This time, none would stop her. This time, she would ascend the titanic steps and cross through to the realm of the gods unhindered. The daemons that prowled and waited for the unwary variously hissed and spat at the Blood Queen of Khorne as she ascended, but they dared not approach. Those who served the god bowed in respect for their rightful queen.

As she came to the step where she had fallen all those years before, she knelt and briefly raked her talons across the dark stain where her body had once lain. It was a permanent reminder of her trials, of all that she had undergone to reach the pinnacle she had reached.

Standing, her head held high with the pride and arrogance worthy of a daemon princess, she strode through the coruscating madness into the unfathomable realm of the gods.

She never could fully articulate what it was she saw when she stood before her master's throne. A veritable sea of skulls and bone, stretching as far as the eye could see in all directions, rising upwards to support the throne of brass upon which he sat.

Blood red images of her recent butchery assailed her mind, the destruction of the tribes, the burning of the Vale and the explosion of gore as she had torn the head from Edan's shoulders.

'Did you doubt my fidelity, my lord?' Valkia threw down the skulls that she had gathered and they tumbled down the mountain to rest, forgotten, at the bottom. In time, they would decay and be unrecognisable. But Valkia had already lost interest in them. The head of her traitorous half-brother with its broken spine lay on the plain of bones, the unseeing eyes staring into eternity.

A tide of murder, destruction and warfare filled her consciousness. Ceaseless carnage and a field of battle that stretched on into eternity. There would be no end to the bloodshed until the stars themselves grew dim and fell from the sky.

The vision thrilled her. This was what she had been born for. This was what she *was*. The right arm of slaughter personified.

'Aye, my lord,' she said, leaning on her spear and staring out across the eternal battle. 'There will always be blood.' She turned and took in the enormity of the presence that dominated the throne. 'Blood for the Blood God.'

EPILOGUE

THE FIRE THAT Kormak and his chosen warriors set razed the sprawling camp of the Schwarzvolf to the ground. The animal enclosures, the training grounds... everything that had taken so long to build up was destroyed in a comparative blink of an eye.

Fierce and unchecked, the fires raged for several days, dying out only when the snows became heavy enough to smother them. Thick, acrid clouds of black choked the skies for miles around. The snow came down thick with ash, staining the landscape in grim blackness that lingered until the second snows restored unblemished white to the world.

When the hard winter passed, when the ice receded, the true extent of the destruction wrought on the Vale was finally revealed. The earth was as dead as the carpet of stiff corpses that littered the former settlement, piled high where the battle had taken place. Fire, blight and the touch of daemons had withered the once-verdant valley and turned the soil a noxious black.

On the orders of his mistress, Kormak had spared one thing only and Valkia's throne had escaped the purging fires unscathed. It had been returned to its rightful owner in the realm beyond and over the years became lost in the skulls she chose to decorate it with. Her brother's skull disappeared into the countless others she brought to her consort over time, but she retrieved that of Eris, mounting it on her throne in a silent acknowledgement of her daughter's final tribute.

The years passed, melting into one another in a blur of time. Five, ten, twenty years during which the memories of the Schwarzvolf faded gradually. Fifty, one hundred years... and more.

Nothing would grow in the Vale and the surrounding region. The unyielding earth would give no life to seeds that found their way there and over time, the poisons in the ground seeped into the trees and copses that bordered on the old Schwarzvolf lands. They twisted and contorted into mockeries of their former selves, taking on eerie, horrific shapes that conjured up images of tortured bodies.

Cursed, they called it. The name of the Vale was lost, swathed in the mists of time until the area where a long-forgotten tribe had once lived became known as Bloody Hollow.

Legends grew; stories of how the valley had become cursed by the gods. Some touched the edges of truth but for the most part, memories of the Schwarzvolf passed into history forgotten. The people of the tribe were nothing more than echoes of the past.

All but their leader.

Legends persisted of a terrible daemon scourge that scoured the lands in the guise of a woman. Legends that told of the history and deeds of the mistress of skulls. The story of the self-proclaimed warrior queen who had conquered and allied the warring tribes of the north under a single banner.

The tales told of a cold beauty that was much coveted by the living and the damned alike. How she had been cursed by her own people to die in her most triumphant hour and how the dark god of battle had raised her again to fight on in his name.

Wide-eyed children listened to the stories around campfires, searching the skies warily for a glimpse of the winged harbinger. They learned swiftly that to spy the Blood Queen was a prelude to war. Time continued to pass and then they learned that stories were sometimes cruel reality.

Wherever there were people, there was inevitably conflict. And even though warriors might claim lofty goals or noble ideals, in their secret hearts they craved the glory that could only be claimed from the taking of life. They were Khorne's creatures whether they acknowledged it or not.

But the armies that rolled out of the Chaos Wastes carved a gory path wherever they went and raised their voices in open adulation to their thirsting god. The memory of the Schwarzvolf may have been long gone, but the memory and knowledge of Valkia the Bloody remained. Wherever there was war, she would arrive, leading an army of unnatural creatures into glorious battle.

And afterwards, when all that remained on the fields of slaughter were the dead, the dying and carrion birds, Valkia would stalk around the bodies of the fallen, marking out those who earned eternal reward and above all else, reaping skulls for her master's skull throne.

Sarah Cawkwell is a north-east England based freelance writer. Married, with a son (who is the grown up in the house) and two intellectually challenged cats, she's been a determined and prolific writer for many years. Her first novel, *The Gildar Rift*, was published in 2011. When not slaving away over a hot keyboard, Sarah's hobbies include reading everything and anything, running around in fields with swords screaming incomprehensibly and having her soul slowly sucked dry by online games.

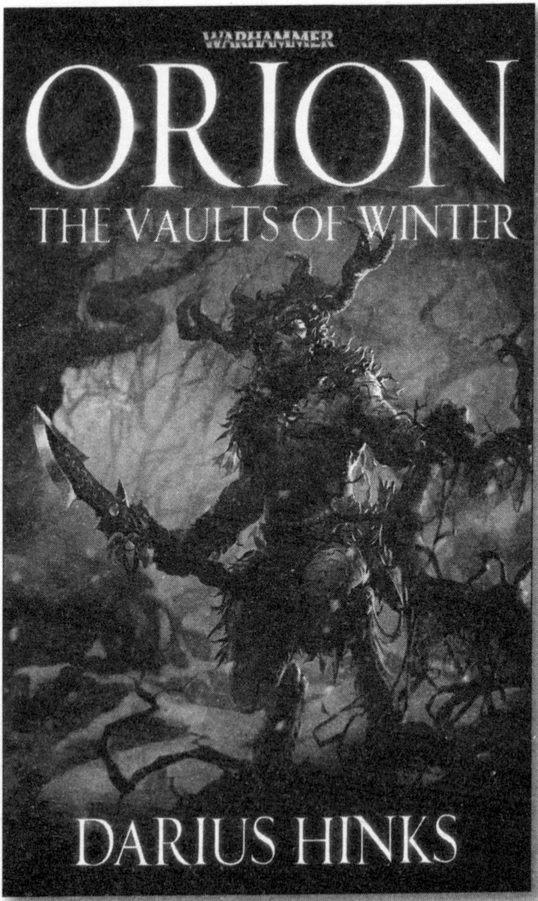
WARHAMMER
ORION
THE VAULTS OF WINTER
DARIUS HINKS

An extract from Orion: The Vaults of Winter
by Darius Hinks

SILVER LIGHT POURED down through the branches, filled with the power of the infinite. It shone first upon a circle of priests, flashing across their wooden masks and in the bottomless pits of their eyes. Then, as the moons aligned overhead, the light fell on the figure kneeling at their feet: a trembling, scarred ruin with shattered antlers and a broken, bleeding fist. The tree had endured the ritual countless times and, as the soul of a god descended through its branches it shivered, recognising the dreadful hunger of Kurnous, come again to taste blood.

There were nine disciples, their droning chant led by the High Priest, Atolmis, whose spear was resting on Orion's shoulder. At the crescendo of their song, he drew a knife and dragged it across his naked chest. The other priests followed suit and, as the blood fell, they caught it and hurled it over Orion's back. The blood slapped against his skin, the moonlight flickered and Orion shuddered in pain.

The priests closed their eyes, sensing that Kurnous was amongst them, and knowing it was not their place to look upon divinity.

As the blood ran down his back, Orion's bones cracked and elongated. He gasped but did not cry out, remaining kneeling, despite the agony.

Atolmis began the song again, raising his voice to drown out the sound of Orion's splintering bones. It was a droning round that was joined after a few moments by another voice.

Ariel stepped slowly into the Oak of Ages with her head lowered. She was dressed in a long white mantle, girdled by wreaths of larkspur, and in her hair she wore a chaplet of delicate blue vervain. She carried a cloak that shimmered in the moonlight; an intricate weave of leaves and spun gold that rippled between her fingers, shimmering like water.

The song reached another solemn crescendo as Ariel entered the circle and stood over her immortal, blood-drenched lover.

Sensing her presence, Orion tried to stand. At first he was unable to rise. His body was still wracked by a series of jolting changes and he stumbled, dropping heavily back to his knees.

Ariel looked pained, but remained motionless.

Orion tried again to rise and this time he succeeded. He towered over his disciples and his queen, swaying slightly as he looked up at the shafts of moonlight. Then he turned his gaze on Ariel. His face was contorted by pride and pain, but he managed a nod of recognition.

She nodded in reply, still singing as she floated

gently into the air and placed the cloak of leaves over his shoulders.

Orion's spine gave one last crack as he shrugged the cloak into place. He was now nearly ten feet tall and as he looked down at his disciples power rippled from his flesh, filling the chamber like a heat haze.

At a nod from Atolmis the priests stepped back into the recesses of the chamber, fading into shadow as Orion walked past them. The final transformation of his flesh was complete and as he approached the centre of the tree he stretched his enormous limbs and smiled. There was no trace of his injuries and he could feel his oak apple heart pounding in his chest, fierce and virile. The weariness that had overcome him in the Vaults was a memory.

At the centre of the tree there was a natural alcove and a broad, uneven shelf of root. Lying on the wood was a gilded horn on a strap of vines and, next to it, there was a spear, its blade inscribed with an intricate network of knotted runes. Orion took the horn and slung it around his neck. Then he lifted the spear, tested its weight and turned to face Ariel and the priests.

'The Wild Hunt has begun,' he said, striding from the tree.

Hundreds of nobles were assembled on the moon-lit dais outside, clutching torches and wearing masks of birch wood, painted to resemble the snarling faces of animals. As Orion emerged, they threw petals before his hooves and garlanded him with flowers, but he was deaf to their prayers, peering through the ranks of masked figures, looking for something.

After a few minutes of staring into the darkness, he raised the gilded horn to his lips and let out a long, lowing note.

The nobles gradually fell silent until the only sound was the crackling of their torches and the echoes of the horn blast.

Then, from deep in the trees, there came a reply: a chorus of baying howls, ringing out from every direction.

Orion blew his horn for a second time and, around the edges of the clearing, the shadows rippled into life. Grey, rangy hounds emerged from the trees, sniffing and growling as they caught the scent of his divine blood. They padded around the masked figures for a while, moonlight flashing in their eyes. Then they began circling Orion, regarding him with cool, wary, intelligence.

Behind Orion, Atolmis stepped from the Oak of Ages and saw the hounds. He revealed his yellow incisors in a grin. 'Kurnous has risen,' he howled, thrusting his spear into the air. 'Let the Wild Hunt begin!'

The nobles raised their torches into the air and joined their voices to the cry of the hounds. 'Orion!' they screamed, delirious with bloodlust. They drew knives and spears and crowded around their king, howling his name like a warning. 'Orion!'

Orion: The Vaults of Winter
Available September 2012 from *blacklibrary.com*,
GAMES WORKSHOP®
and all good book stores.